HUNGRY FOR YOUR LOVE

HUNGRY
FOR YOUR
LOVE

An Anthology of Zombie Romance

Edited By

LORI PERKINS

HUNGRY FOR YOUR LOVE. Copyright © 2009 by Ravenous Romance. All rights reserved. Printed in the United States of America. For information, address St. Martin's Press, 175 Fifth Avenue, New York, N.Y. 10010.

www.stmartins.com

Book design by Rich Arnold

ISBN 978-0-312-65079-7

First published in electronic format in the United States by Ravenous Romance™

First St. Martin's Griffin Edition: October 2010

10 9 8 7 6 5 4 3 2 1

FOR THE BOY AND GIRL ZOMBIES OF CAMP NECON
WHO SAID IT COULDN'T BE DONE
AND DOUBLE DOG DARED ME

CONTENTS

INTRODUCTION | *Lori Perkins—ix*

ROMANCE AIN'T DEAD | *Jeremy Wagner—1*

REVENANTS ANONYMOUS | *Francesca Lia Block—20*

I HEART BRAINS | *Jaime Saare—39*

EVERYONE I LOVE IS DEAD | *Elizabeth Coldwell—61*

THROUGH DEATH TO LOVE | *S. M. Cross—73*

EYE OF THE BEHOLDER | *Stacey Graham—83*

FIRST LOVE NEVER DIES | *Jan Kozlowski—89*

MY PARTNER THE ZOMBIE | *R. G. Hart—104*

UNDYING LOVE | *Regina Riley—125*

CAPTIVE HEARTS | *Brian Keene*—156

APOCALYPSE AS FOREPLAY | *Gina McQueen*—164

JULIA BRAINCHILD | *Lois H. Gresh*—181

KICKING THE HABIT | *Steven Saus*—199

ZOMBIFIED | *Isabel Roman*—206

WHITE NIGHT, BLACK HORSE | *Mercy Loomis*—232

INHUMAN RESOURCES | *Jeanine McAdam*—246

THE MAGICIAN'S APPRENTICE | *Stacy Brown*—265

SOME NEW BLOOD | *Vanessa Vaughn*—278

LAST TIMES AT RIDGEMONT HIGH | *Kilt Kilpatrick*—294

FIRST DATE | *Dana Fredsti*—329

LATER | *Michael Marshall Smith*—348

ABOUT THE AUTHORS—359

INTRODUCTION

They said it couldn't be done.

And like the undead, I rose to the challenge.

This anthology was born in July 2009 at the twenty-ninth Northeastern Writer's Conference, affectionately known by its regular participants as "Camp Necon." Every year since its inception, Necon has what we also affectionately call "that damn vampire panel." But this year, we had a zombie panel instead. The revolution had begun.

As soon as the panel opened, someone brought up the question of whether or not the zombie mythos could possibly have the staying power of the vampire appeal in American pop culture.

And I said yes.

As soon as the word had left my mouth, the audience responded, "but you can't have zombie romance."

And I said yes, you could.

As soon as I got back to the Ravenous Romance office, I informed my colleagues that we would be doing a zombie romance anthology. They were emphatically skeptical. We posted the thesis on Facebook and hundreds of readers said they couldn't imagine romance with rotting corpses.

Oh, ye of little faith.

The zombie mythos is the perfect metaphor for the end of an era, for a society beset with change it doesn't understand but knows is here.

Vampires were the cultural embodiment of the end of the millennium: seductive immortals with (literally) cutthroat greed. Then came the recession and the end of the Bush boom, and with it came the realization that we were all worker drones paying off our bloated mortgages, bloodsucking corporations and even each other.

We are the dead.

So, in these pages you will find zombie tales that span the possibilities and boggle the brain. Jeremy Wagner's *Romance Ain't Dead* and Michael Marshall Smith's *Later* are two of the most romantic stories of lost love you will ever read. Dating the undead? Try *I Heart Brains* by Jaime Saare and Elizabeth Coldwell's zombie threesome in *Everyone I Love Is Dead*. Love among the dead? Take notes from Francesca Lia Block's *Revenants Anonymous* or S. M. Cross's *Through Death to Love*.

And what about undead exes? Gina McQueen's *Apocalypse as Foreplay* gives you one take you'll never forget. Then there's Jan Kozlowski's *First Love Never Dies*. And leave it to zombie master Brian Keene to show us how we can find love and revenge in the time of the zombie apocalypse in *Captive Hearts*.

But it's not all George Romero's zombie hordes in these

pages. Old-fashioned voodoo zombies make their presence known in Isabel Roman's *Zombified* and Mercy Loomis's *White Night, Black Horse.*

There's even a tale of zombie noir in R. G. Hart's *My Partner the Zombie,* and some classic paranormal romance in Regina Riley's *Undying Love.* And if Lois H. Gresh's *Julia Brainchild* doesn't make you laugh, well, then you *are* a zombie.

And just because this is a Ravenous Romance title, we have some zombie smut for you from two of our favorite RR authors. Dana Fredsti lets you know just how hot and bothered you can get from zombie hunting in *First Date* and Kilt Kilpatrick gives us the unforgettable erotic zombie escapades of a high school senior in *Last Times at Ridgemont High.*

There's something for everyone.

Enjoy.

LORI PERKINS

HUNGRY
FOR YOUR
LOVE

ROMANCE AIN'T DEAD

Jeremy Wagner

I love my dead wife. Wait, let me rephrase that. I love my *zombie* wife. She's not dead or alive. She's *reanimated*, brought back from death after drowning in Lake Michigan this past summer.

I'd better explain.

My wife, Sheri, and I have been married for twenty years. We're in our late forties and live in Winnetka on Chicago's North Shore. We're quite wealthy. I owe my fortune to major successes in real estate while Sheri's fortune comes from her deceased parents' multibillion-dollar medical-supply company. Sheri's an only child and her trust-fund releases and six-figure dividend earnings blast into our joint bank account every quarter. Needless to say, we don't work day jobs. We enjoy our marriage full time.

I've never been in such love with a woman. We met in college. By chance, Sheri happened to be at a bar my friends and I frequented. When I first saw Sheri, I was sucker punched by Eros. She was amazing to me: short and curly blond hair, toned body with all the right curves, green eyes from another world. I'm eating my heart out just thinking about the first moment we met. When I first saw her, she stood out in vivid, living color while the world around her turned to grayscale. I've never seen anyone the same way. Since then, I've forgotten every woman I met before her and I've never looked back.

Sheri's my proof of love at first sight. Also, we've proven love ain't dead, even if my better half is considered dearly departed.

Sheri's demise and return to the world of the living started when we went to the Ravinia Festival in Highland Park. We hunkered down on the grass on a beautiful summer evening with a basket full of cheeses and prosciutto paired with bottles of Laeticia Pinot. We became tipsy while watching, and dancing to, Tony Bennett. It was a blast.

We returned home at midnight and Sheri wanted to stroll down to the sand of our beachfront property. When we reached the beach, she got the idea to go skinny-dipping. I declined because Lake Michigan is ice cold year-round. Even on the hottest days, this Great Lake is freezing.

Sheri said, "You're a freaking wimp, Bruce." She kicked off her heels and took off her blue Escada dress and undergarments. I laughed and sat on the sand with another bottle of red wine, admiring her sweet backside running toward the water. She squealed and dove under. She came up wet and smiling in the moonlight. She said the chilly dip sobered her up. I waved the bottle of wine at her.

I watched Sheri backstroke farther away from the beach. Then I heard the sound of an engine. Sheri asked me what the sound was and I wasn't sure.

Minutes later, the sound grew louder and I made out the shape of a yellow speedboat with its lights off, hauling ass in the moonlight. Before I could yell and summon Sheri back toward shore, the boat roared past our beach and nailed my wife in the head. The boat never stopped.

I dropped the wine bottle and ran to the water. I dove in and swam out to Sheri. I found her floating facedown in the water, bleeding from her head. I turned her over, screamed her name, but she never responded. I towed her back to shore and began mouth-to-mouth resuscitation. She was DOA.

Sheri looked calm and restful in my arms. She didn't breathe and I couldn't hear her heartbeat. I assumed the boat had killed her on impact or she had drowned. Maybe a combo of both did it. Moments later, I rose and picked up Sheri in my arms. I carried her back to our mansion, remembering how I once carried her into our honeymoon suite. The memory was enough to break my heart to pieces.

Inside the dark house, I set Sheri down on a large Westchester leather sofa and covered her with a blanket. The room filled with moonlight. I walked in shock to retrieve my cell phone from the kitchen. I was about to call the cops when I heard the doorbell ring. I glanced at my watch and wondered who was at my front door at this hour. Soaking wet and shaking with cold and loss, I went to the door and flicked on the outside house lights.

To my surprise, I found my next-door neighbor, Doctor Wyclef Moliare, waiting for me. "Wyclef, what's going on? It's late."

"I heard screaming from your beach, Mister Bruce. Everything okay here, mon?"

I studied Wyclef. He wore khaki cargo pants with a bright white T-shirt emblazoned with artwork for a Chicago 5K Run, and no shoes. I always considered him a cool guy. A tall, mahogany-colored man with short dreads and about my age, Wyclef was a purebred Haitian. I remembered him as a real success story, coming to Illinois straight from Port-au-Prince as a teenager, later going to college and becoming a leading brain surgeon.

"Sheri's dead." I began crying. I hung my head, helpless to aid my beloved Sheri and helpless to stop sobbing.

"Take it easy, mon." Wyclef gave me a comforting hug before moving farther into my house with no regard to invite. Without looking at me, he said, "Where's your wife?"

I sniffled and wiped strings of snot from my cold nose. "She's . . . she's in the living room. On the sofa."

I watched Wyclef dash for the living room. His speed and attitude alarmed me and I ran after him. In the living room, I found him kneeling next to my wife's body, checking her pulse and vitals. I felt an odd prickle when he threw the blanket off of her naked corpse. "Hey, Doc. Now, wait—"

"What happened?" Wyclef continued his appraisal of Sheri's body.

"She got hit by a boat. She was taking a midnight dip and some fucker in a speedboat nailed her."

"You get the numbers, make of da boat?"

"No." The thought of the asshole getting away made me crazy. "Whoever it was, was driving fast with lights off and just kept on truckin'. Probably didn't realize . . ."

I started crying again, releasing big lost-love sobs as the weight of my soulmate's death crushed me. Through my tears, I saw Doctor Wyclef nodding and studying Sheri without looking at me. His physical inspection of my dead and nude wife unnerved me. I was thankful when he put the blanket back over her, tucking it around Sheri with a caring touch.

He got to his feet and looked at me. "How long ago this happen? When I hear the screams?"

I nodded and after a minute of wrestling with my overwhelming grief, I mustered coherent words. "Yeah. That was me screaming out there. Tried mouth-to-mouth, but she was gone."

"You call the police? Ambulance comin'?"

"No. You rang the doorbell before I got to my cell phone."

Wyclef looked down at me and grabbed my shoulders with his large hands giving me a tight squeeze. His dark brown eyes were wide and serious. "You love your wife, mon?"

"Of course. Christ, Wyclef. What kinda question is that?"

"Forget da hospital and police. They ain't gonna help this one. You want her back?"

I looked into those fierce Haitian eyes and wondered what the hell he was getting at. "I want her back more than anything. What are you saying?"

"I'm saying, my friend, I got ways to bring your loving wife back from da other side."

Losing Sheri and hearing my neighbor talk of reviving her from the grave was too much. I felt my legs weaken and Wyclef grabbed me and helped me to a leather chair. I hunched over and put my hands to my face. I breathed deep and regained control. "What in the name of Johnny Freaking Appleseed are you telling me? You sound like a goddamn nut."

Wyclef stood over me and laughed. It wasn't a malicious laugh, but it boomed and sounded scary even though the tone was lighthearted. He spoke in an assuring and baritone voice. "I can get her back. But we have to act quick and you got to believe. You believe in Vodou? You know, you call it Voodoo."

I wasn't sure how to answer this. Sheri and I are Jewish and never subscribed to any other religions or beliefs. To even consider anything related to witchcraft or being satanic was laughable and absurd to me. "No, Wyclef. I don't believe in that crap and I'm baffled as to why you're asking this. Sheri's dead and with God. I think it's time to call the cops and find out who killed her."

"Wait, mon. Listen." Wyclef maintained his deep and calm voice. "Before I came to da States, I was a teenage *bokor*. A witch doctor. That's what got me interested in medicine and led me down my path as a doctor and surgeon."

"A witch doctor?" I found this funny. I always respected Wyclef. He received hundreds of awards in medicine, escalating his reputation and accolades as one of the nation's most brilliant brain surgeons. Plus, the guy possessed great taste in food and music. I just couldn't see him dancing naked around a fire in

Haiti, making zombies and shrunken heads. "You gotta be kidding me."

"I learned many old secrets growing up in Haiti. I learned secrets of the dead. I saw medical science coupled with the spirit world. I've made zombies and I've raised zombies from dead bodies whose souls have moved on to da other places."

Again, I couldn't imagine this. "You've got one of the most reputable practices in Chicago. What would happen if your clients or the press knew you practiced black magic?"

Wyclef smiled wide and revealed his large white teeth and the significant gap between his incisors. He didn't answer my question but said, "Did you know Chicago was founded by a Haitian-born black slave in the early seventeen hundreds?"

I shook my head.

"Ya. It's true, mon. Voodoo is nothing new to da North Shore. Though it's funny you won't find as many blacks living in the North Shore today as we once did in the seventeen hundreds. Ironic, no?"

I shrugged my shoulders, knowing wealth has a lot to do with the racial diversity being nil in the North Shore communities. I felt compelled to mention Lake Forest was chock full of ebony players in the Bulls and Bears, but I held my tongue.

"I go to my house and come back with what I need." Wyclef looked serious now. "You let me do my 'ting and you'll see, Mister Bruce."

I thought about it. I had nothing to lose. Either his absurd claim to bring my wife back would happen or it wouldn't.

Then I'd call the cops and start making funeral arrangements. "All right. Get whatever you need. I'm a skeptical man, Wyclef. I'll try it your way and then I'm calling nine-one-one."

"I be right back." Wyclef's long legs carried him away.

I turned and looked down at Sheri. She looked at peace. With her relaxed features and her damp blond hair, she remained beautiful. I kissed her cold cheek. I told her how much I loved her. I told her how much she meant to me and how the world and my life would never be right without her. I began crying again and held her small body close to mine.

I was still holding Sheri when Wyclef returned. In one of his big arms, he carried a large cardboard box. In his opposite hand, he clutched a wooden cage with a clucking chicken in it. I thought of how the village of Winnetka didn't allow people to keep farm animals. I wondered where Wyclef got the chicken and where he kept it. *Were there others?* "Looks like you got your hands full."

Wyclef set the box and the cage down on the living room floor. He stepped away from his belongings and moved furniture and rugs until part of the hardwood floor was uncovered and bare.

"What're we doing?" I shivered, trying to imagine what we'd be doing on the floor. "You need anything?"

"Let's get Sheri on to da floor here." I laid Sheri down on the couch and stood up. Wyclef said, "I'll grab her feet and you take her by her top."

I walked around, knelt and eased my arms under Sheri and

grabbed her by her armpits. At the count of three, Wyclef and I lifted my wife from the couch. She was light and easy to move. To my dismay, the blanket fell off her in the move and we placed her naked body on the floor. I was going to grab the blanket for her when Wyclef said, "Leave da blanket be, Mister Bruce. She gotta be naked to da world right now."

"Does your wife know where the fuck you are right now?" I blurted this without thinking, not meaning to inject such a hard tone in my delivery.

Wyclef smiled and placed his reassuring hands on my shoulders. "Mister Bruce, my wife knows where I be. She praying for Sheri. She sends good vibes here to help your wife come back."

I dropped my head, feeling bad and sad about all of this. "Sorry."

"No worries, mon."

He walked over to his box of tricks and his pet chicken. I watched him dig through his box. He returned with several large black candles and a mason jar full of dead flower petals. He set these items down and moved Sheri around on the floor, spreading her arms and legs wide, splaying her out on her back. I no longer felt weird or overprotective about what he was doing.

Wyclef placed the candles in specific spots all around Sheri's body. He lit the candles and soon the moonlit room filled with candlelight. I watched the doctor open the jar and sprinkle dead flower petals all over Sheri's naked body. He placed the empty jar on the floor and turned to me. "Mister Bruce, I want you to sit and hold her head in your hands."

Before I could ask why, he turned away to retrieve his caged chicken. I did as instructed and sat between two candles with my legs crossed and looked down at the top of Sheri's head and her upside-down face. With a loving touch, I cupped the back and sides of Sheri's head with my hands and stroked her beautiful face with my thumbs.

Wyclef returned and set the cage on the floor next to me. The chicken inside clucked away, cocking its head in every direction. I watched him remove his shirt. His ripped upper torso shined in the candlelight. He opened the cage and removed the chicken. Then he said something to the bird in a foreign language. I watched with disgust as he gripped the chicken's neck with his large fist before snapping his arm and decapitating it.

"Jesus Christ, Doc. What the hell are you doing?"

Wyclef ignored me. He seemed to be in his own world.

I continued holding Sheri's head while watching Wyclef with morbid curiosity. He dropped the chicken head to the hard wood floor and held the chicken's body as it jerked in his grip. I watched him chant and pour chicken blood on his face and down his chest and stomach. Then he squatted down, chanting away while moving Sheri's body and the candles around like a crab. He set the now-motionless chicken carcass on the floor and picked up the head. Before I could object, he dabbed Sheri's forehead, cheeks, and lips with blood from the torn chicken neck. He raked her bare belly with chicken claws before dabbing his own face with chicken blood.

"Start saying Sheri's name, Mister Bruce. I want you to say

her name again and again like a mantra." Wyclef pulled out two sticks of incense and lit them on a candle flame. He held a stick in each hand, waving them back and forth as he continued squatting over my wife. "Here we go, mon."

My mind filled with a few questions. *What are we doing here? Are we going to jail after this?* I already knew what we were doing and why. I began speaking Sheri's name out loud over and over again.

Wyclef continued to squat and crab-shuffle over Sheri's dead body while waving incense smoke and chanting in some foreign tongue. I continued the mantra of my beloved's name while watching everything. Wyclef's eyes rolled back and his baritone voice grew louder while his movements became more wild and intense. He stomped with heavy feet and started yelling. He made it hard for me to concentrate on my repetitive speaking. The volume and dark tone of Wyclef's voice mixed with strange words he shouted and enforced with violent and frenzied motions. It felt most unsettling.

Wyclef reached a vocal crescendo and uttered, *"Jumbie . . . nzambi . . . da Bantu!"*

On his last word, I was looking down into Sheri's face while caressing it and speaking her name. Her chest gave an unexpected heave and her eyelids flew open to reveal milky white eyeballs staring straight into my own. Then all the candles blew out from an unseen blast of netherworld wind and left us in the dark.

"Wyclef! She's moving!" I knew I sounded hysterical. I was

creeped out, sitting in the dark living room with my deceased better half squirming beneath me. "What's going on, Doc?"

"Relax, mon."

My eyes focused in the dark. I watched Wyclef sit on Sheri's stomach. He fumbled for something, then lit up what looked like a hellacious-sized doobie. He locked his lips on Sheri's mouth and blew a giant puff of smoke into her.

"Shit!" I jumped when Sheri began coughing and making odd gurgling sounds. "What did you do?"

"She's back, Mister Bruce. I blew spirit protection into her so's no udder folk try hitching a ride with her from da udder side."

I raised an eyebrow at this spooky little comment. "Uh, right. I'm not worried about ghosts. You heard her. She coughed. It's a goddamn miracle." I felt an immediate need to got to a local synagogue to pray and give thanks.

"She coughed, but dat was just da release of spirit smoke. It kick-started her animation. She's not breathing, Mister Bruce. She never will again."

This was something I didn't want to hear. I felt an urgency to see. I didn't like being in the dark. "Can we get some real light in here? We gotta see what's going on."

Wyclef got to his feet and pulled my wife with him. I remained seated, watching with unbelieving eyes as Sheri stood on her own, naked and in the dwindling moonlight of the living room. She looked beautiful.

"Get the lights, mon."

I jumped to my feet and flicked on the living room lights.

Wyclef helped Sheri to the couch, sat her down and wrapped the blanket around her once again. I took a seat on the other side of her and hugged her tight.

My new mantra was, "I love you, baby." I said this nonstop, wanting Sheri to know I was here. I began weeping again. I rocked my wife and kept bawling her name, but she offered no verbal response. I looked at her with tears flowing down my face and was startled at what I saw.

"Hey, Doc." I spoke and my voice hitched with cracking words. "What's wrong with her eyes?"

I looked into Sheri's blank and pale face. Her features were slack and wooden. She didn't look like she was breathing but I knew she was on this side of the grave because she sat up with her eyes open. Her eyes troubled me the most—they moved but were lifeless. They held no light and no twinkle. The once-beautiful green was replaced by the ghostlike, milky-gray color of a ripe corpse.

"Sheri's zombified, Mister Bruce. When she departed from dis place she go to da udder place. When she comes back to you, she lose part of her spirit and some of da mortal traits she once had."

"Well, what the fuck, Doc?" I felt anger and distress at this bit of news. "I wanted Sheri back. I wanted my wife back one hundred percent. That's why I went through with this crazy Voodoo shit. I didn't want a zombie."

"Guess we shoulda talked about dis."

"Shoulda? What in the name of Johnny Freaking Appleseed

were you thinking? You asked if I wanted my wife back. I said yes. Now Sheri's a vegetable. I love my wife, but I woulda left her dead if I knew this would happen."

"Let me tell ya about zombies, Mister Bruce. Sometimes dey come around with some qualities dey once had. Sometimes dey recognize you." Wyclef offered a smile but lost it to a frown. "I won't lie. Sheri's not gonna be da same like before. She won't be talking. She's a zombie, mon, and she got part of a soul but no real life in her. She just here to be with you and that's it."

These new facts brought many questions to my mind. "How does she stay animated?"

"She doesn't need food. Some zombies, dey try and eat human flesh, but those are da ones who come from the bad side. Ones who go away too long and get corrupted, dey from a horror movie, mon. You don't want one coming back."

"So, she can't breathe and doesn't need food. Hopefully she won't eat me. What else should I know?"

"Her periods are over for good."

"Guess she won't need a gynecologist." I stared at Sheri and felt my heart pang. I didn't want my baby to be a lost soul. Mixed feelings filled me as I considered a future with a zombie wife. "She's got nothing to say about any of this, Wyclef. Maybe she doesn't want to be like this. She's not gonna live a normal life."

"She's not living a life, Mister Bruce. She's dead."

"Thanks, I needed that."

"Mister Bruce, my neighbor, I consider you a friend. I can

tell you're finding this hard to accept. All of dis. But you trust me, no?"

I thought about it. I wondered if maybe I jumped the gun in my panic and traumatized sadness when I allowed Wyclef to do his black magic on Sheri. Though a real consultation would have been nice, I trusted the man. I guess you don't get second opinions with witch doctors. "I trust you, Doc. I'm sure this ain't your first rodeo."

"That's right, mon. I grew up in Haiti with Voodoo being a normal part of life. Have faith in my words when I tell you dat even though Sheri's reanimated and zombified, she can feel your love, and she can take comfort in your company. Your wife can keep you company for the rest of your life. It's all about love and how much her companionship means to you."

I felt doubt at this. Though I accepted the implausible fact of Sheri dying and returning from the dead, I couldn't choke down how a walking corpse felt any emotions. "You sure? How do you know?"

"I've seen zombies absorb true love into their stock-still hearts, mon. I've seen zombies reach out and grab a lover's hand and even embrace another." Wyclef turned grim. "Then again, I seen a zombie bite the cheek off of her husband in Haiti. But dat was one of da bad ones, Mister Bruce."

"I'm not getting a warm fuzzy feeling. What bothers me is that Sheri's personality is gone. We won't be sharing ideas about movies or music. She won't tell me she wants to go to a museum or a farmer's market. Her spark is gone. I basically have a Real Doll on my hands. I should just get a dog to talk to and play with."

Wyclef remained grim. "Don't go getting pets, Mister Bruce. Dogs and cats go crazy around zombies. Dey know when someone's dead and walking and dey don't like it."

"Great. Parks and nice neighborhood walks with my zombie wife are out of the question."

"Don't let this bother you a bit." Wyclef smiled. "You gonna have plenty to do together."

"What about the long term?" I wondered what would happen to Sheri if I died and she remained on Earth. "If I pass on and she's still a zombie, then what's gonna happen to her? Our retirement funds ain't gonna do her any good."

Wyclef began laughing and slapped me on the shoulder. "Mister Bruce, you gave her mouth-to-mouth, no?"

"That's right."

"You blew your mortal breath into her, mon. She's got a piece of your life inside her. She gonna die with you when you go to the udder side. That's how it works."

This idea made me smile. I found it . . . romantic. Sheri expiring at the moment of my own death reminded me a bit of the tragic *Romeo and Juliet,* though Sheri and I were never "star-cross'd" lovers, but rather soulmates meant to be together—even under zombified circumstances.

"I go now." Wyclef picked up his candles and chicken parts

and boxed them up. "Where's your cleaning supplies? I'll get this blood and feathers off da floor."

"Don't worry, I'll handle it. Just get home to your wife. Please shower first."

Wyclef let loose a booming laugh. "Okay, Mister Bruce. I'll do dat."

Questions filled my head again. I looked at Sheri and I loved her more than ever now. I turned to my neighbor as he collected his things. "One last question, Doc."

Wyclef wiped chicken blood off his face and torso with his shirt and threw it in the box with his other items. "Yes?"

"What about rot? I mean—"

"Don't worry. She gonna stay fresh. But you need to wash her, Mister Bruce. Don't let her get too nappy."

"Right." I thought of tending to Sheri like an invalid, but I pushed the negatives away. I watched Wyclef with box in hand heading for the door. "Need a hand?"

"No." He reached the door and opened it. He turned and said, "You gonna be fine, Mister Bruce. You got lots on da brain and you be thinking how unnatural all dis is. But don't despair, it all works out and you'll find your way. I seen dis many times."

"Okay." I breathed easier though my chest and heart felt heavy. "What am I gonna tell people?"

"Don't worry, mon. It'll work out. Plus, I got your back."

Wyclef blasted me with one last smile and was out the door.

I turned to my beautiful Sheri, my zombie wife and kissed her cold cheek. "Let's go to bed, love."

Sure enough, Wyclef had my back. He assisted and gave Sheri an official Doctor Wyclef Moliare physical and mental evaluation. He provided substantial paperwork supporting his diagnosis that my wife suffered massive head trauma and remained catatonic. *Catatonia*: another word for zombie, I guessed.

In the following months, there was much explaining to do and a lot of changes made in my marriage.

My parents came up from Arkansas and saw Sheri once since her return to the living. I explained how she experienced a debilitating head injury and how her speech and motor skills were impaired. My parents believed me. They comforted me, hugged and kissed Sheri and conveyed their sympathies and advised me to be strong.

Sheri's few friends were told about her accident with the boat and I reiterated how she'd suffered a terrible head injury and would never be the same. I used Wyclef's medical records and word to endorse all the bullshit I told everyone.

After the first six months passed, I didn't hear from Sheri's friends outside of holiday cards and an occasional e-mail wishing us well.

Despite my reservations, Wyclef assured me I could be intimate with Sheri without being a deviant or doing anything illegal since my wife was "technically" alive in an animated state. But this was the same guy who said she was dead and a zombie. The words *dead* or *zombie* don't help my libido any, but I got past it and I make love to Sheri often.

Sheri's been wrapping her arms around me on her own. She once nibbled on my ear and I jumped, thinking it was *Dawn of the Dead* time. It turned out to be innocent and unexpected in a delightful, yet macabre way. Perhaps she has a flicker of loving inside her? I don't know, but I hope.

I've taken the liberty of placing green contacts into her eyes in order to lose the undead gray and bring back the sweet color of her gaze. I bathe Sheri every day in her favorite bubble bath and scrub her with her favorite body wash while whispering sweet nothings to her. I also dress her in her favorite outfits, spray her with her favorite perfume, and I play her favorite bands on the iPod dock every day just to give her a sense of herself and the things she left behind when I lost her in Lake Michigan.

That's true love in my book.

I love my dead wife. Again, let me rephrase that. I love my *zombie* wife. I love Sheri more than anything in the world and we're together and living life—well, one of us is. I wouldn't trade it for anything. She's my soulmate, the love of my life and she owns my heart. I believe our love will outlast time itself, even after the physical marriage is dust.

'Til death do us part? It didn't work out that way.

REVENANTS ANONYMOUS

Francesca Lia Block

I saw him at the Revenants Anonymous meeting I had started attending. I heard he was going to be the speaker the following week so that night I managed to pull myself together enough to put on a cute outfit of tight black jeans, high-heeled black boots, and a white shirt that still smelled faintly of bleach. I had even put on makeup so I wouldn't look so pale, and flat-ironed my black bob. Around my neck I wore a giant silver heart-shaped watch on a thick silver chain, as if to imitate what I no longer had inside my chest. I was pretending to be un-dead (meaning *not* dead, rather than one of the undead) because my sponsor, Rachel, had told me to act "as if." It had worked for her. She was now successfully employed and had a nice, if somewhat clumsy, boyfriend who took her on vacations and told her she was beautiful and that he cherished her. I, on the other hand, couldn't sell a story to save my life (pun intended), in spite of having won the big screenwriting contest just out of college, and I hadn't kissed anyone for two years since Brian left.

When the guy walked in to the church basement where the meeting took place, I grabbed the heart locket and held on tight.

The guy was very tall and wore his (dyed?) black hair in a low pompadour with thick sideburns. His eyes were strikingly blue with long eyelashes that made him look a little stunned. He had large, masculine features, a high forehead with some frown lines carved into it, high cheekbones, and a full mouth. I had heard on a talk show once that very masculine-looking men have extra testosterone that can make them more likely to behave like players. I wonder if that applied to revenants as well, since we really didn't have testosterone. He was wearing black jeans, a white shirt, black motorcycle boots, and a white T-shirt. *Twins*, I thought. (To be fair, he had worn the same thing the week before and I was imitating him.)

His eyes slid over me briefly and he went to take a seat. We said the Serenity Prayer and then he began.

"I'm Ed, and I'm a revenant," he said.

"Hi, Ed," everyone droned.

"I've been coming to these meetings for ten years now. When I first came, I literally had pieces of flesh hanging off my body. You could see the bones poking through here," he pulled down the neck of his T-shirt to reveal his clavicle, "and here." He pulled up his T-shirt to reveal a prominent hipbone above the line of his jeans. There was black hair on his chest and stomach.

"The way it started, I'd given up on my music. I was working the bar at a strip club and doing it with every sally I could find and getting drunk off my ass every night. Then I met this one girl, this stripper. She treated me like shit. I couldn't get enough of her. I had to go out of town for a few weeks to visit my dad who was dying and when I came back she had broken up with me. So I just went ape shit. I followed her around begging her to come back. I drank twice as much and started snorting blow. I served alcohol to one too many drunks and he had a car crash that night and died."

The audience grimaced collectively, sympathetically. Ed went on.

"I went back home to see my dad. He had cancer and it was eating away at him from the inside out. I sat at his bedside but I really didn't feel that much and I didn't understand why. When he finally died, I didn't feel anything. Then I started having these dreams where he was touching me. Then I stopped dreaming at all. By then I was officially one of us."

I thought, *Boy, do I wish I'd met him when I was alive, before my heart got so fucked with. I'd rather have him kill it than all those shits that did.*

"And then I found these rooms," Ed was saying. "Like I said, I was literally dripping skin. I was craving the meat."

A low groan went up from the room.

"I had lost my job and all my friends. Since then I've started recording music again and I've started a business so I don't have to bartend. It's other people's music, I'm engineering. It's not my stuff, but it's a start. And I'm taking care of myself. I'm showing up to meetings, even on days when I have to drag myself off my corpse ass and shamble in. I have a sponsor and a sponsee. I don't think about the meat. I've started talking to women again. When I feel really dead, I do something like pet a dog. I know it sounds lame, but I pet a dog. Or I take a walk in nature. I never thought I'd be saying that in front of a room full of people before, but whatever, it's true. I even do yoga now. And I can listen to music now, not just for work. It used to be impossible because it reminded me of how I used to just be able to hear the first chords of certain songs and start crying and how now I can't cry, but I listen anyway. So all I want to say is, even though I'm still a revenant, I'll always be a revenant, that's what the big book teaches, but there's hope. There's hope, man. Thanks for letting me share."

He stepped down and there was some slow, heavy-handed applause. I tried to catch his eye but he kept his head lowered as he took his seat. The guy next to him, Malcolm, the secretary, used what looked like tremendous effort to high-five him.

We went around the circle and when it came to me I said, "Hi. I'm Casey and I'm a revenant."

"Hi, Casey," they all said, including Ed—I wasn't looking but I could distinguish his deep voice.

"I just want to thank the speaker for sharing," I began, still not looking at him. "It's very inspiring to hear that. I've only just started coming to these meetings. The last relationship I was in was two years ago. It screwed me up really bad. My mom had just died and I kind of glommed onto this guy but he felt suffocated and split. I couldn't eat or sleep. And I couldn't write anymore." I thought about making the joke about not being able to write to save my life, but I didn't know if it was in bad taste, and besides, it wasn't all that funny. "Anyway, that's when it happened. Now I'm doing computer sales from home. I don't like to go out. I have to stay away from the meat." Everyone hummed. I stopped. "Anyway, thanks for letting me share."

When I finally looked up, Ed was watching me. I thought I felt my face get hot but that couldn't be. I must have been imagining it.

When the meeting was over Malcolm invited everyone to his home in Silverlake for a party. The house was a broadbeamed green wooden Craftsman with a big porch overlooking the lights of Sunset Boulevard. Malcolm built a fire in the fire pit and we stood around under the cold stars. Like most revenant gatherings, no one said much. A few were making a pathetic attempt at dancing, but it was really just shuffling their feet and occasionally nodding their heads. Still, it was better than what I could do.

I was gripping an empty glass—sometimes it helped me feel human to have something in my hand—when Ed came up to me.

"I enjoyed your share," he said. "Casey, right?"

I nodded.

"I'm Ed."

I shook his hand. It was huge, with silver rings.

"What's this?" he pointed to my heart watch.

I suddenly wished I hadn't worn it; it seemed desperate, like something a revenant that wanted to be human too badly would wear. A poseur revenant. "Oh, nothing."

"It's nice. Too many people stopped wearing watches with

the cell phones." He held out his broad, bony wrist. He wore an old-fashioned silver watch. "It was my dad's."

"But I thought . . ." I began and stopped myself. I didn't want to be rude.

"I know. I think my dad fucked with me when I was a kid. But he was my dad. He didn't know what he was doing. This helps me to remember to forgive him."

I nodded. I thought about the silver engagement ring Brian had given me. It was a really cool ring, engraved with tiny leaves and flowers. Sometimes I wanted to wear it but I couldn't because it reminded me of how much I hated him and then chunks of flesh would start peeling off my face and shit. I wondered if I could learn to forgive him.

"So your mom died recently?" Ed asked. His voice had a tender quality that I couldn't recall hearing in another revenant.

"Yes. She had cancer, too." My voice, on the other hand, was dry and flat.

"It's a motherfucker."

I nodded.

"And you're young to lose a mom." There was the tenderness in his voice again.

"Not that young," I said. "I was twenty-five when this happened two years ago."

"You mean when you went revenant? That's young to be one of us."

"What about you?" I asked.

"Well, I was thirty, so I'm technically forty now."

"You look good," I managed to say.

He winked. He actually winked. I'd never seen a revenant wink before, at least not in a sincere way, but more of in a spastic way like they were trying to imitate a human. Ed actually looked human. "You, too."

The flames of the fire pit were heating up my face to the point where I had to back away. That was a surprise—I was never hot anymore. I must have been imagining it. Then I felt Ed's hand touch my wrist and I imagined a flaming up there, too.

"Would you like to grab a 'tea' some time?" He made quote marks around the word *tea*—we really didn't drink it.

I nodded without thinking and he took out his cell and programmed in my phone number.

"I'll call you, Casey," he said and I wondered if he was really one of us at all. Just like there were revenant poseurs, there were some humans who posed as us because it was trendy and seemed cool to them. God knows why.

He told me to meet at the L.A. County Museum. I was a little nervous to be out in such a public place with all the meat walking around but I said the Serenity Prayer over and over as I drove west along Wilshire. I was wearing a black sundress and wedgies and I'd put on extra lotion to keep the skin from peeling on my shoulders and arms. I got there first and watched Ed walk up the wide, low stairs under the portico toward me. He had flat mirrored shades on so I couldn't see his eyes. His shoulders were broad and his arms were a little too long for the white button-down shirt he wore. His legs, in jeans, were long, too. I felt really short, even in my high shoes.

"You look nice," he said, kissing my cheek.

"So do you," I replied. Rachel had said that if I felt uncomfortable making conversation, I could just sort of repeat what the other person said with a twist. I wondered if that would get me in trouble somehow.

"Do you want to see the exhibit?"

"Do you want to see the exhibit?" I replied.

"Yes I do."

"I do."

"Good."

"Good."

"Casey," he asked gently. "Can I ask you something? Are you nervous?"

"Are you nervous?"

He cocked his head at me. "No. I'm fine. I thought you seemed interesting at the meeting. I'd like to hear about your writing and whatever. You don't have to be nervous with me."

"Okay," I said. "Thanks."

He took my hand and led me toward the ticket booth. It was startling to have him touch me. Most of us didn't ever touch.

We went to the Pompeii exhibit. I wondered what it must have been like for the archeologists to find that stuff under the earth, under the ash. What it must have been like to dig up a marble god, a whole fresco of a garden with fountains and birds and flowers painted in pale shades of blue and green. You couldn't feel dead when you saw that.

We circled around a statue of a satyr playing lasciviously with a beautiful nude girl. She had her fingers in his face and was twisting her torso as if to get away from him but they were both laughing. When Ed and I got closer we saw that the girl was a hermaphrodite, with breasts and a small erect penis. I felt something move through my body and I hardly knew what it was because it had been so long.

"Roman kink," Ed said, and we laughed.

I hadn't heard my laugh in so long that I didn't recognize it at first. It sounded kind of nice, though.

There were some giant horse heads on pedestals. Ed looked into their eyes but I had to stare up into their noses.

"You have a better view," I said. "All I see are nostrils. But I'm used to that, being so short." I realized I had actually made a joke—a shitty joke, but a joke—aloud.

"Oh, now I'm embarrassed," he said, coyly, covering his nose and we laughed again.

Toward the end of the exhibit I wandered away from him over to an alcove where a giant statue of Aphrodite carved in white marble stood with her arms outstretched. I stood under her and closed my eyes.

When I opened them, Ed was beside me. "Whatcha doin'?"

"She's beautiful, huh?" I said softly.

"But do you think love looks like that?" he asked, staring up at her perfect white curves. "Or do you think it's much more dangerous looking?"

"Probably. But I like to imagine it's like this," I said.

We weren't talking like revenants; it was weird.

We left the museum and walked out into the sunshine. After the air conditioning the day felt warm. But then I realized I was probably imagining the feeling of warmth. The sun could trick you like that if things were going well.

We sat at the café and ordered a salad to share, which we didn't eat, of course—it was just for show. We could have gotten chicken but sometimes you dig into it in a way that's not appropriate—it reminds you of the meat—and there were a lot of people around. Ed told me about his job recording music, how he had gone to music school, used to be in bands. He said he still thought about writing songs but then he gave up because he was too old to be a rock star.

"You're not!" I said. I was surprised and a little embarrassed at my own vehemence. "You look great. You look like a star."

I could have sworn I saw Ed blush, but then his face was pale again.

"You have to be a kid to make this work," he said. "Seriously."

"But you could still write. You could still play. For yourself and your friends." I wanted to say, *I'd like to hear you,* but I stopped myself.

"Nah," said Ed and I realized that he really was a revenant; he wasn't a poseur as I had suspected. That's what we revenants did. We gave up before we had even tried.

"What about your writing?" he asked.

"I won this big contest out of UCLA and then it was all downhill after that," I said.

"I hear you. Basically you're dead at twenty-five in this town."

"Literally," we said together and laughed, again.

We walked down a slope and along a shaded path beside a fountain. White roses floated on the shallow water. There was something vaguely bridal about them. I wondered who had strewn them there. I felt a slight shiver up my spine and it surprised me.

"Do you think we have souls?" I asked Ed. "Because that's what I used to write about mostly—souls. But now I don't think I have one."

He squinted at me and chewed thoughtfully on the handle of his sunglasses. "I don't know, to be honest. I don't think we're supposed to, technically."

I looked at the white petals trembling on the surface of the dark water. "But those roses. When I look at them, in the water like that, I feel something. But I can't find words for it."

"That's why those Romans made art, right? Why we write music, isn't it? Or write stories or whatever, poetry?"

"But we don't," I said. "Anymore."

He took my hand again—mine felt tiny inside his—and headed through a red lacquer Japanese archway. I had the same startled sensation I'd had before when he'd touched me. "That's going to change," he said.

On the way to our cars we walked around the tar pits with

the statue of the father and the baby Mastodon standing on the edge of the bubbling black water while the mother Mastodon drowned in the tar. She had been drowning like that for years—I'd seen this statue when I was a little girl and it was already old by then. The baby had been screaming for all that time. It made me think of how I felt when my mother died, how she sank into the pit of cancer and I couldn't save her; all I could do was stand there and scream silently and turn to stone.

Ed walked me to my beat-up Honda and hugged me good-bye. I raised my mouth to kiss his cheek but he turned so our lips met. His mouth was a lot bigger than mine and it smelled like tea tree oil and peppermint. A lot of revenants favored those scents to disguise the way we smelled, which wasn't always pretty. But Ed tasted good. I hoped I tasted okay to him. I'd used some breath spray after the restaurant even though I hadn't eaten anything—doing normal things like using breath spray after going to a restaurant made me feel like I belonged.

"I'd really like to hear your music," I said. And then wondered if I'd offended him because he'd told me he hadn't played since he'd changed.

But he didn't seem offended. He smiled at me. "Only if you read me something you wrote."

So that was it—we'd made plans to see each other again, sort of. At least as close to making plans as most revenants get. But

I didn't hear from him. Not that I was surprised—that was typical. It was kind of a miracle we'd gone on a date at all. If that was what it was. (He'd texted me to meet him at the museum that time, and I'd just written back, *c u there*). I didn't get another text and I was beginning to think I was a complete ass for assuming I'd see him again or that he had been sincere about having him read him my writing, when the next Saturday night, he showed up at the meeting in the church basement. (The church didn't know exactly what kind of meeting it was; I guess they assumed we were A.A.) Sometimes revenants pretended they didn't know each other from week to week—it was hard enough for us to get out of the house and be around other revs— but he greeted me warmly and said my name. I felt him watching me during the meeting.

When it was his turn to speak he said, "Hi, I'm Ed, and I'm a revenant."

"Hi, Ed."

"I had a really good week. I met this nice person and we did a nice thing at a nice place. I felt almost alive. Maybe I did feel alive. It's been so long, I'm not sure. But anyway I'm just grateful to be here. That's it."

I could have sworn this time, for sure, that my face got hot.

After the meeting we went for fellowship at the coffee house next to the church and he sat next to me but he didn't talk to me much. He was talking mostly to some pale, tattooed young girls, one who had scars on her wrists and one with a purple bruise around her neck. He seemed to have a positive effect on them; the one with the scars on her wrists even laughed stiffly, like she was imitating laughter, but still. I found myself wondering again if he was the real thing or some human on a mission to save us.

He walked me to my car in the church parking lot. The chrome shone in the fluorescent light. The air buzzed with electricity and crickets. The night was warm and smelled of pollen.

"Do you want to hear a song?" he asked.

"A song?"

"I wrote one this week. After we hung out."

I tugged on the heart around my neck. "Of course." I realized how that sounded—like I thought he had written the song because of me. "I mean of course I want to hear it."

So we went to his place, a small bungalow with a courtyard full of banana palms and climbing jasmine. Inside, the walls were painted baby blue and hung with a variety of guitars. Ed lit some candles and we sat on the couch and he took an acoustic down. He slung it on and leaned forward. The fabric of his jeans strained against his knees, ready to tear. He looked at me.

"So you used to write about souls?"

I nodded.

"This is a song about souls."

He sang it to me. It was dark and tough and bluesy. His voice was deep and warm and really, really good. His body rocked back and forth. Sometimes he threw back his head and opened his mouth wide and I saw his teeth, which were a little big but made him look sexy and fierce. I noticed that the incisors were slightly sharp, almost pointed.

Hot, I thought.

I hadn't thought that word in years.

After he was done with the song, I applauded. He grinned.

"I like it," I said. I wanted to say I love it but I didn't want to sound like I was posing as a human.

"Hey, hey, glad you like it, Miss Casey."

"Do you think we used to have souls?" I asked, thinking about his lyrics—the parade of ragtag souls marching through the town.

He leaned back and put the guitar pick in his mouth, chewed on it—he liked to chew on things, it seemed. "Yes. For sure."

"And do you think people's souls continue on after they die?" I asked.

"Yes, ma'am."

"So then where do you think our souls went if we don't have them now?"

He took the pick out of his mouth, made a face at it and flicked it down on the table. "Good question. I don't know, but I think they must be somewhere."

I couldn't stop asking him things. I wanted to keep asking and asking and find out what he believed. It felt like so long since I'd had a man to ask about anything, one whose ideas I wanted to hear, anyway. "Do you think souls recognize each other, or if your souls connect and when you die, do your souls recognize each other when they meet again?"

"Well, they aren't personalities. They're something else. So I don't know exactly what remains and what you recognize. But I think there is some kind of recognition, or some kind of connection, maybe? I don't know."

"Because you sort of seem familiar to me," I said. I was so talkative all of a sudden! The way I used to be.

"That's funny because you seem familiar to me, too, girl."

"But not like someone I actually knew, more like there's just something about you."

"I know what you mean."

Maybe we knew each other when we were alive, I thought. Then I remembered something. A band I'd gone to see at McCabe's Guitar shop when I was a teenager. The lead singer was so cute—I'd been stricken staring up at his big, sexy mouth, his handsome, grimacing face. He almost looked like it hurt him to sing, or like he was having an orgasm. After the show—it was hard to remember much about my life—but I think I went up to him and I think we talked. He'd seemed to want to talk to me but I'd gotten scared and hurried off when another girl came over. (I'd never thought I was pretty back then; now I look at pictures of myself when I was alive and think, *not bad—what were you complaining about?* Plus I was writing at that time, I cared about things, I didn't crave the meat.) I'd looked back and seen his eyes watching me still—blue eyes with black Maybelline-long eyelashes—but I only walked faster.

Now Ed leaned forward and put two fingers on my neck. I thought I felt a pulse there, under his fingertips, but how could that be? I was dead as a doornail. I hadn't felt anything in years. I was a zombie and that was one thing I knew for sure. The only heart I had was the watch locket around my neck like the one the Tin Woodsman got from the Wizard of Oz. But then I wondered if I'd made the whole thing up—the revenant thing. Maybe I was still the same. Maybe I was just broken, but not irreparably. Maybe we all were and this revenant thing was just another trend, like kids pretending to be vampires because they thought it was cool. But it wasn't cool to be dead. And maybe, just maybe, I was still alive.

Ed lifted my hand and pressed my fingers against his neck. It felt rough and his Adam's apple was huge. But he had a pulse, pooling there in the thick of his neck. I was sure of it. He moved his head forward and slid his hand behind my head, under my hair, grasping the strands between his fingers as he leaned to kiss me. I shuddered with happiness under the pressure of his lips and tried not to smile and ruin the kiss with my teeth. Slowly we slid down until I was lying on the sofa and he was above me and I felt his erection through his jeans. I melted between my thighs. My heart was pounding—there was no mistaking it. He reached up my back and unhooked my bra. Then he pulled my T-shirt up, tugged my bra away, and fit his mouth over my breast. I arched and pressed up to meet him and I could feel the whole weight of him on top of me fitting into all the right places even though he was almost twice my size. I liked the way his weight almost knocked the wind out of me—it meant I was breathing. Gasping, I took his head in my hands and kissed him as he fumbled with my jeans and pushed himself up against my panties.

"Are we going to do this?" he asked me. "I wanted to wait. But I don't think I can wait. It's been like ten years."

"We're going to," I said firmly.

"Wait?" he asked. He sounded worried and sad but resigned.

"No, not wait."

A long, slow smile spread across his face.

We fucked because, basically, we had to. You don't pass up a chance like that, to feel human, to feel alive, not when you've been dead for years. Even if it was just a temporary reprieve, I didn't care. I howled with joy as he rubbed his cock against my clit and slid inside me, pressing his tip repeatedly up against the soft pad of my wall. More and more; I didn't want him to stop. I clenched around him tighter and tighter to keep him there. Then he went rigid and cried out; his come was spilling inside of me and I was releasing in waves and crying real tears and when it was over he took my face and settled it on his chest and said, very gently, "Welcome back, baby."

I wondered if he was talking about me or my soul, or his.

The next day I woke up in his bed and saw his big face lit up by morning. I kissed his cheek—there was stubble—and he pulled me closer to him, still half asleep. I sniffed his armpit; he smelled sweaty and warm like a man. I wanted this moment to go on forever—the sun through the window, his scent, the rumpled sheets, my body tucked into his—but I wasn't even sure if I was ever going to wake in his bed again; you never know what's going to happen. Still, I was alive. I had a soul.

To prove it, when I got home I sat down to write this story.

I HEART BRAINS

Jaime Saare

1

Derrick stared at the man nestled in the wheelchair, giving him a lengthy once over. His body was a thing of beauty—tall, broad, athletic. The fine crevices obtained by hard work and muscle definition were obvious, the outline of a rock-hard six-pack visible. Even nicked from a recent shave, his face was just as good, and his short black hair neat and tidy.

Too bad the motherboard upstairs had fizzled and died out, leaving him in this shitty fucking predicament.

About as shitty as mine.

The small folder resting on the table beside him listed pertinent information. His age: 28. His height: 6'2". His weight: 205 lbs. His known allergies: none.

It was like a Best Buy for the brain dead.

So wrong on so many levels.

"Can I help you, sir?" A sales associate approached, wringing his hands.

The showroom was nearly empty. Only one other person was in the area, and he was in the same pickle. The body that held his interest was much younger, in the early twenties, with a nasty-looking scar over his forehead. A large muted television featuring a continuous loop of football was placed directly in front of the wheelchair, the table with his information and stats placed next to him like a playbook.

All the bodies had an area just for them, playing off their strengths. The women were displayed as risqué as the management dared, while the men were groomed to perfection.

It was laughable and depraved at the same time.

Derrick motioned at the once healthy and vibrant man and asked, "How did it happen?"

"Carbon monoxide," the clerk answered readily.

That got his attention. He stopped staring at the all-but-living body and focused on the small pudgy man hoping to bring in a fat commission.

"Suicide?"

"I'm afraid so."

Protocol dictated that the fine upstanding employees of Bodies For Your Brains didn't divulge those sorts of intimate details—reminding the clientele that the "product" was once a living man or woman not too much unlike themselves didn't help sales—but he could see the gleam in tub-o'-lard's black beady eyeballs.

He wanted to share what he knew.

"Why?" Derrick whispered and glanced around, as if the fat

fucker was revealing the secrets to Atlantis instead of how a guy decided to off himself.

You know, therefore you must tell, he screamed with his eyes and mannerisms, standing before the salesman like a revered mystic on a holy mission. *The fate of the world rests on your shoulders. Use the force, Tub-o. Let it guide you.*

"Well." Fat man peered around and lowered his voice. "His wife found him in the garage after he bet everything they owned on a long-shot horse that broke its leg out of the gate. That's why he's here."

"She's a scorned woman?"

Tub-o nodded eagerly. "And then some. I was here the day she brought him in with the release papers. She was the most beautiful thing I'd ever seen, with long legs"—he moved his hands down his stumpy body and brought them back up again, cupping his man boobs "—and the nicest pair of ta-tas this side of Dollywood." He sighed and shook his head. "Then she opened her mouth. I haven't heard a woman talk like that since my Aunt Ermer gave my Uncle Mortimer hell for driving the widow Parker home."

"So she's fine with donating his body?"

"Absolutely."

"Good to know."

He walked in a circle, studying what once remained of—he leaned forward and read the cheap paper name tag—Eric Joshua Bradworth. The body was good, in incredible condition, and he was running out of time.

Glancing down at his own skin, he struggled not to cringe. Once blue veins were now turning black, the surface no longer smooth and silky but becoming dry and parched.

The zombie virus was in full swing.

He'd learned within hours of his expenditure—following the car accident that severed the femoral artery and bled him dry—that he wouldn't be seeing those heavenly white gates. God had other plans in store. But if he didn't get his brain inside another body, the only thriving portion of him would slowly start to decompose, and then he'd be singing along with a well-known straw man while searching for the Wonderful Wizard of Oz.

Goddamn the government and its twisted chemical weapons gone awry.

"When did it happen?" the attendant asked casually.

"Just this morning," he answered.

"Damn, man. That's got to be tough. But if you're here, that means you're ahead of the curve. It could be worse."

"You mean I could be like the other assholes without a sizeable bank account to procure a body?"

"You said it, not me." His rat-sized eyes narrowed and his portly belly rippled as he shifted his feet. "Are you interested in buying or will you shop around?"

He walked to Eric's wheelchair and kneeled, staring at the body he would control and the face he would assume. It could have been worse. The guy wasn't ugly and he'd died of something that didn't affect viability or fuck up his face or limbs.

He would be able to continue with his very physical lifestyle, having only the impediment of learning to maneuver and control a body both taller and wider than the one he was accustomed to.

But there was one deciding factor that would put it to the test.

Rodent-eyed associate frowned when he moved closer and placed his hands between the legs of the invalid, accessing the package just between. In a normal setting, he wouldn't be caught dead copping a feel of another man's cock and sack. But since he was dead, and the body didn't belong to anyone at the present moment, he felt his heterosexual status was still on the up and up.

When satisfied with the answer he sought, he asked, "What are the terms of sale?"

"Uh, what?" Tub-o stammered and quickly looked away when Derrick peered up at him and smiled, behaving like the sick bastard Tub-o thought he was.

Fucking prick.

"Oh, the terms of sale!" He recovered nicely, providing a businesslike face. "No refunds, no returns. The body comes with a certificate of health and a yearlong membership to the Bodies For Your Brains gym. You are responsible for procuring the surgeon of your choice if you'd like someone other than the doctors retained for the company."

Derrick thought it over and glowered at the hand that was turning grey. His entire body was rotting. Soon he would fall apart. A million dollars was an obscene amount of cash to pay for anything, but in this case, it went far beyond any connotation of medical necessity. He took a moment to thank his parents for investing in Hilton Hotel and Resorts when they started decades ago. Otherwise, he'd be another working stiff that fell directly into the stereotype when rigor mortis set in.

"I'll take it," he said, rising to his feet. "Where do I sign?"

Tub-o smiled cheerily and he had to resist the overwhelming temptation to press a finger into his Santa Claus–sized belly to see if he would giggle like the Pillsbury Doughboy.

"Over here, sir."

He walked to the cheap plywood and aluminum-plated desk, taking the seat directly across from Tubs. A large wooden plaque told him the associate was actually Thaddeus Harris.

Derrick bristled at the irony.

"Thaddeus Harris?"

"Yeah, so?"

"As in *The Police Academy* Thaddeus Harris?"

The unfriendly smile on Tubs's face said it all. "I'm a lot like the Harry Potters of the world that existed in anonymity before a certain boy wizard took the name to new heights."

"Must suck."

Obsidian eyes flashed knowingly. "I'm sure there are things far worse."

Derrick notched his chin and gave the man props. "Touché."

A few clicks on the trusty Dell on his desk and Thaddy boy started listing off what Derrick guessed was the standardized version of a check list. No returns, no exchanges, no liability to the company after the donor left the property, no feeding the body after midnight . . .

"Oh," Tubs said, frowning at the screen.

"Oh?"

"There's a stipulation here. It's one of our lesser-used clauses. I'm not even sure if it's right." He wrestled his girth from the chair and gave a thin smile. "Would you excuse me for a moment?"

He didn't really pay attention when Tub-o bustled away, too wrapped up in just how fucked up his life had become. He was a respectable businessman, operating a successful brokerage firm passed down through the generations. Life had been good—excellent, even.

Well, almost.

Losing his girl to a bedpost-notching best friend was a blow to his self-esteem, but they'd all worked through it. If Tanya was looking for greener pastures, let her have them. She'd learn her lesson when Tom moved on to his next challenge.

Death changed a lot of things, including bitterness.

This time, he would find the right woman. And when he did, he would never let her go.

"Excuse me, Mr. . . . ." Thaddeus waited for him to introduce himself.

"Quinn, Derrick Quinn."

"Mr. Quinn," Thaddeus said. "There is one minor stipulation the wife checked, and after taking a look at the hard copy, it's definitely not a computer error. Sometimes it happens when there are children left behind, but in this particular circumstance, it's rather odd."

Figures.

Just when he thought he had a handle on the shit, he got thrown another curveball.

When Tubs wasn't forthcoming with the stipulation in question, he demanded, "Well? Spit it out, Thaddeus. What does she want?"

The belly bracing the clipboard in hand quivered like Jell-O and he fidgeted uncomfortably. "She wants to meet the buyer."

2

Olivia DeMarkus Bradworth wasn't in the mood for a date. The last time she agreed to one, she wound up married to a schmuck who had the body of a Greek god and shit for brains. But since the holy creator got it wrong the first time, she figured it was her moral obligation to set the wrong things right.

She smoothed her hair, examining her face in the rearview mirror. The short blond strands were still slick from the straight iron, and the smoky MAC pigments ensured her mushroom blue irises popped. She scowled and shook her head. The dark circles underneath were still visible, but in the time it took to change from her Hooters uniform and drive to the posh LaMer restaurant in Lovington, she was lucky she looked as good as she did.

"Oh, get on with it," she sneered at her reflection. "He's a zombie, for Christ's sake!"

The stipulation regarding her introduction to the buyer was something she assumed would take place inside Bodies For Your Brains. The plan was simple: meet the brain, tell the brain it had best take advantage where the other brain had not, bid the brain a fond farewell, and collect the cash. But she quickly learned the meeting would take place on her time, in a place of the purchaser's choosing. Apparently, this newest flourishing medical industry was as cold and callus as the people they catered to.

Which says what about you?

"Damn it!"

Snagging her purse in one hand and the keys in the other, Olivia climbed out of her beat-up Honda Civic. She slammed the door as hard as she could and sighed in relief when the latch caught and held on for dear life.

Thank you, Jesus.

Her poor vehicle was on its last nut and bolt. Bitterly, she remembered it would have been retired months ago. Too bad her naïve ass didn't bother trusting her husband as much as she loved him.

As in not at all.

Mustering up as much pride as she was able, she strode across the sidewalk, noticing the expensive vehicles parked next to her pitiful jalopy. Someone opened the door for her and she tried not to squirm. Even wearing her best, she paled in comparison to the normal patrons of the establishment.

"Can I help you, miss?" The hostess, while keeping her voice polite, observed her critically.

"I'm meeting someone."

"Who are you meeting?" she asked, peering down at the reservation list.

"Derrick Quinn."

"Oh." The hands on the paper visibly trembled and she gave a very weak smile. "This way, please."

They walked past the tables and booths, to an area a sign indicated was reserved. As Olivia approached, she saw a dark head bob, as if trying to see her as well. Then she rounded the corner and got the shock of her life.

The z-virus was a cruel fucking bitch.

The man was obscenely good looking, with features straight out of *GQ*. He must have died recently because his skin, though ashen, still retained a hint of tan. His dark brown hair was worn long, brushing past his chin, and his goatee was neatly trimmed.

From the blatant approval in his stare, he found her equally acceptable.

"Mrs. Bradworth?" Derrick stood and walked around the table, pulling out a chair. "Please, would you take a seat?"

Olivia's body operated on auto pilot. She walked, one Payless shoe-covered foot placed in front of the other, and then she sat.

"I appreciate your meeting me here."

She shook her head and cleared her throat. "No problem."

A waitress arrived and she nodded meekly when he ordered, unsure of what to say. He was polite where Eric was brash, cultured where Eric had been raised on MTV and Nick at Nite. His entire ensemble screamed affluence and wealth, and knowing he could probably eat in a place that would cost her a week's worth of tips at the hoot and holler intrigued her.

He's dead, you idiot. All that's left is the brain. Get a grip!

"I heart brains," she muttered, envisioning a shirt with smiling zombies and messy brains on a platter.

Those friendly green eyes narrowed. "Excuse me?"

Bolstered by agitation, she repeated, "I heart brains."

"Is that supposed to be funny?"

"I was thinking that maybe Café Press might be a good place to supplement my income. Just think about it. 'I heart brains.' You could have the plate"—she lifted her own off the table as a simulation—"with the brains and the zombie offering it for dinner. With the recent pandemic, it could make a million."

"You are going to make a million, Mrs. Bradworth." He quickly corrected himself, "Or what's left of it after the company you consigned your husband's body to gets its share. I'm sorry for your loss, by the way."

"Don't be so quick," Olivia snapped at the blatant insult. "Eric was an asshole who only cared about one person—*himself*. If it were me that kicked the bucket, he'd have signed my body over before the death certificate was certified official."

"If he was so terrible, why didn't you divorce him?"

"I was going to, you arrogant piece of shit." The words came out before she could prevent them and she slapped her hands over her mouth, eyes wide at her variable temper.

What she'd just confessed could end everything.

"Well, well, well. It appears you have a few secrets of your own, Mrs. Bradworth."

"Don't call me that." The words were muffled against her hand.

"Come again?"

"I said don't call me that!" she snapped, lowering her hands. "It's Olivia DeMarkus, not Bradworth. I've reverted to my maiden name."

The waitress returned with the wine Derrick ordered and two glasses. She poured the dark red liquid carefully and left the bottle on the table before she vanished.

"This is a very good year. You'll enjoy the texture and flavor—"

He caught her staring and she blushed cherry red. Her fingers wrapped around the stem of her glass clumsily and she rushed to bring it to her lips, hoping he didn't ask her what in the hell she was gawking at.

"What were you looking at?"

She didn't close her eyes, but she did cringe and wilt a little on the inside.

Damn.

She placed the glass on the table and said, "I didn't know you could drink anything."

Derrick seemed to think about that for a moment. Then he confessed, "I've been advised that consuming liquid or food after a forty-eight-hour period won't do my body any favors, but I'm hoping that won't be a problem after our dinner has concluded."

An exhaustion she wasn't aware of overcame her. The poor bastard seated across from her didn't deserve a lengthy schooling on how to treat a woman. Even if he took the damned body, he wouldn't be Eric. Her former husband, God rest his useless ass, was long gone.

"You know what? We don't even have to take it that far, Mr. Quinn."

She reached into her purse, grasping the paper with her signature waiting just inside. When she extended it to him, he frowned and gazed at it.

"Why did you want to meet with me if you'd already made the decision?"

Olivia snorted. "Because I wanted to make sure you had half a brain. Eric certainly didn't. A body like that shouldn't go to waste. Not a second time. It's not fair to the female populace. We have enough shit to deal with without being deluded by a pretty face concealing an empty locker."

He smiled and asked curiously, "An empty locker?"

"Yeah, as in you hear the continuous echo of nothing inside the vacant space."

The chair caught as she shoved away from the table and she cursed her inability to end the evening with a graceful exit.

"Don't go."

Derrick's words caught her off guard, and when she peered up at him curiously, she froze. The sexual heat in his eyes had fuck all to do with getting into *Eric's* body.

"You're a beautiful woman, Olivia. It's a shame the man you married didn't know how to appreciate it. If I hadn't died this morning I'd take you home, drape you across my bed, and show you exactly how you deserve to be worshipped."

Wow.

Her entire body swooned and her nipples went hard beneath the satin and lace she'd hidden them behind. Eric had never gotten her this hot, not in a million years, and this guy didn't even have to touch her.

I wonder if that mouth tastes as sweet as it purrs.

Hello! He's dead, you idiot!

Derrick situated himself across from her, but this time he kept his elbows on the table. As if he both needed and feared the nearness. "Tell me about yourself."

She laughed nervously, heart hammering against her sternum. "What do you want to know?"

Those glorious green eyes of his remained steady on her own.

"Everything."

3
—

THE CARIBBEAN: FOUR MONTHS LATER

God, she was beautiful. Her blond hair shone like wheat in the sun, and her tanned body was rounded in all the right places. She rotated on her towel, offering him a view of her uncovered breasts and a fleeting flash of her hairless sex. The areolas were darkened by exposure to the sun, the nipples small, glorious, and erect.

Derrick groaned as his cock swelled and throbbed, reminding him of all the work it had taken to reach this point.

Rehabilitation following brain surgery was serious fucking business. The nerve endings had to work properly in order for his brain to direct and guide the body it was now programmed to. It took two weeks to regain his balance, another two to walk correctly, then months of physical therapy to help him learn all the basic fundamentals.

The goddess in the sun sighed in bliss, and he smiled, basking in her beauty.

He and Livvie had kept in close contact throughout the ordeal, exchanging letters and late-night phone calls. They knew each other as well as any two people could, even if they had yet to meet face to face following the procedure. She was as exquisite as he knew she would be that first night—beautiful on the inside and out. A hard life had forced her into a stupid situation and a bad marriage, but she'd lived and learned from it.

Now she had her whole life ahead of her, a future that wasn't tainted by financial debt and ridiculous obligation. Eric's sacrifice came with more than one benefit. The money he gave her in death meant she could start over.

She could start fresh.

His eyes took in the sexual fantasy she created and felt a painful tug in his heart.

He loved her wit, her playful banter, and the way she breathed into the phone just before she told him goodnight.

Self-doubt resurfaced when he glanced into the nearby window and saw the man staring back at him. The face, while slightly different, was still the same. The goatee changed it somewhat, as did the longer hair that obscured the fading scar across his hairline.

But would she still see Eric? Or would she see him?

They discussed it at length and she swore it didn't matter, joking, "Eric's body, your brains. How could a girl go wrong?"

He took advantage of the sun, knowing she would be nearly blinded by the bright rays. Tons of scheming had finally brought them to this moment. Now it was time for things to come full circle. Olivia thought she was enjoying time on a secluded isle as a belated birthday present, while he knew she would finally accept or reject him as the man he was.

The sand shifted beneath his feet, alerting her to his presence, but he didn't hesitate.

"Hello, Livvie."

He waited for her to acknowledge him, heart rammed in his throat, praying the name that drifted from her lips belonged to him.

"Derrick?"

The profound relief he experienced prevented coherent speech. He dropped to his knees beside her and placed an arm on either side of her head. Then he did what he'd waited months to do. He lowered his head and kissed her heart-shaped lips. Her throaty moan told him everything he needed to know and more.

She wanted him too.

He reached one hand behind his shoulders to remove the thin cotton shirt, pulling it over his head and tossing it to the ground. Their mouths met once more, tongues lapping and exploring as eager hands did the same. Her taste was sweeter than he imagined, and her skin was softer than lush silk. The weight of her breasts filled each of his palms, her nipples perfectly sized for his thumbs.

He tore his mouth free from her lips and struggled to breathe. "I've wanted this for so long."

Her fingers caressed his goatee and she smiled, whispering, "So have I."

Shifting slightly, he settled his weight between her out-stretched legs, the barrier of his swimming trunks keeping him from pressing entirely against her. She cradled his head as he fondled and teased her nipples with his fingers, teeth, and tongue. He gave each breast equal attention, rotating the pebbled tissue between his thumb and forefinger before smoothing the outer edge with light, lazy circles.

"Please," she groaned, writhing madly beneath him. "Don't tease me."

Phone calls they shared came to mind, sex sessions so intense they left him yearning for the real thing. Hot silken flesh was so much better than the rough calluses on his hand.

"You've teased me for months, baby. It's only fair."

Her infuriated wail broke his resolve and he released her breasts, sliding down her body. Truth was, he wanted to taste her as much as she wanted to be tasted. Intimate conversation revealed many things, including Eric's lack of interest in oral sex. The bastard had made her feel bad about herself as a woman, making her believe it was her fault and something was wrong with her.

Good thing he had no such qualms.

Going down on a woman was the ultimate display of trust. She was allowing him to venture to a place on her body that made her feel vulnerable.

And damn if he didn't feel honored by that.

"Relax," he soothed when she tried to hide herself. "Let me see you, Livvie."

"But—"

"But nothing." He lifted his head and met her anxious eyes. "Do you remember what I said I wanted do when we finally met like this?"

Her throat convulsed as she gulped and nodded.

"Then let me give you pleasure. Trust me."

Her thighs quivered when she relaxed and rested her head back on the towel. Her fingers twined together on her stomach, bubblegum pink nails burying themselves into the back of her hands.

Slowly, he spread her thighs, groaning in awe at the sight awaiting him. Her lips were swollen, the pink folds beneath glistening in the sun. He wanted to bury his face in her weeping core until she lost control, but he forced himself to go slowly.

The first deep stroke of his tongue caused a whimper. The second wrought a soft cry. He took his time, tasting her as he promised, lapping at her tenderly. When she thrust against his mouth without restraint, he worked his middle finger into her, pressing until his knuckle met the giving softness of her.

"So close," she breathed. "God, Derrick, I'm so close."

"Come for me."

He used his free hand to move the hood away from her clit and pulled the swollen nub into his mouth. Her body convulsed and she screamed his name, writhing in the ecstasy that only came from oral stimulation. She was beautiful when she came, uninhibited and expressive.

"That was . . . You are . . . I can't believe . . ."

"I'm glad you liked it, baby. I know I did."

He waited until she lifted her head to place the fingers that were deep inside her body into his mouth to lick them clean, and the heat in her eyes told him the embarrassment she experienced was long gone. She rotated on the towel and flipped over, crawling to him on her knees. Her hands went to his trunks and she tugged on the elastic waist.

"My turn."

His mouth went dry and his cock pulsated miserably.

"Whatever you say."

He flopped into the sand when his body was as bare as hers, landing on his back, and hollered when her hot mouth closed over his aching flesh. She used her hand to work the root she couldn't swallow, sucking greedily while working the base of his cock with her tongue. Never had a blow job been this good or this satisfying.

How did I ever live without this woman?

He held off for as long as he could, which was only minutes.

"Stop," he groaned. "I want to be inside you when I come."

She allowed him to slide free from her shining lips but mumbled, "You were inside me."

"I want to be inside you here." He reached for the slick folds of flesh between her legs and pressed a finger inside. "I want that tight sex of yours squeezing me, to feel you clamping down around me."

Snagging his shorts, he quickly retrieved the condom stowed inside.

"Have you had sex with someone else?" There was no condemnation in her voice, but there was a pain he hadn't anticipated radiating in her eyes.

"Hell, no." He palmed the line of her jaw with his free hand.

"Don't you know how I feel about you, Livvie? Haven't you figured it out by now?"

"I thought I did," she whispered. "But you didn't say anything . . ."

He dropped the condom and captured her face in both hands. "I love you."

Shyly, she murmured, "You do?"

"So fucking much it hurts."

She smiled and produced an unexpected burst of laughter. "I love you, too."

He reached for the condom again and she stopped him, pulling him over her body as she rested in the sand. "You're not the only one that's been waiting for this. I've been on the Pill for months now."

"Well damn, woman. Why didn't you say so?"

He moved between her outspread thighs and thrust into her, going balls deep. She cried out, arching her back and grasping at his shoulders. He pumped his hips, taking her hard and fast. The moment she climaxed, he allowed himself to follow, spending his seed deep inside her body.

"You're incredible," he murmured, pressing a kiss to her temple.

"You're not too shabby yourself."

"Are you hungry?" He smoothed stray stands of hair from her face. "I brought fresh crab and shrimp from the mainland."

She sighed. "That sounds wonderful."

He pulled away from the temptation of her body and rose, sliding on his trunks and offering his shirt when she blushed at her lack of clothing.

"No one's out here," she explained. "And I don't like tan lines."

"I'm not complaining."

She rotated the large garment around and froze when she saw the words written on the front. There was no zombie standing with a plate of brains. Instead he went for simple and understated.

"'I heart brains'?"

"Your idea, remember?"

Her beautiful lips curved. "You remembered that?"

Stepping in front of her, he eased the material around her head, waiting as she pushed her arms through the sleeves. Then he whispered, "I remember everything when it comes to you."

Bending at the waist and taking her hips in hand, he claimed her lips, tasting the sweetness within. She went soft against him, raking her fingers across his skin and welcoming his tongue as it delved inside.

Becoming a zombie was a bitch, but salesman Tub-o pudge was right, it could have been a hell of a lot worse.

So what if he had a different body?

He had the brains.

And he got the girl.

EVERYONE I LOVE IS DEAD

Elizabeth Coldwell

I always vowed I would never date a zombie, until Mark turned up dead. Or should that be undead? I'm still not sure of the distinction. And if you're confused by this, think how I felt. But I suppose I should start at the beginning.

It must have been about eighteen months ago when the first of the zombies started turning up. No one was really sure where they came from: some people said it was due to genetically modified food, others that it was caused by the radiation from cell phones or from living too close to power lines. Still others claimed it was all part of a big conspiracy engineered by the lizard people secretly in charge of the planet. You can still see them even now, arguing themselves into knots about the subject on late-night cable TV shows.

Whatever the cause, the first time one of these shambling, rotting husks pushed its way out of the cemetery dirt and started making its way in search of civilization, people were naturally terrified. They'd all seen the films where zombies gradually take over the world, killing and eating the brains of their victims until only a few hardy souls are left to make a last futile stand for mankind.

Only it turned out that while zombies were eager to feed, they didn't necessarily need prime human rib. They were just as happy with the brains, offal, and other parts of domestic animals which would otherwise have found their way into low-grade burgers and sausages. Once that had been discovered, it was easier for them to establish their place in society. Naturally, the reaction to the appearance of the zombies varied from country to country. In Haiti, those who had originally wished them dead locked their doors, buried their heads under the bed sheets, and prayed they would live to see the morning. In parts of Africa and Aboriginal Australia, the zombies were worshipped as venerated ancestors. In Britain, they were ruthlessly hunted down and decapitated, that being the only reliable way to kill a zombie.

Here, the government decided that the sensible thing to do was to allow them to find jobs and pay their taxes, just like everyone else. Otherwise they would all have been sitting around on welfare, and given the state the economy was in that just wasn't a viable option. There were certain restrictions—no zombie could work anywhere which dealt with the processing and handling of food, or be around animals or children—but after awhile you no longer really noticed that the guy repairing your shoes or the woman behind the counter at the dry cleaner had a certain graveyard pallor and a blank-eyed, uncommunicative demeanor. Indeed, sometimes it was hard to tell them from the person who'd been working there before.

And, of course, it wasn't long before you saw mixed-mortality couples openly kissing and holding hands on the streets. For some girls, dating a zombie was the perfect way to upset Daddy, far more shocking than running around with the big, black quarterback on the college football team could ever be. I didn't see the attraction myself, although a couple of my friends enthused about the unique delights of lying in the arms of the undead. They claimed that once you'd tried it, you would never go back, but I wasn't even a little bit zombie-curious.

Then one cold February evening, I was serving the last couple of customers before the coffee shop shut for the night when a familiar figure shuffled slowly through the door. My heart fluttered up into my throat for a moment as I realized I was looking at Mark—or, rather, what had once been Mark. His formerly glossy brown hair was dull and lifeless and his skin had a distinct greenish tinge, but despite the fact that he was clearly dead, he was still undeniably handsome.

When the zombies first started returning, I must admit I had wondered what would happen if someone I had known was among them, but I had been thinking more of a dead relative than the man whom I would always consider the one who got away. Mark and I had been one of those couples everyone had said was destined to be together, but it had just never happened. When I had been single, he had been in a relationship, or the other way around. He had gone to college on the West Coast, while I had stayed on the East. And then, just when we were both single, available and living in the same city once more, with seemingly nothing to stop us having a long and happy life together, Mark literally dropped down dead in the street one evening, killed by a heart condition no one had known he had. I was devastated, sobbing all the way through the funeral and grieving for months afterwards, but in time I had recovered and accepted I was simply never going to see Mark again.

Until now, as he was standing at the counter asking for a large sour-milk cappuccino.

"Mark!" I exclaimed stupidly, aware that my voice was too loud, too forced in the quiet surroundings of the shop. "How've you been?"

"Oh, you know," he said, his voice slower and more guttural than when he had been alive, "not too bad, considering I've been dead for—what, four years?"

"Yeah, time really flies. So, are you working?"

"Yup, I got my old job back at the bookstore over on Twenty-third. I think they were kind of glad to see me back—once they'd got over the shock."

"Well, it is good to see you," I said, surprising myself by how sincerely I meant this. Looking at Mark was stirring up feelings I thought had been buried along with him. "Maybe we should go out sometime, catch up on everything that we've . . . oh, you know what I mean."

"Sure, that'd be nice." He picked up his coffee, started sloping over to a vacant table, then turned—a process that took him a little while, as though he still wasn't totally in control of his limbs. "Tell me, Millie, are you seeing someone at the moment?"

"Yes, I am," I admitted. And as I watched him shuffle off to drink his coffee in a secluded corner, I wondered whether I should tell that someone about my unexpected encounter with Mark, and about the feelings I now realized I still so clearly had for him.

So later that night, as I lay in bed with Brody, I came clean. Brody was the best thing that had happened in my life since Mark had gone. I'd met him at the point when I'd finally decided I had to spend time around people who hadn't known Mark, who hadn't hung out in the same places he had and who could help me to move on. Someone had invited me to a gallery opening in the East Village, and that's where I had got talking to Brody. Lanky and blond, with eyes the cool blue of a mountain lake, he couldn't have looked more different than Mark, but that was part of the initial attraction—it meant I couldn't easily make comparisons. Not only was Brody cute, he was intelligent and well read, qualities I've always admired in a man. He worked for a small publishing house who specialized mostly in academic publications, but had ambitions to one day write a novel. By the end of the week we were an item, and a couple of months after that we moved in together. Of course, I never forgot about Mark entirely, but being with someone as clearly besotted with me as Brody was helped to ease the pain.

I dropped a gentle kiss on his forehead. "The strangest thing happened today," I said. "Mark came in for a coffee."

Brody looked at me, startled. "Mark? You mean he's . . . ?"

"Back, yes. I know, I can hardly get my head around it. And because I promised I'd never keep any secrets from you, I have to tell you the weirdest part." I took a deep breath. "As soon as I saw him, I knew I was still attracted to him."

"Seriously? You've always said you'd never be one of those girls who went chasing after a dead guy."

But Mark's not *a* dead guy, I wanted to tell him, he's *the* dead guy. Brody, however, didn't give me the chance to say anything. He pressed his lips to mine, kissing me passionately.

"What would you rather feel?" he asked. "Warm lips like mine"—he kissed me again, to emphasize the point—"or Mark's cold ones?" His hand moved down between my legs, parting the lips of my pussy so he could tease my clit. "Fingers that know how to take you to the edge of ecstasy, or ones that aren't properly under control?"

He straddled my body, and I spread my thighs eagerly as his cock head nudged at the opening of my sex. "And, most importantly, do you want this cock inside you?"

"Yes, Brody, yes!" I almost screamed, as he plunged up into me with his hot, virile length. Mark would never be capable of fucking me as hard as Brody could, of filling me with his fertile seed, but as the first fierce sparks of orgasm shot through me, I knew I still really wanted to find out what sex with Mark would be like.

A publishing convention was taking Brody to Chicago for a couple of days, so in his absence I arranged to have dinner with Mark. He'd chosen a zombie-friendly trattoria close to his apartment, and when I arrived he was already seated at a discreet corner booth, well away from the undead couple having a blazing row at a table near the door. It was a little hard to make out what was being said, given that the pair of them were rather more decomposed than most and her jawbone didn't seem to be properly connected, but the gist was obvious: he was dumping her. Seemed like relationships didn't get any easier even after you were dead.

I ordered a bowl of linguini, and Mark went for what was described as the charnelhouse special: a plate of sloppy meat with what looked uncomfortably like a piece of windpipe sticking out of it. Vaguely repelled by the whole scene, I asked myself what on Earth I thought I was doing here, and then Mark looked at me with his dark, rheumy eyes and my reservations melted away. So many times I had dreamed of sharing a romantic candlelit dinner with him, and now here we were, clinking wineglasses in a toast to each other and chatting together companionably.

As we ate, I filled Mark in on everything that had happened while he had been out of my life, telling him about friends we had known who'd got married, or had started raising a family. He told me he was aiming to raise money so he could go traveling, though he aimed to stay well away from Britain, given the country's less-than-welcoming attitude to the undead.

Soon, it felt as though no time at all had passed since the afternoon I had made plans to go for a dinner like this with Mark, only to receive a phone call a couple of hours later to let me know he was dead. It didn't matter that one of us was alive and the other not. At this moment, we were just two really good friends on the cusp of becoming lovers.

There was, of course, the small matter of Brody standing in the way. Mark insisted on being told all about him, and I obliged. "You should meet him," I said. "You'd really like him."

"Do you love him?" Mark asked.

"Yes. Yes, I do." I drained the last of my coffee. "He's bright, he's funny, he's an amazing lover. He's all the things I've ever wanted." *All the things I know you would have been,* I almost added.

"But you're still sitting there, thinking of what it would be like if we were together." Mark put his hand on top of mine. It was the first time I'd ever been touched by a zombie and, remarkably, I didn't immediately recoil. "You know if you come home with me it will change everything forever, don't you?"

I nodded, prepared for anything which might be about to happen. Nothing more needed to be said. We paid the bill and made the short walk to Mark's apartment. It took a while, as we were moving at Mark's pace, but with his big arm wrapped around my shoulders I was completely comfortable. We got the odd scandalized look from people who still weren't happy with the idea of mixed-mortality couples, but I didn't care. Let them think what they wanted; I had been given a second chance with Mark, and if I didn't take it, I knew I would always regret what might have been.

Behind Mark's closed front door, I surrendered to my desires. His skin was cold to the touch, but no colder than the night air outside. All the comparisons Brody had made the night he'd fucked me in the ways he said Mark never could came flooding back, but I was so caught up in the thrill of finally being with Mark after all this time that it really didn't matter. He pleasured me with all the skill he could muster, everything slow, everything measured, and my body opened for him willingly.

Afterwards, I knew I had crossed the line. Cheating on Brody with anyone was something I had never planned to do, but with Mark? How would I explain that? And if I didn't tell him and he somehow found out, would he make me choose between the two of them?

If I covered my tracks carefully enough, I thought, Brody need never know. I could keep on seeing Mark whenever he was away and it would just be our dirty little secret. But Brody and I had built a relationship on being honest with each other, and in the end I just couldn't lie to him. When he got back from Chicago, I sat him down and told him I'd been for dinner with Mark. The expression on my face let him fill in the blanks.

Strangely, he didn't react the way I'd expected. There was no row like the one I'd witnessed between the couple in the restaurant, no threats to leave or flat-out declaration that everything was over between us. Instead, he asked me to invite Mark over to our apartment one evening. "I want to meet him," Brody declared. "I want to see what a dead guy could possibly have that I don't. God, talk about the living envying the dead."

What could I do but agree to his request? Brody could tell I was upset by everything that had happened, and he took me in his arms, kissing my tears away. Gradually, the kisses grew more intense, until we were peeling off our clothes, suddenly hungry for each other. Brody threw me down on the bed and buried his head between my legs, licking the petals of my sex until they blossomed, allowing him to enter me with his strong, hard cock.

As he fucked me with long, powerful strokes, my legs wrapped tightly around the small of his back so I could pull him further into me, I knew I couldn't break up with him. What we had was just too good to throw away. I needed Brody, but I was sure I needed Mark, too. Maybe a meeting between the two men would be for the best; it might help to clear up some of the confusion I felt.

Mark came over to our apartment a couple of nights later, bringing a bottle of red wine. He had on the same grey suit I'd seen him wearing at each of our previous meetings; like all zombies, he didn't seem to be comfortable in anything other than the clothes he'd been buried in. I introduced Brody to Mark, then went to the kitchen to find glasses and put the kettle on. I'd left a jug of milk out overnight to go sour, just in case Mark fancied a cup of coffee.

The three of us sat a little awkwardly making small talk in the living room, Brody and Mark eyeing each other up like a couple of prize fighters.

When Brody started talking about the latest manuscript he was editing, Mark chipped in, "So how much do you enjoy your job then, Brody?"

"Well, obviously it's not as satisfying as working on my own book would be, but . . ."

"You see," Mark said, "this is why you and I, and Millie, too, for that matter, really aren't so different from each other. I serve people in the shop every day, people who look down on me because they're alive and I'm—I'm like this. But all those people who aren't really doing the job they love, or work for a boss they can't stand or are stuck in a relationship that's gone sour—well, every day they die a little bit more on the inside. And in the end, they aren't any better off than me, after all."

Brody looked at Mark with something approaching respect. "You know, I think I'm beginning to realize what Millie sees in you. And it's obvious you're in love with him, Millie. Just the way you look at him tells me that. But I have no intention of giving you up without a fight. I'll do whatever it takes to be with you, so what the hell do we do to sort this out?"

I looked at Brody, then Mark. How could I choose between the living and the dead? I loved Brody's passion and vitality, but I had tasted dark, forbidden pleasures with Mark and I didn't want to give them up. If there was only some way I could walk on the dark side with Brody—and that's when the answer hit me, elegant in its simplicity.

Brody died a week ago tonight. It was a beautiful death. He swallowed a quantity of sleeping pills, washed down with the bottle of champagne he'd been saving for the day I accepted his marriage proposal, and I held him in my arms as he quietly slipped away.

Mark was there, too, to bite him as he faded into unconsciousness. It's the one sure way, the doctors say, to turn someone into a zombie. Given Brody's powerful desire to be with me, whatever it takes, I know it won't be too long before he's pushing up through the dirt they so recently shoveled over his coffin and knocking on the door of this apartment, ready to join Mark and me in the most unusual of threesomes.

I'll admit I don't know exactly what the future will bring, but I'm dying to find out.

THROUGH DEATH TO LOVE

S. M. Cross

"It's a good strategy," she says. "You just have to make it your own, put your mark on it. We all use fillers to maintain our turn, to signal interest and attention. Frankly I've never heard that particular one put to such elegant use."

It's a bit disconcerting actually; a hunger sound slowed and softened, an "mmmmmmm" with the slightest breath in front, an oddly appealing mix of rampant desire and precarious restraint. Fear and anticipation flutter against her stomach walls, a delicious feeling she hasn't had since high school.

The fear isn't surprising since it hasn't been that long since zombies and humans were predator and prey. The world has changed a lot in ten years, economic necessity turning the lemons of a near depression into the lemonade of a miraculous global economic recovery, all thanks to ex-consumers who no longer are dead but not ex-.

No, the fear she gets. It's the anticipation that startles her, a delicious frisson sweeping over her, something akin to reading a horror story late at night all alone, hearing a thump and a bump, and the accompanying mix of dread, despair, hope, wanting and not wanting, tumbling together. And isn't that the essence of attraction, the fear of ends, the dread of them, the despair at all that has passed and yet, when confronted with the promise of what could be, the hunger rising, the risk you're willing—no, forced—to take?

"Now let's see how you are doing with your oral motor exercises." These are drudgery; there's no way around it, but critical if he's to keep his speech intelligibility, not to mention a prosody that's more music than growl. Speech therapy for zombies is all about compensatory strategies, blurring the lines between dead and living so we can all just get along.

As he goes through the exercises, following each with production of the target sound in a word and phrase, she carefully observes the pursing and retraction of his lips, the movement and accuracy of his tongue, the lovely, miraculous dance of speech, one motion following on the heels of another, future sounds shaping the present, molding the memory of the past. He's so fluid it's startling, nearly human in rate and rhythm. Shows you what's possible with money, opportunity, and force of will. One thing you have to admire about zombies is their single-mindedness. They may not get points for imagination, but for sheer stick-to-it-tiveness, they can't be beat.

Yes, he's had every opportunity and it shows. Beyond a slight hesitation now and again, a gesture that seems more appreciation than inability, as if he chooses to linger as opposed to being forced to it, his speech is nearly human. There's not an ounce of self-consciousness in his attempts; even his mistakes seem delightfully purposeful, designed to enchant. You've gotta love a man with this much aplomb, even a dead man.

"You're doing wonderfully."

"Mis-s-s-stakes," he sighs.

He's so hard on himself, another zombie trait she can't help but admire. It pushes him toward excellence, being all he can be, resolving to do better next time, always sure there will be a next time which, because he's a zombie and already dead, is pretty much guaranteed. No they don't give up and they never take no for an answer. If at first they don't succeed, they try and try and try again. She finds herself blushing at where this thought leads, watching his tongue dart forward for production of a "t," then disappear for an open vowel, only to emerge slightly thrust between perfect teeth, capped to hide deterioration, giving him a killer smile. Who would have thought the word *tooth* could be so damn sexy?

She shakes her head to get back on track. This is therapy, not a date. She hears him focus on an "s," try and miss it, an almost that only her trained ear can discern, and of course his more exacting one. Sibilants are always going to be trouble for him; they require motor planning that takes a toll on a system past tense instead of present. The lips want to retract, the death's head grin, distorting his "s's", making them sound more last gasp than full of life. And therapy three times a week can slow the loss but never stem it. She's explained this all to him, yet every week he returns for his Monday, Wednesday, Friday sessions, her last appointment, and frankly the highlight of her week.

"Perfect," she insists. "Charming," she adds. It is charming and sweet these small faults in a body that will never age quite like the living.

"Bias-s-s-sed," he says, his lips retracting into a wide grin. He forgets himself in real emotion, and because of that she can't find it in her heart to correct him. He wants so to please her. It's been a long time since a man has made her pleasure his.

"Maybe. But there are worse things." She laughs, and he smiles, a wide, childish, "cheese" of a smile, so endearing she'd kiss him then and there if they were other than what they are.

"You ready to practice your conversational skills, Robert?" she asks, thinking a change in task and subject is just what they need to get back on track.

He nods stiffly as if he's afraid his head might detach from his body. It won't. He's still fresh. He's careful, though, just the same. It gives him an old world quality that carefulness, reminiscent of more genteel times, of gentlemen and ladies. She's not really sure how old he is. Embalming does that to a zombie. He was in his late twenties when he died, in prime physical condition, and it shows. He won't live forever, but he does have a fair span of able-bodied death ahead of him, certainly more than she has life. There are worse things than turning zombie. He's proof enough of that. She stands; he follows her lead. She understands this is a compensatory strategy, this mirroring that mimics interest, attraction, love. And that's how she reads it at the heart of her, even while her head notices how well his occupational therapist has done her job. It's as if they've found the best in humanity, she and her fellow therapists, and passed it on, modern-day Pygmalions, making the perfect men in death they cannot find in life.

He holds her jacket for her. She slips her arms through the sleeves, thinking how long it's been since this simple courtesy was offered her. Again, it's more than likely some sort of therapeutic "homework," although good manners can't be discounted. Zombies like rules, like to know what's expected and possess an admirable follow through. And yet there's something so appealing in this courteous gesture, something so natural she wants it to mean something more than shaping and task analysis, breaking behaviors down to their components and teaching each scope and sequence to ease fitting in. His successful integration into society depends on it. The living dead are tolerated but still not quite accepted, except in L.A. In L.A., everyone's accepted; perhaps why it's the zombie capital of the world.

"Coffee?" she asks.

They practice out in the community these days to help his generalization. Coffee's a universal, with date and business potential. And with a Starbucks on every corner, carryover is that much more likely. Of course, he doesn't drink coffee, not really. He could, but it messes with a digestive system that needs one thing and one thing only: brains. It's a trick, really, a strategy, part of any good zombie rehabilitation. Keep a glass in front of you. Lift it. Set it to your lips. Leave room for cream, add that and sugar, humanness located more in gestures and preferences than the necessities of life—eating, drinking, breathing.

"S-s-s-s-stronger." This is surprising. He usually lets her direct therapy. A bar is out of the question, of course. Not ethical.

"Don't forget to use full sentences," she reminds him in a slightly apologetic tone, evading the question. He'll take it as a rebuke and she doesn't mean it that way, just a reminder, her job. As for the bar, well, it's not like given the choice she wouldn't want to go somewhere with a bit more ambience than the local coffeehouse. She knows these trips into the community aren't dates, even if they sometimes feel like it.

"How about dinner, then?" He offers this compromise with a smile, the kind she cannot refuse, the one so wide and open, childlike and honest, offering himself up in that perfect span of pearly white.

"Well done, Robert. Lovely phrasing. Very clear. Dinner?" She pauses, considers his request.

Dinner teeters on the edge of impropriety but doesn't cross over. Besides, she should be working with his feeding skills. Hand to mouth is the occupational therapist's realm, but lips to gut are hers. Biting, chewing, swallowing, jaw retraction: all are legitimate therapeutic goals and necessary if he's going to take his place as head of the family empire.

Dinner can be therapeutically justified. Okay, maybe rationalized is more accurate. She definitely won't charge his insurance plan. He will pay for dinner but this extra time will be her treat, like going Dutch, like college, both so poor this the only way to be together more often than not.

"I don't know a local restaurant that caters to your particular needs." She won't say *brains,* can't say it. That word reminds her of all he is and all he isn't. Besides the absence of a beating heart, the need for this particular kind of sustenance seems to mark the true difference between living and revenant, between zombie and man.

"I do." It's the "I" that decides her, the Cartesian acknowledgement of the difference between brain and mind, the Augustinian assertion of self. There are the mindless, shambling dead, and there are the thoughtful undead, men and women of heart and soul, certainly more human than not. Robert is definitely one of the latter.

"You've been planning this. You knew I'd accept."

"I hoped," he says, remembering to use a full sentence as well as that small, bold pronoun that makes mammal man.

They stroll down the street, a leisurely pace that hides his stiff joints, the slight lurch in his every step. She has taken his left arm, the one slightly crooked, the muscles of it in definite need of an extra physical therapy session or two to get better extension and a wider range of motion. It's gallant though, that arm, as tender as the stroll. The sun is setting, splashing the sky crimson and vermillion. It's a flattering light for her and for him. The greenish tinge of his skin, so prominent under fluorescents, mellows in this light, turning flesh-toned in the glow. And whatever stares come are not from those wondering at zombie and woman strolling arm in arm, but at two people walking a distance they could so much more easily drive.

His head tips to the left, towards her. His nose drinks her scent in a long, audible inhalation. "Mmmmmmmm," he murmurs, exhaling, a yearning hum that sends chills down her spine.

"Mmmmm," she responds, not just flattered at his desire, but aroused.

She's good enough to eat. She can hear it in his voice, feel it in the brush of his mouth against her hair. That she feels the slight skim of his teeth against her scalp only adds to her longing, his restraint admirable and extraordinary given his hunger and needs. Has a man ever given up something so necessary thinking her even more essential? Since the Zombie Wars and Zombie Peace, dating has frankly been a nightmare. Every man pulls out the line, "for the good of the species," sometimes mere seconds after "hello" and "pleased to meet you." How many times has she sat in a Starbucks with a stranger on a first date to test the waters, one that never moves past, "let's get it on for the good of mankind," "you're not getting any younger," or her personal favorite, "I'm a rare commodity. I've got options," the implication clear that she doesn't?

Well, apparently she does, good ones.

He helps her off with her jacket, pulls out her chair. Only when she's settled does he take his seat across from her, his eyes never leaving her face. She tells herself he's gazing into her eyes, and maybe he is, although now and again she catches his eyes wandering up toward her hairline. He forces them back to hers after each lapse, accompanied by an apologetic shrug, a resigned sigh. It's sweet how hard he tries, how he wrestles with his nature, determined to be more human than not, for her sake and for his. It's hard to resist and why should she, anyway?

It's some time after the main meal, a few stray bits of Synth-brains still clinging to his plate, a few limp bits of salad on hers, that she decides to agree to a second date and whatever else may come. She watches him regretfully eye the remnants on his plate, forgoing the satisfaction of a final lick and slurp, denying himself the last bit of neural goodness to make a good impression. She's definitely going to turn vegetarian. You can't watch a zombie eat brains, even synthetic ones grown in Petri dishes just for this purpose, and not reconsider meat in any form. Even tofu may be out, unless it's blended or extra firm. The slightest jiggle and wiggle makes her nauseous, too reminiscent of the last sixty minutes of zombie-meets-brains. Still, it's a small thing to give up really, a minimal compromise, the kind good relationships, the best, are full of.

She watches the way he eyes her skull, surreptitiously of course, but obvious to anyone who spends any times with the living dead. No, she'll never be able to fall asleep in his arms, not without a helmet at least. Yet even that seems a small price to pay for a man who takes such care, wants and needs, as any man, but is patient enough to enjoy the pursuit as much as the getting. She won't ever have to worry about him falling asleep after making love. And while she's not sure about children, there's much about zombie human interactions that's still unknown. There's always adoption, a human girl, a zombie boy, or vice versa, the perfect integrated family.

His hand stiffly slides across the table, waits, palm upward, for hers. "Happy?" he asks.

"Yes," she replies, a completely honest response. She is happy. She slips her hand into his, cool and comfortable—unexpectedly pleasant, actually, more than you'd think from something long dead. But then his dead isn't, not really—a subtle but critical difference.

"Tomorrow?" Can a zombie wear his heart on his sleeve? If so, then Robert does just that, his heart and soul waiting for her answer.

"Full sentences . . ." she starts but then stops herself. She's not his therapist anymore, can't be. "Okay. Not dinner, though. Let's save that for another night." She's going to have to work up to meals. As it is, she's not sure if she's going to keep this one down.

"Maybe the park? I love walks."

"Walks. Mmmmmm," he replies as if he can't wait.

It's a nice thought, that's he's as eager as she, that this isn't about brains or loneliness, but something more. And who's to say it isn't true, that he can't wait, that neither can she? Stranger things have happened, stranger loves have found each other, risked, and lasted.

There are worse things than falling in love with a zombie, making a life with someone not quite living and not quite dead. They're proof enough of that.

EYE OF THE BEHOLDER

Stacey Graham

Anna left the theater with the theme song swelling her head. Escaping through the fire exit door, she skirted around couples holding hands as they whispered about the credits. She had candy stuffed into her bag and a soda stain on her skirt. Who would care if she stuck to the shadows? Stepping out of the alley, she attempted to hug the dirty brick walls lining Times Square and avoid the tourists dressed in their best vacation gear, price tags still attached to the collars.

Eyes fixed on the filthy oil-and-God-knows-what stained concrete beneath her feet, Anna crossed Broadway, her hands clutching the cheap purse she'd bought on Canal Street weeks before. The smell of formaldehyde still clinging to the fabric, the bag reminded her of her last boyfriend—small, stinky, and not worth the money she'd spent on it—but she loved it. It was unfortunate that the chemicals used in making the bag had created an adverse allergic reaction, seizing Anna's ability to breathe and slowly suffocating her a few days later. When she awoke in the morgue, she held the purse in a death grip, not content to release the faux Coach bag she'd died for, even in the half-life of the undead.

Through the excessive noise of the car horns and music of a half-naked cowboy, Anna's eyes strayed from the pavement to a pair of lovers, caught in the harsh illumination of the street lamp that clashed with the gaudy lights of Times Square, their hands wandering and lips smashed in unnatural angles against skin. Anna lingered too long watching, mentally betting against herself on how long it would be before one of them took a breath, one that didn't include the other's carbon dioxide. Her head turning back a moment too late, her body crashed into the figure dead ahead. As her cheek assaulted the soft gray wool of his suit jacket, she felt her skin tear away, leaving a rough spot that would take forever to patch up in the morning.

Awesome, she thought. *How much more putty does a girl have to go through to leave the house lately?* Clutching the torn skin on her face with her fingers, Anna turned to apologize. Zombie maintenance was getting expensive. Soon she'd be filling the holes with Spam in order to make it to the corner store, she thought with a wry grin.

"I'm sorry, I didn't see . . . what are you doing?" she said. The man in the suit was on his hands and knees in the deepening twilight, searching the ground for something.

"Don't step on it! I can't get another one and those things squish. Sounds awful." His hands groping blindly, she dropped beside him to help. Her eyes darting under the tabloid paper boxes, their innards stuffed with news of the apocalypse, she heard him chuckle. "I finally get a girl to notice me and she's helping to find an eyeball."

"I've heard worse pickup lines," she joked. Having a bond with someone who understands the delicate nuance of rotting flesh and protruding cheekbones made up for any awkwardness over missing orbs. Dropping her purse to the ground to get a better look under the paper boxes, she heard a distinct *pop*.

"Oh crap, I'm sorry." With a grimace, she raised her bag to find the squashed remains of a blue-veined eye stuck to the bottom of her fake Coach hobo bag. Peeling what was left from the leather, viscous eye goo leaving a trail from the bag, she gave it to the man now standing over her, one hand covering the gaping hole in his face.

"Blech. I hate it when this happens, it was inevitable, however." His auburn hair tousled from the hunt and patches of dirt on his knees, he looked more of a teenager than a grown zombie male slowly losing his parts due to a clumsy girl. Smiling at her now, she saw how his face was losing elasticity around the mouth, giving him a lopsided grin she hoped he was going for.

"Hold on, I can help." Digging into her bag, Anna withdrew a small wad of putty. Picking out the Tic Tac and a stray flimsy bubble of lint, she rolled the substance into a ball. Standing on tiptoe, Anna smiled into his good eye as she popped the putty into the hole and drew down his eyelid to a sultry half-lidded angle.

"I feel like I'm winking at people. The crazy guy on the corner just gave me the finger," he said.

Her hand still on his chest to steady herself, Anna was reluctant to step back. Since her untimely demise, most people avoided her due to the slight head roll and drooling. He made no move to extricate himself from her touch, and she wondered if rigor mortis had set in his legs. With a fetid sigh, Anna released her hold on him and turned away. Anna had had little luck with men while alive; why should it change now that she had pulse issues? Reaching down to pick up her beloved bag, she felt the cold fingers of her eyeball victim grasp her hand, drawing her back into his arms.

"I can't move quickly anymore so chasing you down for a date is impossible." His words were spoken low and rough. Anna knew his vocal cords were disintegrating, giving him a sexy timbre. "But can I take you out for a bite to eat? I'm Michael, by the way." Pausing to consider what zombies found appetizing, Anna wasn't sure she could sample the buffet of humans stretching out before her in Times Square.

"Anna," she said, pointing to herself. "I'm full, really. I ate a small family earlier and you know how they can make a girl bloat," she said. Smiling up at him, her lips straining over teeth in rotting gums, Anna didn't mind how the garish lights of the city bounced off her mottled skin, creating an aura of mystery and rancid fascination. She felt beautiful for the first time in years and it had only taken death to prove it to her. "How about a tour of the city instead?"

Holding out his hand to hail a cab, he looked back to smile only to shake his head in amusement as a bus removed it from his wrist as it sped by. Horrified gasps from the top tier of the tour bus turned to sounds of vomiting as shoppers buried their heads in the black bags filled with ill-gotten goods from Canal Street. Anna knew that black bag well; it had housed her own death warrant, but she was powerless to warn them. The hand, now flattened in the street, was a lost cause.

"This has to be the worst first date in history," he said. Tucking his arm into his suit jacket pocket, he grabbed her fingers with his remaining hand and said, "Let's walk from here."

Down the street, music flew from an open doorway. Its rhythm hard and heavy, it drew in crowds of the living and undead, both unable to resist its beat. Anna and her date walked past the doorman and into the club—apparently you don't question a man missing an eye and a hand—and into the smoke-filled room. It was difficult to determine who was still breathing and who had just passed over by the look of the patrons. They all had the twitch of the dead after working in the city all summer.

"What do you drink?" Michael asked.

"I don't anymore. It just runs down my face since I can't close my mouth all the way," she said. It was better to warn him if this was going to go any farther.

Making his way to the bar, Michael ordered two beers—one with a straw. He was thoughtful that way. Anna carried over the cold brown bottles to a table that cleared immediately, its occupants not eager to share space with the undead. Not wanting to waste a minute, she took a quick sip of the beer, wiped her face on her sleeve and grabbed his hand, pulling him to the tiny clearing the owners called a dance floor. He took Anna in his arms, and she felt only the cold embrace of romance.

"I hope they don't play 'Thriller.' I hate that song. People keep asking me to do the Claw at parties. It gets old fast," Michael mumbled into her hair. His good hand caressing her back, she felt his body jerk in time to the music, she wasn't sure if it was intentional or not.

In the hot, dark club, two lost souls found each other amid the lonely living. Neither was eager for the music to end as they swayed to the movement of the night. Anna imagined her heart was beating again and for a brief moment, she felt alive. The other dancers moved away in disgust as the new lovers discovered that beauty was indeed in the eye of the beholder. Which just happened to be in his pocket.

FIRST LOVE NEVER DIES

Jan Kozlowski

Sometimes it sucks working as a cop in the town you grew up in.

Danielle LaFontaine had been one of the prettiest and smartest girls in my high school class. But after ten years of bad decisions and worse luck, including our little global zombie epidemic last year, she was neither of those things anymore. What was left was only a sanded-down, dried up carapace of a woman. The only apparent life left in her was the feral survivor's intelligence that glittered in her eyes as she scrabbled to find a way out of this latest disaster.

"Okay Danielle, the patrolman said you had something you wanted to share with us before they take you to booking."

"Ryan Walborn . . . I remember you from high school."

"It's Detective Walborn, Danielle. And this is my partner, Detective Shana Mason. It's late and we don't have a lot of time. If you've got information for us, spit it out."

"All right, *Detective* Walborn. Like I was saying . . . I remember you from high school. And I also remember you used to spend a lot of time sucking face with that little Lassiter girl."

"Thanks for the trip through the high school yearbook, but . . ."

"Well, I got something about her old man that might interest you, especially since it involves what really happened to the mayor last week."

Shana and I exchanged glances. "You have our attention."

"First you got to do something for me."

"Danielle, you know even possessing zombie fluids is an automatic fifty years, and dealing it doubles it down."

"But it wasn't like, the real shit. It's just fake stuff I mix up and sell to the mutants who think shooting it up is their rocket to nirvana."

"All the same in the eyes of the law. Sorry, there's not a lot I can do."

"Even if what I've got concerns the mayor, Lassiter, and a meat train?"

"She's bullshitting us," Shana said.

"Maybe not. Let's hear what she has to say."

"You going to help me out?"

"*If* the info is good and you're not playing us . . . who knows, the evidence might take a little detour on its way to the station, but no guarantees. Deal?"

"Yeah, I guess it'll have to be. This is what I know. Lassiter's always been the go to guy in town for hardcore kink. A real eight-millimeter beserker. Back before the virus, he was famous for his S and M, bondage, and kiddie-diddler parties. You name it. If it dripped slime, this guy was up to his dick in it."

"So how come we've never heard of him before?" Shana asked.

"How old are you, five?"

"Danielle . . ."

"All right. Sorry. He is unfamiliar to you fine members of the law enforcement community for the usual reasons . . . friends in high places and lots of cash changing hands, especially around re-election time.

"Anyway, when the virus hit, for about a minute and a half people stopped caring about getting their rocks off. Then, when they started getting horny again, there was a brand-new wide world of perversion to explore."

"Like meat trains."

"Among other things, but trains are the big money makers. As soon as we figured out how to keep the Zoms from killing us, people like Lassiter figured out how to use them as fuck toys. And Lassiter, since he already owned a full-service dungeon complete with cages, restraints, and the kind of equipment they needed to make it work, became the guy to go to if you wanted to ride."

"So I take it the mayor was an avid locomotive enthusiast?"

"Yep, as often as he could shake his security detail. Except for last week, when something went wrong. I heard the Zom he was tailgating was getting a little overripe and when it twisted around to bite at him, the strap sawed straight through its torso and the top half of it sheared right off. When it landed, it grabbed the mayor's leg and took a big chunk out of it before

Lassiter busted in and blew its head off. I heard His Honor still had his dick in its ass when he got bit and they had a helluva time getting him disconnected before they whisked him away."

"Well, that explains why he suddenly took off on that family vacation so close to re-election time."

"Yeah, I guess any day now we'll get word that he was a victim of a tragic accident out of state somewhere," Shana added.

"I take it what happened to the mayor hasn't put a damper on Lassiter's operation?"

"You know how it is with these pervs," Danielle said. "If anything, it's made Lassiter's services even more popular. They like the danger, the thrill of doing something other people died doing. They're even asking for more decayed ones now, ones way past their expiration dates. He used to 'retire' them after about six months or so, less if they saw a lot of wear and tear, but now, even if they're almost a puddle of goo on the floor, somebody will pay big to do something nasty to them."

"Well, it sounds like you've got some solid intel on an active operation. It's good, but I don't know if it's worth possibly losing my career over."

"Never figured you for the type to fuck a girl over when she was down, Detective. But since we've got a history, I'll throw in one more nugget that might get your dick juicy. Lassiter's not alone in the house. His wife and daughter still live there. No one's talked to either one of them since before the infection, but they've been seen on the property."

"Are they alive?" I asked.

Danielle shrugged. "He won't let anyone get close enough to see. He keeps them locked down tight, but nobody knows if he's keeping them in or keeping everyone else out."

"You know the guy. If you had to guess, are they alive . . . or not?"

"Just a guess, but I'd bet that the old lady's gone zombie and he keeps her around like drug dealers used to keep pit bulls. Maybe even sets her out to patrol the place at night. The grounds are completely fenced in, electrified, razor-wire, the whole anti-zombie security package."

"And Mandy?"

"She's probably still alive, much to her dismay."

"What's that supposed to mean?" I asked.

"You dated her all through high school, you mean you don't know?" Danielle asked.

"Know what?"

"You're a *cop.* Put it all together, Einstein. Her *father* is a sex freak. Who do you think was his favorite victim? Who do you think he used for his first kiddie-diddler parties? Who do you think he tried his new toys and furniture and equipment out on?

"But of course that was before the infection," she added. "Now, who knows? He could still be using her. He could be saving her for a big Pay-Per-View event. Or maybe he's not into live flesh anymore and he's going to auction her off. Lots of possibilities, none of them good, not when it comes to Lassiter."

"All right. Enough," I said. "Danielle, let the officers take you to the station. I'll take care of everything else. But this is the last time. Find a different profession, retire to a private island, I don't care, just get the hell out of town."

"Until the next reunion, you mean . . . right, Ry? You know I could *never* miss our big one-O coming up. Hey, we could double date, I bet I could dig up someone . . . and make sure to ask Mandy when you see her!"

Her cackling followed us down the hallway, but it was Danielle's speculations about Mandy's life that kept banging through my brain as Shana and I walked to the car.

"Ryan, you okay?"

"Nope. Definitely not okay."

"You want to talk about it?"

"Nope," I said. "I want to *do* something about it."

"You gonna go get her?"

"Yep, but I'm going to drop you off back at the station first. No sense you getting mucked up in all of this."

I expected an argument from her, but all she did was give me a crooked smile and show me two small glass medicine bottles she had hidden in her pocket.

"Well, considering I'm the one who remembered to grab the evidence against Danielle," she said, "I'd say I'm already up to my mucking eyeballs in this, so we might as well head over to Lassiter's house and put an end to all this shit."

"Okay. Thanks, partner."

"*De nada*. How about backup?"

"Given that we don't know who Lassiter's friends are, it

wouldn't be smart to trust anybody at the department," I said.

"How about stopping at my place and picking up Alice on our way . . . and some extra weaponry?"

"You must really want to do this, letting me borrow your beast *and* raid your private armory."

"What can I say, Mandy's story struck several nerves," she said. "Daddy dearest needs to go bye-bye, hopefully in the most painful, time-consuming, and humiliating way possible."

I glanced over and noticed her granite-hard expression. "Shit, you too?"

"No, not me," she said. "A girl I knew in school. She tried to tell and no one believed her. *Her* dad was a doctor. He started drugging her to keep her compliant. She hung herself from the ceiling fan in his waiting room one day when she was fourteen."

She paused, then went on. "I was the last one to talk to her. We were working on a social studies project together. She wanted to pass the notebook back to me so I could add her research to the paper. After she left my house, I found she had written me a fourteen-page letter telling me everything her father had done to her all these years. She never mentioned she was going to kill herself. I thought I'd see her the next day at school and we'd talk about it."

"Jesus. That's a lot for a fourteen-year-old to handle. Did you turn the letter over to the police after you . . . found out?"

"Yeah. I figured they'd put the guy in jail, there'd be a trial, something . . ."

"But it all just went away, right?" I asked.

"Yep. He never even saw the inside of the police station. The letter disappeared. I was only fourteen and she was gone."

We drove the rest of the way in silence, lost in our own individual regrets and what-ifs.

Alice, a large brown-and-black German shepherd, met us at the door. She was trained as a zombie detection dog, an indispensable specialty that evolved from her original cadaver dog training. Dogs like her could smell decomposing flesh a minute after death a mile away and Alice was the best of the best. She'd already saved our asses a number of times over the past twelve months.

After giving Alice her required quota of love and adoration, I followed Shana into her gun room. Once it had been a normal, ordinary bedroom, but she had lovingly refurbished in early John Rambo meets any Robert Rodriguez movie. Handguns from tiny, pearl-handled .22s all the way up through her array of 9mms and .45s adorned one wall, while two other walls featured her collection of long weapons, rifles, shotguns, automatics—culminating in her pride and joy, a hand-held rocket launcher, just like the one Michael Douglas used in the movie *Falling Down*. The other wall held drawers filled with ammunition, loaders, kits and other accoutrements.

"What are we taking?" I asked.

"It's your party. Take anything you think we can use."

It took an hour to collect and load everything into the car. The hardest part was leaving room for Alice, who filled the back seat with her hulking presence. The sun was just coming up as we rolled across town to the Lassiter homestead.

We drove past the house once slowly and parked one street over. Lassiter's house was fairly isolated for central New England suburbia, surrounded by woods on three sides and a long gated driveway out front. Danielle had said the whole place was fenced in, electrified, and razor-wired, which weren't unusual upgrades for those who had survived the initial attacks.

"I assume you have a plan for storming the castle . . ."

"I told you that when Mandy and I used to date, her father wasn't happy about it," I said. "So we spent a lot of time sneaking her in and out of the house. Even back then he was into heavy security, but like most people, the one thing he always failed to do was look up."

"Look up?"

"Yeah, *up*. The house is surrounded by old-growth trees. Great for keeping prying eyes out, but even better for getting up and over fences as well as flying above Daddy's radar."

"That's all well and good for you, Monkey Man," Shana said, "but what about Alice and me? I failed rope climbing in gym and Alice left her wings attached to her special-occasion collar."

"Give me some credit. I grabbed Alice's harness, saddle-bags, and a blanket we can use for a sling. There's also rope in the trunk. Mandy and I did the up and over so often, we had a whole series of ropes and ladders permanently set up in the trees."

"You think after ten years, they're still there, and functional?"

"The ropes I used were top of the line climbing ropes and we hid them pretty well, but we won't know for sure until we get in there."

We grabbed everything we could carry, packing Alice's saddlebags with some of the smaller stuff, and headed in.

Unlike most of the world, nothing much had changed in this little stretch of woods in the past ten years. Paths were fainter and a few of the trees had fallen over, but there was little evidence of human presence or interference.

It didn't take us long to run up alongside Lassiter's property lines. The big metal fence rose out of the underbrush, barbed wire glinting in the early-morning sun. We followed it along the perimeter, checking for breaches and doing recon on what was going on inside. From what we could see, all was quiet, but Alice let us know there was definitely decaying meat some-where close by.

I found the access tree just about where I remembered it. Mandy hadn't been much of a climber when we started seeing each other, so by necessity this tree featured a lot of large, low branches that got us about ten feet up before having to switch over to a rope ladder that took us up into the much bigger oak that spanned the fence.

Following the old *Romeo and Juliet* route was harder than I remembered. Shana and I had a few scary moments when ropes were too frayed or missing, but we took it slowly and carefully, and eventually all eight of our feet touched down safely inside Lassiter's compound.

We tried to stick to the edges and keep obstacles between us and the house's windows, but there came a point when there was nothing to do but make a flat-out run across a big chunk of open yard in order to reach the back of the house.

We were halfway across when I heard Alice's deep warning growl and saw her cut off to the right. Shana saw it too and we peeled off after her. Alice had picked up the Zom's scent and led us right to them. There were three of them milling around a fenced enclosure about the size of a large dog run. Off to the side, a wire-covered, human-sized chute connected it to the house.

"What do you think? Is that our way in?" I asked.

Shana craned her neck to check out the cage's perimeters. "I don't see any insulators or battery boxes, so Lassiter didn't bother to electrify it. I'm going to say, yeah, this is probably our best bet. I'll get rid of the meat, you get the bolt cutters for the cage."

Shana attached the silencer to her piece and popped off three brain buster rounds. Her shots were dead center and all three Zoms went down quick and clean. Ten seconds later we were through the fence and checking out the door and the chute for locks and booby traps.

Sometimes guys like Lassiter fall into the same trap as the drug dealers used to. They figure they've got these vicious beasts running around protecting the place, so they don't need to take regular everyday security precautions. They get sloppy about closing and locking doors and windows, figuring nobody's ever going to get past the guardians, so why bother? Guys like that make my life as a cop a lot easier.

Lassiter, unfortunately, was not one of those sloppy guys. The door that led from the cage into the chute was easy enough to breach. But the door that led from the chute into the house was solid steel, with no locks, handles, or buttons on this side to allow humans in. Obviously no one was ever meant to use this door as an entrance.

"Shit, dead end," I said.

"No pun intended, I suppose," Shana said, staring hard at the door as she ran her fingers around the edges. "Hold on a second. I think I've got it."

Shana pulled a screwdriver out of Alice's magic saddlebags and went at the hinges on the door, which surprisingly were completely exposed on this side. Zoms don't use tools so I suppose it never occurred to Lassiter to cover this particular base. Within a couple of minutes we had the pins out and were ready to pull the door away.

"Ready?"

"Go."

The door came down, our guns came out and we moved quickly into the house. Alice wasn't alerting to any new threats, but she was moving slowly, swinging her huge head from side to side. I had worked with her long enough to know she was searching for something she knew was out there, just beyond her sense range.

The house still had an early-morning quiet feel to it. Like its residents weren't accustomed to acknowledging the brighter half of the day. There were four doors on this lower level, besides the one we came through. When Mandy and I were dating, they led to a family room, a half bath, the furnace room, and the garage. We checked them out: three were empty and the family room was padlocked from the outside. Whatever was in there wouldn't be getting out any time soon, so we agreed to move upstairs.

The middle level consisted of the kitchen, dining room, and living room, all in an open-type floor plan. Nothing unusual except the amount of filth and garbage banked up in the corners. It looked like whatever food was consumed in this place didn't need cooking or refrigeration. All clear. One more level.

Shana and Alice finally made Mrs. Lassiter's acquaintance as we reached the upstairs hallway. She charged out at us from the bathroom, but in the second between our guns going off and the bullets blowing through the back of her skull, Shana and I both registered that not only had she been moving at a pretty good clip, but she was armed with an axe and had been quite clearly cursing us out.

"Shit," both of us said in unison.

"She was alive when we shot her, Ryan. Danielle was wrong. What if she was wrong about everything? What if she fucked us over just to get out of doing time? What if we just broke into a fucking law-abiding *civilian's* house and gunned down a woman who was protecting herself from fucking *intruders*?"

"Calm down. Shit. Let's just take a breath. Okay. First of all, law-abiding civilians don't keep fucking zombies in a kennel out back. Second, Danielle told us she was only guessing about Mandy and her mother."

"If that bitch is fucking us over, I'll hunt her down and . . ."

BOOM.

The muffled gunshot echoed down the hall, followed by a scream and what sounded like furniture being thrown around. Shana, Alice, and I ran to the last door at the end of the hall. Alice alerted, so we were prepared for a Zom, but when we opened the door, no way in hell were we prepared for the scene playing out in front of us.

Lassiter lay sprawled on the floor, rifle on the rug next to him, blown-out lamp off to one side. Curled over him like a hungry vulture was a naked, bloody Mandy, ripping his torso to shreds with her bare hands. She was so intent on her prey she never even acknowledged our presence.

Shana recovered before I did, but instead of following protocol and firing off a kill shot, she dragged me backwards out of the room, slamming the door shut behind us. We sat in the hallway listening to slurping and smacking noises for what seemed like a very long time, tears running down both of our faces.

"Do you want me to handle this?" Shana asked, breaking the silence.

"No, this is all mine."

I got slowly to my feet and walked to the door. The feeding sounds had stopped. Usually right after a good meal, they were a little slower and marginally easier to handle. They never really slept, but temporarily fell into something like a post–Thanksgiving stupor.

I opened the door carefully. Mandy wasn't near the body any longer. She was curled up in the corner on the far side of the room, about as far as possible from her father's remains.

She must have seen me come in, but she didn't move. She just sat there, her thin body slightly bloated by what was probably more food than she had ever been allowed to consume. I raised my arm and lined up the sight.

"I'm sorry about everything, Mandy. I love you. I've always loved you."

And I pulled the trigger.

When I finally stopped sobbing and went over to check Mandy's body, I swear, the half of her face that was still intact was smiling.

MY PARTNER THE ZOMBIE

R. G. Hart

I sat behind my tan oak desk watching our new client drip on our carpet. The carpet was just dry cleaned yesterday.

My partner, Matt Butcher, sat opposite me behind his desk, his dark eyes watchful. I sensed he was waiting for my indignation to explode, but I wasn't about to give him the satisfaction. The steady drone of traffic on Bleeker Street three floors below our office windows filled the silence. It was early in the day so delivery vans were busy making their rounds.

"Mr. Jens," I began, keeping my tone even, "how is it you're so wet?"

His round face and coal-black eyes turned from Matt to me. He was a small man. Some would say he was a midget. Having seen every oddity this world can offer—and some of my best friends are midgets—I prefer the term little person.

"I require the services of a private investigator, but I'm not sure I came to the right place." Jens's eyes flitted to Matt, then back to me. "Is he gonna eat my brain?"

I laughed. "No, Mr. Jens. Matt's a vegetarian. He only eats tofu brains." I glanced at Matt. One side of his generous mouth curled in a half smile and the corners of his eyes crinkled. I confess I shiver every time he smiles. Truth is, I'd loved Matt since the day I met him. Too bad he didn't share my feelings. Zombie and redheaded PI loving just wasn't in the cards, I guessed.

I saw Jens scowl at me. He obviously didn't appreciate my twisted sense of humor.

"Sorry, Mr. Jens. A little joke." I eased back in my tan oak captain's chair and shifted my weight. I'd been sitting too long and my *gluteus maximus* was sore. The concord grape–colored chair cushion had long ago been mashed into uselessness.

"Truth is, my partner is a fifty-fifty zombie."

Jens blinked. He didn't get it. Not surprising, considering that in my line of work I didn't believe half of what I was told either. "He wasn't fully zombie when he escaped from the undead factory." Yeah. Right. More like the island where the *Mambo* created her zombies.

"Ever hear of Zombie Away?" he said sarcastically.

I shook my head. "Allergies."

Jens *humprfed* and crossed his arms over his chest. "I was told, Miss Armstrong, your agency was the best. Now I'm not so sure." He waved a dismissive hand at me. "A zombie and a model? I mean, *really*, how would anyone ever take you seriously?"

I narrowed my eyes and rose from behind my desk. I was pleased when he took a step back, but winced when his runners squished more water onto the carpet. I rounded the desk and went to the coffee maker we kept on top of an army-green filing cabinet. I poured myself a mug.

"Mr. Jens, I have not, nor have I ever been, a *model*. I used to be a federal agent with the Legal Investigative Protection Service and have brought many criminals to justice. Surely you've heard of the Zero case."

Jens's brow creased, his eyes skeptical. "Yeah. I've heard of it."

I walked back behind my desk with my mug in my hand. "Well, Matt and I were heavily involved in that case." Of course I didn't tell him I left the L.I.P.S. because of that case. It was need-to-know information and that he didn't need to know.

"Okay." He paused, then suddenly his words spat out machine-gun style. "I'm soaked because I was pushed into a tank of water from forty feet up. Someone's trying to murder me."

Jerry Jens is a circus midget. At least that's what the billboard next to the ticket booth screamed in large red and purple letters. I glanced at Matt and grunted. He was wearing my favorite grey pinstriped double-breasted suit and grey felt fedora. Man, did he look like a professional private dick right out of a Raymond Chandler novel. Cool.

I was wearing my usual uniform of black spandex leggings, four-inch spiked heels, and billowy cotton sweater. I wore a bulky sweater because I hated it when men talked to my breasts as if they were microphones. A thirty-eight C cup could be a real detriment in my business.

Jerry had gone home to change, but he'd given me a card for Maxmillian Q. Quiet. Quiet was the general manager and ringmaster of the Dingaling Brothers Circus. The much traveled circus was camped on the edge of town.

We approached the ticket booth to find the oldest woman I had ever seen seated on a stool behind a wall of dirt-smudged Plexiglas. There was a half moon–shaped opening just above the counter for the exchange of money for tickets. Her weathered face was a perfect representation of the Grand Canyon. "That'll be seventeen fifty," she said in a gravel-crunching voice.

She didn't look up when I handed her Quiet's card. "We're here to see Mr. Quiet."

The old woman's sky blue eyes finally lifted from the *Racing Form* she'd been reading to peer at the card, then at us. Her world-weary, unemotional eyes flitted between Matt and me. "Staff entrance is round back."

I smiled. "We're private investigators. We really need to speak with Mr. Quiet. It's a matter of life and death." Yeah, I know, a little dramatic, but sometimes theatrics can take you a long way. Especially when you're dealing with theatrical people.

"Why didn't you say so?" she said, her tone heavy with sarcasm. "Once you're inside, turn left, then make a right at the second tent. Follow the tent until you come to a row of trailers. In the fifth trailer from the left you'll find Maxie."

"Thanks."

She nodded, then turned her attention back to the paper. I retrieved Quiet's card and we started to walk away when she called me back. I went back and leaned toward the window as the woman motioned me closer with one crooked finger. "Yes?"

"Don't tell Maxie I sent ya."

I glanced at Matt. He shrugged. I looked back into the old woman's blood-webbed eyes. "Yes, certainly."

Once inside the entrance we were greeted by the smells of fresh cut grass and sour hay.

We soon came to the line of trailers just as described by the old woman. What she'd failed to tell us about was their elaborate paint jobs. Each trailer was painted in a different theme. Some had grey-skinned elephants with their trunks curled back, others had pretty girls in elaborate Las Vegas showgirl costumes astride pure white horses, while others bore images of smiling clowns and balloons. They were truly works of art.

There had to be at least forty trailers standing side by side. Matt counted to the fifth trailer from the left and motioned for me to follow him. We approached Quiet's trailer with Matt in the lead. I love a man who takes charge. Even if he's an undead man.

In contrast to the other trailers with circus-related images, Max Quiet's trailer was covered in rainbows and unicorns. Strange. Why the difference?

Matt rapped his grey knuckles on the door. Silence returned as the echo of Matt's knock died from inside the trailer. Matt frowned, then pounded on the door with his fist.

Finally a foghorn-like voice responded, "Who goes there?" This is Quiet? I don't think so.

"It's Aloha Armstrong and Matt Butcher, Mr. Quiet. We're with Abby-Normal Investigations, sir. We—" Before I could say anything more, the aluminium door flew open to slap hard against the side of the trailer. The door missed Matt with inches to spare.

My jaw hung open at the sight of him. Like Jens, Maxmillian Q. Quiet was a little person.

Quiet invited us into his trailer after I explained why we were here. He seemed genuinely surprised concerning an allegation of attempted murder. We didn't mention Jerry Jens's name yet.

Matt and I each took a seat on one of two grey-green over-stuffed chairs across from a matching sofa. Quiet sat on the sofa.

We'd caught him with his pants down. Literally. He was still dressed in boxer shorts—I was so thankful he didn't wear briefs—and a ratty sleeveless undershirt.

His beady eyes shifted between us. His child-sized feet fidgeted like he had to pee and his chipmunk cheeks were flushed. I nodded to Matt, indicting he should lead the questioning. He shrugged, took off his fedora, and placed it in his lap. He then cleared his throat. Matt was a man of few words. I liked that about him. Being questioned by a zombie had to be at least a hundred and forty-two on the intimidation meter.

"Mr. Quiet." Matt paused to pull out his notebook from his inside pocket, then flipped it open with a flick of his wrist. So *Star Trek*. So cool. His brow wrinkled as he studied the page. "A Mr. Jerry Jens visited our office this morning." He glanced up from the page to look at Quiet. "Do you know Mr. Jens?"

Quiet fidgeted, then said, "Yes. But I don't know anything about any murder."

Matt's eyebrows arched in sync. *You go, guy.* "Who said anything about murder?"

"You said . . ." His hazel eyes shifted to me. "*She* said Jerry said someone tried to murder him."

Matt nodded. "But if the victim isn't dead, then it's attempted murder. A fine point to be sure, but Mr. Jens has engaged us to find the person responsible for the *accident* this morning."

Quiet frowned. *Uh-oh.* The intimidation meter had just slipped a few notches. "Say. Who are you people, anyway? Are you cops?" Quiet rose from the sofa and crossed the room to stand in front of me. I can tell you a little person wearing only boxer shorts and an undershirt reeking of stale beer and cigarettes is not a pleasant experience.

I smiled as sweetly as I was able, hoping my charming side, such as it is, would quell the tiger in his tank. "No, Mr. Quiet, we're not cops. As Matt explained, we came here because Mr. Jens hired us to find out who tried to kill him." I shrugged my shoulders slightly. "We're hoping you'll cooperate with us."

His eyes became like black beads in a snow bank. "Why didn't he go to the cops?"

"He did," said Matt. "They didn't believe him."

Quiet snorted, then padded across the seventies' era forest green shag carpet toward the small kitchen. "Coffee?" he offered.

I looked at Matt, then back at Quiet. Matt frowned at me and slapped his notebook closed. I leaned toward him and whispered, "Patience." We locked eyes. His shoulders relaxed and he nodded. Matt's one serious flaw was his lack of patience. Not a good thing in the PI business.

"Sure." I shifted my gaze to Quiet and grinned. "We would."

Building a bridge of trust between us and Maxie Quiet was going to take time. Problem was, my instincts were screaming that time was growing short. And my instincts are never wrong.

Max—he told us to call him Max—brought us steaming pastel mugs filled with freshly brewed coffee. Mine was dark, like my men. I eyed Matt. Actually, I like my men tall, grey, and handsome, actually.

Max handed Matt his coffee with the two milks and five sugars, since he has a bit of sweet tooth. Zombies don't have to worry about their figures, like we alive folks do.

Max finally returned from the kitchen carrying a mug as colorful as ours. He took a generous sip and closed his eyes, smiled, then eased back into the embrace of the thick sofa cushions with a sigh. "Sorry if I was rude before, Aloha. It's just that we run this place on a very tight budget. Even a hint of bad publicity is going to hurt our bottom line."

"I understand, Max." I frowned. "Who would want to hurt Jerry?"

Max didn't hesitate. He blurted, "Uno." There were no doubts in this guy's mind who was responsible.

Matt scooted forward in his chair. "Uno who?"

A mischievous smile crossed Max's thin lips. "Not who. What."

Matt and I shared a puzzled look.

Max sighed. "You mentioned Zero earlier."

I nodded. "What about him? He's serving his time on the American Prisons reality show." I grunted and shook my head. "It's the last place I would wish on anyone."

Max rolled his eyes. "Yeah. Terrible." He paused, then said, "Anyway, Zero's oldest son is Uno. He's as much of a megalo-maniac as his father and just as reclusive."

"So?" said Matt, a trace of impatience in his voice, "what has Uno got to do with Jerry Jens?"

Max eyed Matt dryly. "Jerry and Uno are brothers."

We found Jerry in his apartment on Syler Street. The building was sixteen stories with no elevator. Jerry lived on the fifteenth floor.

Still huffing, puffing, and gasping for breath, we arrived at his front door. Matt was bent forward at the waist breathing hard. We both smelled of sour sweat. "We . . . gotta . . . get clients . . . who . . . live . . . on the first . . . floor," he gasped.

My heart pounding in my ears, unable to speak, I nodded. I looked up as the apartment door opened. Jerry. He was dry and clean-shaven, dressed in a purple track suit minus shoes. "Hey, guys. What took you so long?"

I'd called ahead saying we'd be here in ten minutes. That was before I knew about the Olympic walk-up competition.

Jerry stepped back. "Come on in."

I puffed my cheeks, then entered the apartment with as much dignity as my trembling legs allowed. Muscles I didn't know I possessed ached.

The apartment's floors were hardwood and the walls were painted pale blue. The air smelled of peaches. Matt shuffled in behind me. Great. I rolled my eyes. Just when Jerry was convinced Matt wasn't going to eat his brain, he shuffles like a zombie.

The door clicked closed behind us. "Let's go into the living room," Jerry said with a sweep of his hand.

I grunted my agreement. We followed him into the living room. One wall was a floor-to-ceiling window that overlooked the city. The window was tinted to diffuse the sunlight so the apartment didn't get overheated.

"Nice place," I said, my voice harsh.

We sat on the brown leather sectional facing the windows. My heart rate finally normalized and I was tempted to think I might even live.

"I call it home." Jerry sat on another section of the sofa. The sofa sighed as I sank into the soft leather. Boy, did it feel good to sit down.

"The circus must pay pretty good," said Matt.

I shot him an angry glare. As far as I'm concerned, it's rude to talk about how much someone makes—or in my case, doesn't make. I frowned. I nailed Matt with my we're-gonna-talk-later-dude look. He ignored me again.

Jerry laughed when he recognized the annoyance in my eyes. "No. Not at all. I receive royalties from Zombie Away."

Uh-oh. Not that again. I looked at Matt, uncertain how he'd react. Sure Matt had used Zombie Away, but since in his case it needed fifty-four treatments to work and he was allergic, it just wasn't gonna happen. "I'm happy the way I am. Live with it," he had said when I mistakenly made Zombie Away my last-stand ultimatum for any shot at a relationship between us. This was before I knew he was allergic. I'd planted my foot firmly in my mouth and I learned shoe leather leaves a bitter after-taste. It was the darkest day of my life.

Jerry frowned. "Matt, maybe after this case is over I can arrange some free treatments for you. What do you say?"

I held my breath. "No. Thank you," Matt said.

His words put the final nails in the coffin of my hopes and dreams. Jerry shrugged. "Okay. It's your loss." Yeah, *his* loss.

Matt retrieved his notebook and a pen from his suit pocket as before. "Tell us about your brother, Uno." His pen was poised over an empty page.

I exchanged an oh-brother look with Jerry. "Doesn't believe in foreplay, huh?" I offered him a weak smile. Jerry sighed, then launched into his story.

Jerry and Uno were twins raised by different mothers. Their early years were spent on a dude ranch near El Paso. Zero used the ranch as a cover for his plans to take over the world.

When Jerry was ten, like every boy his age, he dreamed of running away and joining the circus. Which he did. When I asked him how Zero never found him, he said he changed his name to Jerry Jens. His birth name was Dos. With a handle like that I'd change my name too.

Uno found him six months ago when he came to the circus looking for mindless security guards who would follow orders without question. They argued and Uno threatened to kill him unless he signed over the Zombie Away royalties.

I finally understood what Uno was up to. With Jerry gone, the profits from Zombie Away would finance the takeover of the world. While Uno embraced his father's mad dreams, Jerry rejected them. But Jerry never believed his brother would really kill him—until yesterday, when he was thrown off the high dive platform.

After we'd left Jerry's apartment behind, we headed south on I-16 toward Wallenberg.

"I've been thinking," Matt said after several minutes of quiet between us. I could almost see the smoke coming from his ears. Secretly I hoped it wasn't spontaneous combustion. "It's strange Uno would only try to kill his brother. Why didn't he just shoot him? Why throw him from a diving platform?" He paused and his grey features formed a scowl. "Seems a little less than foolproof to me."

My '75 Mustang squeaked and popped as I steered it into the left lane and stomped on the accelerator. The four cylinders screamed as we slowly crawled past the Franken-Goo Reclamation tanker truck.

I nodded. "Yeah. That is odd." I glanced at Matt. His fedora was tipped at an angle and the last rays of the setting sun gave his skin a slightly golden tinge. Way cool. "Who did he say grabbed him?"

Matt pulled out his notebook and scanned his notes. "He didn't know. Whoever it was threw a sack over his head. He did say he smelled bananas, though." Matt winced and wrinkled his nose. "Then all he smelled was used jock straps."

"Uggg. Gross!" I chuckled.

Matt looked thoughtful. "Don't fresh zombies smell like bananas?"

"Yeah, you're right." I steered back into the slow lane in front of the tanker truck to let a Smart Car speed by us. The driver of the Smart Car gave us the one-fingered salute as he passed. Nice.

It was dark when we arrived at the turn off to Wallenberg. As we came to the stop sign where the off ramp met the main road into town, we found a police roadblock. Three state police cruisers and one Wallenberg sheriff's car were parked in the middle of the road. Their rollers made the surrounding grasslands shine alternately blue and green.

I steered us to the side of the road and parked on the gravel shoulder. I shut the engine off and pocketed my keys. I'd brought along a jean jacket to wear over my sweater. The evenings can get cool this time of year.

I pressed the button on the side of my Timex and the round watch face lit up. Nine fifteen and seven seconds.

"Hey, Aloha," Matt called. "Look at this." He was standing in front of a dark green road sign. In white block letters were the words *Wallenberg 2 Miles* and an arrow pointing to the right. Only "Wallen" had been crossed out with red felt pen and the word *Zombie* inserted. Wallenberg was now Zombieberg. This couldn't be good.

I looked around and saw a group of cops standing next to a police cruiser parked farthest from where we stood. I saw one of them had enough gold bars on her epaulets to be a rear admiral, so I knew she must be in charge.

As I approached the gaggle of law enforcement officers, she looked at me, her hazel eyes intent and questioning. She looked familiar.

"Aloha Armstrong?" Her pale face broke into a toothpaste-model smile. She took off her peaked cap and shook her hair loose. Her dark curls cascaded about her shoulders.

"Perky Peters? Is that you?" I ran up to her and wrapped her in a bear hug. "It's been too long." The Perkster and I were roommates at The L.I.P.S. Academy. It was old home week.

I released her and we stepped back to scan each other up and down. "You look well," I said. I probably looked like something the dog left behind, but Perky was a cop, a *real* cop. Who woulda thought?

"I'm great." She nodded at the bars on her right shoulder. "I'm the chief of police. Me. Can you believe?"

One of the four male cops standing in a group near the bumper of the cruiser snorted. Perky ignored his sarcasm. "So what you been up to?" she asked.

"I own my own private investigation company, with my partner, of course."

Perky shifted her gaze to peer over my left shoulder. "Who?"

I turned to see Matt had been handcuffed and was being seated in the back seat of a blue and white state police cruiser.

"Hey! What's goin' on? My partner's the zombie!"

Perky filled me in.

We sat in the front seat of her sheriff's car. The soft chatter of radio checks disappeared as Perky turned down the volume with a twist of the knob. Her normally bright hazel eyes were dull and drooped at the corners. The roadblock had been up for eighteen hours now. Perky's perk was definitely on its lowest setting.

Her cruiser had to be the cleanest police car I had ever seen. Not one stale donut or empty coffee cup in sight. Weird.

"Someone set up a zombie factory in town and is turning everyone they can get their hands on into zombies." Her mouth formed a grim line.

Oh crap. She was serious? When I said someone had a zombie factory I was just kidding. I didn't expect anyone would actually build one. Welcome to the *Twilight Zone*.

"But who?" I said.

"A megalomaniac is who," the Perkster said. She gripped the steering wheel so hard, her knuckles were white.

"It's Uno, right?"

Her bloodshot eyes shifted to me and her brow was creased by a frown. "No. Of course not. Uno's my boyfriend. He was the first one turned." Her gaze shifted to the two lane blacktop road ahead. Her voice dropped to a whisper. "They always go after the nicest man in town first."

Now if you don't think I was shocked, then you haven't been following along. "What? Uno?" I shook my head. "No way. He's a creep."

Perky turned to glare at me. "Watch it, pal. You're talkin' about the little guy I love."

I grinned sheepishly. "Sorry. It's just we have information that suggests Uno tried to murder his brother."

As an eyebrow arched Perky said, "Brother?" She snorted. "You mean that miniature-megalomaniac-from-Muskogee, Jerry Jens? Are you kidding?"

"What about Maxie Quiet? He said Uno was a really bad guy."

"Zombie," she said simply.

I sank back into the seat as a knot formed in the pit of my stomach. Uh-oh. We'd been had. Jerry was the villain, not Uno.

After I explained that Matt wasn't a factory-made zombie but a one-hundred-percent-organic-magik-made-orginal (and that I loved him), Perky had him released. We were standing beside her cruiser when the town, visible just over a crest in the road, lit up with searchlights. A loudspeaker began to encourage all to come to the circus. Every day was free day, the speaker said. Free tickets could be quite an enticement.

We had to stop Jerry's mad plan.

We devised our own plan. Matt would go in as the under-cover zombie. Made sense since he was the only zombie PI we had. Not that I was happy he was going in alone. We were a team, after all.

Matt would sabotage Jerry's zombie factory to allow time for the crop dusters to arrive.

Perky had contacted the Zombie Away people and they agreed to provide a squadron of crop dusters to spray Zombie

Away over Wallenberg. Mega corporations don't like megalo-maniacs who besmirch their good name by turning everyone in the world into zombies and hoarding the world's supply of their product.

"But doesn't Zombie Away take three treatments to work?" I said.

Perky shrugged. "They said this was the new and improved version. They say it works the first time, every time."

Matt looked unfazed but I was worried. The drop was taking place at eleven fifteen. It was ten forty-five now. He had thirty minutes. If he didn't get out in time he'd be sprayed and the al-lergic reaction to that much Zombie Away would very likely kill him.

Since I might never see him again, I took his arm in mine and led him into the grassy field beside the road. The crickets chirped around us. I wrapped my arms around his back and pulled him into me. I gazed into his eyes as a smile curled at the corner of his mouth.

"You want to talk about sumthin'?" he whispered.

His heart beat rhythmically against my chest when he wrapped his arms around me. "Matt. Do you remember what we talked about?"

"We talked about a lot of things." Seeing the flash of disap-pointment on my face he added, "Yes, I know *exactly* what you mean."

"I want you to promise me if you survive this you'll recon-sider your decision."

He hesitated. "Okay. I promise."

At that moment I knew he didn't expect to survive.

I heard the drone of aircraft engines high overhead before I saw them. A grey-haired state cop yelled and pointed as the sixteen biplanes became visible, basked in moonlight.

I glanced at my Timex. It was only five after eleven. They were early.

I scanned the road and didn't see any sign of my Mustang. Matt had taken my car to drive into town. He was to find Jerry's lair and stop the zombie factory in any way possible, then hightail it out of there.

After what seemed like a month, I saw my Mustang headed for the roadblock. It was eleven twenty. Shrouded in shadow were the outlines of two passengers in the front seats of the car.

The car stopped with a squeak and a rattle. The engine died. The sounds of crickets chirping drowned out the sound of my heart beating in my ears. In the distance I heard the rush of traffic on the interstate. My senses, my nerves were tuned in. I saw a set of beady eyes shining from the back seat. *Jerry Jens, you are so goin' to the big house.*

Finally the passenger door opened and a blond man got out. He was wearing Matt's clothes, but that couldn't be Matt. Could it?

I rushed to the car but pulled up when the man in Matt's clothes smiled. "Matt? Is that you?"

He nodded. I leapt into his arms. We pressed our bodies into each other, sending thrills of passion through me. Our lips pressed into each other's. His body heat warmed me in the cool night air.

Matt was alive and he wasn't a zombie anymore!

We broke contact but hung onto each other as if our very lives depended on it. I wanted to be hugged by him forever. "How?" I breathed.

"I don't know," he said.

"I do," said a very deep, very male voice behind us.

I swivelled my head to see a tall man with broad shoulders, mouse brown hair, and a dimple in his right cheek. His green eyes sparkled. Perky had one arm around his waist and he was dressed in tan Dockers, a red golf shirt, and Nike's. Perky looked, well, perky.

"Our new formula is hypoallergenic." He grinned and held out his hand in greeting. "Hi, I'm Uno."

Reluctantly, I untangled myself from Matt and shook hands with him. Matt did likewise.

"I thought you'd be . . ." My words trailed off. I was gonna embarrass myself for sure.

Uno and Perky both laughed. "Ain't genetics grand?" said Perky.

I smiled and glanced at Matt. Yeah, genetics were grand.

We'd stopped the bad guy, saved the world, and Matt I would have our shot at love.

All in all, a pretty good day for me and my partner the zombie—or should I say my partner who used to be the zombie?

UNDYING LOVE

Regina Riley

Nothing puts a date off like the smell of formaldehyde and graveyard dirt.

Dee tried to turn her attention to the inventory of said graveyard dirt, but all she could think about was how she was spending another Saturday night alone. It was her own fault, she supposed. She'd never played well with others, and other magic users even less so. Maybe it was her sour disposition, or her headstrong attitude. Or maybe it was simply because of her reputation for dealing so closely with the dead.

Drawing her from her reverie, a voice asked, "Isn't it a bit unusual for a witch to have an office?"

Dee looked up from her desk to find a man standing in her office doorway. "Not when she doesn't want strangers traipsing about in her home."

"May I come in?"

Dee paused to inspect the stranger more closely. Tall and lean, he wore a suit so deeply black it threatened to completely suck the low light from the room. His skin was alabaster pale, and his hair was a brush of raven's wing across his strong brow. He smiled, displaying a row of handsome teeth, delicate and opalescent. And most likely pointy.

Her eyes drew to suspicious slits. "Are you a vampire?"

"Does it matter?" he asked.

"Yes actually, it does." She brushed a stray strand of auburn from her face and frowned. "If it didn't matter, I wouldn't have asked. Close the door on your way out . . . hey, I didn't invite you in!" She shouted the last bit in surprise because, although she hadn't invited the vampire beyond her threshold, he entered her office anyway, closing the door behind him.

"Don't worry, good lady," he said. "I'm not a vampire."

"Then why ask for admittance?"

He shrugged. "Just being polite."

"No man is that polite anymore."

"I'm not like most men you know." He smiled again.

"*Touche.* Have a seat, mister . . . ?" She let the question fall short, fishing for a name.

"Joshua Bane." He proffered a hand.

"Mister Bane. I'm Deetra Jones," she said and stood to shake his hand. As he grasped her palm, she noticed the odd feel of his skin: smooth but taut, like silk stretched tightly across a bone frame, with neither the warmth of the living nor the chill of the dead.

"It's a pleasure to meet you, Missus Jones," he said. He lifted her hand to his lips, which were as lukewarm as his skin, but their contact left her burning all the same. She also got a familiar tingle from down below. She pushed away the rising warmth and nodded at him.

"The feeling is mutual," she said. "And it's *Miss* Jones."

He cocked his head in surprise. "You mean some lucky man hasn't lured you to the altar?"

"Not yet." She smiled at the idea. "And you can call me Dee."

"Why?" he asked, still clinging to her hand, "when Deetra is such a beautiful name, for such a beautiful woman."

Dee looked to the ceiling and huffed. She thought for a brief moment that he might be different, but no. He was just another pale jerk in a too-black suit. She pulled her hand away, sat, and asked, "Are you sure you're not a vampire?"

He smiled even more widely this time, and revealed his perfectly white but perfectly point-free teeth. The lack of fangs did little to kill her doubt, but his gorgeous smile did everything to stoke her fires. Vampire or not, there was no denying he was one handsome man. She locked her green eyes onto his and that warm tingle returned. A slow burn that threatened to set her pants on fire.

"What can I do for you, Mister Bane?" she asked. She returned her attention to the paperwork on her desk, and away from his deep brown eyes. And square jaw. And perfect smile. And kissable lips.

"Please," he said. "Call me Joshua."

"Okay, Joshua. What do you want?"

Joshua cleared his throat. "I was told you would help out a man in my kind of situation."

Dee was pulled into the misery of his voice. She wanted to ask what had left him so pained. Who had hurt him so much? And what could she do to heal his ache? But instead she asked, "What kind of spell?"

"I need to find someone. Someone I haven't seen in a very long time."

Dee looked back up to him. Of course he was looking for someone. She should have known. "I don't do location spells. I do hexes, curses, and bindings. I do blessings and cleansings. I do money spells and love spells and the occasional enlargement-of-certain-private-parts spells. But I don't do locations."

"Don't? Or won't?"

"Won't."

"Why?"

"Expense. Location magic isn't cost effective for a small-timer like me. Unless you can front the eight hundred I'll need in supplies."

He shook his head. "It's really important that I find this person."

"It always is. Good luck finding her." She returned to her work.

Joshua's jaw hung open for a moment before he spoke again. "How did you know I was looking for a woman?"

Dee's knowing smile answered for her.

"This isn't about making her love me," he said. "We have unfinished business."

Dee lost her smile. "I don't deal with assassins, Mister Bane."

Joshua huffed in frustration as he sat on the bench and ran

his hands through his dark hair. "It's not like that either. I have a message to deliver to her. And I have to do it in person." He rubbed his hands together. "I was told you specialized in helping people like me. He said you even give special discounts."

"People like you?" she echoed. Her eyes returned to their narrow suspicion. "Where did you find out about me?"

"A necromancer named Maggot gave me your name and address."

"Son of a . . ." Dee whispered under her breath. She had dealt with Maggot in the past, and every single time she regretted getting tangled up with him. When she wasn't running from the conventional law for some lame hijinks he'd talked her into, she was busy worming her way out of his grimy paws. Out of the whole supernatural world, trust her to get stuck with a backwoods death magician as a not-so-secret admirer. But he did send her a stream of steady business, even if they were charity-case corpses.

"Why would Maggot send you to me?" she asked. "He only deals with the . . ."

Dee let the thought trail off as she stared hard at Joshua. No way. He didn't look the part. The neat hair. The dazzling smile. The clean clothes. The lack of stench. Not to mention the fact that she had just spent the last ten minutes flirting with him. No, there was no way he could be—

"Dead?" he asked. He held up his hands as if in defeat and smiled weakly. The gesture made him look adorable, instead of lifeless.

"You're sure you're not a vampire?"

"Why do you keep asking me that?"

"Because you don't look or act or smell like a zombie."

Joshua winced at the word.

"Sorry," she said. "I meant one of the newly risen."

"That's a quaint term." His sarcasm was thick enough to swallow.

She shrugged. "It's more P.C. than I care to be, but I know you guys hate the zed word."

"You have no idea."

Actually, she had every idea. She had dealt with the dead for so long she felt like she understood them better than the living. But a thing like Joshua she had never even seen before, much less understood. "How come you don't—" she started to ask.

He cut her off with one word. "Magic."

"That's all magic?" she asked.

"Yes, magic got me up and walking and magic keeps me from falling down again. But more to the point, magic keeps me . . . how should I put this?" He paused and rubbed his chin in thought.

"Fresh as a daisy?"

"Thanks."

"Don't mention it. I'm impressed. I've never seen this level of magic applied to a corpse before."

"Again, I am unlike any corpse you will ever meet."

And she believed him, until her business sense stomped her

sympathy into submission. "How do I know you're not just fishing for a good price?"

"What?"

"I do give special discounts to the newly risen because most of them are in a tight fix."

"So you do pro bono work?" he asked, his voice tinged with hope.

"Not for just anyone. How do I know you're not just some Joe Blow looking to get a special rate by playing dead?"

His faced screwed up into a pinch of disgust. "Why would I do that?"

"Won't be the first time someone's tried it."

Joshua put his hand over his heart and said, "I give you my word as a gentleman that—"

"It doesn't make sense," she said, cutting him off in mid-pledge. "Why would someone drop so much magic into one walking cadaver? The implements alone would have cost him more than I make in a whole year."

"Deetra, please. As unbelievable as it is, I'm telling the truth. I'm as dead as the next corpse."

Dee wasn't convinced. There was something funny going on here and she intended to get in on the joke. "There isn't a spell slinger on the Eastern Seaboard I know who would waste this kind of magic on just one zombie. Who's your master?"

A dark brooding came over Joshua. "I don't have a master."

While it was uncommon for a zombie to be without a master,

it wasn't entirely impossible. Usually the dead came back for three reasons: stupidity, cheap labor, and revenge. Joshua looked clever enough to know he was dead and didn't look like the kind of guy one brought back just to wash the dishes. That left one option.

And Dee didn't like the thought of getting mixed up with it.

"Who raised you?" she asked.

"No one you would know," he said.

"Now hold on. Just because I'm a small-time witch doesn't mean I don't know some big-time folks."

He waved away her concern. "None of that is important. I have to see Emily and I have no other means to find her. I have no money and nothing of value. I have tried to indenture myself in the service of others but no one will deal with the likes of me. You're my last hope."

"Well, hope on, buddy."

Joshua rose from his seat, lowered to one knee, and hung his head low. "On bended knee, Deetra Jones, I beg of you. Please help me. Help me in this, my hour of need, and I swear I will do whatever you ask of me in return." He lifted his face to her. A terrible and wounded look filled his dark eyes.

Normally, Dee would have poked and prodded that wounded look until she got the answers she was looking for. But for some reason she couldn't do it. He looked so sad and pained, as if he had seen the inside of pure torture for years beyond her understanding. Her heart ached at the thought of adding to his torment.

But, as they said, business was business.

She stood, parked her hands on her hips and looked down at him. "Give me some proof that you're just an average working stiff and not some slob trying to get one over on me, and maybe, just maybe, I'll think about helping you."

Joshua smiled again as he stood from his kneel, and nodded. He slipped off his jacket and tossed it onto the bench behind him.

"Well?" Dee asked.

But the man kept silent and continued with his smug smile. He unknotted his tie, slipped it free with a whisper of fabric against fabric, and tossed it onto his jacket. He undid the cuffs on his black, silk shirt. Then he began to unbutton it all the way.

"Whoa there," Dee said. "What do you think you're doing?" Not that she was opposed to seeing the man half naked. In truth she would love to see the man all naked, but that was neither here nor there.

"You want proof?" he asked as he worked the last button and yanked the tail free from his pants. "Here's your proof." With that, he pulled his shirt open wide. The silk slipped over his pallid shoulders and dangled from his half-bent elbows.

As pale and smooth as the rest of him, his upper chest looked to be cut from marble while his abs boasted a six-pack Dee could have drank from all night long. But out of the glorious vision that was his bare chest, Dee's eyes fell and rested on the single imperfection: a fist-sized hole in his left pectoral. She leaned low to peer deeper, and saw her office door on the other side. Everything was gone, including his heart, leaving a black encrusted gap in its wake.

"You should know," he said softly, "that I don't show this to just anyone."

She straightened, swallowed hard, and asked, "What killed you?"

"You won't believe this, but it was poisoning."

Dee closed her eyes and gritted her teeth, suspecting as much. The handiwork before her was as clear as a signature, and the thought of its architect made her very blood boil.

"Are you okay?" Joshua asked.

Dee clenched her fists and forced the anger to pass. She tried to smile. "When do you want to do this thing?"

"As soon as possible."

"Then get dressed, because we've got some magic to make."

He gasped. "You'll help me?"

"I think I have to." She pointed to his chest and shook her head. "I'm not a doctor, but in my experience poison doesn't leave huge holes in people. Taking a man's heart? That's not just black magic, that's cruel."

"I don't understand." He returned his shirt and closed it, much to Dee's dismay.

"Joshua, you're not just a zombie, you're cursed. Even if you break whatever mojo is keeping you on your feet, your spirit will never truly rest until your heart is returned to your body."

"I had no idea."

Dee was sure he had some idea, but wasn't in the mood to argue. "I haven't seen the likes of it for a while."

He ran his hand over his chest, smoothing down his now-buttoned shirt while arching his movements around the gap. "I don't care about my well being. I need to find Emily. And soon."

Dee pursed her lips together and tipped her head to one side. "I can almost bet that wherever your lady friend is, you'll find your ticker."

His eyes grew wide. "Do you think so? I suppose it makes some sort of sick sense. But again, none of that matters right now. She does."

Dee smiled. It was clear how he felt about his mystery woman. Dee wished, one day, someone would think of her like that. "Love her that much, do you?"

Joshua lost all of his excitement in an instant. "I did. I mean I do. It's just been such a long time. I . . ." He let the idea fade as he sat and cradled his head in his hands.

His sorrow was infectious and once again Dee ached for him. She stood and went to his side. As she sat on the bench, she resisted the urge to run her hands through his hair, to take his hand into hers, to hold him. Sure, he was handsome and polite and aside from the fact that he was one of the walking dead, he was already in love.

But Dee was always a sucker for romance, even if it wasn't her own.

Joshua looked to her and said, "I'm sorry. After you've offered me such kindness, I feel like I'm holding back on you. It's very hard to explain."

"Then don't," she said. "As the hired help, I don't need explanations. Or some dead yo-yo going on a self-pity binge when I'm trying to work. Understand?"

He gave her a weak smile. "Yes, ma'am. And you're much more than just hired help, Deetra. Much more." His eyes sparkled as he spoke her name.

Dee's heart fluttered at his flattery. But she reminded herself that even men who were spoken for could still flirt. "You just remember those words when the bill comes due."

"The bill," he said with a sigh. "I don't suppose you give credit?"

Dee paused and took a long, hard look at the man. "No. But I do accept favors."

The sinful grin that spread across the dead man's face made Dee wonder just how in love he truly was. "I promise you anything, anything at all, if you just help me find her."

"Good," she said. "Because what I'm about to do for you will cost you for the rest of your un-life."

There was only one man who could help Dee get the materials she needed without wanting cash up front. What he would charge her this time, she could only imagine. Dee dialed the number, took a deep breath as it rang and nearly hung up when he answered.

"I was startin' to wonder when you'd call," Maggot said across the line.

"Tell me," she said. "Did you send him to me because you felt sorry for him, or because you knew I would need help with the spell?"

"Why can't it be both? You get to do your gallant thing, and I get ya right where I want ya."

Dee knew better, but clamped down on the bait anyways. "And where do you want me?"

"On the kitchen table, for starters. Then the couch, then the living room floor—"

"If you think you're going to lay a hand on me—"

"Now that hurts, Deedee. You know I were just joshin'. I thought you knew me better than that."

Dee sighed. Maggot might be a lecherous freak, but he did have a good streak somewhere in that dried-up bag of bones. "I'm sorry, I'm just frustrated."

"I know, honey. That boy's done been through the ringer, ain't he?"

Dee eyed Joshua and agreed.

"And just for the record," Maggot said, "I sent him your way 'cause I knew you'd help him pick up the pieces. You know I'm all thumbs if the recipe don't include at least three dead things. Besides, everyone in a hundred miles knows you can't be beat when it comes to proper magic."

The spell work wasn't the issue for Dee. The equipment was. A location spell required a quarter ounce of pure gold dust, and that was just the start of a very long and very expensive list. "But I can't afford—"

"I know that too, pun'kin. That's why I prepped some goods and sent 'em with the stiff. Didn't he give 'em to you?"

Dee put her hand over the phone and nodded to Josh. "Did Maggot send something with you?"

Joshua's pale hand struck his worried brow as he realized his forgetfulness. He went to the hallway and returned with a small cardboard box. It bore the legend "Stuff Fur Deedee" and had Maggot's grimy fingerprints all over it. The man had just left a couple hundred dollars' worth of implements just lying around in the hallway.

Dee smirked and reminded herself to scold him later. "Yeah, I got it. I'll repay you as soon as I can."

"Darlin'," he said. "You don't owe me nothin' but a smile."

"Thanks, Mag."

"A smile across the table while I'm eating a home-cooked supper would be lovely."

Dee rolled her eyes. "We'll see."

"It won't even be a real date. Just you payin' me back, all nice like. See?"

"I have to go, Mag."

Maggot's voice dropped to a whisper. "Deetra, listen close, little girl."

Dee fell quiet at the sound of her proper name.

"You keep me updated about that boy, you hear?" he asked.

"I will," she said.

"And you watch your cute little behind, pun'kin. There's something goin' on with that kid. Somethin' bad."

"I know. Thanks again, Mag. I owe you big time." Dee could hear the dry stretch of his wide smile.

"I know, honey. Maggot might not got much upstairs but he do have a long memory. Yes, sirree. A long memory."

She hung the phone up on his wicked cackle. "Looks like we got our goods."

"I'm sorry," Joshua said. "This package completely slipped my mind. I'm afraid I find myself forgetting things from time to time."

"Yeah, having a half-rotten mind will do that to a guy. Still, you're more coherent than most zee's I see. The only thing we are missing is something that belongs to her. Something that would help us get a fix on Emily's essence."

"It won't be destroyed, will it?"

"No. I just need it for a focus."

"I might have something." Joshua slipped his hand into his pants pocket and pulled free a small velvet box. He held the box out to Dee and said, "I never had the chance to give it to her, but it always belonged to her. Will it do?"

Dee cracked the lid on the box, already knowing what she would find inside. Perched between two layers of silk was a thin gold ring. A wedding band. Any doubt Dee had about Joshua's dedication to Emily washed away. Dee smiled and slipped into her professional mode, and out of her flirting one. "That will do just fine. Let's get started."

"Where do we do it?"

Dee shuddered at the question and fought to keep her mind

out of the gutter and focused on the job at hand. "We don't do anything. You sit on that bench and watch me."

"Yes ma'am." The zombie did as asked.

The spell work, while expensive, was simple. Dee had a knack with certain magic that could have made her a superstar in the field. But she never wanted fame or fortune. She just wanted to be left alone. Usually. The handsome form of Joshua, as he lingered at the edge of her casting circle, made her think twice about her self-imposed abstinence. It was a shame he was taken already. She could think of a few places to take him. On the kitchen table maybe, then the couch, then the living room floor—

Less than twenty minutes later, Dee had Joshua's answer.

"I have an address," she announced.

"So quickly?" he asked.

"Magic's simple if you know what you're doing. You should see me sling a hex. I once rendered a man from hairy to bald in ten seconds, flat."

"Wow." Josh was duly impressed. "Remind me to never make you mad."

"If you do, just be quick with the apologies." They laughed as she wrote the address on a slip of paper. She handed it and the ring to him and said, "You were closer than you thought. It should be fairly easy to find."

"Is it very far?" he asked as he eyed the address.

"About an hour's drive."

He looked up to her with a sheepish grin. "How long is that on foot?"

Dee looked to the clock on the wall. It was well past ten and that late-night dinner was getting further and further away. She huffed as she grabbed her keys. "Come on, big boy. Let's go find your lady fair."

"I couldn't ask you—"

"You're not asking," she interjected. "I'm offering." Dee slipped on her coat and went to the office door. She opened it wide and turned back to look at him. "Now, are you coming or not?"

That sinful grin returned and Dee could only wonder what the mind behind it was thinking as the body followed her out to her van.

"I hope you like to hear people sing," she said as she buckled up.

He shot her a curious glance as he clicked his belt into place. "I enjoy live performances, but it has been a while since I've seen a band perform."

"That's all well and good, but I meant just regular people."

"Regular people? As in?"

"Me. I tend to get carsick very easily and while driving is the key to keeping me level, I find singing helps distract the nausea. So unless you want to end up with a lap full of puke, you'll be a good boy and put up with it."

"By all means, sing away."

Dee spent almost the entire hour doing just that. It wasn't so much a serenade as it was a performance to a captive audience. Literally. But Joshua seemed to enjoy her renditions of various artists, favoring the older songs, which he sung along

to himself. As they neared their target, Joshua turned down the volume mid-chorus, which left Dee belting out her appreciation of a certain-colored submarine all by herself.

She drew the chorus to its natural close and eyed him. "What's on your mind?"

"Why do you do it?" he asked.

"Car sickness. I told you already—"

"No," he said with a chuckle. "I mean why do you help people like me?"

She had been asked this on more than one occasion, and usually dodged the answer with trite comebacks and clever witticisms. But without thinking about it, she found herself telling Joshua the truth.

"My grandfather taught me everything I know about magic," she said. "He was the best. At least to me. He always had time for people. No matter how much they could pay, he would always help if he could. A week before my eighteenth birthday, he passed away."

"I'm sorry."

Dee shrugged. "He was old. It was expected. But what we didn't expect was to see him again."

"As a zombie?"

"Yeah. He had been feuding with our neighbor for years over the property line. One foot to the right of the fence post, gramps said. One foot to the left, Ferguson said. So when gramps kicked the bucket, old man Ferguson hired a necromancer to raise him. He brought gramps back and put him to work on

that single foot of land out of spite." Dee gripped the wheel until her knuckles were white with anger. "I still remember that day I came home from school and saw him pulling weeds from around the fence."

"It must have been horrible."

"It was. I tried to fix it. I tried everything he taught me, but I was too inexperienced. I couldn't break a spell like that. I even went to every magic user I knew, but I couldn't afford what they were asking. We were so poor back then. In the end, I went to the necromancer who raised gramps. I offered him . . ." Dee paused and swallowed the swell of sickening memories. "Everything. I offered him everything, Joshua. And he laughed at me. He said business was just business. That he didn't want to get a reputation as a man unable to keep his word." Dee glanced at her passenger, and his look startled her. His face was twisted in a mask of hatred, gritting his teeth while his nostrils flared.

"That black-hearted monster," he said.

Dee appreciated his anger more than he could know. "My family spent three long weeks watching him fall apart and there wasn't a damned thing we could do about it. I swore then that when I got older, I would be just like Granddad. That I would help anyone, regardless of their ability to pay me for it. Especially the dead."

"You're a testament to his generosity."

"Thanks, but I'm really just a pale reflection of it. The day I saw his corpse staggering around that fence post I promised myself that I would never leave anyone else in the same lurch."

They both went quiet for a few moments, the seriousness of the discussion clipped short by her accidental pun. Dee was the first to giggle, followed closely by a chuckle from Joshua. Dee let out a loud laugh which set Joshua into a full-blown cackle. The pair of them filled the car with easy laughter.

"Did I really say lurch?" she asked between giggles.

"I'm sorry," Joshua said, "but that was just rotten."

Dee rolled her eyes. "Are you mocking my deadpan humor?"

"I don't know about humor, but it's certainly not grave."

"If you're going to spend any time with me, you'll have to keep a stiff upper lip."

"Of corpse I will."

"Okay!" Dee shouted between peals of laughter. "Okay! I give. Enough with the puns. They'll be the death of me."

Joshua smiled wide as he wound his laughter down to a few occasional titters. They settled into a comfortable silence as Dee slowed the car to a stop beside the curb.

"Here we are," she said. She leaned across Joshua to get a good look at the sign she had parked beside. "Autumn Evenings?" Beyond the sign sat a small, sad-looking, single-story building. The brickwork was patchy, the roof was in need of re-shingling, and the outer woodwork was screaming for a fresh coat of paint. It had the look and feel of its true nature, a run-down retirement home. "She's in there."

"Are you sure?" he asked.

Dee cut her eyes at him. "Are you doubting my magic?"

"No, ma'am."

"Your friend lives here. She might not be here right this moment, but this is where she calls home."

He unbuckled his belt and sighed. "I can't believe she ended up here."

Dee couldn't believe it either. No wonder he had a soft spot for the whole caring thing. His lady love was either a live in nurse or a nurse's assistant. "Look, it's late. Maybe we should come back tomorrow."

"No. I need to see her now. I've waited so long." He climbed out of the van and stalked toward the dark entrance.

"Joshua!" she shouted behind him as she climbed out of the driver's seat. "Wait up, daddy longlegs."

Dee wondered how they were going to get the attention of the staff when the place was so obviously closed for the night. But to her surprise, someone was waiting at the door. A tall redhead in a tight, white uniform smiled as they approached. Was that Emily? Dee's stomach dropped to her knees as she realized he was about to hook up with his woman, and Dee would once again play the third wheel.

"Can I help you?" the nurse asked.

"I'm here to see Emily Lane," Joshua said.

"Of course," the nurse said. "We've been waiting for you."

Dee saw Joshua's shock, but the nurse must have missed it. Dee had to admit, she was a little shocked herself.

"This way," the nurse said, and held out her hand.

Joshua nodded and followed her lead. Dee, forgotten in the excitement of the moment, fell in line behind him. Down the quiet corridors they walked, their steps echoing on the cold tiles as they went. Urine and sweat and age rose to fill Dee's nostrils, as well as that old familiar stench of death and decay. She wondered if there was a zombie on staff, but decided that the smell was coming from everywhere. She supposed that you didn't have to be dead to be a zombie. Just abandoned like an old, forgotten photograph; a thing to be dragged out at holidays and then pack away again until the next important date. In some small way, she was glad her grandfather didn't have to see this side of old age.

As they reached the end of the hall, the nurse stopped outside of the last door on the right. "It won't be long now. I'm glad you could make it. Please let us know if we can get you anything." The nurse paused and placed a hand on Joshua's shoulder before she added, "I'm very sorry."

Dee couldn't have thought such a pallid man could have gotten any paler, but what little color Joshua had to his face drained completely. He pushed past the nurse and into the room beyond.

"Emily?" he asked in a quiet voice, before the door closed behind him.

"Spouses are just as welcome," the nurse said.

Dee narrowed her eyes. "I'm not his spouse."

"You're her granddaughter?"

Dee shook her head. "Just a friend. Of his." She almost said Joshua's name, but her sense of danger kept her tongue still.

"Ah. We didn't even know Miss Emily had a grandson before tonight. None of her nieces or nephews mentioned him. I'm just glad he could make it before . . ." The nurse let the unspoken words fill the gap as she left Dee alone outside the door.

Dee was confused. She didn't want to interrupt the love-birds' private reunion, but enough was enough. She needed some answers, and now. She gathered her righteous irritation to her and pushed the door open.

What lay beyond was typical of the old-style hospital rooms in its sterility and joylessness. The white walls were spotted with age and neglect, as was the equipment scattered about the place. Joshua was seated on the edge of a small bed, leaning over the still form of a sleeping elderly woman. Even in her advanced age, Dee could see the traces of beauty the woman once bore. But ever more present was the overpowering funk of death. The woman's chest went nearly concave with every breath.

Joshua had the woman's frail hand in his strong one, strok-ing her paper-thin skin in slow, loving strokes. He looked up from the sleeping oldster with tear-filled eyes, and nodded at Dee. His voice hitched as he spoke. "Come in. She's resting. I think she's almost gone."

The sound of his breaking voice stirred the woman. Her eyes fluttered open, and rolled around to rest on the sight of Joshua. In a weak voice she asked, "Josh?"

"Emily," Joshua whispered.

"Oh my Lord, Josh. Is that really you?"

"Yes, my angel. It's me."

A gorgeous smile spread across her aged face, lighting up the room and lifting years away from Emily. "I must be in heaven, then."

Joshua reached out and caressed her face. "Not yet, my love. But you will be. Heaven thinks they have angels now? They don't know what an angel is."

Dee's breath caught in her throat at the tender sight.

"Everyone said you were dead," Emily said.

"I was without you," Joshua said.

"I waited so long."

"I know."

"I kept the church reserved. For three weeks. But you never came back."

Joshua closed his eyes and pressed her hand to his face. "I wanted to. Oh God, Emily, I wanted to."

"You haven't aged a day," Emily said as she ran a trembling finger over his cheekbone.

"Not by choice," he said. "I wished we could have . . . together . . ."

"I don't want to know what happened," the woman said. "Do I?"

Joshua thought about it for a moment, then shook his head.

"Was it that horrible man?" she asked.

"Yes," Joshua answered.

The answer seemed to satisfy Emily's curiosity, but only inflamed Dee's.

"You always knew where to find trouble," Emily said. She

coughed a few times, and returned to her thick wheeze. "I got married."

"I hoped you would," Joshua said, his words belying the sorrow on his face. "Did he take good care of you? You always deserved the best."

"He died young," Emily said. "I quit after that. Twice was too much. Why are you here? After so many years, why come back now? I must look so horrible and old and—"

"No," Joshua said over her lament. He cupped her face in his hands. "You're beautiful, my angel. You always will be. I came back because I had to tell you that I never stopped loving you. And I never will."

"I love you," Emily said. "I always felt you out there, somewhere. They said you skipped town, said you were dead. But in my heart I knew you were there. I felt you."

"I felt you too." He patted his chest. "Emily, your love kept me going, all these years."

Emily smiled as a pale crimson flushed her wrinkled face.

"I have something for you," Joshua said as he pulled the box from his pocket and slipped the ring free. Emily gasped and for a moment Dee thought the excitement might do the poor thing in. Joshua gingerly took his lady by the hand and slid the ring onto her finger.

"I do," Emily whispered.

"As do I." He leaned low and kissed the woman with such passion, such fire that Dee was sure he would crush the poor lady's fragile bones. But Emily held up, kissing him just as fiercely in return. Dee felt a pang of guilt as she watched the age-gapped lip lock. She dipped her head under her hand and turned to the door as the sounds of their kiss drifted to her. The room soon fell quiet as the passionate moment passed.

"You," the old woman said.

Dee turned to find Emily looking at her. She smiled at the elderly woman.

"You watch him," Emily said. "He can't take care of himself. Never could."

"I'll try," Dee said, surprised at the crack of her own voice. She didn't even realize she was crying until the salt of her tears reached her quivering lips.

Emily turned back to Joshua. "She's very pretty."

"Not as beautiful as you, my love," Joshua said. He caressed her face again. "No one ever was, or ever will be."

"I have to go now," Emily said.

"Please don't," Joshua said. A single tear broke free and rolled down his pale face. "Not so soon."

"I'm sorry. It's time."

"Emily. Please don't leave me."

She reached up and slowly daubed at his weeping eyes. "I'm glad we could say goodbye this time."

Joshua nodded but said nothing else.

Emily drew a rattling breath and in a single burst of excitement said, "I have something for you too. A box for you. Under the bed. That man sent it to me a few weeks after the wedding. My mother told me to throw it away, but I kept it all these years because I knew. Somehow . . . I knew . . . you'd come back . . . to me." After she spoke the last words, she closed her eyes and fell still.

Joshua sat in silence for a minute, just looking down at his lost love as his tears dried. He leaned low and kissed her on the forehead, the eyes, and the lips one last time.

"I love you, Emily," he whispered. "Godspeed you to your eternal rest."

Joshua got to his feet and retrieved the wooden box from under the bed. Clutching it to his breast, he silently passed Dee and exited the room. Dee pointed the fingers of her right hand to the corpse and laid out one quick motion, a sigil of her own design, ensuring that Joshua would never see his lady love up and about now that she was gone.

Dee caught up with Joshua halfway down the hall. As they passed the nurse's desk, each woman in white nodded their sympathies without even asking what happened. They knew when the reaper had done his deed, just as Dee could smell death in the air. She and Joshua were well in the car and halfway back before he spoke again.

"Thank you, Deetra," was all he said.

They rode for a little longer in silence, until Dee couldn't stand it any more.

As if sensing her frustration Joshua said, "Go on. Ask your questions. You deserve much more than anything I can offer you."

"How long have you been dead?" she asked.

"Seventy-three years," he answered.

"I see. Do I want to know what happened?"

"Let's just say I dug my own grave. One should never embezzle when one is the accountant for a necromancer."

"That was a punishment for stealing from him?"

Joshua nodded. "He killed me on my wedding day. He knew for weeks, but let me ride it thinking I had beaten him. I was surprised when he asked me over for drinks. Said he wanted to celebrate my nuptials. He isn't a celebrating kind of man."

"Few necromancers are." Dee thought of Maggot, and how lucky her friendship with him really was. She would have to be nicer to him in the future.

"A few arsenic brews later and I'm a walking corpse. Then he fixed me up so I would never go sour, as he put it. Not living, never dying, and all this knowing my Emily was growing older and older and would eventually die without me. His last punishment was to take the one thing that led me to steal from him."

"Your heart."

Joshua nodded. "We didn't have the money to start a life together, so over a few months I cooked his books, hoping he wouldn't notice."

"You stole for her."

"And died for her."

"All because of that black-hearted monster."

Joshua narrowed his eyes at Dee.

"Silas Croomer was the same man who raised my grandpa."

"I'm so sorry," Joshua said.

"No," Dee said. "Don't be sorry. Be angry. Be furious. Be pig-biting mad as hell and not want to take it any more. But don't be sorry. Don't you ever be sorry again."

This finally got a smile from the dead man. "Yes, ma'am."

"How did you get out from under Silas? Did he die? Please say he's finally dead!"

"No, unfortunately not. He bound me to his second cousin who lived up in Vermont. Roger was a good man, surprisingly enough, but all the while my absent heart ached for Emily. He wanted to set me free so I could go to her, but we both knew Silas would just kill all three of us. So Roger fixed the spell to slip at his death. I am no longer bound to him, or Silas, or anyone. Except you."

"Me?"

"I owe you everything. If you hadn't stepped in I would have missed my chance to say goodbye to Emily again. I can never repay you for what you've done. Please accept my servitude instead."

"I can't."

"Please, Deetra. Don't make me beg again."

Dee nodded to the locked box. "But you have your heart now. You can rest."

"Is that what you truly want?"

She sighed. What she wanted was to have a chance at him, now that he was on the market again, so to speak. She also wanted him to be happy, and she knew that the one thing the dead wanted more than anything else was to find eternal peace. "Yes. Put your heart back and when we get home I'll work on lifting your curse and the zombie spell. You can finally join her, where you belong."

"You are unlike anyone I have ever met, Deetra Jones. There is not enough karma in this universe to pay you back for this deed." And with that, he snapped the rusted lock and opened the box. He looked inside for a moment, then started to laugh.

"What's so funny?" she asked. He held the box to her and she glanced inside. It was empty, save for a few words scribbled at the bottom. "Come and get it," she read aloud. She supposed Joshua was laughing because there was nothing else he could do.

"Silas was always the sly one," he said.

"You mean he was always the asshole." She blew an exasperated breath and strummed the wheel with her fingertips.

"What do we do now?"

"We don't do anything. You just sit there and be quiet while I try to work this out."

"Yes, ma'am."

"And cut that out."

"Yes, ma'am." Joshua smiled.

Dee eyed the dead man and his dashing smile. She supposed, maybe, she had been on her own for too long. It had been years since she had a familiar, or help of any kind. And he did offer. "Would you like to work for me?"

"I have to. I owe you my fealty."

"I didn't ask for your servitude. I asked if you wanted a job. As in a paying job."

Joshua was silent.

"Would you like to work for me?" she asked again.

"I'm dying to," he answered.

Dee smirked, laid her foot down heavy on the gas and flipped a bitch in the middle of the quiet road.

"Where are we going?" Joshua asked.

"To see a man about a spell," she said.

"You can't be serious. Silas will kill you where you stand."

"I'm not talking about Silas. I'm talking about Maggot. He's the man to see about locating dead things like, oh, the heart of a seventy-year-old corpse."

Joshua closed the box with a chuckle. "You are single-minded, aren't you?"

"No honey, I have an eight-track mind. They just don't make the tapes any more."

The pair of them laughed for a bit.

"I really appreciate all you have done for me," Joshua said.

"You'll get a chance to make up for it," Dee said. "It might take a while to find your missing ticker, and until then I have loads of things that need doing." *Including me*, her mind finished for her.

"Yes, ma'am."

"Stop that! I'm your friend, not your master."

He nodded his assent, but Dee had a feeling he wasn't going to stop.

And, truth be told, she kind of liked it.

CAPTIVE HEARTS

Brian Keene

"Maybe I should cut off your penis next."

Richard moaned at the prospect, thrashing on the bed. The handcuffs rattled and the headboard thumped against the wall, but Gina noticed his efforts were growing weaker. That was good. Weak was better. She wanted him weak—enjoyed the prospect of such a once-powerful man now reduced to nothing more than a mewling kitten. Even so, she'd have to keep an eye on his condition. She didn't want Richard too weak. He'd be useless to her dead.

"Please, Gina. You can still stop this. No more."

"Shut up."

The room was dark, save for flickering candlelight. The windows had been boarded over with heavy plywood. Gina had done the work herself, and had felt a sense of satisfaction when she'd finished.

Richard raised his head and stared at her, standing in the doorway. He licked his cracked, peeling lips. His tongue reminded her of a slug. Gina shuddered, remembering how it had felt on her skin—the nape of her neck, her breasts, her belly, inside her thighs. Her stomach churned. Sour and acidic bile surged up her throat. Gina swallowed, and that brought another shameful memory.

"Just let me go," Richard pleaded. "I won't tell anybody. There's nobody left to tell."

She studied him, trying to conceal her trembling. He had bedsores and bruises, and desperately needed a bath. Richard's skin had an unhealthy sheen that seemed almost yellow in the dim candlelight. His hair, usually so expertly styled, lay limp and greasy. One week into his captivity, she'd held up a mirror and shown Richard his hair, and asked him if it was worth the ten thousand dollars he'd spent on hair replacement surgery. He'd cursed her so loud she had to stuff a pair of her soiled panties in his mouth just to stifle him.

Gina winced. She could smell him from the doorway. He stank of shit and piss and blood, and with good reason. She'd stripped the sheets from the bed, yanking them right out from beneath him when they became too nauseating to go near, but now the mattress itself was crusted with filth. The bandages on his feet covering the nine stumps where his toes had been were leaking again.

"Where would you go?" she asked.

His Adam's apple bobbed up and down. "They said things were better in the country. The news said the government was quarantining Baltimore."

"Not anymore. It's everywhere, Richard."

"Turn on the news. They—"

"There is no news. The power's been out for the last five days."

Richard's eyes grew wide. "F-five days? How long have I been here, Gina?"

"That's easy. Just count your piggies. How many are missing?"

"Oh God, stop . . ."

"I'll be right back."

She went down the hall. When she returned, she was dressed in rubber gloves, a smock, and surgical mask. The bolt cutters were in her hand. She held them up so that Richard could see. That broke him. Richard sobbed, his chest heaving.

"Don't worry," she soothed. "I cleaned them with alcohol, just like always. We can't have you getting an infection."

Gina retrieved her wicker sewing basket—the last gift her mother had given her before succumbing to breast cancer three years ago—from atop the dresser, then stood over the bed. Richard tried to shrink away from her, but the handcuffs around his wrists and ankles prevented him from moving more than a few inches.

"Listen, listen, listen . . ." He tried to say more, but all that came out was a deep, mournful sigh.

"We've been over this before," she said. "You won't die. I know what I'm doing."

And she did. While most of her fellow suburbanites had fled Hamelin's Revenge—the name the media gave the disease, referencing the rats that had first spawned it—Gina had remained behind. She'd had little choice. There was no way she'd have abandoned Paul. Richard was already imprisoned by then, so she didn't need to worry about him escaping. She'd ventured out after the last of the looters moved on, armed with the small .22 pistol she and Paul had kept in the nightstand. Gina had never fired the handgun before that day, but by the end of that first outing, she'd become a capable shot. Her first stop had been the library, which was, thankfully, zombie free. Alive or dead, nobody read anymore.

Her search of the abandoned library had turned up a number of books—everything from battlefield triage to medical textbooks. She'd taken them all. Her next stop had been the grocery store. She'd scavenged what little bottled water and canned goods were left, then moved on to the household aisle, where she'd picked up rubber gloves, disinfectant, and as many cigarette lighters as she could carry. Finally she'd hit the pharmacy, only to find it empty. She'd had to rely on giving Richard over-the-counter painkillers and booze instead. She hadn't thought he'd mind, especially given the alternative.

"I just want to wake up," Richard cried.

Gina positioned the bolt cutters over his one remaining toe. "And I just wanted to provide for Paul."

"But I di—"

"And this little piggy cried wee wee wee—"

CRUNCH.

Richard screamed.

"—all the way home."

He shrieked something unintelligible, and his eyes rolled up into his head. He writhed on the mattress, the veins in his neck standing out.

"You brought this on yourself," Gina reminded him as she reached for a lighter to cauterize the wound.

Richard had been her boss before Hamelin's Revenge—before the dead started coming back to life.

Gina and Paul had met in college, and got married after graduating. They'd been together three years and were just beginning to explore the idea of starting a family when Paul had his accident. It left him quadriplegic. He had limited use of his right arm and couldn't feel anything below his chest. Overnight, both of their lives were irrevocably changed. Gone were Gina's dreams of being a stay-at-home mom. She'd had to support them both, which meant a better job with more pay and excellent health insurance. She'd found all three as Richard's assistant.

Gina had spent her days working for Richard and her nights caring for Paul. Richard had been a wonderful employer at first—gregarious, funny, kind, and sympathetic. He'd seemed genuinely interested in her situation, and had offered gentle consolation. But his comfort and caring had come with a price. One day, his breath reeking of lunchtime bourbon, Richard asked about Paul's needs. When Gina finished explaining, he asked about her own needs. He then suggested he was the man to satisfy those needs. She'd thought he was joking at first and, blushing, had stammered that Paul could still get reflexive erections and they had no trouble in the bedroom.

Then Richard touched her. When Gina resisted, he reminded her of her situation. She needed this job. The visiting nurse who cared for Paul during the day didn't come cheap, nor did any of his medicines or other needs. Sure, Gina could sue him for sexual harassment, but could she really afford to? Worse, what would such a public display do to her husband? Surely he was already feeling inadequate. Did she really want to put this on his conscience as well?

Gina succumbed. They did it right there in the office. She'd cried the first time as Richard grunted and huffed above her. She'd cried the second time, too. And the third. And each time, Gina died a little bit more inside.

Until the dead came back to life, giving her a chance to live again.

She'd called Richard before the phones had gone out, telling him to come over, pleading with him to escape with her. They'd be safe together. They could make it to one of the military encampments. Could he please hurry?

He'd shown up an hour later, his BMW packed full of supplies. He smiled when she opened the door, touched her cheek, caressed her hair, and told her he was glad she'd called.

"What about your husband?"

"He's already dead," Gina replied. "He's one of them now."

Then she'd hit Richard in the head with a flashlight. The first blow didn't knock him out. It took five tries. Each one was more satisfying than the previous.

The thing Gina had always loved most about Paul was his heart. Her mother, who'd adored Paul, had often said the same thing.

"You married a good one, Gina. He's got a big heart."

Her mother had been right. Paul's heart was big. She stood staring at it through the hole in his chest. Paul moaned, slumping forward in his wheelchair. She'd strapped him into it with bungee cords and duct tape so he couldn't get out. He was no longer dead from the chest down. Death had cured him of that. He could move again.

She moved closer and he moaned again, snapping at the air with his teeth. Gina thought of all the other times she'd stood over him like this. She remembered the times they'd made love in the wheelchair—straddling him with her legs wrapped around the chair's back, Paul nuzzling her breasts, Gina kissing the top of his head as she thrust up and down on him. Afterward, they'd stay like that, skin on skin, sweat drying to a sheen.

Paul moaned a third time, breaking her reverie. She glanced down and noticed that another one of his fingernails had fallen off. She couldn't stop him from decaying, but when he ate, it seemed to slow the process down.

She reached into her pocket, pulled out the plastic baggie,

and unzipped it. Richard's piggy toe lay inside. It was still slightly warm to the touch. She fed Paul the toe, ignoring the smacking sounds his lips made as he chewed greedily.

"We'll have something different tomorrow." Her voice cracked. "A nice finger. Would you like that?"

Paul didn't respond. She hadn't expected him to. Gina liked to think he still understood her, that he still remembered their love for each other, but deep down inside, she knew better.

Eventually, Gina grew tired. Yawning, she went around the house and snuffed out the candles. Richard was still passed out when she examined his newest bandage. She double-checked the barricades on the doors and windows. Finally she said good-night to what was left of the man who had captured her heart, while in the other room, her captive awoke and cried softly in the dark.

APOCALYPSE AS FOREPLAY

Gina McQueen

There are fifteen of them left outside my bedroom window, and I am running out of bullets fast.

God *damn*, why did I have to be born so popular?

And where in the hell is my man?

This whole zombie plague/collapse-of-civilization thing is going down stupid fast, pretty much the way the movies always told us it would. Guy gets up. Bites another person. They get up. Bite somebody else.

Thank God I was raised around guns, with both Mom and Dad backwoods hardcore survivalists. I grew up on a firing range, never taught that it wasn't a young woman's place to squeeze the trigger and aim like you mean it.

As such, it never occurred to me that I couldn't blow somebody's brains out if push came to shove. Be they male or female. Republican or Democrat.

Alive or the next thing to it.

Thanks to my Mom, I never knew limitations. Thanks to my Dad, I never thought of men as the bad guys. (Except maybe government men. And Ray helped me get over *that*.)

Thanks to these guns, I never had to split the difference. Right up until now.

That said:

BLAM! Jerry Whicker's forehead implodes, firehosing what little brains he had out the back of his skull in freshets of wet papier-mache confetti. He collapses like the wannabe prom date he was.

Never liked that Jerry. Had fended him off since high school. Another jerk who never got the word no. Eternally nursing the hope I'd one day be *just self-loathing or drunk enough,* if only he hit on me every chance he got.

Those days are gone forever. *Aim for the brain* is the new game in town. Blowing holes in their guts is a waste of time and ammo, the practical equivalent of polite conversation.

As of right now, *no means no.*

Not no, thank you.

No with a capital BLAM!

Jerry hits the lawn and stays there, directly in front of the Rev. Stanley Simmons: to my mind, the least sexy man in town, an inveterate starer at my God-given breasts who seemed to think he'd gotten the Pentacostal version of papal dispensation for that act. Good to know he hadn't been plowing evangelical boys with the Lord's tallywacker, I must admit, but if I had a daughter, he wouldn't have been giving her Bible lessons.

BLAM!

Rev. Stan is already tripping over Jerry when his red third eye opens, more expressive than the others. It makes him arc majestically as he falls—pelvis out, head back, arms flailing up as if groping for Heaven.

"Good luck with that," I say, reloading.

Thirty-seven down, thirteen to go.

I wonder if my man is ever going to show.

In George Romero's *Dawn of the Dead*—Mom and Dad's favorite movie, circa 1979—the zombies descended on a shopping mall. Why? Not because they wanted to shop in the conventional sense, but because it was a place that was important to them. Somewhere they wanted to be.

I guess I should be flattered.

I know I'm not the only desirable young woman on Donnybrook Terrace, and thank God for that, though I'm terrified for Susu and Jackie and Dot, who couldn't defend themselves if the zombies were made of Xanax and low-fat yogurt.

Just as I'm sure that many of the most desirable men are, even now, being surrounded by the feminine dead.

Hubba is hubba.

And hunger is hunger.

BLAM! There goes that dipstick from Lance Automotive. I always knew he had a thing for me. Scraggly beard and scrawny body, always leaving his monkey suit unzipped, like I was somehow barely repressing the desire to lick the grease off his sweaty pot belly. Guess again.

Then BLAM! Sweet old Mister Finster from next door, and a pang of inescapable heartbreak. I want to believe that he's here just out of convenience—even in life, he didn't get around so hot—but I can't help reading his wide-open robe as a repeat of last December's wardrobe malfunction, when he asked me to change the light bulb in his bedroom because he was too weak to unscrew it himself.

One more limp dipsy-doodle down.

And, from somewhere up the street, the distant sound of gunfire.

"Oh!" I gasp, shocked and embarrassed by my girliness. Take a look at myself in the bedroom window glass. My makeup is smeary with tears and sweat, and my hair is a riot, but I tell myself that I still got it goin' on.

That he is gonna love me, when he fights his way through.

That those are his gunshots, blowing their way back home to me.

BLAM! Another single shot from my 98 Bravo, having dialed back from semi-automatic hours ago. Precision is the key. But precision eludes me this time.

I take the left eye out of little Pat Diggins.

Poor kid. Horrible family. Always wanting a hug. At ten, it was cute. By seventeen? Waaaaaay past creepy.

The shot spins him around, but doesn't take him down.

"I'm sorry," I say, though the sad little boy I knew is as gone as the parents he is better off without.

The next shot works better.

A dozen to go.

And from the street comes *blam blam blam*, three in rapid succession. Whoever it is is on a roll. Sounds like a .357 Magnum.

Please let it be him.

I take aim at the remainders, closing in on the window now. Some are woefully close to home, in far more ways than one.

For example, I always liked Willie. Super nice. From the health food store. Always had great advice on fresh produce. A warm and lovely smile.

Right now, he's probably got more red meat packed between his teeth than he'd eaten in the past thirty years.

BLAM!

Doug, my boyfriend from seventh grade. First guy I ever kissed. Turned out remarkably dull, but never less than sweet to me . . . until now, drooling black blood down his drab bank teller's suit.

BLAM!

Oh, Danny. Lived together three years, him cheating on me all the while. So handsome, so charming, so much fun to be with that it was almost worth the drama.

He must have died early, because he sure looks ripe. Never thin, but omigod—in death, he has put on some serious water weight.

It splooshes as I pull the trigger.

BLAM!

Then, from around the corner, here comes Ray in a spray of gunfire.

The first thing I look at is his beautiful face. There's no blood on it. That's a very good sign. His expression is one of intense concentration, no small measure of anxiety notwithstanding.

I love how smart and capable he is.

I knew he knew I'd be waiting for him.

Ray is tall, long, sculpted, and lean. A college basketball star and Gulf War soldier before he became a federal agent, he lives through his body the way most people only live through their dreams.

He is an active man. Powerful. Disciplined. Engaged.

And oh, so tender, when the push comes to lovin' . . .

I never thought I could fall for a government man. They were Fascists and vultures, pure and simple. Didn't matter which party was minding the store. They just wanted to eat what was ours.

That was how I was raised. That was what I believed.

So when the feds came to my ranch-style suburban home and started asking questions about Mom and Dad, and their alleged signing of some crazy petition that they probably knew was dumb at the time, but they were *just really angry*, way back in '02, my hackles were raised. I wasn't rude, but I was firm.

I love my parents, I told them. I don't live with my parents. They have a life of their own. They're good Americans. They're not trying to overthrow anybody. They just want to be left alone. And so do I.

The first guys they sent were officious and stiff, and what they gave was what they got back, in spades.

Then they sent Ray.

God bless America.

It wasn't just how damn fine-looking he was. From the start, I recognized he wasn't trying to nail them. He was just burrowing through the bullshit of a paranoid nation to weed the legitimate terrorist threats from all the other little blips on the possible threat index. That was his job.

And I could tell he was clocking me, too.

"We live in a dangerous world," he said.

"I know."

"It could all come apart at any second."

"Exactly."

"We need to keep track of what matters to us," he said, blue eyes shining deeply into my own. "Keep each other safe. Take care of each other."

"Otherwise, we're all alone," I said, leaning closer. "And that's no way to live."

Ray smiled, his lips amazing. "No, it isn't."

"So what, if I may ask, matters most to *you*?"

"Ah . . ." Ray actually sat back and thought about it, his eyes skimming heavenward before locking back on mine. He sighed once again deeply, unconsciously licked those lips, and said, "Oh, you know. Other people. The people you love."

"So who do you love?" I wasn't being a smartass. At least,

not entirely. I actually suddenly wanted to know. "Are you talking *everybody,* in a Socialist do-gooder kind of way?"

"Or a Christian way?" He laughed. "Sort of. Yeah. Absolutely. That's—you'll pardon the expression—the whole motherfucking point of any attempt to make the world a better place."

"*Language!*" I cautioned in mock dismay. "Are you allowed to say shit like that, in a federal capacity?"

"Extreme times demand extreme measures," he said, winking. "So yeah, but . . . No. I mean, of *course* it's not all just some vague dumbass hippy-dippy love of the idealized commonweal. But that's definitely part of it."

"Do tell." I was enjoying his chatter. But mostly, I was enjoying his company. His proximity.

The way he was looking at me.

"You're a human being, right? You love people."

"Yeah. Sure."

"But you love some people more than others."

"Yes, I do."

"So let me ask you this," he said, leaning into me, as I leaned into him. "Does *loving certain people more than life itself* make you (a) love the whole of the human race? Or does it (b) only make you love those certain people?"

Now it was my turn to think about that. And it only took a second.

"Both," I said. "Just more the one than the other. And thank you for asking."

"Why?" He grinned, searching. Just confirming the evidence trail, like a good investigator should.

"Because it made me really like you."

"I like you, too," he said, as our noses touched. "Sunshine."

And the second he said my name out loud, in just that way . . . well, baby, it was on.

The courtship that followed went quickly from formal to truly love-tastic. The second he declared my Mom and Daddy off the list, we fell into each other heart and soul, body to body, mind to mind. All subsequent interpersonal investigation was off the record, and off the hook.

I gotta be honest: for a couple of days there, I honestly thought about following him back to D.C.

Then the dead got back up, four hours ago and counting. And almost everything seems to have changed, except for the fundamentals.

If there is a God—and I believe that there is, weirdly now more than ever—then God is love.

And God, I love that man.

"Ray! Baby!" I holler, heart a bass drum in my chest. "Over here!"

"*Sunshine?*" Like me, he has barely dared believe. Watching his joy and relief is like a baby's first Fourth of July, all unexpected fireworks and glee.

"Come around the side!" I continue to yell. "They're all kind of focused up front here, so you should be able to get around 'em, no problem!"

He hesitates, still in the street, gun hand aiming back from whence he came. "Sunshine baby?" he says. "It's not gonna be quite that simple."

Then the horde of zombie women appear behind him.

Dear Lord, there have to be forty more, of all conceivable shapes and sizes, ages, and walks—make that shambles—of life. In his short time here, he has clearly gathered some admirers.

Jealousy rears its ugly head, and puts his face squarely in my sniper sites: not because I want to shoot him, but because I want my hypersensitive scope to show me every single flicker of thought or emotion going on in his face. See if there are any secret shames trailing him that I might want to know about, sooner rather than later.

I see nothing but love and determination, staring right back at me.

Then I jig to the right, draw a bead, and divide Penny Hager's eyebrows by one thick squirting red inch.

She drops. Ray starts running toward me.

And the last dozen zombie men in my front yard all turn toward him with fresh and unsettling intensity.

The first wannabe rival Ray separates from his forehead is Elmore James: not the blues singer, just the asshole named after him. Ray pops him clean, watches him cave, pivots left, blows a hole in John Dixon, feints to the left, dribbles Pete Seymour's graymeat down the back of his ruptured skull.

It's like violent ballet, so graceful and smooth. I can see how he must have been a vision on the courts.

I want to open fire on the rest, clear the field, and put a dent in the wave of undead hussies. But I'm down to my last several rounds.

And the fight has just become a lot more intimate.

My bedroom has a porch outside. The torches are prepped in a metal bucket right inside the door, rags soaked in kerosene draped right around the hacked-off dining room table's legs.

I grab one, fire it up, pocket the lighter, throw open the door, and pull the .357 from my sling holster.

One hand thunder and one hand lightning, I burst out into the yard.

My calculations are correct. There's nobody around the side. They're still waiting for the Bravo to fire from my bedroom window, because that's how fucking dumb they are.

I'm not even sure who the first guy I set on fire is, or was. I guess he must have liked me, because he's here. Or maybe he was just hungry.

But I'm thrilled by how quickly he goes up, becomes a flailing warning flag. The other zombies recoil. I torch the next one, spin it back toward its friends, then set fire to another pile of corpses on the ground.

Within seconds, my lawn is a funeral pyre. I accept it, as I accept the end of the world I've always known.

Then Ray's arms are around me.

And he's kissing me hard.

And I almost set us both on fire, because I want to hold him so badly.

"Take this," I say, pulling back and proffering the torch. "I got more."

"You're knockin' me out."

"That's why you love me."

"You better believe it," he says, taking the torch, and twirling just in time to make Bob Zortman's face ignite in fatty yowling sparks.

I run back to the bedroom, grab a pair of torches, spark the first off the last, and wade back into the fray.

Ray has herded the last men back toward the street, where the former women have caught up with them at last. I drop one torch on the pile of bodies closest to the sidewalk, start shooting ladies in the head.

BLAM! There goes Lisa from Bed Bath & Beyond, out on Route 37. What she's doing here is a mystery to me. A mystery liable to go unresolved.

BLAM! Of course Cindy Fitch would be here. Little snooty blonde Daddy-runs-the-country-club beeyotch. She was probably trying to get Ray into her private racquetball court for some sweaty one-on-one.

Not in this lifetime, cupcake.

BLAM! BLAM! BLAM! Between us, we mow down a row. But more are still coming. We wave the torches around to back them off. This will not last forever.

There has got to be a better way.

"Ray?" I say. "How you doin' for ammo?"

"I got four shots left," he said.

"I brought us a couple of extra clips," I said, slapping my jacket pocket with the gun hand while I set real estate cougar Ruth Mellman's heavily hair-sprayed head on fire. "But we need to make a move here, for certain."

"Whose van is that, parked at the curb?"

"The Mexican gardener guys."

"Are they still around?"

"Right here," I say, kicking Raul, splayed out on the sidewalk before me. He was the first poor bastard I had to watch get eaten, and the thirteenth one I shot. The rest of his crew was down as well.

Raul was legal. His friends were not. My parents would not have approved.

But I really liked those guys. I really, really did. I playfully flirted with them all the time, got 'em laughing, got to know them well enough to know they all had wives and families they cared about. So it never crossed the line. Never got weird. Was always respectful and fun.

"Okay, then," Ray says, as I feel my tears start rolling, thinking about their families now, and wondering what they'll do.

Thinking about my Mom and Dad . . .

And in that tiny spacing-out moment—so fast that, in normal life, you'd barely even know it happened—a dead hand grabs ahold of my hair.

All of a sudden, I'm face to face with Dorothy Sutton.

This is a woman I've known my whole life. My high school librarian. Friend of my parents. An inspiring person, all the way around. Kind and thoughtful.

There are maggots in her eyes.

Who do you love? Ray's voice, inside my head. Imitating my question to him.

"I love you," I say, and press my barrel to her head, saying goodbye to what's left of her the only way that I know how.

Now I'm back on my game. BLAM! Watching her fall, and thinking about Ray's van inquiry. The dead are all spaced out around it.

I think I finally get his drift.

One, two, three, I drop the last three zombies between us and the van's engine block. He's already taken care of two others. The space has cleared.

He empties his last two shots into the gas line, like a pro.

"RUN!" he says. And I do. Back toward the house. Looking over my shoulder.

Then he tosses his torch and takes off as well.

It takes almost forty seconds for the van to explode, the squirting gas igniting and spreading mayhem far and wide. Sheets and scraps of metal pierce and bisect already dismantling corpses, pieces of whom festoon the yard and pavement.

Ray stands, as the mushroom cloud plumes, looking sexy as hell in the sunset. Beyond him, the crowd has thinned to less than a dozen still standing. And several of them are on fire.

We make short work of the rest. The extra clips come in handy.

For a moment, there is actual peace.

We look at each other. The last ones standing. Alive. So alive it is almost obscene.

"So now what?" I say, trembling.

"Well," he says. "If it's okay with you, I think it's a good time to meet your parents."

I think about Mom and Dad, on their forty acres of land. Out in the boonies. Fifteen minutes by Jeep. By foot, a little longer. We'll just see how it goes.

One thing for certain: they've got munitions out the ass, and a buffer of woods between there and civilization.

Plus, I'm dying for them to meet him.

"I would love that," I say.

"Are you sure?"

"Are *you* sure?"

"From what you say, they are wonderful people."

"Yes, they are."

"Will they trust me?"

"No," I say. "Not at first. You'll have to charm them with straight talk and utter sincerity, just the way you did me."

"I'll give it everything I've got," he says.

"And what about the rest of the world?" I ask him, already terrified by whatever answer he might have.

"Well . . ." he says, surveying the wasteland of Donnybrook Terrace. "I think they might be on their own for a minute, till we get our strategy worked out. They don't have Internet out there, do they?"

"Of course!" I say. "Secured satellite. What do you think they are, primitives?"

He holds up his hands. "I'm just askin'!"

But the question remains: *what about the rest of the world?* It's a big one, and a terrifying one at that.

I know this war has just begun. That it might take years. And that Ray is sworn to fight it.

I know, too, that my fate is sealed. I'm too damn good at this to just sit on the sidelines.

Most of all, I know that—if we can just keep fighting side by side—we can handle this thing. We can bring our country back.

And if it's truly all over the world, we can handle that, too.

Just as long as we're together.

Down the street, a couple of late-comers straggle into view. There will be more. It is time to get a move on.

"Baby?" he says, wrapping an arm around me. I snuggle in tight.

"Yeah?"

"How long do you think it's gonna take us to load up?"

"Everything's packed but the Bravo and that one last torch . . ."

"You're shitting me." His eyes are wide.

"No. I—"

Then he kisses me so hard that the soles of my feet start to throb.

When he pulls back, my eyeballs almost pop out of their

sockets—not just from suction, but from the magnetic pull of his all-enveloping gaze.

"Sunshine?" he says, almost incredulous himself. "I have fought alongside some serious motherfuckers, okay? Unbelievable soldiers. Agents trained out the Academy wazoo in the logistics of urban warfare."

"Uh-huh."

"But for you to have your shit dialed so tight—with zero warning—is just staggering to me."

"Well, thank you," I say, slightly light in the head.

"I swear to God."

Then he kisses me again.

The best kiss in the world.

This time, when it breaks, he hugs me tight as can be, so tight it almost hurts. I squeeze him exactly that hard back.

"I can't imagine this without you, my glorious Sunshine," he whispers in my ear. *"My gorgeous, glorious, unbelievable Sunshine."*

I let that shudder through me.

He kisses my ear. I kiss his throat. We kiss each other's lips until the moaning of the dead is almost as loud as our own.

"And to answer your question?" he says, pulling back. Wicked grin on his face. "As to who do I love?"

"Yes?" I say, as we both point and aim.

Then he tells me, as we fire together.

Apocalypse as foreplay.

"I love you, too," I say.

JULIA BRAINCHILD

Lois H. Gresh

"Dick, I want you to meet Julia Brainchild."

My producer, Harold Latootski, was all aglow. Beside him was a young woman, maybe twenty-five years old. His hand was on her elbow, and a beautiful elbow it was.

I propped my spatula on the fry pan. So this was Julia Brain-child, author of *The Art of French Brain Cooking* and blog mistress extraordinaire. "Enchanted to meet you. Please, call me Richard."

She held out a hand. It was delicate and as white as chalk. The nails were pearly and the color of farm-raised salmon.

I bent, kissed her fingers: cold but fragrant, a citrus bouquet that reminded me of my grandmother's scent. With my eyes lowered, I scanned her body, but in a way she wouldn't notice. The peach pencil skirt showed off slim hips and long legs. Matching four-inch high heels. Nice breasts beneath a creamy cashmere sweater. Classy, as I'd expected Julia Brainchild to be.

She quivered slightly, released her fingers from mine. "Richard Ashford, the American brain food expert. I've watched your show many times. You're very good with simple matters." She paused. *"Qualifié."*

"Why, thank you. From you, that's quite a compliment." I wasn't sure what *qualifié* really meant, but it sounded good.

Harold smoothed some hair strands over his bald scalp and whisked lint off his thousand-dollar suit. I figured he was anxious to leave and get back to whatever it is network producers do. But then he dropped the bomb: "Dick, I've hired Julia to co-host *Brain and Soul* with you."

No way.

Pretty as she was, with those turquoise eyes and waves of tawny hair to her shoulders, Julia Brainchild was exactly what I *didn't* need on my show.

"My show isn't about butter and cream and sauce. We're about health. Brains are pure protein and no fat. Americans love 'em."

Harold countered, "Julia's *the* world's expert on brains, plus she's photogenic as hell and will attract new viewers to the show, Dick. Young male viewers, for example."

But my ratings were through the roof. "McBrains are bigger than ever, you know that. Teenage boys like McBrains better than pizzas."

"I've heard your Kentucky Fried Brain is doing well, too," said Julia Brainchild.

Was she on my side? Startled, I added, "Then there are my BLTs—brain, lettuce, and tomato sandwiches. Pure protein. For God's sakes, Harold, we're bigger than any diet since—"

"*South Park*?" asked Julia.

I frowned. "South Beach. And we're bigger than Atkins ever was, too."

She said, "I know you are Brain Burger King, Richard. But it might be fun to"—she batted her eyelashes at me—"to add some zest, some *épice*, to the American diet."

She lifted my spatula—

my spatula!—

—and stirred the Fruity Brain Crispees in my pan.

"Work with her." Harold's tone was sharp; he was ordering me, and in his glare was a threat. Julia Brainchild was famous. I was disposable. Any short order cook who worked out in the gym a few hours a day and had a nice face could fill my shoes. I was just Brain Burger King because of Harold.

I took my spatula back from Julia Brainchild. "We air in a few hours. I'll be teaching Americans how to make healthy breakfasts and snacks."

Her turquoise eyes flared with excitement. "Brain snacks, oh yum!" She licked her lips.

Julia Brainchild was getting off on the thought of my recipes.

I could barely contain my surprise. What a thrill! Against my better judgment, my body took charge and I felt myself getting hard, my stomach starting to flip-flop as it did whenever I got aroused.

Maybe this wouldn't be such a bad thing after all.

She worked with me for hours before the show aired. She tasted my Fruity Brain Crispees, gasped with delight; nibbled on my Brainola Bars, declared them to be *savoureux*, savory. By two o'clock when the crew showed up, we were giggling and trading secrets about Grilled Brain Kebobs (mine), Lobes Benedict (hers), Brain McNuggets (mine), Brains Normandy (hers), and past lovers (ours).

"In three, two, one . . ." Jason, one of our crew, gave me the "on the air" signal.

It was a half-hour show. Live.

"And now, it's Chef Dick Ashford and the lovely Miss Julia Brainchild!"

Julia smiled at the camera as if she'd done this a million times. Then she picked up one of my spare aprons—white cloth, covers everything—and winked at me. "I cover all my special parts," she said, "so the creams will not spray me."

The guys operating the equipment turned red. My brain went on hold. "Today," I managed to say to the cameras and to the diet-crazed American public, "on *Brain and Soul*, we welcome French art and love to our dishes. You all know Julia Brainchild, and today, she's going to help us make Honey Roasted Brain n' Oats. It's good for the digestion, good for your heart, and it tastes like candy."

"Oh, Richard . . ." Julia smacked her lips. "*You* are like candy. Isn't he, dear viewers?"

"Yes, well, choose a brain, maybe cow or goat—"

"Or," said Julia, "quail or ostrich—"

"Yes, or quail or ostrich, as Julia suggests in her French way. Soak the brain for at least a few hours."

"Two point one five hours, to be precise," said Julia.

"Yes, that would be good, then roast the brain—"

"No, Dicky dear. *Richard.* Braise the brain in a light sauce of lemon and butter, *then* roast it."

And on it went. No matter what I said, Julia interrupted with her French cooking tips. She contradicted everything I said. And all the while, she managed to wriggle her body next to mine, sending shivers through me, and she managed to make me say things like "a fine Beaujolais would go well with this brain" and "sautéed ganglia in bean sauce at your place tonight?"

By the time the show ended, the technicians were all abuzz: Julia Brainchild was a big hit. Harold rushed in with the news. People were already Twittering about the sexual tension between Dick Ashford and Julia, the fun quips, the dynamite she added to my recipes. Blogs already had thousands of comments. And the part when she whipped off the white apron and pranced around the stove and counter, showing off her legs, that body, those breasts, that face—

Well, already, stills of her were all over the internet, vids on YouTube. Julia Brainchild was the next Heidi Klum, Pamela Anderson, Angelina Jolie. Already, requests were hitting Harold for Julia to pose in the *Sports Illustrated* swimsuit edition.

"You want to get coffee?" I switched on my sexiest grin, beamed my crystal green eyes her way. Most girls couldn't resist me when I pumped up the charm. I was well over six feet tall, packed with 215 pounds of hard flesh and muscle, and I'd been told my face was what really got me the job as Brain Burger King. How could she resist?

But she acted coy. Smoothed her hands over the cashmere sweater, making her breasts stand out more. Turned and pretended to putter with the pots and pans on the set, so I could get a better look at her butt in that tight pencil skirt. Leaned over the sink, playing at washing the spatula, just to entice me with the view.

Then abruptly, she was upright and turning towards me, those turquoise eyes filmed with lust, or so I thought, and those lips parted ever so slightly.

"You love the brains?" Her voice was low and seductive. She stepped closer. One step. Two. Now inches from me, her eyes fixated on mine.

I bobbed my head. "I do. I do."

"Ah, most men do not understand this love for brains."

Lots of women want you to tell them you love them for their brains, but with Julia, the meaning was totally different. She pressed her cheek to mine and shuddered as I said that canned thing that all men say at some point in their lives. "I love you for your brains, Julia."

She laughed, the citrus scent moving closer, then she whispered in my ear. "Love so soon, Richard? But we've only just met." I didn't feel her hot breath on my ear, which was strange, but the words alone set me sizzling even more. I was hard and ready to go, and I knew she felt it because the peach skirt and the creamy sweater were right up against me. She was on fire. I was on fire.

"*Petit cerveau,*" she said. Then she laughed. "*Tete de linotte!*"

Was she complimenting me, remarking on my big hard penis? I didn't know French, still don't. So I said, "And you are the most beautiful woman I've ever seen, Julia. Your eyes are stunning, your hair, your lips . . ." And I moved in for the kill. I grabbed her head with both hands and kissed her, long and hard. Our tongues met, intertwined, licked. She wrapped one long leg around me, shoved me against the stove. Her body was in flames, but cold to the touch. I knew she was on fire, knew it, and yet the pearly white skin had the chill of thawed beef.

I couldn't convince her to see me that night. She came up with one excuse after another. She had to perfect the Consommé Brunoise. The Brain en Croute took time. Brain Bouillabaisse with Rouille required one final step, the fennel seeds and saffron threads.

I ate dinner alone. A double order of large fries and a thirty-two-ounce super-sized Coffee Mate Deluxe. I watched cartoon reruns for hours. *South Park.* Finally fell into a stupor, then a deep sleep around 3 A.M.

The following afternoon, I was late to the set, but it didn't really matter. I could make brain dip and chips in my sleep.

Julia wore a light blue skirt and aquamarine silk blouse. The blouse was semi-transparent. The blue and aquamarine really set off her eyes, which blazed like fine gems. I couldn't take my eyes off her.

"Richard?" She made my name into a caress. "You're watching me." Then she was close again, scraping her fingernails down my face and neck.

A groan rumbled up my throat.

She tipped my chin up, then passed her tongue across my lips.

I shouldn't, she was a seductress, she wanted my job, she was better with brains than me—

But I couldn't help myself. My hands were on her waist, my mouth clamped to hers, both of us writhing with desire. All I could think was: *I need more, more, more . . . now, now, now.*

"In three, two, one . . ."

We were getting the "on the air" signal.

We pulled away from each other. Julia's eyes were wide. She tucked her shirt back into her skirt, straightened, and smiled for the camera.

I wasn't wearing my apron.

I always had my apron on before I went live.

I was digging beneath the counter for it when I heard:

"And now, it's Chef Dick Ashford and the lovely Miss Julia Brainchild!"

I bet the bloggers are going wild with this, I thought, as I scrambled to get the apron on and appear as if nothing had happened between me and Julia Brainchild right before the viewers saw us.

We debated diet orange soda versus Perrier water.

We argued about Brain on the Cob versus Brains Riviera.

She insisted we make Eiffel Tower of Brain, the ultimate French dessert for special occasions. I refused.

"Brain food is smart food," I said. "And smart food is healthy food. A nice brain steak on the grill. No salt, no sauces."

We bickered about Brains Monte Carlo, where diners took their chances, not knowing about Julia's secret of using a mystery brain: camel, fish, or boar, you never knew.

"All you need is catsup," I said.

"All you need is wine," Julia said. "A Rothschild, an Ott Chateau de Selle, perhaps a Frontignan."

And when the show was over, Harold ran in and told us the ratings had soared higher than ever before, that the network wanted to sign us both for another two years of *Brain and Soul*.

"Viewers love it!" he cried. "The romance, the tension, the brains! It's wonderful!"

But it was no longer about health food and dieting. We were insanely attracted to each other, that was clear. It wouldn't take much, I decided, to seduce her. Then she would be totally under my spell, and I would rule again, with her on set to follow my commands and make lovely chitchat about French brains without threatening my superior views.

I would seduce her with the one brain dish that nobody else could possibly make. The dish my mother had passed down to me from my ancestors. Something special, something *not* French that Julia would already know.

It took two weeks of preparation. In the meantime, we kissed, we groped, we nearly made love right before the shows aired, but always Julia stopped me before I could strip off her clothes and have her. And always, she refused to see me after the show was over.

I would have Julia Brainchild.

I bought the brains, two of them: alpaca and llama. I soaked the brains for twenty-four hours. If not prepared correctly, this dish would kill. Pickled raw brain ceviche, a rare delicacy: extremely dangerous like the Fugu puffer fish. You eat bad brain ceviche, you get neurological diseases, go mad, and die. I pickled the ceviche for twelve days to kill all the bacteria. It sat by my bed in a giant crock filled with lemon and lime essences, onion, garlic, minced chillies, and a drop of vinegar. I watched *South Park*.

And I waited.

On air, we flirted, we cooked, we talked brains.

Finally, when the ceviche was ready, I told her. "Julia, I have a surprise for you, a special dish I've been preparing for weeks. Please, you must come tonight and let me treat you with it."

She hesitated. Her eyes clouded. "But I can't, Richard."

"Yes, you can, Julia."

"What kind of special dish is this?"

"*Brains*, Julia."

"What kind of brains, Richard?"

"Alpaca and llama."

She gasped. A hand flew to her mouth. "Oh! Oh, Richard, how did you know? That is my favorite."

I'd struck gold. Yes. Finally, she would succumb to me. Finally, she would be mine, all mine, and *Brain and Soul* would be my kingdom again. She would be my queen. I loved her.

"How is it prepared?" she asked.

Satin sheets. Bear rug.

"It is prepared, the special dish, as ceviche," I said.

She, who never flushed at all, paled to an even whiter shade than before. She staggered back against the stove, gripped the handle. *"Alpaca and llama ceviche?"*

"You know of it? It's not French," I said.

She nodded, swallowing rapidly. "It's not in *The Art of French Brain Cooking.* I never speak of it. You're right, it's not a French dish."

Of course, my Julia would know this rare specialty. She was a world expert in cooking brains, French or otherwise.

"I will come," she said.

And my heart started thumping like crazy, and the blood rushed to my head.

She.

Would.

Be.

Mine.

I rushed home, cleaned up the apartment as best as I could, made sure the bed had the black silk sheets, tidied the bear rug at the foot of the bed by the TV. I lifted the lid from the ceviche crock. Took a little taste. Perfect. We would dine here, then make love all night. Perhaps I would propose marriage to her on *Brain and Soul*. Not tomorrow, though, but soon.

She arrived at seven, kicked off her heels, and threw her arms around me. I kissed her neck, and she tossed back her head and begged me to nibble further and yet further down. I did. I nibbled down to the buttons on her blouse, opened them, nibbled down, down, slid my fingers under the top of her bra. She smelled like tangerines and limes, like my grandmother. It was odd, but somehow sexy and comforting at the same time. Her skin was cold, as always.

I carried her into the bedroom, gently set her on the bear rug. "It's been so long," she said, "since I've made love. You will be gentle, won't you?"

"Always, my sweetest."

I'd rip her clothes to shreds and fuck her till she screamed.

I fumbled with the remaining buttons, slipped off her shirt. Unzipped the skirt, slid it down. Peeled off the pantyhose.

My clothes were off in less than five seconds.

I surveyed her. She was perfection. No blemishes anywhere. Perfect pearly white skin, pink nipples, tawny hair.

But then she pushed at my chest. She tried to sit up. She grabbed at her clothes. "No," she cried, "I can't do this, I can't!"

"But why?" My erection started to shrink.

"I . . . my skin, it's too fragile. It might flake off."

Say, *what?*

That had to be the lamest excuse I'd ever heard from a girl. "I'll be gentle, I swear," I said.

"No!" She was crying, backing away from me, her butt moving across the bear rug. Scrabbling to dress herself.

For God's sakes.

I'd give her the ceviche. That would do it.

I gave her my bathrobe, then wrapped myself in a towel. I calmed her down. She cried on my shoulder, telling me she'd not let a man this close to her in many years.

"How many years?" I asked.

Flustered, she said, "I don't know. Maybe sixty."

I laughed. She was so adorable. Sixty years. Yeah, right. "You're like, twenty-five years old, Julia."

"Oh." She nodded. "Uh-huh. I meant, sixty *months.*"

I didn't believe that, either.

But whatever, she would be mine, that was that. I would fuck her all night, she would be queen to the Brain Burger King, and Harold could make some big PR announcement about our engagement. Not tomorrow, but soon.

I opened the crock, showed her the ceviche. She nearly fainted from joy. "My mother's friend taught me how to make this when I was a little girl," she said. "She was Peruvian, but we were all very poor, so my mother and her friend had to substitute rabbit brain for the alpaca and llama brains. Rabbits were easy to come by in the French countryside, you see."

"I can't believe you've actually had this dish—in any form, actually. It's a family secret. I never make it. And I don't know anybody who's ever had it."

Julia Brainchild was obviously perfect for me. Here was a beautiful woman, sexually intoxicating, untouched by any man for years, twenty-five years old, the world's expert on brain cooking, and she knew of the alpaca and llama ceviche!

I drank in the aroma of the ceviche: citrus and spices. I admired the perfect little wedges of brain that I'd diced for hours and hours.

We cuddled on the bed, pillows behind our backs. Her robe fell open. She didn't notice. My towel unwrapped. She didn't notice.

I held a spoon of ceviche to her lips.

She flicked her tongue. It dipped into the ceviche. "Ahhh . . ." A long sigh. She grabbed the spoon and stuck it in her mouth, chewed for what seemed like minutes, then swallowed.

"More!" she cried.

I scooped a bunch of ceviche into a bowl, gave it to her with the spoon. With her robe fully open now, her breasts bobbing as she gulped, she swallowed chunk after chunk of my special family ceviche.

And finally, a slight bluish flush rose to her cheeks. She handed the bowl and spoon back to me. Tugged the robe around her body to hide everything again.

"You have Peruvian ancestors?" she asked.

"No." I explained that "My mother was American, but my

grandfather, Julian LeBlanc, originally came from France, or so I was told. I have no Peruvian ancestors that I know of."

"LeBlanc?" She leapt off the bed, pointed a finger at me as if accusing me of something.

"Well, yeah . . . so, what of it?" I hopped off the bed, grabbed her by the waist, and pressed her to me. I stared into her eyes.

"Richard, we cannot be, you and I, we cannot do this anymore."

"Come on, we're made for each other, Julia. You know that, and so do I. What on earth is the problem?"

"I know your recipe. But you made it incorrectly."

"You're breaking up with me over a recipe?" I drew back from her, stared in disbelief. This woman was crazy.

"You omitted the one essential ingredient, Dicky."

And now she was calling me Dicky again?

"A pinch of alpaca testicles," she said flatly. "That's the ingredient that makes the ceviche an aphrodisiac."

"And you know this *how*?"

The whites of her eyes were dimming to gray. The white of her skin was beyond a pallor now, it was tinged with blue. Everywhere. The pink nipples were lavender, now purple.

What was happening to her?

"This is an ancient Inca priest recipe," she said. "They used it as an aphrodisiac. My mother's friend, the Peruvian, listed the ingredients, all of them, including the alpaca testicles, over and over again. I helped my mother make the ceviche. With the rabbit brain."

"But so what?" I yelled. "What does this have to do with you and me, and getting engaged and married on *Brain and Soul*?"

She laughed. I saw that her teeth were cracked and yellowing by the minute. "We can't get married, you silly, silly *petit cerveau*! You *tete de linotte*!"

I pulled on my pants and shirt, shoved her skirt and blouse at her. "Here, you might as well get dressed, Julia. I think you're sick, and I mean that in a loving way." I paused. I did love Julia Brainchild, but her mind was nuts and her body was clearly not well. I would take her to the finest doctors. Then we'd finally get on with it.

"I died in childbirth, Dicky. Long ago. A hundred years ago, in fact. Nobody knew that ceviche recipe except my mother, and both she and her friend died with the secret. It was passed down only to me."

"And to me," I said. Then I thought, *did she just say she died a hundred years ago? What the hell?*

"Don't you get it?" She staggered toward me. Her gait was choppy, almost like a lurch. "I *died,* Dicky. In childbirth. Apparently, the child lived. He must have been Julian LeBlanc, your grandfather. You see, Dicky, LeBlanc was the name of the man who fathered my child!"

Psycho . . .

I took her elbow to lead her to the door and get her back to her apartment. She needed a good long rest, then a very good psychiatrist. But as I touched her elbow, the skin flaked off her arm.

I dropped my hand. Stared at her. "You are . . . ?"

"I prefer to think of myself as the Living Challenged."

"A zombie?"

"It's why I specialize in French brain cooking. I've had years to perfect my recipes. If I make love, if I let myself go too far for too long, if I let myself go all the way, I revert to the form I had when I reanimated. Hence, the blue skin. I must leave you, Dicky."

Yeah, maybe that was a good idea. This Julia Brainchild was one whacked-out chick. Harold might force me to work with her, but beyond that . . . forget it.

"Dicky, I did love you. But you see," she said, "I'm your dead great-grandmother."

I shook my head. "You're crazy, Julia. Come on, let me take you home and I'll see you at work tomorrow."

"You forget, I'm the star of that show, not you."

And I saw the cracked yellow teeth, the gray whites of her eyes, the skin falling off her face, the breasts sagging then deflating like balloons sucked dry of air.

I saw the knife in her hand. Classico-Emerol stainless steel, model 287631A.

The blade flashed.

I grabbed her wrist. It fell off her arm and with it, her hand and the knife.

Could I kill her, a zombie? Was it possible? How? Every zombie movie I'd ever seen showed that people could never kill them—not with fire or decapitation, not even with machine guns.

My mind was racing. I stalled for time. "Can't we work something out?"

"Yes, Dicky, we can. You see, I do love you, Dicky."

"We can still do the show together, I promise," I lied.

"Yes, Dicky, we can. I know you love me, too, Dicky."

Then she leaned and her tongue flicked out and touched my cheek. The yellow teeth nibbled. I felt the heat dribble from my cheek to my lips, and I tasted blood. *She'd bitten me.*

"We'll do the show forever, Dicky. Just you and me. And brains. And now that we are one, the same, it's time."

"Time?" I squeaked.

"Fuck me, Dicky, fuck me till I scream. You won't care if my flesh flakes off. Ha! And I won't care about yours, either!"

There was no need to announce an engagement the next day, or any time soon. I was stuck with Julia Brainchild forever. We were two of a kind now. I'd fallen in love with my own great-grandmother. And as we, two rotting corpses, dished up health food to the diet-crazed Americans, we could binge on all the cream and butter and lard and fatty sauces we wanted. As long as they were simmering on brains.

KICKING THE HABIT

Steven Saus

I almost didn't hear her say hello over the guard's screams.

He wasn't just screaming because of me. He took a nasty header into a pit while fleeing across the construction site. His right leg was bent at a nasty angle. If you took the time to look, there was probably bone sticking out somewhere. I wasn't looking at his leg.

My eyes locked with his as I lowered myself into the hole. Or to be honest, he looked at my eyes. I stared at the grey matter a few inches behind his. Despite the decay, my stomach rumbled and my salivary glands tried to summon a few drops.

"Hello?" she called again. Her voice echoed off an abandoned backhoe. "John?"

That got my attention. Friendly greetings were rare enough since I rose, but someone calling me by name—well, that was really odd. It was a nice change from the usual greeting of "Oh dear God, no!" or maybe "Quick, get the shotgun!"

She stood on the other side of the pit, silhouetted against the moonlit sky. The jutting forms of two cranes framed her body against the clear night sky, creating an illusory archway behind her.

That was what I recognized at first: It was Maria's pose in an arch, just like the prom picture I'd stolen from the funeral home. Casual, relaxed. Except in the photo she was still a few hours away from being dead.

She lurched around the edge of the pit, turning as she shuffled so she kept me in sight. The moonlight shimmered on her skin. My memory filled in the soft lines of her face and edited out the patchwork of stitches and scars from the accident. Her gown billowed lightly around her arms in the breeze as if carried by the guard's whimpering cries. I had never thought about her rising. Never considered I would see her again someday.

"Maria?" My voice was raspy and hoarse. I'd like to say it was just emotion, but part of my esophagus had rotted away a few weeks ago. "I remember you."

It needed to be said. Too many memories slip away after death. More slide away when the hunger strikes us. I don't remember my parents. The memories of Maria were still there and fresh. The stolen summer evenings, the times we'd meet after school, the good three years we'd spent together. And the memories after that.

The corner of her mouth lifted, a scar keeping it from becoming a full smile. "When you left for college, I said I would always remember you." She had given back my ring on my parents' doorstep. Neither of us cried at the time. We couldn't cry now.

The guard remembered his gun. He shot me a few times, the

flash illuminating the rent-a-cop uniform against the red clay. As the slugs punched through my ribs, I got a good look at his face. He was young, maybe the same age as when I shot myself.

His shots didn't hurt, not like when I'd done it, but it knocked me back into the slick mud. Just annoying. I stood up, reached down, and took the gun from him. His eyes rolled back like a malfunctioning Ferris wheel. He collapsed, squelching into the bottom of the pit.

"Finally," I croaked. I kicked him a few times to make sure he would not get up anytime soon.

I climbed out of the hole. Maria still wore the prom dress they'd buried her in. Her hair was mostly there, though much of the cartilage around her nose was gone. And there was the half-repaired damage from when Scott drove them and a half a bottle of whiskey off the road on prom night. The angry crude stitches cut across her right wrist and forearm; her exposed collarbone glinted in the silver light.

"What happened to you?" she asked. Her hand reached for the gaping hole in the back of my head.

I shoved the words through my throat. "You said you would remember me. You were gone." My dry tongue skittered across cracked lips. "I said I would follow you."

The guard let out a soft whimper. I looked back down into the hole. The hunger was strong, and the guard—more boy than man, really—was near. Remembering to draw breath, I croaked at her, "I will share him with you," and I swung my legs into the pit.

"No!" she cried, and I glanced back at her.

She glared at me. "You don't have to eat him," she said. "There is another way."

The snarl snuck past my lips, straight from the gnawing need in my gut. She had to understand. She was like me. It didn't matter what I thought of it. The dry heaves afterward, the days of guilt—none of it was enough to stop the hunger.

I was close enough to the guard that I could almost taste the soft texture of his brain. It was so strong I wanted to gag and drool simultaneously, though I could do neither. I dropped into the pit.

"John!" Her voice was still enough to make me pause. "There are others of us who have given it up. We'll help you."

I tried to concentrate. The boy moaned softly. If I still had a pulse, it would have been racing. Aware brains, afraid brains—oh, they are the best. For a brief moment the fresh neurotransmitters flood your tongue and everything else dissolves in pure ecstasy. For a moment, you forget everything. For a moment, you forget what you were forced to become. I took a step toward the boy. The cool night air fluttered up the slit in my tux, through the hole in my skull.

"John." She was almost pleading now. "Come with me. We'll help you. You don't have to feed like this. You don't have to be alone."

I looked to see if she had a weapon—some way that she could take advantage of me. I wanted to eat, not be eaten. When I first rose, I was out of the ground before the man buried beside me. He had worked as a first meal, even if he had been too salty for my taste. Still, Maria had never lied to me in life, no matter how much I'd wanted her to. Not even when I begged her to on my parents' porch, when I asked her to just lie and say she'd wait for me. I looked again at her.

Her body was in worse shape than mine, but I had only burst out the back of my skull, not shattered my whole body. She saw me hesitate, and both corners of her mouth rose. Despite the scars, her smile was still the same.

She held her hand out to me, to help me up from the pit. "I'll wait for you this time, John."

I looked at the boy, and looked at her. My lungs tried to take a deep breath. It just seemed the thing to do. I turned to face her, took her hand, and prepared to be hungry for quite some time.

I saw the stitching around her wrist fail a moment too late. I held her hand in both of mine, the guard a soft cushion for my undead pratfall. I looked back up at her at the top of the pit; she looked down at me. I held her severed hand up, and she wriggled it in mine, and there was nothing left to do but laugh.

That was three months ago. Now we travel through the Midwest. She has packed the gown into a bag on her shoulder. She changes clothes whenever she can find a fresh supply. She prefers to wear sundresses in the city, but changes into sweats when we're between towns. I left my tux in a trash can somewhere outside Toledo. Instead I wear a hoodie and jeans, and rotate T-shirts from bands that were popular before we rose. I got a hat to keep the wind out of my skull. Our companions follow our example. They wear newer clothes snatched from abandoned strip malls or thrift stores.

It gives us an advantage. The clothes are often enough to avoid trouble with the locals. They are used to looking for shambling folks wearing the latest in undertaker fashion, not folks in regular clothes. Maybe they think we're just homeless drunks. We don't stop to ask.

We raid factory farms. I never liked the things, even when alive. But they're good for us now. Chickens, pigs, other livestock, all caged into an amazing density of brains per square feet. It's a deep delight to wade into a mass of beakless, terrified chickens. As our feet squish through their waste, we break their necks and crunch their skulls in our mouths. Chickens as methadone, I guess.

Sometimes it's not enough. Bob stayed clean for nearly a month. He had taken to wearing tweed jackets, lecturing us on the hidden beauty of *The Grapes of Wrath* like the professor he used to be. We found Bob crunching through a little girl's skull. He sat on the remains of her dollhouse, eyes glazed over, shoveling the grey stuff into his mouth. I had to put him down when he tried to eat Maria.

Despite the occasional relapse, we keep trying to convert others to our cause. Sometimes they're people we knew. Recognition helps us then, but often they're perfect strangers. Humor breaks through the slow mental fog of the undead. We have a routine down. "Need a helping hand?" I yell, and toss Maria's hand to them. Every time we get another one clean, her eyes shine—a little bit with the preservative we spray on each other, but also with the memory. Maybe my eyes shine too.

The addiction is still there. The monkey—like us—never dies. We cope with that as best we can. Maria takes my hand when I get the shakes. I press the remains of my lips against hers when she keens into the night. We make do.

Tonight, it's another chicken farm. The farmer's family is holed up in the basement, their tempting brains safely out of reach. Our family shambles into the pens to feast on avian brains. Maria is beside me. We look into each other's eyes, chickens clucking in panic around us, and smiles crinkle our stiff flesh. I can't be away from her any more. I need her. If we're apart, I feel the hurt deep inside of me. Her hand slides into mine and gives it a squeeze. I know she feels the same way.

I know we've really only traded one kind of hunger for another.

And that is enough for us.

ZOMBIFIED

Isabel Roman

Yum.

There was no other word for it. Mr. Tall, Delicious, and Doctor-fied had just introduced himself as her co-inheritor of a no-doubt ramshackle former plantation on Martinique. At least this trip wouldn't be as boring as Rebecca Davis originally imagined six months ago when her lawyer called her with the news.

Through some convoluted distant family connection, she and the gorgeous man before her were now on their way to the Caribbean. It was Rebecca's first real vacation in two years, and she'd originally been annoyed she had to share it with a stranger.

Now, with Griffin Stoddard, *Doctor* Griffin Stoddard, standing before her, she changed her mind.

Visions of the two of them in a very private hotel room overlooking a picturesque vista rather than traipsing to wherever the mansion was located entered her thoughts.

Yum, indeed.

"A pleasure to meet you in the flesh, Doctor Stoddard." Rebecca smiled. Her smile felt a little like the cat who ate, or was about to eat, the canary. She didn't care.

Too many pleasurable things to count flashed through her mind in the time between spotting the handsome doctor and now. How many, she wondered, could they accomplish before leaving Martinique? And did they really need to see the old mansion?

"Griffin, please," he said.

His hand was large and warm against hers, firm as he shook it. He looked slightly old-fashioned with his blond hair and bright blue eyes. She half expected him to kiss the back of her hand.

He didn't. She found herself slightly disappointed with that. Still, Rebecca's palm tingled long after he released her hand. They stood before their gate at Baltimore/Washington International Airport, the bright fall sunlight angling across the floor as other travelers mingled around them.

Just then, the boarding announcement echoed over the speakers, and Griffin gestured for her to precede him.

Once inside the plane, he hoisted his large black duffel into the overhead compartment at their first-class seats. Unable to resist, she watched his arm muscles, how his shirt stretched across his chest. Distracted, she didn't realize he'd sat next to her until he leaned in.

"Quite the adventure we're in for," he whispered as the first-class flight attendant made his way toward them.

"Is that so?" she asked, the wicked glint in her eye leaving no doubt about her interest.

"Absolutely." His answer was quick, as if he'd been thinking the same thing. But then he smiled, relaxed beside her. "Receiving a letter from a French lawyer about an inheritance that isn't an Internet scam or in Nigeria is an adventure in my book."

It was his wink that almost had her forgetting their extremely public setting. The fact that her FBI credentials would probably not prevent them from being kicked off the plane should she jump the delicious doctor next to her had her forcibly buckling the flimsy airplane seatbelt.

Rebecca forced herself to keep her hands in her lap as the male flight attendant took their drink orders. Oh, but how fun it would be to lick some gooey tropical concoction off the doctor's chest.

"Your room or mine?"

Instead of verbally answering, Griffin picked her up. Her legs wrapped around his waist as he carried her across the floor. Rebecca barely noticed the view before he placed her on the bed. Quickly rising to her knees as he stepped back, taking his addicting scent with him, she ignored everything but Griffin and pulled him down.

Those large hands she'd admired the entire flight here, and the all-too-brief stopover in San Juan, slid under her top. Mouths fused in a rush of fire and need. She unbuttoned his linen shirt, and ran her hands over the smooth paleness of his chest. Her fingers tingled at the sensation, and her breath caught at the feel of his skin beneath her palms.

Kissing his chest, tongue darting out to taste him, Rebecca whimpered as Griffin squeezed her upper thighs, moved his hands to her backside and up her spine, taking her tank top with him.

Rebecca abandoned herself to his hard muscles and the texture of his skin as it rippled under her questing fingers. This was passion—pure, unadulterated passion. And he was such a beautiful creature, she couldn't help herself.

Her mouth clamped down on his nipple as she unbuckled his pants. Griffin undid her bra and she wiggled free to shove his pants over his lean hips. Immediately twisting around, she pushed him onto his back and straddled him, wearing only a thin scrap of panties and her flat sandals.

The look in his eyes as she knelt before him was hot and hungry, and her heart pounded in anticipation. No regret stirred within her as she took what she wanted, what Griffin's demanding kisses and sure hands promised the both of them. Quickly stripping him, she crawled up his body.

"Delicious," she murmured. Strength, restrained power, and unbridled passion waited for her. All for her. "I need you now." His hands secured her to him, his eyes a burning blue in the dimness.

Legs clamped tight around his waist, Rebecca pushed down,

rotating her hips against him. His hands gripped her, stilling her for a moment, but just a moment. Those long talented fingers of his skimmed along her breasts, nails scraping over her sensitive nipples, then down her belly, smoothing over the silken material of her panties.

"You look like Aglaia," he murmured, tangling his hands in her long curly hair. "The youngest and most beautiful of the Three Graces."

Surprised, Rebecca smiled, touched at the sentiment. "That's sweet." She thanked him, touching her lips to his in a soft kiss. Sweet or not, no matter how she appreciated his words, or that he even *knew* the names of the Graces, she wanted him—no, she *needed* him.

Maneuvering her body onto his, she teased his rock-hard erection, touching him, caressing his skin with her hands and body.

"Rebecca," he growled. Grabbing her waist, in one quick move he rolled them so he hovered over her.

Griffin pressed against her entrance, moved only the tip against her. He kissed her hard, stealing her breath, and she moaned as he released her from his powerful touch. Grabbing her beneath her knees, he pushed her legs back almost to her shoulders. With erotic slowness, his blue gaze watching her intently as she shivered with the anticipation of their joining, Griffin entered her. Stilling for a moment, now completely encased in her, he paused and she relished the feel of this connection.

Whatever this was between them, it was strong.

Her breath came in short gasps. She curled her nails into his arms, arching into him, silently begging him to move. He pushed her legs further back, leaned down, and kissed her again.

Moving within her, pumping slowly at first, and then in a steadily increasing rhythm, he entered her again and again. Rebecca's breath hitched, her passion coiling tighter, her body ready to explode. Griffin's hands trailed down her, teasing heated flesh, making her ache for more. She wrapped her legs about his hips, straining closer as they clawed at each other. Passion built and exploded, and built once more.

And still, they couldn't get enough of each other.

Rebecca yelled his name as her back arched in a mind-blowing climax. She clamped around him, gripping his arms tightly, thighs clenching around his hips. Feeling his body tense over her, hearing him rasp out her name, she reached up and held him close as they both peaked.

Long, long minutes later, she opened her eyes and tried to remember how to speak. Happy to stay like this for the foreseeable future, Rebecca turned her head. Griffin watched her through half-open eyes.

"I vote for staying here tonight." His deep voice rumbled along her skin.

Nodding as his hand skimmed over her hip, Rebecca agreed. "The lawyer can wait."

"We'll never get there at this rate," Griffin commented as he finished buttoning his pants. They'd pulled their Jeep into a secluded path off what passed for a main road in Martinique for a quickie. Fleur de Martinique Plantation was in the middle of the island, and even with the rental's GPS, he wasn't certain they'd be able to find it easily.

"You're right," Rebecca replied. "I just find it hard to keep my hands off of you."

Griffin shot her a grin as he started the engine on their Jeep. Though he'd never been to this particular island, he'd driven through several Caribbean ones and a Jeep with four-wheel drive was always best.

Another hour, two wrong turns, and the condescending GPS recalculating the route later, they arrived at what was presumably their inheritance.

"It's got potential," Rebecca finally said.

"Doesn't look at all like Collinwood," he agreed.

She slanted him an amused glance. "*Dark Shadows*?"

Griffin shrugged. "You have a better comparison?"

"No," she sighed, dark eyes sparkling in the dimness of the turnoff. "Though I'm certain there are ghosts wandering the halls. Hmm," she added as they sat there, staring at the monstrosity. "Maybe Brad Pitt's house from *Interview with the Vampire*?"

"Good one," he laughed. "You've got that whole tropical feel, the dense rain forest. I can see that."

"I even have my own Brad Pitt." She turned to look at him, wiggling her eyebrows up and down.

Griffin returned her smile but said nothing. Then, before either could be distracted further from their destination, he released the brake and started down the rutted drive. It was just after noon, yet the sun was blocked from view by dozens of thick trees, their overhang forming a bower that reminded Griffin of Sleepy Hollow. Switching on the headlights and feeling absurd that it was necessary, he watched a small unrecognizable animal dart across the lane.

The sun dappled the yard around the house, spots of bright Caribbean sunlight not doing a damn thing to dispel the murkiness that hung over the property.

"This is reminiscent of every horror movie I've ever seen." He shook his head as another bump loomed in the middle of the road.

"One," Rebecca said and laughed, an oddly carefree sound in the gloom of the driveway, "I promise not to sprain my ankle. Two, you've got someone with you who knows hand-to-hand combat. And three . . ." She paused, peering through the windshield. Her smile faltered. "Perhaps I *should* have packed my gun."

"I don't think you can shoot ghosts," he said. Swerving to avoid yet another pothole in the middle of the dirt path, he cursed. "Then again." He parked the car and opened the door. Rounding and opening hers, he added, "Probably not a bad idea."

Taking her arm, Griffin led her up the stone steps. He was surprised to notice they weren't cracking, rotting, or completely gone.

"If it weren't so far from everything," Rebecca said as he struggled with the key the lawyer had given them, "we could make it into a hotel."

"And serve what?" he asked. "Damn it!"

The key slipped against whatever covered the hole, and he banged his knuckles. No blood; he probably wouldn't need a tetanus shot, which was just as well. If he left now, Griffin damn sure wasn't returning to this place anytime soon.

"Serve?" Rebecca asked as she took his hand and examined the knuckles.

Griffin forgot the tongue-in-cheek comment he'd been about to make as Rebecca's lips brushed each knuckle individually. "Serve breakfast and ectoplasm?" he managed.

"Exactly," she whispered, her dark eyes looking up at him from beneath thick lashes. "If you survive your first night, the second's on the ghost."

"Not a bad marketing campaign," he agreed. She let go of his hand, and he tried the key again. "If we can get the ghost to cooperate."

More cursing, another clash between his knuckles and the door, and Griffin finally opened it. He was beginning to suspect there was a reason, other than what the lawyer implied, for him not joining them on this journey.

"I wouldn't even know how to go about paying them," Rebecca said.

Just then, the door opened with a creek. Griffin pushed it as wide as it'd go and stepped through. The lawyer said the electricity was still connected, so he felt against the wall for a light switch. Finding one, he flipped it up.

Light flooded the foyer. Dust danced in the breeze from the doorway, but otherwise it wasn't the house of horrors he'd expected.

"The place doesn't look as bad inside as it does from the out."

"I was just thinking that," he commented, stepping through to the interior.

It wasn't well kept, and a thick layer of dust clung to everything, but the electricity worked, and they'd also been assured by the lawyer that the water was still on.

"Maybe," he said, turning to her, "we won't need our camping gear."

Rebecca laughed, an easy sound, as she joined him in the foyer.

"Definitely looks like something out of a flick." Her voice echoed throughout the empty mansion. "An old Hollywood period piece," she amended, "not a horror movie."

Griffin shrugged. "Did the lawyer, what's his name, Mr. Desmarais, say anything about the owners?"

"Not to me." She walked in a circle, looking up the staircase. He wondered if she always did that—part of her FBI training—or if she just couldn't stay still.

"But I did some digging." Rebecca stopped moving and turned to face him. "I meant to share with you."

"Not that we had time when we first arrived." Griffin smirked as if she needed a reminder, but the heat in her dark eyes told him she didn't. She remembered well enough what they'd done the moment they'd checked into the hotel.

"Not that we had time," she agreed in a husky voice. Clearing her throat, she said, "Basic stuff—sugar plantation founded in the late eighteen-thirties, my family lived here, yours lived in Fort-de-France, this and that happened, and it was a joint venture up through the early twentieth century."

"And the last relation died three years ago," he added. His own lawyer had told him that. Repeatedly.

"Exactly," she said and nodded, stepping closer. "Took Mr. Desmarais this long to find us."

Spreading his arms wide he said, "And now we have this palace."

"Come on, Brad Pitt," Rebecca grinned. She grabbed his hand and tugged. "Let's check out all the rooms. Maybe there's treasure under the floorboards."

Three shrunken voodoo heads, a single gold doubloon, an ancient German Luger, and one and a half wooden legs later, they gave up. The rest of the house was as dusty as the entryway, so they opened the shutters, unpacked their camping gear and set up camp before the unused fireplace.

Before Rebecca knew what was happening, Griffin's lips were on hers and they made love in an abandoned mansion in the middle of Martinique. It was the most pleasurable day she could remember spending in a long while.

"No pirate treasure," she sighed, propping her head on one hand and looking at him.

"No, but lots of dust."

Rebecca frowned at his frown and traced the line of his jaw. "What do you expect?" she asked. "The place has been closed up for years."

She swept her arm out to encompass the end tables, coffee table, piano, and old-style chairs—some wicker, some old enough to be certifiable antiques. Not that she had any real notion of what a certifiable antique looked like.

"Dust is created by human skin," he mumbled. Shaking his head, he grasped her hips and pulled her atop him. "Are you sure you want to stay here for the night? Or do you want to drive back?"

"Nah." She kissed his lips. "Let's just stay here. We haven't explored a fraction of the place. Plus . . ." Her lips trailed along his jaw, and Rebecca wondered when she'd become so fascinated with a man's jaw line. "Plus we'll just have to drive back out tomorrow. What's the point?"

"Definitely not an ordinary woman," he said against her mouth. "Most I know would rather head back to the hotel than stay here. In the middle of nowhere."

"Hey," she said, smiling, "at least we have electricity."

The night was warm, and Griffin found himself dozing as they sat on the back porch, Rebecca next to him as they watched the stars. Having grown up in Northern Virginia, he never really had the chance to appreciate such a view.

"What's that?" Rebecca asked, breaking the comfortable silence.

Griffin looked to where she pointed, far to the left, but could only make out lights from a neighboring house. "Neighbors. How unfortunate."

She chuckled, but didn't take her eyes off the lights blazing in the darkness. Griffin watched her for a few minutes, then shrugged and went back to looking up at the stars.

"It's weird."

Looking back down at her, he laughed. "The fact we have neighbors?"

"No." She shook her head and looked up at him, dark eyes nearly impossible to see in the night. "The lights weren't on before. I couldn't even tell there was a house over there until they blazed to life."

"And how is that weird?"

"It's two in the morning."

"Maybe they're vampires," he suggested with a grin. He didn't know her well enough to say anything beyond that. Didn't know how suspicious she was, what her job at the FBI entailed, so kept to horror movie references.

Instead, he settled back against the newel post on the steps. There hadn't been any chairs for them, or any he deemed sturdy enough, to hold his weight.

"It's still weird."

"Maybe they also inherited the mansion, finally found the place with the condition of the roads here, and are now exploring." He didn't believe it any more than her look indicated she did, but Griffin had no other explanation.

"Maybe."

He couldn't tell how much more time passed before a scream broke the stillness of the island night.

"Did you hear that?" he demanded, suddenly wide awake.

Tearing his gaze from the suddenly not-so-beautiful night, he watched Rebecca slowly nod. "Yeah. It's the scream from every horror movie ever produced in history."

"Exactly. Little *Halloween* with some Freddy Krueger thrown in." His words belied the pounding of his heart.

"I was always partial to Jason from *Friday the Thirteenth*," she said. But Griffin noticed she wasn't as relaxed as she sounded. Her hand blindly groped at her side—for the gun, he surmised, that she wasn't wearing. "Sure, he had like a hundred and eighty-two sequels, but . . . damn it!"

She glanced at her hip, confirmed what she already knew, and locked eyes with him.

Another sound, a scream-screech sound, cut through the night.

"Could've been an owl," he offered.

"Could've been." She nodded, already standing. "Where was that antique gun we found?"

Moments later, they were back in the attic. Rebecca tore through boxes as he angled the bare bulb in her direction as much as possible without burning his fingers.

"Got it!" she called, holding up the German Luger as evidence. "No cleaning kit, but I did find several bullets."

"Good enough," Griffin said as they went back downstairs to the veranda. They were being ridiculous. Talking about horror movies, scaring themselves like a bunch of kids around a campfire. Nonetheless, he detoured into the front room where they'd left their camping stuff for a flashlight.

"You know," he said, "it was probably just an owl or some other indigenous creature."

"Agreed." She gave a short nod. He could see the federal agent in her now: the practiced movements, the clean motions. She loaded the Luger with ease, though it didn't look like it'd been cleaned since World War II.

"I doubt that'll even shoot," he said. They were now on the veranda, the night once more silent around them. "It's a movie prop."

Rebecca chuckled, but gripped the gun firmly.

This time, the scream sounded definitely human. And it didn't stop. The sound echoed around them, continuing long after human lungs should fail from lack of oxygen.

"We have to investigate that, don't we." It wasn't a question. The scream continued on, sending chills up his spine. Griffin spent time in a downtown D.C. hospital emergency room. This was worse than anything he'd ever heard there.

"Yup." Rebecca glanced over her shoulder. Even in the darkness, he could see the steel in her eyes.

"Let me find a shovel or something," he conceded.

There was nothing lying in the yard or around the sides of the house, so Griffin raced back inside and into the basement, doing his best not to think of the *Texas Chain Saw Massacre*. Horror was a favorite genre, but after this, he wasn't so sure he'd look at them the same way.

Gripping the shovel, he met her at the back door. Rebecca stood with her back to the house, her gaze on the building across the fields, gun held firmly in both hands. When she saw him, she laughed, shrugged, and nodded to the house. "Let's go."

Holding the flashlight before them, he walked beside Rebecca as they traipsed across the uneven ground. The other house was further away than it had seemed from the veranda.

Griffin pulled up short. There was a man in front of them. He hadn't been there before, Griffin was certain of that. The flashlight was pretty strong and yet the man loomed out of nowhere. The screaming stopped, and an eerie silence descended on the field. He had a feeling it wouldn't last.

"Excuse me," Rebecca said in an even voice. No answer. "Excuse me!" she said more forcibly. Turning to him, she asked, "Know any French?"

"*Parlez-vous* English?" Griffin offered. "*Merci beaucoup*? I took Spanish in high school, Latin in college and medical school. Never French."

"Sir, we heard . . ."

The man never moved. In fact, Griffin wasn't certain he even heard Rebecca.

There was another scream, a short burst of sound that barely registered given the complete lack of reaction from the man before them.

He had a bad feeling when she put her hand on the other man's arm, and he wished it was jealousy. Not usually one to fear the night, something about this night on this island creeped him out. About to step forward and stop Rebecca from touching the other man—though he couldn't voice his reasons for such an act—Griffin halted midstride when the man finally turned.

His eyes were sunken in his pale, pale face, devoid of all emotion. His limp hair, which looked like it could fall out in a stiff wind, hung about his face in strings, and his mouth stayed half-open, slack. In short, he looked like no living thing Griffin had ever seen.

"If I didn't know better," Griffin whispered as Rebecca took a sharp step backwards, bumping into his chest, "I'd say he was a corpse. But since it's medically impossible . . ."

"So you are seeing what I'm seeing." Rebecca glanced at him, then back to the man who hadn't moved before them. "*Night of the Living Dead*?"

She didn't move, raised her gun slightly, but he wasn't surprised to see her gamely try again. "Excuse me," she said, voice a little less sure, "but do you know . . . um . . . ."

"The pivotal question," he quipped, praying the Luger fired. "What *do* you say to a zombie?"

Apparently not that. The zombie, or whatever it was, lunged at them. Griffin reacted. He kicked the zombie—or whatever—in the groin and pushed him backwards. Trying not to grimace like a girl that he'd just touched a zombie, he moved to the side. Rebecca had raised her gun, and he didn't want to be in the line of fire.

"I'm a United States federal agent!" Rebecca shouted.

"Are you serious?" he asked her, but took another step back. Just in case.

"I'm supposed to say that," she defended, but hadn't taken her eyes off the prone, er, man.

In a move far too fluid for the, ah, undead, the zombie was on his—its?—feet and clawing at Rebecca. Griffin moved, his only thought to protect her.

"Move away!" Rebecca shouted.

The Luger fired. Surprised that it did, he shook his head. The shot echoed in the clearing, sharply contrasting with the screams still coming from the house. The zombie fell backwards, lying still in the high grass.

"No silver bullet? Beheading? Stake? How do you kill a zombie?"

Griffin cautiously walked a step forward. The zombie hadn't

moved. He took another step. "Apparently," he said, "a special World War II bullet."

"Don't touch it!" she warned.

"I wasn't going to fall into that trap," he promised, but did take another step closer. It was his medical training.

Enthralled, he crouched beside it, careful to keep half an arm's length out. "If we can get it back to the States, I can publish this."

"We have to keep on."

"We did our duty," he pointed out, but stood.

"Come on Doctor Moreau, we're heading for the house."

"And to think, yesterday morning going to Martinique was such a good idea."

"If we get out of this alive," she agreed, "I'm going to find that lawyer. He'll be sorry."

"I never thought I'd have to crawl through the mud on a vacation," Rebecca mumbled.

Griffin slithered next to her, shovel gripped in one hand, flashlight in the other. He'd turned it off, he noticed, the closer they got to the brightly lit house. For a doctor, he was more practical than she'd have given him credit for.

"Now what?" he asked once they were lying next to a long floor-to-ceiling window. There was no curtain on it, but then who besides them was out here at two in the morning to see the lights?

"Find the source of the screams," she whispered back.

"I got that," he snapped.

Rebecca looked sideways at Griffin. For a man who had just crawled on his belly through the mud, he looked pretty damned sexy. She wanted to lean over and kiss him, but practicalities and all. Instead, she nodded upwards. "I'll go first."

"Good," he grunted, shifting to crouch against the wall, shovel at the ready. "You have the gun."

Snorting an aborted laugh, Rebecca peeked around the stone-wall, scanning the interior as quickly as she could. Not seeing anyone—or anything—she eased forward. As far as she could see, there was no latch on the window, and she didn't want to risk drawing attention to them by breaking the glass.

Silently motioning for Griffin to follow, she sprinted to the next window, but encountered the same thing. On the third try, she stopped before French doors, and eased one open. It wasn't locked, but again, she chalked it up to the complete isolation of the house.

Really, she just refused to consider any other option. If she was back in D.C., that'd be different. Here . . . with zombies . . .

"Ready?" she asked.

"As I'll ever be." Griffin nodded.

They slipped inside. Rebecca could feel Griffin behind her, a solid, reassuring, *alive* presence that did much to steady her against such an unknown. Gangs, gangsters, thugs, she could deal with. Zombies?

"Maybe the letter from the lawyer really was a scam," she muttered.

"I was just thinking that same thing." Griffin's voice was light, given the situation.

Her hand gripped the doorknob to the door separating the empty room from whatever else lay in the house. "Ready?"

Griffin nodded, and she swung the door open as fast as she could. It made a horrible screeching noise, but just then the screaming began again.

"What is he doing to her?" Griffin demanded.

Rebecca shook her head. She had no answers, and was afraid what they'd discover when they did find the source of the scream.

Down the hall, to the left, and that's when they found them. Dozens of the creatures. They stood in a haphazard array, not walking, not talking, not even moaning in an undead kind of way. They just stood there.

Rebecca raised the gun.

"Wait. They're not reacting." Griffin pointed the shovel to the group who hadn't even noticed their presence. "Damn, they're the Borg."

"Okay." She took a deep breath. "All right. Let's go, then."

Utterly disgusted, she held the gun ready as they slipped by the zombies. It was true; they didn't react. One or two looked right at them, but Rebecca didn't want to take the chance they'd charge if she maintained eye contact, and moved past them as quickly as she could.

Griffin followed her as they walked down another hall and to a set of steps. The door was wide open, lights blazing from the basement as well. Both sides of the stairs were walled, so Rebecca took the chance and descended them.

"This is a bad idea," she said halfway down.

"Can't turn back now," Griffin pointed out.

"Wasn't going to," she shot back, "but it's still a bad idea."

The last step and she peeked around the corner. Blinking, she tried to process what she saw.

"He looks like a mad scientist!" Griffin whispered from above her.

It was exactly what he looked like. Wild Gene Wilder hair, a white lab coat, computers, machines she couldn't begin to name, and a woman on the table. One look told Rebecca it was too late for the woman. She was already a zombie.

"Seriously?" Rebecca ducked back behind the wall. "He's really wearing a lab coat?"

He opened his mouth to comment, closed it, tried again, then shrugged. "I have nothing to say to that."

Incredulous, she hoisted the gun higher and said, "Just to recap before we charge in and attack the mad scientist and his zombie hoard: we came down to the Caribbean, to this gorgeous island. Inherited a spooky mansion in the middle of nowhere that just so happens to be next to another spooky mansion that houses zombies and apparently a mad scientist."

Griffin smiled, and she could see he tried hard not to laugh and draw attention to them.

"Trust me, this isn't an ordinary case."

"No." He shook his head. With the shovel at the ready, he

nodded to where the aforementioned lab coat–wearing mad scientist stood over his latest victim. "Ready?"

Rebecca nodded and rounded the corner, gun aimed at the only other living being there. "You're the living, breathing cliché of a mad scientist."

"Who the hell are you?"

"Perfect," Griffin muttered.

"You must be the Americans from Fleur." His accent was heavy French, not from the island Rebecca suspected.

"Good guess," she said.

"What kind of experiments are you doing here?" Griffin demanded. "What have you done to these people?"

"If you took my buyout offer," the mad scientist said, "you wouldn't have been my next experiment."

"I've seen this movie!" Rebecca said. She held the gun steady on the man, eyes never leaving his or the zombie on the table. She was fairly certain the creature was strapped down, but one never knew with zombies, did one. "I could try to arrest you now, but I'm a U.S. special agent and have no powers under the French government."

The scientist smirked. It looked mildly disturbing.

"Plus," she continued, "I have a feeling all this is going to be really hard to explain."

"Pierre! René! Inès! Kill the intruders!"

Frowning, she glanced at Griffin. He'd edged along the wall to the computers, alternating looking at the mad scientist and the beckoning monitors.

Three zombies ambled from nowhere. They came straight for them in a slow, steady pace. Rebecca had known this was a bad idea. She moved to Griffin's side, keeping her back to the wall as the three headed for them.

"I have about four bullets," she said to him, "assuming one doesn't jam the gun. I don't want to end up like those girls in horror movies."

"I don't blame you," he said. Then, catching her gaze, he said very seriously. "I *really* don't."

She nodded and fired at the scientist. One shot clean between the eyes, and he fell backwards. The screams of the female zombie on the table had not abated and Rebecca wondered if the creature knew what was happening. Frantic, now down to three bullets, she aimed at the advancing zombies.

They'd stopped.

"What did you find?" she demanded.

"He's *Highlander*," Griffin said, clicking through file after file. "Trying to live forever."

"Ah, but who wants to live forever?" she quipped, not taking her eyes off the still and suddenly confused zombies. She refused to rethink that thought about confusion and zombies, and kept her gun on the closest one.

"I've seen enough."

Taking her eyes off the undead long enough to look at Griffin, she simply moved back the way they'd come. His expression was disgusted, sickened. Whatever she thought the mad scientist was doing, it was worse. Griffin understood his notes, knew what the man was after. Immortality?

He'd experimented on these people. Later, she'd ask what Griffin found, but for now, she just wanted to get out of this house of horrors alive.

"We can't leave them here to run amok," Griffin said.

Rebecca looked over her shoulder as they ascended the steps. She didn't think there was anyone else in the house—anyone else *alive* in the house—but didn't want to be caught off guard. Plus, three shots left.

"They're already dead," she pointed out.

"Indeed."

"Ashes to ashes," she said, peering around the corner. Empty. "We'll torch the place."

"For the best. I don't know if they're contagious or not, or if that's a Hollywood thing." He didn't sound as if he fully agreed, but what else was there? No one would believe them and she had no idea how to get a group of dead beings out of the house.

His hand on her arm stopped her. "We need to use the equipment downstairs. I didn't see anything else on the way in there, and at least I know it's flammable."

With a sigh, she agreed and they headed into the basement. It didn't take them long to start a fire. Griffin was right; besides the computers and such there were jars of liquid, which proved to be very flammable. The fire spread quickly and burned very hot.

Racing out of the house, she saw a zombie on fire. He stood where he caught fire, and let himself burn.

Back on the veranda of their own house, Rebecca sat next to him on the steps and watched it. They'd called the fire department and could even now hear sirens speeding towards them.

"It's safer in D.C."

Griffin laughed and slung his arm around her shoulders. "Yeah. I'm in for selling this place."

"I can't sign the papers fast enough." She settled her head against his chest and closed her eyes. She could still see the zombies and imagined she heard their death screams despite the distance.

"Ha!" Griffin laughed. "I figured it out. He reminds me of a *Scooby-Doo* cartoon."

"Hell," Rebecca said and laughed, "this night was too weird."

"Hmm, yes. But not all of it."

"No," she whispered, "not all of it." Then, in a firmer voice, "I need a drink."

"Buy you one at the Hays-Adams," he offered.

"I'd like that."

"And dinner," he added.

Rebecca stiffened, then slowly looked up at him. She hadn't really thought about anything between them past this tropical sojourn. Looking up at his intense blue eyes, she found herself nodding.

"I'd like that," she said, resting her head back on his chest. "I'd like that very much."

WHITE NIGHT, BLACK HORSE

Mercy Loomis

I don't know if I can rightly describe it to you, what it's like. When you are seized by the *loa* there is no memory, no knowledge of what passes. The *loa*, the voodoo spirits that act as intermediaries between God and men, are fond of using humans as their horses when they wish to pass on a message or join in a celebration. It's said that the *loa* displace their horse's *ti bon ange*, the little good angel, the spark of their host's personality. Either they hold it safe in their keeping, or no one has been stupid enough to try to steal the soul of a *loa*'s horse.

I would imagine the *loa* would take a dim view of such a thing.

But God knows, I had been ridden before, and coming out of the ground was nothing like it.

The *bokor*, the sorcerer, called me from the earth, and I came.

I was bound. I was beaten.

And the *bokor* stole my *ti bon ange*.

I can tell you all this, for I remember it. It is not the same as being ridden, not at all.

A zombie's baptism is a harsh affair, foul paste for the Host, your own blood dripping down your face. They named me Joseph, and led me away.

Without your *ti bon ange,* you are nothing. No will. No thoughts. Just a mindless, obedient slave. So it's hard for me to tell you what I experienced, because I had no ability to think, and no sense of time.

I don't know how long I'd been working on the plantation when they brought Marie-Celeste to join us. The *bokor* who held my soul now was not the one who had raised me from the earth. That man had been too poor to own the immense fields I and my fellow zombies tended. We worked straight through from sunrise to sunset, because the overseers were afraid to be out after dark.

We were told to work. We worked. We were told to go into the shed. We went. We were told to eat the meager food that would keep our bodies running. We ate. We were told to lie down. None of us slept.

New zombies came. Others left. We didn't notice.

But when Marie-Celeste came . . .

I grope for words. I didn't *notice* her, but I was aware of her presence. While I recognized all my fellows, and the overseers too, for that matter, there was a deeper sense of recognition with her. It wasn't that I had known her before, for I had no way to access memory. Her face was not familiar, nor would I have found it lovely even if I had been able to make value judgments. No zombie is beautiful. The sense of wrongness about us is simply too great for beauty.

The overseers gave us simple instructions. No one paid attention to who went where, as long as the work was done.

When we went out to the fields, Marie-Celeste and I walked together.

When we worked, we worked next to each other.

When we lay down, it was always side by side.

There was no thought to this. Zombies cannot think. But just as I was aware of rain running into my eyes, though I had no opinion about it, I was drawn to her, pulled as if by gravity.

No conscious decision, just a force of nature.

If a zombie could be content, I was.

Again, I don't know how long this went on. But one night, as we lay still and silent on the beaten earth floor of our shed, the *bokor* who owned the plantation came. He looked us over, called Marie-Celeste to him, and took her away.

By chance I had lain down facing the door, so I was able to watch her leave without moving. Though I could not have disobeyed the command to lie down, I feel certain that the connection that had brought us together would've lifted my head at the least, and any movement would have focused his attention on me. Even as it was I felt the pull of her calling me to follow, and for the first time since my soul was stolen I knew conflict, physically drawn to go with her but bound to stay where I was.

I have no doubts the command would have been the stronger of the two forces, but at the moment the *bokor* left, the *loa* Simbi Makaya came into me.

My eyes closed.

It started as the old dream. I stood in my grandfather's temple, a few steps back from the altar, and before it was the *loa* in his signature red and green, stamping back and forth and gesturing wildly with his cigar. Simbi Makaya, my *mait-tete*, the first *loa* to have ridden me.

He was yelling at me, as usual.

It is frustrating to me now, in hindsight, that the one time when I could endure his censure with true uncaring stoicism was the one time when I was too emotionally dead to enjoy it. As it was, since he gave me no commands, I simply let the words wash over me—meaningless ravings.

Eventually he realized this and stopped, puffing thoughtfully on his cigar. "So. You say you do not want to be a *houngan*. You are no priest, you say. You want to be a modern man. Go to university. Work in the city. No time for the temple, no time for the *loa*, no time for your *mait-tete*! Well." He puffed some more and gave me a nasty smile. "Now you have time, no?

"I send you dreams. You ignore them. I send you warnings. You ignore them. I send portents to your family and friends, and you ignore *them*. You get sick, you lose your job, but do you come to the *houngan* for guidance? No! *You move to the city!*" He stomped one foot. "Stubborn!" Then his anger faded, replaced with satisfaction. "Not so stubborn now. Didn't think you needed your *mait-tete*'s protection. So. I take my protection back, and what happens to you? Zombie. Not so much fun, make the temple look like a paradise, no?"

He laughed and took another puff, then crossed his arms and considered me. "But I still want you for my horse. And *him,* Jean-Yves," and here he jerked his head back, somehow indicating the door of the shed even though we were not at the plantation at the moment, "he does not feed me, he does not call the society, he does not do honor to me, the master of magicians! He is soft and comfortable, and forgets his duty. So. I take my protection from him, too."

Simbi Makaya looked past me and pursed his lips. "And also, maybe, Erzulie Dantor has an interest in a certain pretty girl, wants her husband to tell his servant Jean-Yves to let the girl go. But the *bokor,* he does not listen." The *loa* glanced at me, smiling. "Not wise to ignore one's wife, especially when she is Erzulie Dantor. So very fond of knives, she is. So. Jean-Yves, not on my happy list. Even more so than you."

Even a zombie could see where this was going.

He pointed the cigar at me. "I will give you one more chance. I will break the spell that holds your *ti bon ange* from you. After that, well, I will give you no more chances."

He reached for me. Since I had no will to fight him, my body gave just one brief convulsion before the *loa* was in control. Everything went dark.

I came to myself in an unfamiliar kitchen, a salt shaker in my hand and grains dissolving on my tongue. *Chaos!* I had not been able to feel for so long, and now it was all thrust upon me at once. I doubled over, catching myself against a table as my knees went weak, caught up in the *loa*'s retreat and the return of my soul. It was worse than being thrown into cold water, but that was the best analogy I could make. Light and dark flashed through my vision. The breath was driven out of me, my mind overwhelmed by the intense sensations, my muscles spasming.

There was a moment where I thought it would be too much to endure, and I would die in truth. But through the ache of hungers left unsated and limbs that have toiled with too little rest, the presence of my Marie-Celeste burned.

The very thought of her warmed my heart, drove back the riot of feelings until they settled, uneasy and fitful, into their proper places.

She was near.

This knowledge of her did not surprise me in the least. I had always been able to tell which *loa* rode whom, and what neighbor was knocking on the front door. It was part of what made me so very attractive to the master of magicians.

I climbed to my feet on colt's legs and followed my inner compass, my hand still closed tight around the salt shaker.

Listening carefully, hiding as best I could, I made my way through the quiet house. I would have passed by what looked like a closet door if I had not been guided to it. There was a lock on the door, and before I tried it I tapped three times against the lock plate and whispered the charm my grandfather had taught me. The door opened soundlessly when I turned the knob.

The dim light from the hall let me see that this was indeed used for storage, but of the *bokor's* ritual tools. There was the crutch of Legba and bottles of rum and whiskey, candles and skulls and cloths of all colors, top hats and glasses with only one lens, a shelf holding nothing but small ceramic bottles.

Lighting a red candle, I softly shut the door behind me.

Of course, it was her *ti bon ange* that drew me, not her body. Setting aside the one bottle that resonated with her energy, I picked up each of the others in turn. Carefully, for I had never much liked to make use of my gift, I sent a thought to each soul as I held it: *Fly home to your body. There is work yet to do.* Then I sprinkled the bottle with salt, muffled it in cloth, and smashed it against the edge of the shelf.

One bottle was empty. I smashed it anyway.

When all the bottles were destroyed but one, I blew out the candle.

Show me to where your body is, I whispered to Marie-Celeste's *ti bon ange,* and opened the bottle.

Her soul spilled forth, invisible as the air, silent to my ears but loud in my heart. I followed its song through the house to a back bedroom. There were voices on the other side of the door, so I called the disembodied soul back to the bottle and hid in some long curtains nearby.

After a few long minutes the door opened. The *bokor* Jean-Yves came out, followed by a maid, her arms piled high with towels and cloths.

"*Houngan* Stefan will be here tomorrow," Jean-Yves said as they walked down the hall, "and I expect you will have Marie-Celeste properly dressed and presentable by the time he arrives. It wouldn't do for him to decide to refuse her."

The maid murmured something deferential as they rounded the corner, voices fading into nothing.

My hands clenched tight around the bottle and the salt shaker. Jean-Yves planned to give Marie-Celeste away, or possibly trade her, probably hoping that Erzulie Dantor's wrath would follow the zombie's owner instead of her maker. Glaring after him, I crept back to the door.

It was silent inside, so with a brief prayer I eased the door open. The room was dark, but there was enough light coming through the windows that I could make out her shape on the bed. Marie-Celeste lay naked on top of the sheets, her black hair like a wet halo around her head. Her eyes were open but empty. I felt a faint glimmer of the pull that had drawn us together, but what lay on the bed was simply a shell. I held the real Marie-Celeste in my hand.

"Open your mouth," I whispered aloud, and the zombie did. I closed my eyes briefly, reaching out to her *ti bon ange. Fly home to your body.* Then I wrapped the bottle in the sheet. With one hand I smashed it against the bed frame, and with the other I sprinkled salt into her mouth.

With a shrill cry of triumph, her soul slammed into her body.

Marie-Celeste gasped, her back arching, her eyes wide. Convulsions wracked her lithe frame, her hands scrabbling at the bedclothes, head twisting from side to side as her soul sought to reestablish itself. Her expression changed, moving from shock to distress, then agony. Then rage.

I didn't know what Jean-Yves had done to her, but I could feel it, a festering hatred growing like an abscess in her psyche, threatening to sever the fragile connection that remained between her body and her *ti bon ange*. If her soul fled her now, her body would follow its last impulse—destroy Jean-Yves—and she would die.

Though my gift let me feel her mind, her pain and confusion were too great for me to get through. Desperate, not knowing what else to do, I leaned down and kissed her.

In that first long moment, there was no response. My heart cried out in denial, and I kissed her harder.

Then, like butter going soft in the afternoon sun, her lips molded to mine.

Her harsh breaths eased, and the hatred drained out of her.

I pulled away, averting my eyes, because I was suddenly very much aware that she was a zombie no longer, but a person, a woman, naked and vulnerable and trapped beneath me. "I'm sorry, I—"

She grabbed me by both ears and hauled me back down to her. With growing delight she studied my face, a tender, wondering smile dancing on her lips. "Joseph," she murmured, calling me by the only name she knew, and kissed me before I could correct her.

I think she meant it to be a gentle kiss, but it didn't stay that way. God alone knew how long we'd been together in that horrific state, so close but never touching, and even though we'd been unaware at the time, now it was all coming down on us. The zombie's contentment gave way to human passion, infectious and hot like a fever, delirium making us forget where we were, the danger we were in. There was nothing else for me but her soft brown skin and her delicate hands fumbling at my clothes, and the hot, wet pressure as I sheathed myself inside her.

If I had never believed in magic before, that moment would've convinced me.

And too, on the edge of my awareness, Simbi Makaya and Erzulie Dantor twined together, coupling with a frenzied joy that matched our own.

I pushed that knowledge aside and focused on Marie-Celeste, savoring her breathless, pleading moans, suckling at her pert breasts, my hips rocking, rocking, until she cried out, shuddering around me. The pleasure of it broke me and I came, groaning into her shoulder, our arms wrapped tight around each other.

She gave a pleased little laugh and kissed my cheek. "Ah, Joseph," she said again, her eyes shining.

Maybe I would keep the name. Anything, as long as she kept looking at me like that.

I shook myself. "We have to go," I whispered, looking around for my clothes.

Her gaze took in the room with one swift glance, and she nodded, reaching down to the floor and tossing me my pants. I found my shirt and handed it to her. Watching her dress didn't make it any easier to get my pants on. She was so adorable, rolling back the long sleeves, her slim legs poking out from under the hem.

Footsteps pounded down the hall outside. No time to do anything but step between Marie-Celeste and the door before it burst open, slamming into the wall and almost swinging shut again.

Jean-Yves batted it aside, his lips drawn back in an angry snarl. Ceramic shards fell from his fingers.

I suppose I *had* left a bit of a mess back there.

The *bokor*'s gaze flicked over me, the rumpled bed, and fixed on Marie-Celeste with the burning hatred of wounded pride. "You'd deny me, the greatest sorcerer on this whole stinking island, but fall right into bed with a man that I *bought* for half a cask of cheap rum?"

The heat of her anger warmed my back. "I'd sooner bed a leper than you!" she snapped, trying to dodge around me, her fingers hooked into claws. I spread my arms wide, determined to keep between them.

Jean-Yves spared me a derisive glance. "I'll deal with you later," he growled, and threw something at me.

My hand tingled, as if I'd been scuffing through dry leaves and had reached for something metal. Almost without meaning to, I raised my hand and caught what he had thrown.

Nothing happened, save that the presence of my *mait-tete* surrounded me.

"You're not the greatest sorcerer on this island," I said as the *bokor* gaped at me. "Simbi Makaya is."

I could feel the others approaching, running up the hill. With a grim smile I made a fist around the little fetish I had caught, stepped forward, and punched Jean-Yves as hard as I could.

His cheek *crunched* under the blow. He reeled, stumbling to the side.

Away from the door.

I'd learned so few charms before my grandfather had died, before I'd turned my back on the *loa* and the faith that had raised me. But this one I knew. Before Jean-Yves could recover, I slammed the door shut, touched the lock plate.

Click.

The other man righted himself, one hand pressed to his face. "You'd have done better to put yourself on the other side of that door. I'm going to make you wish—"

I threw the fetish at his feet, grabbed Marie-Celeste, and hauled her back toward the far window.

Jean-Yves laughed at the nest of snakes that seemed to appear at his feet. "I don't need the *loa* to dispel my own magic," he sneered, waving his hands at the hissing serpents and causing them to vanish in puffs of colored smoke.

Behind the *bokor,* there was movement at the window that faced down the hill.

I took an instinctive step back, pushing Marie-Celeste toward the window behind us. "You don't want to see this," I whispered.

She refused to budge. "Oh, yes, I do."

The window shattered.

We all crouched instinctively as the glass went flying, and the first zombie was halfway over the sill before Jean-Yves turned and saw his danger. With a horrified cry he sprang for the door, rattling the handle uselessly and trying to undo the locking spell. More of the zombies were pouring through the window, tearing at the frame, silent except for a low rumbling growl that made my skin crawl. The *bokor* dodged past the reaching hands of the first zombie and hurled himself at me.

I braced myself, ready to defend the only other exit, hardly aware of Marie-Celeste's shudders until she abruptly darted past me, leaning down to scoop up a shard of glass. With a harsh cry of "*ke ke ke!*" she drove the shard into the *bokor*'s belly.

Jean-Yves staggered, and Erzulie Dantor left Marie-Celeste just as suddenly as she had seized her. Marie-Celeste convulsed, stumbling into me as I rushed to pull her back. Jean-Yves stared at us, eyes wide with shock and disbelief, until the mob of dead men grabbed him. Panic blazed across his face and then, as hands and teeth began to tear into flesh, the shrieking began.

I stood there with Marie-Celeste wrapped in my arms, until she finally turned and buried her face against my chest. The zombies ignored us completely as we opened the window and slipped out into the night.

The screams continued for quite some time. We made a wide circle of the house, and by the time we found the road, the noise had ceased.

We started down the road, more concerned about getting away from there than deciding on a destination. I'd worry about that once I found out where we were. I had my arm around Marie-Celeste's shoulders, and she snuggled close.

"As soon as we find a place to stop, we need to have a long talk," she said, already sounding tired. "I don't even know anything about you."

"I'm training to be a *houngan*," I offered.

She gave me an approving glance, and I smiled.

Anything, so long as she kept looking at me like that.

INHUMAN RESOURCES

Jeanine McAdam

"You really have got to stop looking for adventure and find a job," my mother told me in a not-very-nice tone of voice. My mother never gave me attitude. I wasn't sure what was up with her.

"I don't want any old job," I groaned. I could feel my fingers tightening around the milk carton I was holding. "And I can't work a desk job," I explained while pouring the milk onto my Frosted Flakes. "I'll lose my mind."

"Claire, you are twenty-one years old," she said as she added sugar to her second cup of coffee. "I won't support you any longer. I've given you plenty of time to find yourself. College wasn't your thing and I understand, but if you want to live here you're going to have to start paying rent."

I sighed big time. As my shoulders went up and down, I could feel a muscle twitch in my neck. I decided to fight back.

"I can't believe my own mother is kicking me out," I countered. Maybe a good healthy guilt trip would get her to back down.

"Don't you even try that on me—" she warned.

"I'm going to apply again to the police force," I interrupted.

"They're not going to take you," she said bluntly. "You can't say things like you enjoy reenacting *Star Wars* if you want to be considered." She looked me up and down. "You should have told them you watch *Law & Order*."

I rolled my eyes. She could be annoying. Maybe she had a point. I shouldn't have said anything about playing Princess Leia but I thought it'd make me interesting. After all, their advertisement at the bus stop said they were looking for diversity.

"What do you have in mind?" I asked her grudgingly. My mother always had a plan.

She smiled. I hated when she smiled like that. All the creases in her face folded up to her eyes and her chin wobbled. "There's a new insurance agency a few miles off Route Seven." She pointed at me. "My friend Irene tells me they need a receptionist."

Office work. It was always nine to five, health insurance, retirement, and a life of stability. That was my mother's mantra. Be more like your sister, she's got a nice job at the bank. Susan was also deadly boring with her loan officer job, white picket fence, and two well-behaved children.

My mother continued speaking, not even noticing my face contorting into a painful expression. "I think this is right for you," she said with a definitive nod of her head. Then she stood, coffee cup in hand. "I've been tolerant through the mountain ranger, ski patrol, lifeguard, and police officer phases." In the doorway she added, "My patience has run out, Claire Defoe. I know you want to live boldly but you've got to pay the bills."

"I'm here to inquire about the job," I said to the pale woman sitting behind the reception desk the next day. When she didn't return my half smile, I decided it was the florescent lights sucking the life out of her. I vowed that if I got the job, as soon as I started resembling her, I'd quit.

Without looking up from the computer screen she moaned, "Ake a sea." She sounded like she had about a dozen marbles in her mouth and that neck brace she wore held her chin firmly in place. After she shifted her eyes towards one of two tweed chairs, I got her meaning. I sat.

About ten minutes later a hunched-over man with skin even paler than the receptionist came out of the back office. He nodded. I nodded back as I watched him ease himself into the chair next to me. It seemed he had low back pain.

"Can you answer the phone?" he asked. His voice was just as hard to understand as the blonde with the ooze running out of her nose.

"Yes," I said.

"Say Sibboleth Insurance," he challenged. It sounded like his tongue was either missing or not working properly. It seemed he couldn't press it against his front teeth to make the shhhh sound.

"Shibboleth," I replied with a particular emphasis on the *sh*. My mother told me they were really picky about the pronunciation of the agency's name.

Most of my job interviewers checked my references, ensured I had a high school diploma and enough stamina for the work. Nobody quizzed me on pronunciation. If this was office work, I didn't like it. As soon as I got my paperwork in order, I planned to reapply to the police department.

On my third day at Shibboleth Insurance a man around my age came through the double doors. My coworkers had gone to lunch and not invited me. Well, what did I care? The best way to describe those two was pathetic. Besides the coughing and wheezing, they both had carpal tunnel syndrome, bad backs, and red eyes. Mr. Nil was now wearing a neck brace and wrist bands like Eliza's.

"How can I help you?" I asked the man with a mop of black curly hair and three different cell phones attached to his belt. He wore his jeans a little short and his eyes were hidden behind thick black glasses. He shifted from heel to heel. "Is Mr. Nil here?" he demanded.

"No, he is not," I said, trying to sound like a receptive receptionist. My mother told me I needed to be bright and cheery to hold onto my job.

"What about Eliza?" he challenged.

I couldn't understand why anyone would want to see my drooling co-worker. Instead of questioning his intent, I shook my head and leaned over the desk. "They're out to lunch and nobody invited me," I added as I let my lower lip fold down. "I'm sure you know what it's like to not be invited to lunch."

Since this stranger was nerdy looking to the max, I figured

he could recognize the feeling. Not that I cared much about lunch. I was just trying to bond with the customer.

After I said that he looked at me more carefully. I couldn't blame him for getting on his high horse. After all, I'd just insulted him. "You're not pale," he said stiffly. "And you've got a sharp tongue." He didn't sound offended by my words—more interested.

"I do not," I defended myself. Well, maybe I did but this was the first time I'd wagged it since joining the Shibboleth Agency. Plus what I said to this stranger wasn't that bad. Exclusion was a universal feeling. At least to me.

Then he reached over and touched my thumb. "Firm skin," he said mostly to himself as I pulled my hands away and folded them in my lap.

"I'm twenty-one," I clarified, slightly offended. Not that a nerd could get under my skin.

"Okay," he said mostly to himself as he took a step back. "They've hired a human."

Then he took another step back and seemed to realize he needed to explain all this to me. But he didn't. Instead he said in a cryptic way, "I'll be back."

He turned and pushed at the door. It was actually a pull door so it took him a minute. As his head bounced against the glass, I couldn't help but notice his butt. It was firm and those black jeans he wore accented him in an athletic way. Not what I expected on a guy who pushed his glasses up his nose at least fifteen times while he stood in front of my desk.

After the nerd left, Mr. Nil came back. "Could you come into my office?" he requested politely. Then he moaned, which was a little weird but I was getting used to it. If I spent my entire adult life at Shibboleth Insurance, I think I'd moan a few times too.

"Have a seaaaa," he said unable to emphasize the sound of the t. I wondered what had happened to his tongue. Maybe he bit it or someone cut it. I couldn't imagine and decided not to ask because now he had a Band-Aid on his chin.

"Did you get into a fight during lunch?" I asked as I curled my fingers around my palm.

"What?" he replied, trying to lift his eyebrows.

I explained quickly. "The bandage on your chin." I pointed at him. "Did someone hit you?"

"No." He shook his head. "It's shingles." It took a lot for him to get his mouth around the word.

"Oh," I replied. My mother would have wanted me to say something like "I'm sorry" or "too bad" but I didn't. It sounded disgusting and I couldn't muster the sympathy. After he asked me a few questions about the phone messages, he told me to go to lunch. He didn't inquire about my visitor and I didn't volunteer the information.

Later, when I was in the café, a familiar voice said, "Hey."

I looked up from my ham sandwich. It was nerd boy.

"Hey," I responded, wondering why he was still hanging around.

"How long have you worked for Shibboleth?" he asked as he sat down across from me and planted his elbow on the table.

Hadn't nerd boy's mother taught him any manners? "Get your elbow off my table."

"Sorry," he replied. The left corner of his mouth lifted as he folded his hands neatly in front of his chest and squared his shoulders.

"Three days." I frowned. Then I took another bite of my sandwich. "You followed me," I accused.

He nodded. "I think you're in danger," he said in a low voice.

Since it was nice being around someone who could pronounce his vowels, I decided to hear him out. Plus I was still feeling a little freaked out by that thing on Mr. Nil's jaw. I leaned forward. "What kind of danger?"

"Do you know anything about the undead?"

As he spoke the door opened and a cool breeze flooded the cafe. My hair blew across my face. I pushed a few wisps off my nose and shook my head. When I first sat down that little bell above the door sounded quaint; now it was creepy.

"What do you mean, the undead?" I asked warily.

"Corpses that rise from the grave?" His blue eyes never left mine. Then he shook his head. "But that's not the case with these two. I think they were bitten because they still have human qualities." He had the tone of someone who knew what he was talking about. "They could be paper pushers counting their days until retirement or flesh-eating monsters looking for their next meal."

This was ridiculous. Besides being a geek with bad hair, this guy was missing a few screws. I rewrapped my sandwich and threw it in the bag. "If they're hungry," I said dryly. "I'll bring them the leftovers."

"Okay," he replied as he stood. He was trying to act casual but he was too much of a type A person to pull it off. "Sounds like you know what you're doing." Then he awkwardly dug into his pocket and threw his business card on the table. His momentum was off and it skidded to the floor. "Call me if anything happens," he suggested, picking it up and putting it under the salt shaker. Then he headed for the door. Again he couldn't figure out it was a push. After a few pulls he finally got himself outside.

The card said, "RAFE THAYER, ZOMBIE HUNTER." Included was his e-mail address, Facebook page, Twitter account, and cell phone number.

That night I looked him up on Facebook. His wall discussed the best way to kill a zombie. One-Eyed William recommended a head shot. Clever Carrie liked a clean cut with a machete, and Dainty Dan used acid. The fight continued until Rafe posted. He agreed with Dan that in the right situation acid could work, but William's and Carrie's weapons were the most effective in disposing Satan's army quickly. His opinion seemed to be final and the thread moved on to determining the difference between a zombie and an office worker.

The group established pale skin, rounded shoulders, and red eyes were common symptoms of a typical office worker, plus coughing and sneezing due to poor air quality. The difference between those punching the clock and the undead was

the skin. If it was peeling or falling off in chunks, most definitely a zombie. Plus they moaned more often than office work-
ers and Carrie posted a chart to aid the zombie hunter in
determining the difference.

I thought of Mr. Nil and Eliza. No, it couldn't be. I told myself Rafe was a crazy person who found others like him on the
Web. I couldn't associate with these people. Even though my
fingers were itching to get on the keyboard and offer an opinion, I knew it wasn't possible. If I wanted any future with the
police force, I had to keep my thoughts to myself. This was
much worse than dressing up like Princess Leia.

I decided to call Rafe instead. Not surprisingly, he picked
up after the first ring. "Hello, Claire," he said, all smug.

"There's a big difference between zombies and overworked
insurance agents," I said without even bothering to engage in
any formal greeting.

He knew exactly whom I was talking about. "I'll give them
the hunched shoulders and wheezing as typical for paper pushers," he said. "But do they have red eyes?"

I couldn't believe how superior he was acting. Didn't anyone tell him that sort of behavior wasn't very attractive?

"Yes," I conceded. "That's because they are on the computer
all day." I wasn't ready to let him win the point. Plus zombies
weren't real. The only place they existed was in bad horror films
and the imaginations of people like Rafe.

"They are turning into zombies," he said.

"Do you have proof?" I asked.

"No, I don't—"

"Well," I interrupted. "I guess this ends our conversation." Then I hung up. Maybe I was rude, but he was a weirdo. Did he even have a job?

The next morning when I pulled into the parking lot at work, Rafe was waiting for me. If I didn't think he was harmless, I would have been concerned. This was the second time he stalked me in two days. If my mother knew about this, she'd make me call the police.

I scratched my head after I got out of my car. Rafe was leaning against a rusty VW Rabbit. His arms were folded over his chest and his legs crossed at the ankle. He looked just as smug as he'd sounded last night. I reminded myself he was a loser.

Without a glance his way, I marched across the parking lot.

"Would you like protection?" he asked the side of my face. He still hadn't peeled himself off his car.

I rolled my eyes and turned towards him. "What kind of protection?" I demanded.

He held something up. A travel bottle in a Ziploc sandwich bag.

"What's that?"

The left corner of his mouth lifted. He looked kind of cute when he did that. But remember, I said kind of. Also, he wasn't my type. I liked outdoorsy guys.

When he didn't answer, I reached for the baggie. He pulled it away. He was taller than me and held it over his head. I wasn't going to give him the satisfaction of watching me jump. Instead

I took a step back. "Look," I warned, "I'm tired of your dorky games and I'm late for work." I turned towards the building.

"It's acid," he said as he scurried up behind me.

"Acid." I started to walk faster. I should have listened to my first instinct and called the police. This guy was a threat. On second thought, if I wanted to join the police force, I probably needed to handle this situation myself.

"I can't send you in there with a shotgun or a machete," he explained quickly. "The acid is in a compact and will disable them so you have time to escape."

I screwed my face up and gave him a funny look.

He shrugged his shoulders. "Listen." He smiled at me. His teeth weren't exactly straight but there was an attractiveness to his lopsided grin that I liked. "Just pretend you've got to mist your face, then turn it on the good folks at Shibboleth Insurance."

He actually seemed to be enjoying this. I didn't feel the same way. "That thing won't leak in my purse?" I asked suspiciously. "I don't want to permanently disfigure myself." It wasn't like I was picture-perfect beautiful, but I did have a cute dimple on my chin and a nice smile.

"No." He shook his head. "It's sealed." He pressed the bottle into my hand.

Just to humor him, I took it. At the end of the day, I planned to bring it back along with the name of a good therapist. A Google search should help me find someone in the area who specialized in delusion.

When I arrived at my desk Eliza moaned at me. Her wrists were still covered with bandages and that neck brace was wrapped even tighter around her chin. Plus she had a new problem. Sores were oozing along her jaw line. Maybe if she loosened the brace it would give her chafed skin a chance to heal.

Around noon, Mr. Nil invited Eliza and me into the conference room for a lunch meeting. It was nice to be included and after grabbing my brown bag, I eyed the Ziploc baggie. *What the heck,* I thought as I stuffed it into my sweater pocket and looked over my shoulder to ensure Eliza hadn't seen me.

Mr. Nil motioned for me to sit at the head of the table. He and Eliza took their places on my left and right. I put my work folder down and pulled out the turkey sandwich my mother made for me. She also packed in three Oreo cookies. I could tell she was happy I had a job.

Deciding the polite thing to do was wait for my co-workers, I folded my hands on top of the table and smiled at them. With a moan of triumph, they grabbed my thumbs and started pulling my fingers towards their mouths. "Hey," I yelled, trying to jerk loose while my Oreos spilled to the floor. With a shake, I was finally able to get Eliza to give up. With my free hand, I reached for my pocket and pulled out the acid. Unfortunately it was still in the Ziploc bag.

"Stop," I demanded as Mr. Nil pressed my index finger against his chapped lips. He was pretty strong and I put my foot on his knee to hold him back. "Damn," I said as I felt Mr. Nil's teeth against my skin. Eliza didn't seem to notice my curses because she was trying to grab at my other hand again. As I worked at opening the bag, I dodged her attempts.

Finally I had my fingers wrapped around the spray bottle. Just as she reached for my pinkie, I pumped a few squirts her way. The acid soaked into the back of her hand and she cried out in agony. In the blink of an eye, I could see her tendons and brown bones.

I realized Rafe was right. They were zombies. Satan's Army of the Undead.

Without hesitation I turned on Mr. Nil. He cried out "acid," and let go of my hand.

"Don't come near me." I held the spray bottle in front of him. "You belong in your grave," I told my boss while I grabbed my purse and backed slowly towards the door.

"Please," he groaned. "Help us." He pulled off the bandages covering his chin. "We need food," he cried while chucks of bloody flesh fell to the table.

My stomach rolled and instead of barfing I turned and ran. I could hear them behind me. "Get her," Mr. Nil told Eliza as I ran through the reception area and towards the double doors.

Rafe was outside, sitting on the hood of his car, and I immediately felt bad for every insult I had lobbed his way. "Start the car," I yelled, deciding I would apologize later. "Start the car," I said again when he didn't react. I glanced behind me and could see the zombies piling up at the glass door. When Rafe saw them he jumped into the driver's seat and turned the Rabbit over.

A moment later I opened the passenger-side door. "They are

zombies," I cried out. Like he didn't know. He peeled out of the parking lot as I closed the door. "They tried to eat me," I said, pulling my seat belt on and waving my hands around.

"Did they bite you?" He took his eyes off the road and studied me carefully.

"Oh no," I cried thinking of the gnawing Mr. Nil did on my knuckles. I held my hand up. There were teeth marks and it was red. "Am I going to turn into a zombie?" I moaned.

"Did he break the skin?"

"I don't know," I cried.

After glancing one last time in the rear view mirror, Rafe pulled over. "Let me see," he demanded. We had stopped next to the river. I could hear the water running as he turned towards me.

"Will they come this far?" I asked.

"No," he said. "They don't like water." He held my finger in the palm of his hand. "Did you acid them?"

"Just Eliza and it was only a little on her hands," I explained. "I threatened Mr. Nil and that was enough to get him to let go of me."

"His teeth are soft. He couldn't break the skin," Rafe said. "So you're not infected."

"I won't turn into a zombie," I clarified.

"No." He hesitated. "But now that he's tasted you, he's not going to give up." He pulled his eyebrows together. "He's going to want to finish his meal."

"You mean." I breathed heavily. "He'll come after me?"

"And if he gets you," Rafe said, grimly putting the car in gear and stepping on the gas, "you'll spend the rest of your days pushing papers at Shibboleth Insurance Agency."

That sounded worse than death. After absorbing that thought for a minute or so, I asked, "What are we going to do?"

"Go to my house," was the answer without explanation.

Rafe lived on the water. It was a big house with a wide front porch and a rolling lawn. There were three or four fancy cars in the driveway. It seemed Rafe was doing well killing the undead. Maybe I could forget about the police force and join him.

We stepped into a marble entryway after he opened the front door and threw his keys in the silver bowl on the credenza. "Ronnie!" a voice called from the living room.

"Mom, I'm busy," Rafe replied.

"Come say hello to my friends."

Rafe turned to me with a pained expression on his face. I decided to not comment on his pseudonym because I could commiserate with the meddling-mother problem. "My mother doesn't know about my zombie work," he explained through clenched teeth. "To keep her out of my business, I have to perform a few social niceties every once in a while."

When we entered the living room, four women were sitting around a card table. I guessed they were playing bridge. Rafe's mother had a big smile, big breasts, and wore tan pants with a pink cardigan sweater.

"Ronnie, how are you?" one of the other women asked in a snarky tone. "Do you have a job?"

Even though we had a lot less money, the words sounded exactly like ones spoken at my house. People could be so mean.

"I'm doing this and that," Rafe replied as he looked at his shoes.

This annoyed me. The woman was insulting him. He wasn't doing this and that, he was saving humanity from those flesh-eating, brain-dead creatures living in our village. "He's doing a lot," I taunted. "As a matter of fact, he saved—"

"Come on, Claire." Rafe pulled on my arm. "Let's go downstairs. I've got a new video game I want to show you."

"What?" I said to Rafe as he dragged me out of the room.

Once he had the basement door open, he turned on me. "They can't know what I do," he hissed. "To them I'm just a jobless, PS3-playing loser living in my mother's basement."

"Why not?" I protested. "You're saving—"

He interrupted me again. Rafe couldn't open a door but he certainly could get his point across when he wanted. I kind of liked that. "Do you think they'd believe me if I told them zombies lived among us?" he snapped at me. "Or do you think I'd be thrown in the loony bin?"

He pounded his chest. "Right now, I'm the only line of defense between the good people of this town and those flesh-eating monsters."

Okay, he had a point. I snapped my mouth shut as he led me down the stairs to his basement. Once we were past the washer and dryer, which I might add were high-end and brand-new, Rafe pushed his way through a door. When he turned on the light I felt like I was in Dexter's laboratory. Computers lined one wall. Maps papered the other and a pink rug covered the floor.

"This used to be my sister's playroom," he said quickly when he noticed me looking at the rug. "She moved to Boston and found an acceptable job."

I nodded. The story sounded familiar.

Rafe treaded across the room towards a grey cabinet on the far side. With a devil's grin, he opened the doors. An array of guns were pegged on a board inside. Light reflected off their shiny barrels and black handles. He pulled out a pistol and turned towards me.

I blinked a few times.

"Do you know how to shoot?" he asked, completely ignoring the stunned look on my face.

I nodded.

"Good," he said grimly. "It's only a head shot." Without asking my permission, he strapped a gun belt around my waist and tightened the buckle at my thigh. I know my reaction was completely inappropriate, but there was some tingling happening down there, especially when his fingers brushed my inner thigh.

"What are our next steps?" I asked and cleared my throat.

"We go back and kill them," he said.

"Okay," I breathed. Suddenly I was in deep. Really deep. I lifted my chin and knew I could do this. After all, wasn't I looking for action?

When we got back to the office things hadn't changed.

"How—how do we do this," I asked Rafe. I ignored the catch in my voice and he did too.

"You put a bullet in the head of the girl and I'll take care of Mr. Nil." He passed me a pair of black gloves. I hesitated in taking them from him.

"Claire, if we don't do this, they will kill again," he said firmly. "We must protect our community."

Since he put it that way, civic duty was something I could feel comfortable with. "Do the police know?" I asked him.

"We won't get arrested, if that's what you're implying," he explained while climbing out of the car. He was two steps ahead of me and looking pretty confident as he swaggered up the walkway to the building. He didn't have any problem with the door when he held it open for me.

Eliza sat at her desk. Before she had a chance to moan Rafe commanded, "Eliminate her."

I lifted my gun, sighted her eyeball, and pulled the trigger. She splattered all over the desk and computer screen. Before I had a chance to say anything, Rafe was in the other room taking care of Mr. Nil. Our job was done.

After we left the building, Rafe put his arm around my shoulder. "I sensed something in you, young Claire Defoe," he said, sounding a lot like Obi-Wan Kenobi. "You did good," he added.

I smiled and placed my head on Rafe's shoulder. "Do you think I'll be doing this again?" I asked as we approached his car. Maybe the police force wasn't right for me. Maybe fighting zombies was my calling.

He nodded. "You've got the talent and there are always zombies to kill." Then he opened the passenger door for me. "Do you want to get something to eat?"

"Are you taking me out on a date?" I teased him. I was feeling a little giddy after putting a bullet through Eliza's head.

"I guess I am." He smiled at me and pushed a piece of hair behind my ear.

Feeling like I had nothing to lose, I leaned over and kissed him. Since he was a nerd, I could tell he didn't know if he should kiss me back. So I let my tongue sink deeper into his mouth and he quickly got my meaning.

Rafe may not know his pants are too short or how to open a door, but he can kiss and he can kill the undead. At that point in my life, those qualities were everything I wanted in my zombie-hunting boyfriend.

THE MAGICIAN'S APPRENTICE

Stacy Brown

Carla Nash just couldn't believe the note she held in her hand.

Dearest Carla:

I've been thinking about you recently. I would love to see you again. Please have my office arrange a flight at my expense and be my guest in Vegas. There's so much I need to tell you.

Love,

Ray Stellar

She was shaking.

Carla had always loved Ray. She loved him in kindergarten when she would chase him into the arts-and-crafts closet and kiss him until he squealed. She loved him in junior high when he would play his exploding chewing gum and plastic dog crap jokes on her. And she loved him in high school when she would allow him to practice his lame magic tricks and sleight of hand on her to impress the cheerleaders who would never give him the right time of day.

But Carla always knew Ray didn't feel the same way about

her. Her best friends said he used her, but she just told herself he didn't appreciate her love yet. After he knocked up yet another tall, thin, big-breasted bimbo, while bedding her on the side, she'd had enough. She moved to the West Coast, where she got her degree in massage therapy, a nice pair of C implants, and a yearlong tan, and broke the hearts of wannabe actors who thought her love was the real thing. But she would always love Ray.

Carla packed her bags and drove to Vegas. She sublet her apartment for the month of June. She just knew this was it, that Ray had finally figured out that no woman on Earth would ever love him like she did.

Ray had a penthouse suite at the Mirage, where he performed six days a week. She loved driving down the strip and seeing those huge billboards touting Ray as the future of magic. She couldn't wait to get there and give him the love she always felt he deserved.

They knew who she was when she checked in. Her bags were whisked away to "Mr. Stellar's suite." She had imagined this moment for years—in the shower, driving through L.A. traffic, rubbing the aches and pains of her Botoxed clients. It was her favorite daydream.

Ray greets her at the door and takes her in his arms, smothering her with kisses. Finally, he pulls away and looks into her eyes, saying, "Carla, I've been a fool. I never realized how much I loved you. Will you ever forgive me?"

But, of course, that was not what happened.

The door to the suite opened and Antonio, Ray's high school sidekick who always unnerved her, greeted her. How could she have forgotten about Antonio? Half the time Ray was begging for a blow job in the back seat of his dad's car, Antonio was driving and trying to watch in the rear view mirror. She could never decide if he was in love with Ray or with her.

"Hello, Carla," Antonio said, leaning in to give her a kiss on the cheek. "You look wonderful." He looked first at her face, then let his gaze travel down her body in an oddly intimate appraisal, one that actually sent a charge through her. She'd spent so much time and money on this new and improved body, it always gave her a thrill when someone noticed just how hot she was now.

She took a good look at him. He was so much better looking—the pimples were long gone and he'd grown out his hair from the crew cut his overbearing parents always made him wear. His once-awkward lean body had been replaced by lanky muscle, and he appeared pierced in all sorts of interesting places.

"You look pretty good yourself, Antonio," she said. And relaxed.

"It's Tony, now," he said. "No one calls me Antonio anymore, except Ray."

She thought she remembered hearing through the Central Valley High grapevine that his parents had both been killed in a fairly gruesome car accident, leaving him pretty well off.

"Well, Tony," she said, rolling his new name around on her

tongue. "I'm kind of surprised to see you're still with Ray after all these years."

"He's my . . ."

Ray breezed into the room from an inner hallway, and spun her around to face him. "Hey, baby," he said, stepping, back and looking her over. "You look hot!"

Ray was not as handsome as Antonio, or even as well built, but he was a natural performer who had finally blossomed— if a man could blossom—into his body. At thirty, he exuded charm. Carla melted.

Carla spent the next two weeks in a Ray trance. They were connected at the hip. He set her up in her own adjoining suite, and bought her every dress and bauble and cutesy stuffed animal she'd ever wanted from him. Aside from performing, Ray never left her side.

Then one night he sent Tony over to tell her she should wear something very special. They were going to have a big night. When she tried to wheedle information out of Antonio, he just shook his head.

"You don't approve?" she asked, hurt by his lack of enthusiasm for them as a couple.

"It's not that. You and Ray mean the world to me." He started to say something, then shook his head again. "Just be careful with Ray. He's a showman."

She wore her new little black Zac Posen dress and a diamond necklace Ray'd given her that said, "Forever." She loved it. She loved him. And she was sure he finally loved her.

Although he hadn't said it yet. But she knew men were like that.

They went to Alex, the most expensive and extravagant French restaurant on the strip, and Alessandro Stratto actually came and talked to them while they dined. Moments like this made it hard to believe this was finally her life.

Finally, after the meal had been served and eaten, Ray took her hand and began to say what she hoped would be the magic words she'd been dreaming of since she was five.

"Carla, I have something really important to ask you. You don't have to give me an answer right away, but you're the only one I could ever ask."

She couldn't believe this was finally happening. God, she loved him so much. She wished she could stay frozen in this moment forever, staring into Ray's brown eyes looking at her so intently.

"I know you love me, and that you've always loved me. You told me once that you would die for me."

Yes, she had said that once, in high school, when he'd literally thrown her out of bed to make room for Eileen Reardon, who chewed him up and spit him out. Carla had put him back together again. It was not one of her favorite Ray memories, and she wasn't overjoyed that he brought it up at a time like this.

"I need you to die for me now."

"What?" She pulled her hand away, and pushed back against the booth they were sitting in. Had she heard him right?

He came around and sat next to her in the booth, then put an arm around her.

"I sent Antonio to study the black arts in Haiti. He's a master now. I need you to let him put you under, so to speak, so you can be in my show. He can always bring you back."

She squirmed away, feeling the steak's béarnaise sauce churning in her stomach. She felt like she did in high school, when she'd learned he'd been sleeping with her younger sister for six months. She felt used.

She stood up and pushed him away.

He fell to his knees. "Please, Carla, I'm begging you. Please do this for me. I'll make everything up to you." His stage voice bellowed and everyone in the restaurant was watching them now. She couldn't help thinking that this was going to be on *Inside Edition* and *TMZ* tomorrow.

She didn't know what came over her, but she said, "Yes, but only if you marry me."

"Whatever you want," he said, and hugged and kissed her. Alessandro came over with champagne. Desserts appeared out of nowhere. Minor Vegas celebrities and old Vegas locals with money came over to congratulate them.

In the morning, she woke up alone, and thought she'd had this really weird dream about Ray asking her to let him kill her.

But when she got out of the shower, Antonio was sitting on her bed waiting for her.

"I can't believe you agreed to this," he said, shaking his head again.

"I love him," she said, trying to explain.

"I know. We all know, but it's not enough."

"He's going to marry me."

"Oh, Carla," he said. "The only one Ray loves is himself."

"But I promised him," she said, suddenly wondering what she had agreed to. "I'm going to be okay, right?"

Antonio stood, took her face in his hands, and stared into her eyes. It was such a surprisingly intimate gesture that it took her breath away for a moment.

"I love you, Carla, and I would never let anything truly bad happen to you, but this is a bad thing you've agreed to. Anyone who truly loved you would never ask it of you, but as long as you love Ray, there is no escape."

"I love Ray," she said sadly.

"I know," he said again. "Carla, please remember this. I can only save you from the fate you have chosen for yourself if you are loved back by someone."

She nodded, not sure she understood.

"No matter what happens, just remember that I love you."

Carla bought a Vera Wang wedding dress. Ray let her redo the Mirage suite in Target Modern. She hung all her new dresses in Ray's walk-in closet and had shelves built for all her new shoes. She was happy.

She did notice that Ray kept her suite of rooms, and she

thought she saw the hotel staff move a coffin into the room at one point, but she understood that the trick she was going to help him with involved her playing dead. He'd had her fitted for a whole bunch of glittering magician's apprentice costumes that showed way too much of Carla's toned flesh, but they seemed to make Ray happy, and more than anything in the world she wanted to make Ray happy.

On the day Antonio was to put her under the spell, Ray asked her to wear one of the sparkly rhinestone Danskin outfits. He even did her hair and makeup, which she thought was a little weird. She looked a little too hooker-ish for her taste, but she knew he was applying makeup to be seen from the audience.

Antonio knocked and came into the suite.

"Whaddya think?" Ray asked, stepping back from Carla as if she were a painting.

"A vision, Ray. I will always remember her like this." He took a camera from his pocket and asked them to pose.

Then he locked the suite doors and said, "Are you ready, Carla?"

"Ready as I'm ever gonna be, I guess." Because she really didn't believe this was going to work. She knew how all Ray's tricks were done. There was no such thing as magic.

Antonio asked her to sit on the new couch. He pulled a cloth bag out of his pocket and sprinkled some sort of ash into his hand. He took her hands and looked into her eyes again.

"Remember what I told you the other day?"

"Yes," she said, nodding her head. He was freaking her out a bit, but it was nice to know that two hot guys loved her.

He blew the ash into her face, and that's the last thing she remembered.

Carla was dreaming. She felt like she'd been dreaming endlessly, and her dreams were not pleasant.

She dreamt that she died. There was a big Vegas funeral, with her body driven down the Vegas strip. She saw her mother crying, and her sister, Valerie, was there too. She saw Ray comfort her as her own coffin closed, and Carla got the distinct impression that Ray and Valerie were going to pick up where they left off in high school.

But her head hurt when she thought too much.

It felt like days had passed. Carla woke in her old suite at the Mirage, without the Target Modern furniture. She tried to sit up, but she had no energy or muscle tone. Everything felt wrong. She tried to call Ray, but she couldn't seem to get the words out.

"*Aaaaaaay,*" she said, and he came running in.

"It worked," she heard him shout.

Ray moved her to a sitting position and smothered her with

kisses, but she couldn't feel anything. But she remembered she loved Ray, and the trace of a smile graced her chapped and over-lipsticked lips.

She saw another man in the room. *Antonio,* she thought. But thinking about him too much made her head hurt.

Because she was starving. All she could think about was eating. She thought about a burger—raw. Or Ray. She wanted Ray.

Ray took her hand. She could smell him. He smelled good, like grilled meat.

"Sweetheart," he said, "you're going to be my new apprentice in this trick. Remember?"

But Carla didn't remember anything. She looked at his tanned hand holding her very pale one and wanted to bring it to her lips.

"So in this trick, I'm going to cut you in half and put you back together in front of the audience, okay?"

Antonio watched them. "She needs to eat," he said.

"Well, then, get her something."

Antonio called room service.

"So, sweetie, I'm going to test this to make sure it works, okay?"

Carla grunted, but it wasn't in acknowledgement. It was out of hunger.

"So, I'm going to cut the tip of your pinkie finger off, and I promise to put it back on, okay?"

Somewhere in the recess of what was left of Carla's mind,

she knew she should say no, but she just couldn't seem to care. All she wanted was food.

"Eeeeeed meee," she demanded.

"Okay, after we try this little experiment, okay?"

Ray took a rather ominous-looking butcher knife and cut her pinkie just below the upper knuckle. It was neatly severed, if there was such a thing. There was no blood. He set it down on the glass coffee table and it wiggled on its own after being cut.

Carla felt nothing. She too was fascinated by her fingertip with a life of its own.

Ray grabbed the errant fingertip and pushed it back on her stub, but it fell right back off again and wiggled.

"It doesn't work like that," Antonio informed him. "You need to glue it back with fresh blood."

Ray turned his nose up. "You do it, not me. I pass out at the sight of my own blood."

Antonio laughed.

Ray picked up the knife and cut Antonio's wrist. Blood pooled. He dipped the severed end in the blood, then pushed the pinkie tip to the stub, where it reattached.

Carla has no sense of time. She is taken from her room and sawed in half and put back together six days a week, with matinees on Wednesday, Saturday, and Sunday, and a day off on

Monday. Antonio feeds her steak tartar and heals her with his blood. Ray puts her in a box every night and leaves her alone. She is always hungry for raw meat and more of Ray.

Sometimes she thinks she can hear Ray laughing in the room next door. There is always the sound of other women around him. He never kisses her anymore. Most of the time, all she can think about is how hungry she is and how much she loves him.

One day, while Antonio is washing her, Carla realizes it is Antonio that she loves. "Luf," she says, as he pours water over her head.

"Yes, I know," he says, thinking she is thinking about Ray again. He can only wash her once a week now, as her skin is so dry and her scalp is almost brittle. The years have not been kind. Neither has Ray. But he is rich.

"Eww," Carla says.

He looks into her eyes and sees it just then. He actually sees Carla's soul return to her body through her eyes.

They both smile, and he kisses her for the first time ever. Carla kisses him back. The spell is broken.

They are so much older now. Years have gone. Carla's body is actually still twenty-nine, but a dried-up twenty-nine. She looks like Antonio's fifty. Ray, on the other hand, still looks boyishly thirty-five. His face is miraculously unlined, though a little bit pudgy.

At first, Carla is angry at the lost years and betrayal. It eats at her. But Antonio's love is as healing as his blood once was. He always takes her hand, and kisses her constantly. He tells her he loves her in everything he does. She never sleeps alone. Carla realizes this is what love should feel like, and that she is loved for the first time.

However, Ray is not pleased to have Carla back. He spent every dime he made and has nothing put away. He never thought he'd have to retire. And he's pissed that both his meal tickets have found each other. This was not how it was supposed to be. But the worst of it is that the Mirage has canceled his contract and he has just days to find a new place to live.

When Ray approaches Antonio with an offer he can't refuse, Antonio knows what's coming. He and Carla are ready for Ray.

Antonio sits Ray down on the couch and deftly blows a spray of ash into his lungs.

If you're driving down the Vegas strip, I'm sure you've seen those billboards for The Amazing Carla and Tony, that goth husband-and-wife magic act with the boy-toy magician's apprentice they saw in half and re-attach every night.

SOME NEW BLOOD

Vanessa Vaughn

"I'm dead," Dan declared, slumping down to take off his shoes. I didn't want to remind him it was true.

At the moment, I felt the same. My commute home had taken a full hour. Several lanes of the freeway had been closed. I still felt hypnotized from watching the taillights inch forward ahead of me.

With a sigh, I sank down onto the bed, pulling off my high heels and dropping them to the floor. Gently, I massaged my tender soles. I hated those shoes. Sometimes they made my feet feel like they might fall right off. Hell, at times my feet *did* fall right off. But in the corporate world, it wouldn't matter if my body was coming apart in pieces. I still had to keep going strong.

Dan's presence in the room felt comforting as he loosened his tie and slid it slowly from around his neck. I liked the idea of having him near me. It made me feel stable. Safe. But he was as much of a zombie as I was these days.

He lifted the remote and switched on the ten o'clock news as we undressed. The flickering light of the screen penetrated the bedroom. The glow did not feel romantic, though, like the flame of a candle might. Instead, the illumination seemed harsh and artificial, like the all-too-bright lights of an operating room.

I rolled up my hose and pulled a floral nightgown over my head. Quietly, I arranged myself under the covers. I turned to Dan. "So how was your day?" I asked.

"Oh," he said. "Same." He made some comments about reports that were due as he settled into bed, then he looked over at me. "You?"

I shrugged and made a noncommittal noise. I didn't really want to talk about work. "I love you, you know," I cooed, touching his chin with the tip of my finger. We snuggled close and wound our arms around each another. It felt good to feel his body so close to me. Of course, it felt almost as good to just lie down and relax after the day I'd had.

We were on our sides facing one another when Dan leaned in to kiss me. I felt his lips as he eased closer. I started to feel his hand inch its way up my thigh. I hadn't really been considering sex tonight, but now it was clear that was where this was leading. I was surprised, at first. We had lost most of our uninhibited newlywed enthusiasm years ago. After a day of work, our tired bodies often responded like death warmed over. But as I felt those fingers edging higher, I started to reconsider. Perhaps he was piquing my interest after all.

I fumbled for the controller and muted the television. The room seemed suddenly quiet with the noise of the broadcast abruptly squashed, but I knew the silence would only feel awkward for a moment. Dan pulled me closer and started to roll onto his back. "Why don't you be on top this time?" he said.

Before I was conscious of what I was doing, a long sigh escaped my lips. I immediately regretted it. "Well, that's great," he said with just a hint of a smile. "I'm glad this is so difficult."

I knew he was half joking about my reaction, but I could tell he was also partly serious. "It's not like you're exactly brimming with energy tonight, either," I offered. That was an understatement. Not only were the two of us not brimming with energy, our lifeless bodies seemed barely animated. "Just tonight, why don't you be on top?" I said, trying to conjure up a flirtatious tone. "I like it when you're on top." I raised my hands slowly to his shoulders and tried to help maneuver myself below him. I could tell instantly I had made a mistake, though.

"Oh, Lucy, for goodness' sakes," he said. He wasn't angry with me, just exhausted. He leaned in to give me a peck on the cheek. Then I watched him twist onto his other side, grabbing a book from his bedside table. "Never mind," he mumbled. "Not tonight. Too tired."

For a moment, I felt obligated to protest. It seemed like one of us needed to jump in and liven things up. I knew that wasn't going to happen, though. Neither of us had any life left. The truth was that lately our lovemaking had seemed less like the explorations of frisky co-eds and more like the motions of automatons grabbing at whatever human flesh was nearest. I could hear it now—the low moans that would escape us, our stiff-armed fumbling as we reached for one another. I had pulled myself out of the grave. I could haul myself to work every morning. But I didn't have what it took to pull our sex life out of the gutter.

Dan was settling into his book. He had turned off the TV and clicked on the little reading lamp at his side of the bed. I did the same with mine. But before I settled in, I grabbed my water glass and padded into the kitchen.

As I was walking back, I passed the large picture window in the living room. Things looked dead out there at this hour. I turned the fragile crystal glass in my fingers and sipped the contents a little. It was only a little past ten, but all the houses on the block were already dark. The only signs of life were coming from the new neighbors next door.

We had been invited there for a party tomorrow. I could see them moving inside their house now. No doubt they were arranging things for tomorrow night.

The woman had seemed vibrant when I met her—almost blindingly so. She gave off quite a sensual impression with her bright red hair and colorful form-fitting clothes. I was used to wearing the dark suits I usually sported at the office. I looked down at my nightgown now and realized that my monochromatic palette had worked its way into my non-work attire, as well. Even the floral print I had on was gray.

I caught a good look at her as she passed her window again—clad this time in short shorts and a tight red top. She was laughing, and as she walked backward past the window I finally got another look at her husband, too.

There was no doubt he had an incredible physique. When I had spotted him, shirtless and toned, moving furniture into his new house, I had stolen looks at him most of the afternoon. I looked him over now and sipped my water, feeling a pull almost like hunger. The man next door was so gorgeous, I wanted to eat him right up. I could see what a magnificent body he had. Judging from the money he had to be pulling in to afford that place, I imagined he also had a mind to match.

I licked my lips as I stood in front of that window, knowing I'd fall asleep tonight thinking about that body . . . and those brains.

The next night, I sat studying my face. I looked like a monster. I knew it. But now I found myself wondering if anyone else would notice. I decided a little concealer would do the trick. With a little luck, I might even be able to fool the partygoers next door into believing I was one of them. With a few dots of makeup, I seemed revitalized. I dug deep in my drawer and even found a little color for my cheeks. Just a small dash of blush gave the illusion of real life glowing under my deathly pale skin.

I could pretend to be stylish, but that wasn't really who I was any more. Dan and I had led such a monotonous life for the past few months that even dressing for a party like this one was a rare event. My little black dress had been hanging behind my other clothes for so long, I literally had to shake a layer of dust off of it. Before I ran it through the wash, the thing almost looked like I had pulled it out of my crypt and not my closet. But by the time I grabbed my purse and threw on a coat, I almost felt like a real person again. For the first time in weeks, we had somewhere to go that didn't involve our regular haunts.

I could see Dan was pleased about our plans, too. We were also both a bit nervous. After all, we didn't know this couple well at all, and had no idea what to expect. We walked over to their nearby house at our usual ambling pace. The wind was cold, and we stumbled slowly, trying to steel ourselves against the chill and the light drizzle of rain. As I raised my hand and rapped on their front door with my white knuckles, I felt a secret pull of excitement. I had imagined being close to my free-spirited next-door neighbors for quite a while, but now the possibility of actually spending time with them made me feel a little anxious. I gripped Dan's hand and he gave me a reassuring squeeze.

The front door opened suddenly, spilling heat and light and music out into the darkness. We were engulfed by the smell of food, the sound of ice cubes as they clinked delicately against the sides of liquor-filled glasses, the illumination from warm lamps and flickering candles, and the blur of dozens of guests. I was out of place, a hibernating creature that had only just clawed its way out of a hole in the earth and now stood blinking at the sun.

"Lucy, hello!" exclaimed our hostess, shaking me out of my momentary daze. She embraced each of us warmly as we shuffled our way inside. The host stood by his wife, collecting our coats as Dan and I shrugged them off in the entryway. Jessica was puffing delicately on the end of a long cigarette. "We're so glad you could make it," she purred. "What can I get you?" She made a sweeping gesture toward the bar and gave Dan a wink.

Dan took a step forward, raising his arms toward our hostess. We hadn't eaten tonight, and the man knew what he wanted. I caught his arm in time, though, and steered him back toward me. I was worried Jessica might have noticed our little exchange. I was also worried that the sight of such fresh people could make Dan start to drool.

Oh, yes, drinks, I thought. *She asked about drinks.* I hesitated a moment. "I'm not sure," I said politely. "What do you have?"

Her husband, Jeff, stepped in. "Come with me," he said smoothly. "I'll show you." I felt relieved he had offered. I moved to his side, ready to follow him toward the bar.

Dan asked Jessica for a scotch. I looked over my shoulder at them as she led him to a nearby table covered with decanters. She lifted one and started to pour a double, but simultaneously she gestured toward a bowl filled with keys.

A sensible precaution, I thought, *to make people give up their keys at such a liquor-soaked party.* We had simply walked over from next door, but most people had probably taken their cars. I could see the need to curtail drunk driving.

I heard the soft clink of our keys as they sprawled among the others. While Dan and the hostess talked, Jeff led me silently to the far corner where there was a much wider selection of cocktails. "What'll it be?" he asked with a smile.

God, he was gorgeous. There was no doubt about it. Watching him lean back casually on the bar and shoot me that grin, I felt a sudden compulsion to discover what his lips would taste like, what his skin would taste like. I didn't know what I wanted exactly, but he just seemed so alive. I felt drawn to him reflexively, like a night creature to a flame.

Yet I resisted the instinct to devour him right then and there. Instead, I tried to focus my energy elsewhere, mulling over the simple question of what to order. I decided to take a chance. "Surprise me," I said coyly, and he liked that answer. I could tell.

"Absolutely, Lucy," he said, brushing my arm with his hand. I felt satisfaction with that light lingering sensation. A slight touch from his skin seemed to alert me to a basic need I had been neglecting, like someone dying of thirst startled to feel a drop of water soak into his tongue. For the first time in a long while, I was being flirtatious—I was being flirted *with*—and I soaked it up eagerly.

I glanced back at Dan and saw him laughing with Jessica. Good. I was glad he wasn't watching this. Jeff stepped close to me and raised a heavy glass filled with liquid. "What is it?" I asked.

"Special recipe," he answered. He had doled it out from the punch bowl behind him. One thing was certain—this concoction was deceptively drinkable, yet strong. A girl could be embalmed with stuff only slightly more potent. As we talked, I reached up and tried to smooth my hair down. I was sure I looked frightful. Coming here, Dan and I had walked through a light rain. I knew my hair had frizzed by now into an uncontrollable shape. I could picture my mass of dark unruly hair and what it might look like. I had done my best, carefully blow-drying it into smooth sections tonight, but on an evening as humid as this, it was no use. I could only do so much to mask my true nature.

Jeff saw what I was doing as I fidgeted with my curls. He was in the middle of another story, but he stopped and caught my hand. "No, don't," he said seriously. "Your hair. I love it just like that." I gave him a disbelieving sideways look. "No, really," he said. "It makes you look fearless. Like a wild thing."

I shook my hair then and laughed out loud. "Well, thank you . . . I think," I said in an amused voice. We looked at one another and the moment lingered, as if both of us were expecting more to happen. We were hovering close. But of course there could be nothing more. No kiss. After all, our spouses were only at the other end of this very room. "Of course . . . maybe just a nibble," I considered, as I eyed his neck.

Jeff ended the quiet stalemate by putting his fingers over mine and gripping my glass. "Refill your drink?" he asked, and I nodded. I hoped my host didn't notice the rolling whites of my eyes as my gaze moved around the room, hungrily examining the guests. For a second, I considered asking one of them to dance, but I quickly reconsidered. My limbs were too stiff. In my post-mortem state, I was far from coordinated. Besides, who knew what might happen if I got too close to one of these people? It would be a little hard to continue to blend in if guests started to lose their limbs.

It startled me when a man stepped up behind me. He rested an arm around my shoulders, and I lowered my new glass from my lips, trying not to spill it. The man leaned in close. "Hi, honey," he said.

I smiled at my husband. I also took a step away from Jeff, trying to make it look like the two of us hadn't gotten quite so cozy. But Dan didn't seem to notice. Jessica sauntered over a split second later. "So," she said, her eyes darting over the two men and me, "Having any fun tonight?"

We nodded and she sparked up another long cigarette. The party was at full tilt by that time. Jessica launched into a story about her new house that set me giggling for the first time in years, and Dan squeezed my shoulder, his body resting close to mine. He was laughing, too. I knew both of us were enjoying ourselves.

At that moment, though, I also caught Jessica looking into my husband's eyes just a moment too long. She touched his arm as she made another joke, and I didn't know what to think. But try as I might, I couldn't force myself to feel offended. The truth was, he was enjoying the attention from this couple and so was I. My husband always made it clear he loved me dearly. He was absolutely crazy about me—and I about him—but it was nice to feel wanted by someone new. It was nice to feel the dizziness of excitement as we talked to strangers who desired us. I remembered a time when we were dating that Dan and I felt like this all the time. I wondered if we could find a way to get that back, or if all of our quiet evenings alone would continue to feel dead.

Just then, Jessica noticed several guests preparing to leave. Despite the loud chatter and boisterous dancing from some couples present, it was getting very late in the evening. She excused herself with a smile, and a small nod toward Dan, and made her way over to the door with her husband in tow.

By that point, Dan and I were already glowing. After several drinks and more flirtatious glances than we'd enjoyed in years, there was definitely more than a little flush to our cheeks. We turned to one another and shared a feeling of disbelief at the way this evening was shaping up. And the night was still young.

The music came to a sudden halt. Every head at the party immediately lifted, scanning the room for the source of the interruption. It was Jessica they found standing by the stereo, her hand raised to request everyone's attention.

"Well," she said confidently. "The time has come for some of us to leave." She looked toward the group of people standing ready by the front door. "Yes," she said. "It's time for us to go our separate ways . . . but I do hope some of us have made some new friends." As she said this last part, she looked at two people near her who were kissing. The woman giggled back at Jessica's remark. "And now," she announced. "My husband will take over from here."

All eyes turned to Jeff who had taken his place by the large bowl of keys. I watched him as he spoke, draining some more of my drink and thinking about how perfect he looked standing there in that collared shirt with his sleeves rolled up.

It was only as I began to sense emotion from my husband standing beside me that Jeff's words began to register. This was a swingers party. *Good Lord,* I thought. *When Jessica asked me how long I had been 'in the lifestyle,' I thought she was talking about commuting to the city!* It was clear now what was going to happen. The men at the party would all draw keys from the bowl—and spend tonight with the woman who matched them.

Suddenly, I felt bewildered. I could feel Dan tensing up beside me, as well. This was unlike anything I had ever gotten mixed up in before. Yet, all the same, I couldn't stop myself from looking around the room and thinking about the possibilities. I felt a smile creep across my face as I noticed Dan looking, too. Secretly, I was thankful he hadn't left the moment all of this began. Far from it. In fact, he was watching all of this unfold as breathlessly as I was.

Every man at the party took their turn, starting with the group by the door. Eventually, the host himself reached into the bowl and came out holding a set of keys held together with a small silver bird. The key ring was mine. Unmistakably. I would recognize it anywhere. A hush fell over the party as he held them up and no one stepped forward to claim them.

Our host knew whom they belonged to, though. When there was no response, Jeff turned and looked at me. He stared me down, and I knew this pairing hadn't happened by chance. He had picked my keys deliberately.

I was sure that secretly my husband loved the idea of going through with something as bold as this. He was longing to pair up with someone at the party and have a wild night alone, just as I was. He was longing to sate himself with any piece of lively untasted flesh he saw here. So was I. But I also knew he couldn't do anything—couldn't even pretend to entertain the idea—until I expressed an interest first.

In a way, there was nothing else I could do. I stepped forward and claimed my keys, taking my place beside our host. My palms felt hot and sweaty, and I realized I couldn't remember the last time I had felt this alive. This was the nervousness of a first date, the blush of a first kiss, and a hunter's resolve all wrapped into one. I watched nervously as my husband and the other men drew keys, but mostly I was thinking about the stranger beside me. Tonight, I would find out how his body felt as I bent it into shapes he had never considered. I would find out how he tasted. As I thought about the possibilities, I could barely stand to wait.

The house emptied quickly. I nodded to Dan as he left. Even Jessica decided to go out with her partner instead of staying in. So in the end we were all alone. The two of us turned the stereo on again, and this time we danced. Our dance was slow, and the two of us didn't speak at all. I curled my arm around the back of his neck. The gorgeous stranger kissed me. And then he said he wanted more.

So I indulged him.

My response was primal. It was urgent. As our kiss lingered, I ran my fingernails hard down his back. I watched him flinch and saw blood on my palm. Then I reached for him, and I didn't hold back. I nibbled at his ear, tasting him in that one delicious spot for now—but eventually I knew I would move on to more vital areas. Jeff was already unbuttoning his pants, expecting me to focus there at any moment, but I had other plans first.

I was determined to find out what was in that head of his . . . one way or another. Did he like me at all? Maybe now I could pick his brain and find out.

Jeff's brains. And they were all mine. Now my fantasy really was coming true. As I gave into my hunger, I wondered if Dan had found someone as satisfying.

That morning, I didn't linger. I took a few swallows of coffee and pulled on my clothes. I looked at the aftermath of the night before and smiled at the impressive mess we had left behind. I wanted to playfully lie back down on the rumpled sheets and tumble there again, remembering the delicious flesh of abs and shoulder blades and thighs I had indulged in the night before. Yet even if last night had been an incredible adventure, I knew this was not where I wanted to be.

I knew what I needed, and I knew who I loved. I whispered a happy good-bye to the body resting on the bed, then made my way back over to the house next door. I raised a hand in front of my eyes and squinted into the orange slant of morning sun as I walked. This time, every step on the way felt light. I was giddy. Girlish, even.

I pulled out the ring of keys and twisted one in the lock. Only seconds later, before I had even closed the door behind me, Dan burst inside. We smiled at each other with excited knowing grins, like two cats ready to pounce.

Dan and I had been stumbling through life as the living dead, but now we felt revitalized. He kissed me right there, hugging me close and lifting me enthusiastically off the floor. When he pulled away, I could see red on his mouth. *Was that lipstick?* I wondered. But it didn't matter. He walked me down the hall quickly. My dress was unzipped before we even reached the bedroom door. He tossed me onto the bed like a shopping bag filled with new toys. I squirmed and watched him eagerly as he quickly stripped off his tie, my eyes asking him for more.

He sprang forward then, pinning me with his body, and we both had much more fun struggling for the prime position on top than we had ever had avoiding it. Eventually, he pushed his way inside, and I balled my hands into fists. He rolled roughly on top of me and held my wrists just above my head.

We had been reminded of what we wanted from one another, and now we seized it. We weren't zombies anymore. As he kissed me back, I knew it was true. All we craved was something spontaneous. All we had needed in this relationship was some new blood.

LAST TIMES AT RIDGEMONT HIGH

Kilt Kilpatrick

For one beautiful moment, I thought I'd walked in on the beginnings of a sex party right there in the teachers' lounge. Mrs. Hastings, the Home Ec teacher, lay stretched out on the table, back arched and stylish skirt scrunched up around her waist, while Principal Caruthers enthusiastically buried his face into her lap, wrestling with her sleek pantyhosed legs. At the other end of the table her pretty T.A., Ms. Foster, held her in a tight embrace and nuzzled the nape of her neck. Mrs. Hastings writhed and gasped as the young blonde pawed her sweater and ran her hands through the older woman's hair for better purchase on her neck and throat. Mrs. Hastings made soft noises as her resistance failed, and she gave up altogether trying to push Ms. Foster away.

Then the moment of wishful thinking passed, and my perception of the scene flipped inside out like a trick of origami. The wonderful retro swinging '70s orgy I thought I was seeing vanished, and I realized what was really happening. It got ugly so fast; the next moment all blood and horrible gobbling noises and poor, poor Mrs. Hastings. I think I must've made some choked sound of horror, because Principal Caruthers and Ms. Foster instantly looked up from their lunch break and spotted me. Their mouths and teeth were stained with blood and sticky twists of half-chewed flesh, and their eyes were an eerie dead-fish-belly white. They let out a ghoulish keening screech that grated on my hackles like the awful shriek of a coffin nail pulled out by a claw hammer. And before I knew it, they had abandoned the remains of Mrs. Hastings and closed in on me. But I'm getting ahead of myself.

Just a few short hours before, the world was still here and it was just another school day in paradise at Pleasant Valley High. Which meant of course that life completely sucked and I was ready and downright eager for someone to just kill me already. The day's allotment of humiliation, boredom, and degradation was being dished out at regular intervals, right on schedule. One particular highlight came in Ms. Baymiller's English class. Now, normally English class was something of an oasis in the howling wilderness of high school for me. Not only was it my best subject, but from my seat I had a stellar view of Dee Dee Carrington, head cheerleader and magically delicious über-babe.

Her short pleated skirts and tight sweaters were legendary, but when she was in her two-piece cheerleading outfit, like today, she was a downright superhero goddess. She was hard not to look at. I loved watching her dazzling honey-blond hair in that wedge cut, the way she tapped her luscious lips with her pencil when she was thinking, the way she sometimes idly toyed with her earlobe with her head lightly cocked to one side, the way she dangled her sandal off her foot as she sat back in her chair. I lived for those days when a chance exposure of skin would let me catch a glimpse of the perfect little dimples down in the small of her back. But what chance did a normal guy like me ever have with a hottie like her?

Pretty Ms. Baymiller, whom I always secretly thought had a quiet classic brunette hotness herself, had been leading us in a discussion of the Romance poets, and was reading from William Blake's "America: a Prophecy." In hindsight, one particular passage stuck out at me:

> "*The morning comes, the night decays, the watchmen leave their stations; The grave is burst, the spices shed, the linen wrapped up; The bones of death, the cov'ring clay, the sinews shrunk and dry'd. Reviving shake, inspiring move, breathing! awakening! Spring like redeemed captives when their bonds and bars are burst . . .*"

In the middle of her recital, a heavy hand thumped me on the shoulder. I jumped at the touch and turned around. It was Todd Brookshire glaring at me, of course. He was the burly, buzz-cut, no-necked star of the football team, and his steely pit-bull eyes held pure menace. He slipped me a note without a word, and jerked his head at me in what seemed to be a command to turn around again. I obeyed and surreptitiously opened the folds of paper. It said:

I WANT TO FUCK U SO BAD

I stared at it, bug-eyed. He flicked the back of my head, hard, and his voice hissed in my ear: "Don't be a spaz, McGowan! Hand it to Dee Dee!" Ms. Baymiller paused for a beat to peer over her book, then continued. No one else appeared to notice. Reluctantly, I folded it up again and as inconspicuously as I could manage, leaned over and stretched out my hand to try to get Dee Dee's attention. She remained oblivious. Slowly, slowly, I reached out and only just managed to poke her upper arm with a corner of the note.

Disaster. Dee Dee yelped in surprise, shrill enough to startle the entire class. She turned on me, her normally delightsome face in a fierce death stare at the intrusion. "Jeremy!" Ms. Baymiller called out, freezing me instantly in place. "What is that note? Bring it here."

"It's nothing, Ms. Baymiller."

"Come on, let's have it."

I panicked. If she read it I was dead. "Honest, ma'am. It's nothing. It's just—" My mind raced to come up with a reasonable alternative. "It's just . . . I—I wanted to ask Dee Dee to the senior prom." *Oh my God*, I thought. *Did I really just say that?* The class erupted in a howl of laughter and Dee Dee's face radiated outraged horror.

"Jerry McGowan, you pantywaist dorkwad geek," she said, dripping disgust. "I wouldn't go to the prom with—*you*" (she accented it like I was a used Band-Aid she just found in her bowl of breakfast cereal) "—if you were the last boy on Earth!" The class hooted again at the unexpected entertainment.

Ms. Baymiller restored order again. "All right now, that's enough." She graced me with a gentle smile and quietly added, "Jeremy, I don't think I need to read the note. Looks like you've got your answer." Her sympathetic look implied she understood the situation was not what it seemed, or maybe it was just my hopeful imagination. I crumpled the note and stuffed it in my pocket, and for the rest of the hour basked stoically in my renewed social pariah status. When the bell rang, Todd paused just long enough to snarl, "You're so dead, McGowan!" and punch me in the shoulder on his way out.

Word of my crushing humiliation in English class was spreading like a viral plague from student to student, along with fresh rumors that the new girls' volleyball coach was a lesbian and that some kid had just up and collapsed in third-period biology class while dissecting a frog—the cause was epilepsy or rabies or evil chemicals or some new super-AIDS strain, depending on who was reporting the news. I dragged myself from class to class as best I could, tugging along the lead weight of my shame through the gauntlet of my peers.

As always, P.E. that afternoon offered still more opportunities to lower my morale. In the locker room afterwards, I decided it was prudent to avoid any more attention for a little bit and hid out in the bathroom. I wanted to wait to hit the showers until everybody was gone. I passed the time giving a mental pep talk to my reflection in the mirror. It wasn't that I was a ninety-eight-pound weakling or anything; it was just that I wasn't into the lame school sports activities. Next year at junior college I'd be able to do cool sports like judo and saber fencing. I would just have to tough out high school a little longer. It sucked finally being a senior, but still being treated like a freshman. And next year I would be a freshman all over again at community college.

I critically examined the gloomy dude in the mirror. Not a bad-looking guy; he looked a bit like a young John Cusack. Unfortunately, the problem was I seemed to be stuck in permanent boy mode, like Michael J. Fox. Was I doomed to age as a Peter Pan man-boy until I finally morphed straight into some ancient leprechaun without ever achieving a respectable grownup adult he-man stage at all?

I finally padded off to the showers to wash up in solitude. Under the forgiving spray of water I was busy drowning my thoughts, so I only half-noticed what might have been a siren going off in the distance somewhere, and yet another typically unintelligible announcement over the school P.A. system shortly after that. But I remained oblivious to it all until I heard the clanging, echoing sounds of movement in the locker room—I wasn't alone in the locker room after all. I wiped the soap from my eyes to see who it was. A knot of dark shapes drew closer, approaching me with unmistakable deliberation. I felt a queasy knot of fear tighten up in my gut. They were coming to get me.

There were six of them, sauntering up like a pack of wolves. It was Todd Brookshire and his entourage of thuggy jocks. They were only wearing towels wrapped around their waists, but somehow that made them even more intimidating, as if they were Roman gladiators or a rogue gang of disgruntled Chippendales dancers. Todd stepped closer and twisted his mouth into an unfriendly smile. "McGowan, you little shit-wipe, you totally fucked up my chances with Dee Dee." *What the hell?* I thought. On what planet did that make any kind of sense?

I was in trouble. My guts twisted again and my heart started beating so loud I was sure they could hear it too. Quick as a rattle-snake, Todd snatched my towel off the wall and began coiling it into a rat's tail. Then he whipped the towel around my waist and caught the ends tight. I was sopping wet, totally naked and completely trapped. He got right in my face and pulled me up close into him, tight against his body, with only his shabby little gym towel separating our groins. Crap! I was so screwed. It felt like his mad dog eyes were burrowing clear into my skull. "I should fuckin' fuck your ass up, but you'd probably enjoy that, wouldn't you, you fucking little fuckwad fagtard? Wouldn't you? Wouldn't you?"

The dull, thumping pain in my chest was real and palpable and roaring in my ears. Then with one last boom, it stopped— and I realized that it wasn't just my terrified heartbeat. I actually *had* been hearing a very real, very loud pounding echoing through the locker room. I suddenly felt myself leave my body. My awareness left the poor naked bastard below getting abused by the gang of closet-case Neanderthals and instead focused on the new sounds getting louder: fleshy, shambling, footfalls underscored by a long, drawn-out death-rattle groan. "Guys?" I said, snapping back into myself. "Guys? Something's wrong. Can't you hear that?" Todd's beetle brow wrinkled in irritated confusion. His backup dancers simply snickered at such a pathetic attempt to escape their clutches.

It was then I caught my first glimpse of the newcomers—the water polo team, fresh from the pool, dripping wet and reeking of chlorine. They wore only their swim caps, goggles, Speedos, and fresh bite marks, still torn and bleeding. Their mouths lolled and their hands were outstretched urgently, as if pleading for help. "Todd!" I screamed in his thick fat face. "Turn around, you moron! They're right on us!" And he did—too late.

His five henchmen went down instantly, suddenly shrieking in fear like little girls as their predators took them. Their screams were incredible, echoing horribly off the tile floor and walls. Todd let me go but before he could even turn to look, they were on us. Two big former aqua-jocks tackled him to the unyielding floor. He hit it hard, with a sickening crunch. The biggest of his assailants lunged down and took a huge bite out of the center of his face, then another, trying to dig its way with its teeth to his soft brains below. Then another zombie tackled me to the ground, too.

He had me undead to rights, but my soapy and drenched buck-nekkid ass popped right out of his grasp like a watermelon seed. I slid around like a fish on the slick wet tile floor, scrambling to get away while he clawed at my torso and legs, trying to reel me back towards his snapping jaws. Somehow my crazy flailing managed to give me just enough space to kick away from him and sail across the floor of the showers like I was cavorting on a Slip 'n Slide. I sprang to my feet and ran for it, hurdling right over one of Todd's screaming, thrashing buddies and making a beeline for the exit. In hindsight, I think my would-be pursuer must have joined in on eating the fallen bully, but I sure as hell didn't turn around to look—in two seconds flat I was out the door.

I all but crashed into a squad of cheerleaders. They squealed "Omigod!" to each other in wide-eyed titillated shock and pointed at me as I skidded to a halt. As they cackled like perky were-hyenas, I was struck by déjà vu. I had been in this nightmare before, standing in nothing but my underwear at school with everyone staring and laughing at me. Naked, dripping wet, and chased by hungry zombies into a pack of tittering sex objects was a new wrinkle for me. But the Freudian analysis would have to wait. Even while I stood there catching my breath in a daze, screams started echoing down the halls. The cheerleaders looked around, startled, then the hordes came around the corner, pouring into the corridor from both ends. There were dozens of them, everyone from the cool and popular to the misfits and rejects: jocks and geeks, teachers, librarians and lunch ladies, band dorks and goths, bathroom smokers and Bible-toters, all horrific, bloodied, and corpse-eyed. They howled for our blood as they spotted us.

My protective ring of cheerleaders screamed and clung to each other for dear life; a bad survival strategy, as it turned out. In no time the dead swarm shambled up and then the zombie tide crashed in from all sides. Blood-splattered pom-poms went flying. I did the only thing a wet, naked young person could do under the circumstances. I ran back into the locker room.

Okay, granted, it wasn't the most well thought-out plan, but I desperately hoped the water polo team would still be occupied with crunching into the twitching, gurgling, still whimpering remnants of Todd and the Toddettes. They were, but it didn't help me any, since I immediately collided into massive Coach Murdock. His head hung at a weird angle, since somebody had bitten off half his neck. The giant snatched me up like I was a burrito and tried to stuff me in his mouth. I screamed louder than the cheerleaders had and started to thrash crazily, trying to keep those huge chompers at bay.

I squirmed and twisted in his arms, and got my leg up enough to stick it into his ragged neck. I straightened my leg as best I could, gritting my teeth as I strained against him. But Coach's grip remained ironclad, and I could feel my fragile rib cage about to pop in his hands. I struggled just to breathe; anvil sparks from the hammering pain inside my skull flew around obscuring my vision, then with an awful, squishy, ripping sound, my foot went right through what was left of Coach's neck. His head popped off and skittered bloodily across the floor somewhere. A full second later, his abandoned body and I came crashing down to the concrete.

Owwww . . . I got to my feet, wobbling a little, and shook my head. My ears were ringing, but I knew I had to keep moving. Why zombies weren't already crashing through the locker room door after me I had no idea, but that was fine by me. I guess the cheerleaders were ample distraction after all. I grabbed the key ring off Coach's belt and sprinted past the rows of lockers towards his office; in my peripheral vision the H_2O zombie team was still busy with lunch, though a few were already stumbling around looking for more. Quickly I let myself into the equipment room, locked the door and ran over to the big window across the room where they dispensed the towels. I was staring a few of them in the face as I slammed down the metal roll-top curtain and latched it, too.

Leaning against it, I slowly slid down to the floor, let out a long sigh and sat there a few moments, catching my breath and trying to process the events of the last two and a half minutes. Clearly, the Zombie Apocalypse was here. I felt strangely calm and accepting of this turn of events. The problem with most zombie movies is that the people in them have apparently never seen a zombie movie. But I, my friends, am a geek and proud, and I've seen more than my fair share of zombie flicks. High school was a nightmare, but this? This, I could deal with.

First, I needed to get dressed, for God's sake. I seriously doubted I could sneak to my locker and get it open without turning into a chew toy, but there were loaner gym shorts and T-shirts. I snatched some and slipped into them. I started to dry my hair—at least there were plenty of gym towels—when I heard the front door slam open and someone very much alive high-tailing it through the locker room, screaming at the top of their lungs. Again, I know it was stupid, but I made a snap decision, unlocked the door and flung it open. *Oh, so that's where the undead horde is, pouring into the building now.* As the screaming sprinter ran up I grabbed her and yanked her in, slamming the door in the faces of the two zombies right on her tail. One just managed to get a hand in; I crushed his fingers and when he pulled back I shut the door and locked it tight. They hissed and clawed and pounded to get in. So much for sneaking out later. I turned to my fellow escapee. "Hey, Dee Dee."

Damn, she was even sexier than her usual perfection, just sitting there against the wall heaving for breath, glistening with beads of sweat, her eyes wide with fear, her cute little cheerleading outfit torn in just the right places.

"J—Jerry?"

"Yeah. Take it easy, you're okay now."

"All those people—they were so horrible . . . Are they dead?"

"Yeah, I think so. Except for the, you know, walking around and eating you, yeah."

She grabbed my arm. "Jerry, they were just *attacking* us. I think they were trying to bite us. They grabbed Suzie and Tiffany, and just started biting them everywhere. All the blood . . ." Her voice trailed off, and I gently pulled my arm loose.

"I know, Dee Dee. They're zombies. That's what they do. Hey, you've got to listen to me now. We've got to find whatever we can in here and then we need to get out of here." They were beating and scratching on the door with no let-up. I was confident the door would hold up a while, but I wasn't so optimistic if they started banging on the towel window's less-impressive metal curtain. Time to take inventory. One big laundry bin with plenty of dirty towels. Significantly fewer clean ones. I started opening the cabinets.

"Jerry, do you think the girls on the squad are all dead too? Should we go out there and help them?"

"Yeah, no, I'm pretty sure that's a real bad idea. I'm kinda amazed you're not dead, to be honest with you." Aluminum baseball bats, hmm, a little light. Lacrosse sticks? Not really with those damn little nets. Discus and shotputs? Tempting but no. Javelin . . . maybe.

"Is *everybody* dead?" She stood up and hugged herself anxiously, looking around at the gloomy institutional florescent lighting, the grimly claustrophobic walls.

Basketballs, volleyballs, dodge balls, softballs, bases, track batons, Frisbees. Worthless crap, all of it. Where were all the football helmets? I inspected a catcher's mask with throat guard. That might work—damn, doesn't fit at all. "I don't know how widespread this is, but I think it's a safe bet that just about everybody here at school is a goner, or already one of them." I thought a moment. "Actually, I'm pretty sure it didn't start here on campus. I expect the whole city is affected. We may be the only survivors for a hundred miles."

She turned and looked at me, bent over in shock and arms out in a pleading gesture. "My God, McGowan, how can you just say that? How are you not freaking out? What kind of robot are you?"

Decent question, actually. The truth was that I was just in denial, keeping focused so we could get through the task at hand. I had no doubt I'd be blubbering like a baby later, but for now I just wanted to keep it together long enough to stay alive. Somewhere deep inside I was very aware that everyone I knew and loved was either dead already or shortly about to be horribly killed. My general antisocial pariah status insulated me somewhat.

"Look, Dee Dee. I'm just as upset as you are. But we've got to be strong now, see? We've got to stay sharp so that we can get out of this alive." I managed to keep my voice firm and tough. Badminton racquets? God, these things are ridiculous! I wondered where the groundskeeper shed was—that place must be chock full of machetes and pruning hooks and those sticks with the nail sticking out for spearing litter. God, one of those would be perfect.

"You're really brave, Jerry. You'll protect me, won't you?"

I nodded absently, hefting a swim trophy and approving the sharp edges of its heavy square marble base. Okay, *that* will bash a skull in nicely, I thought.

"I just wanted to say—I just wanted to say sorry for—for what happened in class today."

Yeah, yeah, I still hadn't forgotten about that funny little pantywaist dorkwad crack, bee-yotch. Jump ropes? Jump ropes . . . must be *something* we can do with all these damn jump ropes . . .

"Jerry? You saved my life, you know?" Whatever. Hey, the lost-and-found box: padlock, padlock, padlock. Math textbook. Hey, these shoes might fit me. I held one up to my foot. Rock on.

"Jerry?"

Something in the soft way she said my name that time caught my attention. I looked over at her. She was completely nude, standing in the pile of her clothes like a statue of Venus, one arm draped gracefully across her chest, the other daintily covering her loins. "I just want to make it up to you." She gently outstretched her hands to me.

I forgive you, I thought.

I turned in a daze, hypnotized by those perfect breasts, those radiant, imploring eyes, those long, beautiful legs. She cocked her head to the side and smiled invitingly. My heart began beating stronger than it had when I thought I was about to be raped in the showers or devoured by undead swim jocks. At that moment it didn't matter where we were or how many dead things just a few feet away were going nuts trying to break in and gobble up our nubile young flesh. I dropped the shoes and approached her with reverence. When we were just a step away from each other, I reached out and gingerly interlocked my fingers with hers, and let her pull me closer. All I could see was those bright eyes, those gorgeous, glistening lips, the nape of her—*holy crap! What is that on her neck?*

I flinched and jerked back. "What the hell? Dee Dee, did you get bitten?" She shot her hand up to her neck and covered the dark wet spot. "What? No! It's nothing. What's your problem, McGowan?" She wrapped her other arm around her breasts.

I tried to grab her arm. "Dee Dee, this is serious. Let me look at that bite now!"

"No! Fuck off!" she yelled, twisting away. "I said it's nothing! It's just a hickey."

"Then just let me look—"

"I said no! And you can forget about any sex, you asshole!" She knelt and snatched at her clothes. "Turn around so I can get dressed!"

"What? You're already naked. What more am I going to see?"

"JUST DO IT!"

"All right, all right . . ." I backed off and reluctantly turned, taking one last wistful glance at her fantastic ass just as she hitched up her panties.

"Turn around, you little creep!"

I left her in peace and returned to my search of the room. The tension in the air hung like psychic smog—palpable, oppressive and inescapable. She sat glowering in the corner with her arms clasping her legs, squint-eyed and sullen. I said nothing either, but inside, my mind furiously weighed hard options. For all intents and purposes, I was trapped in a cramped submarine with a time bomb. If she was bitten, then there was no option: I would have to kill her, either now . . . or when she turned. I had no choice—it was just a question of when, and I had no idea how much time I had left. I needed to watch her.

I went back to work, keeping half an eye on her while I searched. When I finally exhausted the room's contents, I reviewed my haul and outfitted myself in a sweatshirt, what I assumed was a set of lacrosse chest and shoulder protectors, along with some elbow guards, and a pair of baseball catcher's shin guards with built in knee protectors. I armed myself with a javelin, the chunky swim trophy, and perhaps deadliest of all, a screwdriver. I didn't know if any of this would be enough to carry me safely out that door, but before I ironed out the bugs in the exit strategy, I would have to deal with the more pressing Dee Dee problem.

In the meantime, she had taken the stock of clean towels and made a bed of sorts for herself. She lay down and curled up with her back to me, facing the wall, where she quietly sobbed and trembled, and eventually fell asleep to the sounds of zombies clawing the walls. For an hour I watched her, glumly and suspiciously. I knew the rules. I had to kill her. She was the most beautiful girl I had ever known, and hell, maybe the last female left on the whole planet. But I had to kill her.

For what felt like hours, I repeated my mantra and maintained my vigil. I nodded off at one point, waking with a start who knows how long later. I looked over at the body in the corner. She didn't seem to be moving. Or breathing. I stared at her, transfixed. A minute passed. Looked like it was go time. Swallowing hard, my hands sweaty, I reached over and carefully, silently lifted the trophy. I stood up slowly, and crossed the narrow room with cautious steps until I stood over her. She looked so innocent and lovely, as still as an oil painting. I could see just the barest trace of the injury on the nape of her neck. If I could just pull back her collar a little, I could know for sure.

She was as motionless as stone. I crouched down, half unaware of my own hand creeping towards her throat until I barely touched . . . She twitched, and I jerked my hand back like she was a white-hot poker. She began to make an eerie rattling deep in her throat. Startled, I took a step back and raised the inverted trophy like a club. *Kill her. Kill her now.* I took a deep, ragged breath. I tightened my grip, then grabbed it in both hands over my head. *One . . . two . . . three.*

This time for sure. *One . . . two . . . two and a half . . .* I was shaking. Her freaky throat noise stopped, and she was still again. I continued to stare at her, sweat trickling down my forehead. Then I lowered the trophy and backed away, retreating to sit down with my back to the wall on the other side of the room. I dropped my would-be homicidal blunt instrument and let my head rest on my knees as I clasped my legs and rocked back and forth, mentally and emotionally exhausted, eyes closed tight and teary. I was out of ideas, faced with some very grim realities, and all of my options had serious drawbacks. I finally sighed and raised my head, banging it against the wall repeatedly. I opened my eyes again, staring up.

It was just above me. I looked at it in disbelief for a few seconds, then jumped up and pulled out my screwdriver. It was on the ceiling above me, and I realized I could probably reach it with the screwdriver if I climbed onto the counter. Yes, it was an air duct, and if I could get it open in time then it could be my ticket out of here and I wouldn't even have to kill Dee Dee. After all, I reasoned, a zombie didn't have the brainpower to crawl up an air duct and follow me, right? I looked over at her. Nothing. I put the javelin and trophy on the counter next to me, and climbed up. I could just reach the bolts with the screwdriver. I leaned out as far as I dared, and set to work on the grate.

I removed it without too much trouble and set it on the counter. I took the javelin, the trophy, and a baseball bat for good luck, stuffed them awkwardly into a heavy canvas equipment bag, and shoved the whole bundle up into the air duct.

Before I squeezed in there, I paused and looked over at Dee Dee once more. She was still immobile, still beautiful, even with her back to me. Surely no one so lovely could be about to turn zombie on me. I just had to check on her one last time.

I crawled down again, and bent down near her. "Dee Dee?" I whispered gently. If she heard me, she didn't react at all. "Look, I'm sorry about before. It's just been a tough day, you know? I just wanted to say thanks for, well, you know, making the um, offer." Still no response; her eyes remained closed. "Okay, look, I don't know if you can hear me or not, but, well, I'm going to, um, you know, go check out the surroundings, reconnoiter, scout it out." Still no signs of life. "Okay then. Well, I'll be back in maybe an hour or so," I lied, "so . . . so I guess I'll see you then. Bye. Bye, Dee Dee." I wanted to touch her so badly. I reached down to stroke her hair. She growled. Crap!

I backpedaled across the whole room in a crazy crabwalk, jumped on the counter and scrambled up into the opening. There was an awful minute of total vulnerability as I tried to lift myself up, my dangling legs kicking in the air like crazy, thinking the whole time that Zombie Dee Dee would saunter up and start leisurely gnawing on them. But then I made it all the way up and in, and away I went. Good-bye, Dee Dee.

For a miraculous godsend the duct sure was a pain in the ass—and neck and knees, elbows and hands. It was a coffin-tight squeeze with all my new protective gear on, though they were already doing the job admirably. It was hot, cramped, pitch black, and uncomfortable. The hard metal sides echoed and thumped and boomed with my every move, and pushing the canvas bag was exhausting. My first setback came when the tunnel took a sharp bend and I couldn't get the javelin past it. After five minutes of cursing and sweaty blind fumbling, I left it behind with a heavy heart, and kept worming my way slowly forward. At regular intervals I passed over a grate, and could peer down onto scenes of carnage in progress or upturned zombie faces as they groaned in frustration and strained to reach me. I pushed on, and tried to get my bearings along the way. There were occasional side tunnels branching off, but I resisted the urge to explore them; the last thing I wanted was to get lost and start going in circles.

After endless Shawshanking through the ducts, I came to a grate that offered my first break from the horror show. Below were neatly arranged desks, keyboards and monitors, coffee cups, funny knickknacks. There were no bloodstains anywhere. I had made it all the way to the admin wing. The school offices looked like heaven. I fished out the trophy and hammered down the grate. It fell with a satisfying thud. I poked my head down and gave the place a quick upside-down look-see. It was clean. I dropped the equipment bag and lowered myself down to the carpet, feeling just like a ninja.

It felt surreal to be back among normal, quiet, well-lit sur-roundings again. Soft elevator Muzak smooth-jazzed through the air. I thought I could fear faint sounds from somewhere impossible to locate. Wielding my trusty clunky trophy-hammer, I stalked past the cubes towards the doorway that led to the front desk of the school office, if I wasn't mistaken. A sharp acrid smell hit my nose as I went through the doorway. I could see that someone had barricaded the glass front double doors with heavy shelving and a big folding table. Behind the blood-smeared glass panels, nothing but zombies, stymied and gloom-ily loitering, waiting for their chance to get in.

As I stepped around the front desk, I saw the white tiles were stained with a thin, dark, reddish-black puddle spreading out from beneath the body of a highway patrolman—how'd he get here? His uniform was immaculate except for a heavily bandaged hand holding a pistol in his mouth. I stood there a moment, thinking deep thoughts at first, like, what a refreshing change to see a corpse that wasn't moving around and trying to kill you. I wondered: just how hard *is* it to pry a gun from someone's cold, dead fingers?

Then came a crash from somewhere behind me, and I jumped on the body to grab the gun, slipping a little on all the blood. Wow, rigor mortis is for real. Damn if I couldn't pry it loose even to save my life. Crap! Shit! Crap! In a panic, I gave up and instead wielded my trophy again, breathing hard, eyes darting around for attackers. Nothing was coming after me right this second, but I didn't want to get jumped from behind while fumbling with the patrolman's dead body. I stepped back around the front desk, and back into the cubes. There was an-other entrance on the back wall to a hallway behind. I moved up to it. Yes, there were definitely noises coming from there.

I crept up to the doorway and hazarded a quick peek around

the corner. The hallway was clear here, but there were several side passages and noises seemed to be coming from multiple places. I took a chance and turned left, then peered around the corner down a second corridor. There were offices on the left, an unmarked door on the right. I thought I heard a muffled cry from there, so I sucked it up and opened the door.

There they were, just like I told you before: Principal Caruthers and Ms. Foster double-teaming Mrs. Hastings on the table as she squirmed piteously and struggled in vain to put up a fight. It really was quite a sexy sight, in a pervy guilty-pleasure sort of way, until you noticed the blood and the grisly mess on their faces. And until they spotted you.

Principal Caruthers charged me first and I brought the business end of my trophy down as hard as I could right on top of his combover. The sharp marble edge chunked deep into his skull and he dropped dead in his tracks—well, you know what I mean, anyway. Sweet, pretty Ms. Foster, now just about the scariest creature I'd ever seen in my life, screeched like a banshee and tackled me to the ground. She sank her teeth right into my neck, or at least would have if my shoulder guard hadn't been there. Instead she got a nasty mouth full of hard plastic, and I pulled out my screwdriver and fished around in her ear until she stopped trying to rip me to pieces and died for good this time.

I rolled her off me and tried to retrieve my trophy from Principal Caruthers's cranium. Phew, it was in there good; it wouldn't budge, not even when I stepped on his head and pulled with both hands. Oh well, I needed to go get that patrolman's handgun anyway. I stepped back into the corridor, screwdriver at the ready, listening and looking around corners first. But I had already made too much noise. He was so silent, I didn't hear him until he was right behind me.

I caught just a glimpse of movement in my peripheral vision and then he was on me: our school mascot, Peppy the Pleasant Valley Victory Puma. He looked like he had been in a fight with a real puma, with his fuzzy suit torn and sticky with fresh bloodstains.

It was goofy, being attacked by a cartoon character, but he grabbed me with his big mittens and when I tried stabbing him in the brain the screwdriver just kept slipping off his happy oversized puma head. Worse still, the head kept slipping up and exposing his snapping teeth and the dark bib of blood on his furry suit. He had already eaten somebody, and was going to eat me too if I didn't do something quick. He slobbered and gnawed at the rim of my chest protector, trying to get at my tasty skin just beneath it. Bloody drool from his mouth, along with bone splinters and meat scraps, kept dripping into my face. Then came a deafening boom and the puma head flew backwards, along with a good portion of the zombie's head. Eugene, I think his name was. Funny guy.

"Jeremy? Is that you?" said some sweet angelic voice. I turned my head to see what the hell had just happened. It was my English teacher, Ms. Baymiller, kneeling over the patrolman with a smoking shotgun.

"There were seven of us left," she later told me in the nurse's station as she examined me for bites and cleaned me up with a wet washcloth. "There were ten for a long time. Then they snatched one of the secretaries right through the front door while we were getting the barricade up and a couple of the men ran out to save her."

"None of them made it back. The rest of us thought we'd be okay until more help came. We didn't know about how the— this infection spreads, or how fast. Then a few minutes ago, everyone with an injury started acting sick, then became erratic and violent, then, well, you saw what happened.

"Sarah—she was the nurse—she and I were in here looking after poor Eugene. We knew he'd been attacked, but we didn't know he'd been bitten. He refused to take off the costume; he was in shock and hysterical. He kept rocking back and forth, saying the suit was the only thing protecting him. I told Sarah I needed to get more shells for the shotgun from Officer Garcia and I'd be right back. That was the last thing I said to her. I never even made it that far. Everyone started going crazy at once, and Mr. Caruthers came after me. I swung the shotgun at him—hit him, too, and ran for one of the storage closets. I thought I'd be stuck in there for the rest of my life.

"And I would have, if you hadn't shown up when you did." She finished tending to my scrapes and bruises, and regarded me with a thoughtful expression. "Jeremy, it looks like we're going to have to hole up here for the night."

"That's pretty much how I saw it, too."

"And I think it's safest if we stay together in the same room."

"I couldn't agree more."

"I just want you to understand it's just for safety, right? Under normal circumstances, this wouldn't be appropriate, but nothing's going to happen—between us, you understand?"

I put up my hands. "Hey! No worries on my side of the bed. I'll be a perfect gentleman."

She smiled, a little embarrassed, and relaxed a bit. "I know you will. You're a good kid—no, a fine young man. I'm just still in teacher mode. They really drill it into our heads. You know, liability issues, protecting the youth in our care and custody."

Looking at her, I suddenly realized I would never have to write that essay on Romance Era poets now; in fact, probably no one would ever have to write an essay on Romance Era poets again.

We had grim work to do. We moved all the bodies into a utility closet on the far side of the building, and for an extra line of defense, we piled desks and chairs in the two entrances to the front office. If the zombies did manage to get through the barricaded double doors, we knew our little hallway blockade wouldn't keep them out for long either, but the racket would alert us and give us a little time, if nothing else.

We raided the nurse's station and the earthquake kit for

blankets and food, and decided the principal's office would be the best place for us to stay in. The door could be locked and there were secure windows that we could bail out of in a pinch. The teachers' lounge had couch cushions we took to make a comfortable mattress.

By then we were both exhausted and ready for bed. Ms. Baymiller locked the door, and turned off the light, leaving us illuminated solely by a rectangle of blue moonlight. I peeled off my gear and stripped down to my T-shirt and shorts. I turned away so that she could undress; she would sleep in just her blouse and panties. I politely stared at the wall and listened intently to the delicate little rustling sounds while she slipped out of her herringbone pencil skirt, unbuttoned her elegant blouse, undid her bra, and buttoned up again. I was acutely aware of her lifting the blanket and slipping into bed next to me.

"You can turn around now, Jeremy. Thank you." We faced each other in the starry half-light; her eyes were so warm and gentle. She smiled at me. "You did some remarkably brave things today, Jeremy. I'm very proud of you." She hesitated, as if she wanted to say more. "And thank you." She looked me right in the eyes, stretched her hand out to run it through my hair, then leaned forward and kissed me on the forehead. "Thank you, Jeremy." My throat tightened and I couldn't say a word. I could only think of those eyes. I started to bring my hand up to touch her hair, too, but she rolled over. "Now try to get some sleep, Jeremy. We both need it."

Like I could possibly sleep after that. I fluffed my makeshift pillow and lay on my side like usual, but all I could do was watch her lying next to me in the moonlight. She finally slept, making sweet little noises, and I felt like her stalwart defender, keeping watch over her by night. Occasionally there were terrible sounds, crashes, gunshots, screams, off in the distance; sometimes, not all that distant. They made her moan in her sleep like a child, and after a few more she rolled over and buried her head in my chest and nestled her arm against me, still sleeping fitfully. I bit my lip a little, hoping I wouldn't wake her up, and tentatively at first, began to stroke her hair, catching up the loose strands off her cheek and tucking them behind her ear. "Shhh-hhh . . ." I whispered almost inaudibly to her. "Everything's going to be okay."

After a few pleasant, awkward minutes of this, she stirred. Her hand tightened involuntarily, her fingernails dragged gently on the skin of my chest. Under the covers, my body reacted immediately. Her closeness had been making my shorts steadily uncomfortable. By this time I just hoped she wouldn't feel how hard I was now. A deep drumbeat of thunder rumbled and a fireball flared on the horizon, briefly lighting up the room with a bright orange flash. "Jeremy?" she said abruptly, looking up at me in fear.

"It's okay, I think there was an explosion on the other side of town. Maybe a gas station or something."

She nodded, and looked down at her hand on my chest. She left it there, and ever so slightly traced tiny circles with her finger. " Do you think there's anyone else left?"

"I honestly don't know."

She sat up and watched the fire burning off in the distance. I could see the blaze reflected in her eyes. She looked thoughtful, with an expression I couldn't name. As the faraway blaze dwindled down to a candle glow, she looked down at me. "It's warm. Do you want to take off your shirt?"

I forgot how words work and just nodded dumbly. She pulled the blankets down, then reached down and took the waist of my T-shirt and rolled it up. I raised my arms so she could slip it off me. She laid her hand on my chest, and studied me silently for a few moments. "You're beautiful," she said softly, admiring my body with a dreamlike smile.

No one had ever called me that before, or looked at me that way, or touched me the way she was. She ran a warm palm over my chest and trailed it down to my stomach, then brought it back all the way up to my collarbone. I lay there, breathing hard, utterly spellbound by her. She took a moment to adjust herself, sitting up on her knees and facing me fully; the sight of her bare legs was magic. Then she locked eyes with me and without a word, took the blankets and completely uncovered me.

She turned her attention to my shorts, which were tented up ridiculously. But she didn't seem to mind. She reached over and ran her nimble fingers under the waistband and asked, "Can you lift up a little for me?" and pulled them right off me when I raised my hips for her. Setting them aside, she bent over me and gently took hold of my cock. I didn't know it could ever get so big or so stiff. "It's a nice size," she said, pleased.

She ran her hand lightly over my balls and cupped them sociably, then took hold of the shaft again and bent down to bring her mouth to it.

My eyesight fluttered and I felt the most amazing fuzzy tingling sensation arcing from my eyebrows down to my groin when she licked her lips and kissed the head. While one hand slid up and down the shaft, she gently cradled and caressed my swollen scrotum with the other and sucked and licked the head of my dick. I grabbed the cushions with both hands and arched my back with a sharp intake of breath. She paused just long enough to turn to me and say, "It's okay, honey. Go ahead and come for me." That was it for me. What can I say? I shuddered and groaned, and tried not to buck too hard as I came. She kept her grip on me, sucking it all down. At last she raised her head again and beamed at me. "Still with us?" I nodded groggily with half-lidded eyes and a dopey smile on my face. She leaned over and started to unbutton her blouse. "You can touch me," she said, pulling open her top to expose her breasts. They mesmerized me with their sweet roundness and the perfect tan sunbursts of her areolas. The nipples were rigid under my fingertips, and I loved feeling the breast's fullness fill my cupped hand.

Her head arched back as she slipped a hand behind my neck and pulled me up into her chest. I kissed one, then the other, then took her breast in hand and suckled on the firm responsive nipple. She clasped my head and stroked my face and ear, moaning her pleasure as I ran my tongue in circles over the smooth perfect areola, until she couldn't take any more and stood up.

What a magnificent view to see her standing above me, then to watch while she dug her thumbs in the sides of her panties and pulled them down. I could smell the scent of her excitement, and it made my head swim. She bent down and touched my cheek. "I'm going to get on top of you, all right?"

Yeah, it was. She straddled me and lowered herself until she rested on her knees astride my lap with my penis standing just before her. She licked her fingers and worked the saliva around my head and shaft. "Look at you!" she said and laughed. "You're still so hard!" She was right.

"Now just relax. It's okay. Let me do it." She opened herself with one hand, grasping me with the other as she rose up on her knees, leaned forward, and backed into me until she could ease me into her. Her mouth opened with a little quaver as my penis slipped past her slick folds, and we both breathed out sharply. "Thaaaat's it . . ." She groaned. She arched forward and back, holding on to my shoulders for support as she leaned into my chest and rode me. She closed her eyes and let her head loll as she rocked and grinded into me. The sound of her sharp breaths and languid moaning was sheer music to me; hearing it made me prouder than anything I had ever done before.

I reached up to gently knead her breasts; then slid my hands down her sides and held her by the hips, experimenting with what I could do with the angle of my own pelvis. She encouraged my initiative. "Ummm, yes . . . put your hands there . . . yes, just like that . . . yes, ooooh, that's it, I like that. Good . . ." She closed her eyes, and bit her lip with a deep sigh. I grabbed her butt and pulled her into me more. "God, yes!" she exclaimed, then she was coming. What a show; I could feel her whole body tense and the muscles inside her quivering. She stiffened and opened her mouth to cry out silently. She clung to my shoulders and suddenly dropped down and seized my face with both hands to kiss me with her wet, open mouth again and again. At the touch of her lips and tongue on mine, I came again, even harder than the first time. Such a rush. My first kiss.

The moon never seemed so big and full. She lay across me, head resting on my chest, her hand on my heart. I ran my hand through her hair. "Jeremy?"

"Ms. Baymiller?"

"Um . . . maybe you should start calling me Angela."

"Okay."

"Tell me something."

"Anything."

"Are you eighteen yet?"

I kept petting her head. "Yeah, don't worry. Besides, your teaching career has bigger problems." You'd have thought I'd be wired all night. I sure did. But I was sleeping like a baby before I knew it.

I woke up the next morning feeling like a million bucks. The sun was up and birds were singing. It was going to be a gorgeous day. I yawned and reached over for Ms. Baymiller—I mean, Angela. But she was gone. I shot up with a start and called out her name. "I'm right here, sweetheart. Just getting dressed." She was standing behind me on the other side of the room, just out of my sight. I expected to see her in her usual academic elegance, in smart blouse, skirt and heels. But instead there was a Valkyrie in her place: hair pulled back into a ponytail, wearing a sports bra, a set of skateboarder's elbow pads and wrist guards, and some sort of rigid medical neck brace to protect her throat. She had taken scissors to her classic herringbone skirt, and now it was twice as short and slit nearly all the way up. She wore the dead patrolman's motorcycle boots and belt, his pistol back in the holster. She slipped a big bowie knife into her boot. I had never seen a sexier woman in my life.

She checked the shotgun, and set it on the desk next to a line up of all the knives from the teachers' kitchenette. "There are still some good things in the principal's confiscated items box, though it's mostly just illegal fireworks and porn. Have you ever shot a hand crossbow?" She walked up and crouched down to give me a peck on the cheek. "Morning, handsome. Like the new outfit?"

"I really do."

She tousled my hair and grinned. "Get dressed, cowboy. I'm going to go get the keys to Caruthers's Range Rover. It's parked just right there. I think we can reach it with no problem. Then we can go shopping, try to pick up some news on the radio, head for safer ground."

Sounded like a plan, I agreed. She left me to get suited up. Now, where did my clothes go? I found my shorts and was still looking for the rest when I heard a crash from somewhere beyond the hall. I froze, then after a few heartbeats I stepped to the doorway and listened. "Angela?" Nothing. I went back to the desk and picked up the shotgun.

Then I heard her: "Jeremy! Come quick!" As I ran down the hallways, I heard her add, "It's Dee Dee!" *Oh no. I was wrong about them not being able crawl up the air ducts.* "Angela, don't!" But it was too late.

Dee Dee looked like hell, but enough like a lost waif that no wonder Angela came up to help her. The late cheerleader made a keening noise just like a crying child, and stumbled towards her with arms out wide. They embraced just I ran into the room. Dee Dee seized her and buried her head into Angela's shoulders. I raised the shotgun, knowing that if her bite connected, I would have to shoot both of them. But had it? Had her protective gear held up? I couldn't shoot till I knew for sure. Goddamn it! "Angela!"

Dee Dee raised her head from Angela's shoulder and looked at me with tear-filled human eyes. "McGowan?" I lowered the shotgun, unbelieving. She hadn't turned. "You son of a bitch, I thought you were coming right back!" She broke their hug and came at me, but instead of clobbering me, she grabbed me and hugged me too. One miracle after another. "Were you just trying to shoot us, McGowan?"

I ducked the question. "Dee Dee? You're alive? But . . . I saw the bite . . ."

She rolled her eyes. "Jeez, Jerry, I told you it was just a

hickey, already." She pulled down her collar enough for me to see. So it was. It had looked worse yesterday when she was all covered in sweat and blood-splattered and growling at me in her sleep. I guess yesterday wasn't my finest day for decision-making, though it did shape up nicely in the end.

"Jesus—I thought the zombies had gotten you. Would have saved a lot of trouble if you had just shown it to me when I asked you."

"Zombies? What? I didn't even get it then. I got it the night before . . . from Stephanie. We were, um—trying something."

Angela looked at her. "*Stephanie* gave you that? Dee Dee, that's just . . ." she struggled for the right word. ". . . sexy."

And right then, I realized that zombie apocalypse or no, everything was going to work out just fine.

FIRST DATE

Dana Fredsti

I blame E-Compatibility. According to their Compatibility Matching System®, Barry and I were a match made in heaven, or at least the Financial District. I'm here to tell you E-Compatibility sucks.

My date and I sat across from each other in a booth in the Royal Bank next to the window facing Sacramento Street and Embarcadero One. The Bank is a well-known bar with good grub that caters to the Financial District's insurance crowd. I'm partial to their steak salad. Their wine list is eh, but if you're a beer drinker, the Bank is your place. My date, a thirty-something Gecko wannabe with slicked-back hair ten years out of style, wallowed happily in his third Guinness; I sipped on my first glass of an indifferent zinfandel and wished I'd gone home after work. True, I'd be alone in my small studio apartment, but I'd be drinking better wine and not listening to my date blather on about capital gains, due diligence, and profit margins.

I work as an office manager in a venture capital firm and sure, I hear business jargon on a daily basis, but I pretty much tuned it out unless it directly related to my job. I ordered supplies, made sure the place was clean every morning with no coffee cups lying around unwashed, and provided office hospitality by dint of the fact my desk was in the lobby and I actually like people. And did I mention I have a great smile? Seriously. Courtesy of my days on the beauty pageant circuit.

It helps to have auto-smile in one's repertoire, especially first thing in the morning when you haven't had your first cup of coffee and six executives from some potential portfolio company show up a half hour early for an eight a.m. meeting. Helps me say, "Can I get you some coffee or tea?" without "accidentally" pouring the steaming hot liquid of their choice on the laps of the occasional elitist jerk who comes in. It helped now as Barry ("Call me 'Bare,' hahahahah!") did his best to impress me with how much he could talk about himself without once asking me my opinion or any information about me at all. This guy was more self-absorbed than a six-pack of sponges.

Did I mention E-Compatibility sucks?

I mean, honestly, we had zilch chemistry. I could see how some women might find him attractive, but he sent nary a tingle to my loins. My nipples stayed distinctly un-erect, totally uninterested in the man sitting across from me.

And his taste in movies? Jeez, Louise. When I asked him what his favorite horror movie was, Barry's answer wasn't *Dawn of the Dead*, *Halloween* (the original, thank you! I don't acknowledge Rob Zombie's crappy remake) or even *The Grudge*. "That's easy," he said, taking huge bite of his club sandwich. "*Hostel*. I mean, that's just balls-to-the-wall horror—" (I hate that expression and curse Eli Roth whenever I hear it) "—especially the part where the dude blowtorches the Japanese chick and her eye falls out." Bits of rye bread and cheese fell out of his mouth as he talked.

"That's torture porn, not horror."

"Eh, same difference."

I focused on ungritting my teeth, choosing not to reply to such an idiotic statement.

I tried not to watch as a slice of bacon tried to escape Barry's Hoover-style dining, only to be snagged at the last minute between his teeth. He tossed his head back like a seal setting up a fish for the kill and the bacon vanished down his gullet.

"Can I get you another glass of the zinfandel?"

I looked up at our waiter and smiled my first genuine smile of the evening. He was cute, kind of David Boreanz, circa *Angel*, but without the goofy, spiked, over-gelled hair. Plus he had a really cute Brit accent. "Sure. Unless you'd recommend something else." Just a little bit of innuendo there, I admit it.

"You like red?"

I nodded.

"I'll see what I can do." Cutie-boy grinned at me. My body responded with an unexpected tingle of heat between my thighs. An unspoken message passed between us, a mutual interest expressed with pheromones and eye contact.

He turned to Barry, but before he could say anything, my charming date snapped "Another Guinness," with all the manners of a testy three-year-old.

A scream from outside distracted all of our attention.

Suddenly a woman slammed into the window like an oversized bug, her bloodied face plastered in a scream. Her blue eyes, wide with pain and terror, met mine in an imploring stare, as if I could do something to help her from my side of the window. She was close enough to kiss if not for the piece of glass separating us. I watched in stunned disbelief as a heavyset man in a Starbucks uniform ripped into her neck with his teeth and tore out a chunk of flesh. Arterial blood spurted out over the window and the woman slid down out of sight, the bloodthirsty barista battened onto her like a lion taking down a gazelle.

"What the fuck?" Barry stared at the gore-streaked glass. Our waiter shared his look of incredulous horror.

"We have to help her." I was halfway out of the booth before the words left my mouth.

"Are you fucking nuts?" Barry reached over the table and grabbed my wrist before I got up. "She's dead."

I jerked my wrist free. "How do you know she's dead?" I started to stand, but was stopped by Cutie-boy's hand on my shoulder.

"That guy tore out her carotid artery. She's bled out by now."

"And that dude is totally insane." Barry shook his head. "I mean . . ." He looked outside and gulped. "He's eating her."

No way. I slid back across the booth to the window and looked down. The barista's teeth were buried in the woman's neck, his head moving back and forth as he worried a chunk of flesh free—and swallowed it. He couldn't possibly have heard my choked gasp, but his head snapped around and he glared up at me with the soulless bluish-white eyes of a corpse, all color leached out of the cornea. Blood, tissue, and gristly bits of flesh coated his mouth, a flap of skin hanging from his bottom lip.

Our booth was semi-private with tall backs separating it from the ones on either side, so the other diners hadn't seen the incident, but they'd heard the screams. Outside, cars swerved to avoid several bystanders who'd seen the incident and now ran across the street. Others weren't so fast, stumbling towards the Royal Bank as if they couldn't quite control their limbs. A gypsy cab didn't maneuver fast enough and slammed into a woman in a power suit staggering across Sacramento. She flew into the air and landed hard on the street. A red Escalade rear-ended the cab, only to be sideswiped by a Smart Car. The result was inevitable. But then Power Suit Gal staggered to her feet, blood and fluids leaking out of a smashed body, and lurched towards our window. No one could have foreseen that.

I suddenly noticed a growing number of people like Power Suit Gal among the normal-looking concerned bystanders. People with skin a sickly pallor, clothing either askew or ripped, and, well, pieces missing from their flesh. Things dangling out of gaping wounds that should be safely tucked away. Like intestines. It was like one of those stupid 3D pictures, where you stare and stare at it and suddenly see a hidden image within the patterns. In this case, I suddenly saw a lot of fucked-up people. And they were attacking the people who weren't fucked up. And by "attacking," I'm talking full-on, flesh-ripping, gut-tearing, eviscerating mauling.

Shit.

"Zombies," said our waiter.

"You're right," I said.

"Are you both fucking crazy?" Barry looked at us as though we were the ones chewing out throats and swallowing chunks of flesh, like we were responsible for the carnage outside.

"Do you have a better explanation?" I stared at him, incredulous. "That woman just got smushed by an Escalade. You don't get up and walk after that!"

"It's a terrorist attack." Barry nodded emphatically, validating his own words. "Nerve gas. Or . . . or . . . PCP."

"PCP, my ass." Someone screamed near the front door. "Shit." I grabbed my purse and scrambled to my feet. "We have to get out of here. This is a death trap."

Barry shook his head back and forth, back and forth, as if each shake would convince him he was right. "We can't go out there."

"We can't stay here." I scrambled to my feet in time to see several mangled yuppies stagger into the Bank and attack the people nearest the door. "Get your ass up, Barry, or you're going to die here!" I grabbed our waiter's arm. "Is there a back door out of here?"

"Yeah. Downstairs. There's a door into the alley."

"Let's go."

Cutie-boy nodded. "I'll show you the way."

"Barry?"

My date looked up at me, disbelief and outrage in his expression. "This can't be happening."

We *so* did not have time for a generic default proclamation of disbelief. "It's happening, Barry, and you can either deal with it and move your ass now or die here."

Frozen in his seat, Barry watched some real-life balls-to-the-wall horror as two men in Armani ripped apart a group of Irish tourists seated at the bar. Agonized cries of "Jesus, Mary, and Joseph!" gave away their nationality.

I grabbed Barry's arm and turned to the waiter. "Show us the exit."

He took my hand and together we managed to yank Barry to his feet. I didn't like the guy, but I'd be damned if I left him to die on our first date.

We ran towards a stairwell at the back of the restaurant. A tipsy woman was ascending the stairs when we hit the top, her high heels making the trip up an adventure. "Turn around and go back down," I said.

"Huh?" She looked at me, her blue eyes glazed with too much alcohol. "My date's waiting for me."

"So are a lot of things you don't want to meet," I snapped.

She shook her head and shoved past us, oblivious to the screams of terror and pain emanating from the restaurant.

I would have reached for her, but our waiter slung an arm around me and hustled me down the stairs. I liked the way his strong arm felt encircling my waist. Barry clutched my other arm in a death grip and dogged our steps to the basement. Points for survival instinct.

We hit the bottom of the steps and Cutie-boy pointed to the left. "The door out to the alley is back there."

The basement consisted of the bathrooms off to the right, some extra furniture, and some boxes stacked in a corner. Not a hell of a lot.

"Can't we just stay down here?" Barry's grip on my arm was cutting off circulation.

I pointed to the stairs. "No door. We need to get some place we can barricade the entrances."

"And no food down here." Cutie-boy grabbed one of the boxes, ripped it open, and extracted a butcher knife worthy of an '80s slasher film.

"Nice. Got any more of those?"

He grinned and pulled out two more, handing them to me and Barry. Barry took his as gingerly as an arachnophobic handed a tarantula. I seized mine and hefted it, liking the way it felt in my hand. Then I spotted a crowbar lying in a corner. Shoving the knife in my purse, I grabbed the crowbar and gave it an experimental swing. I grinned at Cutie-boy and said, "Even nicer."

"Any ideas where to go?"

I nodded and unzipped a little side compartment of my

purse. I pulled out a cork keychain with three keys and a gray fob dangling from the ring. "My office. It's in the Charles Schwab building around the corner on California Street. If we can get there . . . I think we'll be safe. At least for a while."

"If? *If* we can get there?" Barry's gaze jerked around the room, taking everything in little segments. He reminded me of a somewhat spastic bird.

"At this point," said the waiter, "everything is a risk."

I nodded. "Here's the plan. We go out the back door and haul ass to my building. If someone . . . something tries to attack us . . ." I held up the crowbar. "Once we're in the lobby, I'll open the stairwell and we can get to my office. There's food and water there. We should be okay for a while."

"That's it? That's your plan?" The veins on Barry's neck throbbed. I bet he had high blood pressure problems.

"You got a better one, mate?"

I smiled gratefully at Cutie-boy, vowing to find out his name as soon as we had a second to breathe.

We didn't wait for Barry's answer; the screams from upstairs were building in intensity and growing closer, which meant the mayhem would soon make its way downstairs.

Cutie-boy led the way to the door, slid the deadbolt open, and cautiously cracked the door. I pushed past him and poked my head out, glancing in either direction.

So far, so good. I could hear screams in the vicinity, but the alley was clear of both people and zombies.

"Come on." I stepped outside, crowbar at the ready in one

hand, keys in the other, and thanked the fashion gods that I'd worn low-heeled boots today instead of fuck-me-but-don't-ask-me-to-outrun-zombies pumps.

The men followed me out the door.

"Stick close to me," I said quietly. "I'll get the door open as fast as I can."

I took a deep breath and immediately regretted it; the alley reeked of Dumpster innards and stale urine. "Now!"

I took off at a run towards Front Street, hoping against the odds the street would be clear when we reached the mouth of the alley. It wasn't.

The minute I rounded the corner, I collided with a beefy man who smelled worse than the alleyway. His face—what was left of it—had a grayish pallor. His—no, *its* breath wafted out in a charnel house reek as it reached for me, gore-rimmed mouth gaping to show a full set of hungry, bloodied teeth.

"Oh, *gross*!" I brought up the crowbar and swung it down in an arc, burying the two-pronged hook in its head. The zombie swayed for a second, then collapsed onto its knees, then face-down on the asphalt. I kept my grip on the crowbar and yanked it out as the zombie hit the ground.

"Let's go!" I ran down Front Street towards California, trusting the men to follow me. The door to my office was only a half block and a door away, but given the chaos around us, it felt like miles. I could see other mangled yet still ambulatory people shambling towards us from several directions. Slaughter raged all around us, a mini-apocalypse. I saw the local homeless guy who always perches in front of Lee's Deli get swarmed by several well-dressed Financial District types, blood and guts splashed on their business suits, skirts, and designer shoes. He'd never shake his paper cup filled with spare change again.

I dashed around the corner of California and Front, past the main doors to the Charles Schwab offices to the door leading to the other floors at 200 Cal. Screams, calls to various deities, and the sounds of rending flesh filled the air. Like hell had come to Earth within the space of fifteen minutes. Maybe it had.

Our daily FedEx delivery man staggered down California Street, blood pouring out of wounds on his neck and arms. I locked eyes with him as he suddenly convulsed, like someone with an epileptic fit. I fumbled the keys in my left hand, dropped them as I reached the door with its electronic eye. By the time I retrieved them, Mr. FedEx had changed. His eyes had gone the same dead milky white as the rest of the zombies—and they were still fixed on me.

Shit.

I swiped the little door fob over the sensor. It stayed red. "Shit!"

"What?" Barry stared at me, eyes wide with panic. "It isn't working? You made us follow you out of the restaurant and your fucking keys aren't working?!" His voice rose to a scream, attracting the attention of all the wrong dead people. FedEx dude's gaze shifted from me to Barry. His mouth widened in a ravenous gape and he staggered straight for us.

I looked at the fob; it was backwards. Flipping it over, I swiped it again. The light turned green and I shoved the door open, dashing inside the lobby. "Hurry!"

Barry and Cutie-boy were through the doors right after me. Unfortunately, FedEx zombie (I'll just call him ZedEx) was hot on their heels. Cutie-boy had the foresight to pull the door shut as he ran in, but ZedEx was already partly in and the lobby's glass doors had some sort of air compression system that prevented the doors from being slammed and shattered.

"Shut the door!"

"I'm trying!" This was Cutie-boy.

"Try harder!" I ran for the stairs on the far side of the building's notoriously slow elevator. Decorative, to be sure. But cranky and temperamental, like an aging diva.

"Where are you going?" Barry slammed his hand against the elevator's 'up' button even as I shoved a key into the stairwell door lock.

"Stairs!" I opened the door as ZedEx pushed his way into the building despite Cutie-boy's best efforts to keep him out. Guess lugging all those packages built some muscle.

Cutie-boy staggered back under ZedEx's onslaught, barely keeping his feet. He managed to get one hand under the drooling deliveryman's chin, shoving hard. ZedEx slammed backwards into the glass door, giving Cutie-boy the chance to get away and join me at the stairwell door. I held the door open for Barry, who was still hitting the elevator button with the flat of his hand.

"Barry, come on!"

I don't know if it's because he was inherently lazy or just programmed by years of taking elevators, but Barry ignored me as the elevator doors finally slid open, painfully slow as usual. ZedEx, in the meantime, staggered towards him. I screamed Barry's name as the zombie grabbed his arm and took a hefty bite out of Barry's bicep, tearing through fabric and flesh as easily as though they were soft butter. Barry hollered in pain and outrage, and ripped his arm out of the zombie's teeth.

"You *son*-of-a-bitch!" Barry hauled off and punched ZedEx square in his rotting face. ZedEx stumbled back against the wall and Barry vanished into the elevator. I heard him cursing as the doors slid shut.

ZedEx looked at me as though I was a jelly doughnut and he was a zombiefied Homer Simpson. I pulled the stairwell door shut just as he lurched forward. The door shook as he hit it from the other side, a metallic boom echoing in the stairwell.

Cutie-boy looked at me. "Can that thing get in?"

I shook my head. "Not unless he has a key."

"What about your boyfriend?"

"He's not my boyfriend," I said. "First date."

"Pretty lousy one, by the looks of things."

I nodded. "No joke."

"So . . . is he coming up?"

"He can't get onto our floor without an elevator key."

Cutie-boy nodded slowly. "Do we let him in?"

I hesitated, then shook my head. "He's been bit. If there's

any truth to any of the movies, he's going to turn into one of them."

"So what now?"

"Fourth floor."

We pounded up the stairs, the sound of our footsteps on the metal stairs eliciting a renewed assault on the lobby stairwell door. We reached the fourth floor. I started to unlock the door. Cutie-boy put a hand on my arm. "Are you sure it's safe?"

"Yeah. I was the last one out the door and I locked the elevator, so no one can get off on our floor."

Nevertheless, when I pulled the door open and stepped inside, I proceeded with caution.

The lobby was empty, lights off.

"Hello?"

Nothing.

I turned to Cutie-Boy. "I think we're safe."

He looked down at me and I noticed how green his eyes were, fringed with thick dark lashes. Sea-green. "You're something, you know that?"

"Really?" I felt suddenly shy, pretty ridiculous under the circumstances.

"Yeah." He ran a finger down one side of my face. "You were dead sexy with that crowbar."

His finger traced the outline of my lips and I caught the tip in my mouth, suctioning it in gently, but suggestively. I dropped my keys, purse and crowbar on the floor.

We didn't make it past the lobby couch. Clothes went flying:

his green Royal Bank T-shirt and black trousers, my boots, black silk skirt, and red v-neck sweater. I briefly thanked the clothing gods that I'd worn a nice matching set of Victoria's Secret black silk bra and v-string, even though I don't think he noticed them before yanking them off me and tossing them aside. I did the same to his hunter-green briefs, marveling briefly at the size and hardness of his erection, especially under the circumstances. But then, I was so wet and goddamned horny, maybe there was something to the whole sex-and-death thing. You know, the closer you come to death, the more you want to fuck.

Whatever—when he slid into me, filling me with the long, hard length of his cock, there was no hesitation, no brief readjustment to make sure Item A would fit into Slot B. Everything fit just fine; a tight fit creating a delicious friction that had me digging my nails into his back with each stroke. He put his teeth against my neck, and for a brief second I wondered if he'd turned zombie. Then he proceeded to nibble and lick his way down the length of my neck to my collarbone with just enough pressure to send little frissons of heat to my nipples and groin. I returned the favor by reaching behind him and running my nails down his spine. He shivered with pleasure, creating a corresponding pulse of heat in my clit. I felt my orgasm spark and build, every thrust of his cock turning up the fire a little more until I thrashed beneath him in an orgasm so strong I thought it would shake my body apart. I felt him come as well, a shuddering release accompanied by a low primal growl that made me come all over again.

The best fuck of my life was over in less than five minutes.

We lay on the leather couch, limbs entwined, bodies slick with sweat, our breathing slowly returning to normal. Supporting himself on one elbow, Cutie-boy brushed my hair back from my forehead and grinned down at me. "What's your name, then?"

I laughed. "Angie."

"Angie. Nice. Angie, I'm Ian, and I'm very pleased to meet you." He stuck his hand between us. I shook it, admiring the strength and size of his fingers. I've always liked men with big hands.

"Ian's a nice name too." I played with his fingers, gently running my fingers up and down each one.

"And that feels nice . . ."

"Mmm . . ."

He kissed me then. Slowly, deliberately, warm tongue tangling with mine as he explored my lips and mouth. Fingers found nerve endings on my ear, my neck, the inside of my elbows and the backs of my knees. I felt his cock growing hard again where it lay against my thigh so I reached down and cradled his balls in one hand, using the other to stroke his penis from shaft to tip, up and down with a firm grip and steady rhythm that had him groaning with desire.

"Do you want to fuck me?" I murmured against his mouth, nipping at his lower lip as I continued my ministrations.

Ian growled again, a predatory sound that sent a fresh coil of heat from my belly straight into my clit. He suddenly seized my wrists and yanked my arms over my head. Pinning them there, he drove into me in one strong, deep thrust, at the same time plunging his tongue into my mouth. I would have screamed with pleasure if I'd been able. As it was, I let the waves of yet another orgasm wash over and through me, nearly mindless with pleasure. Little aftershocks rippled through me as Ian thrust his way to his own climax a few minutes later.

Once again we lay in each other's arms. Ian flipped me over so I was on top of him and I rested my head on his chest, letting the sound of his heartbeat fill my senses. Steady. Soothing.

Except . . .

"What's that?"

An irregular pounding overrode the sound of Ian's heartbeat.

We both lifted our heads and stared at the elevator.

Ian looked at me. "Is that your date?"

"It must be."

The pounding faded, followed by the sound of the elevator descending.

"Do you think he's turned into one of them?"

I briefly wondered how I'd become the expert on zombie physiology, but let it go. "I don't know. Do we want to find out?" I hoped Ian would help make some decisions. While I appreciate a man who doesn't try to go all macho alpha male on me twenty-four/seven, I didn't want to be responsible for everything that happened here.

Ian thought for a moment. "If he hasn't turned, we need to

help him. If he has . . . he'll keep riding the damn elevator and thumping on the door. I don't know about you, but that will put me right off lovemaking."

I smiled and not just because he'd made a decision. He'd said "love-making" instead of "sex." That revealed the soul of a romantic. I liked that.

"We can call the elevator up here," I said. "We just need to be prepared for whatever comes out of there."

We put our clothes back on. As I pulled my boots on, the elevator motor hummed as the car rode back up to the fourth floor, along with its passenger.

Boom. Boom. Boom.

"Barry?"

A feral, guttural sound emanated from the closed doors.

Boom. Boom. Boom.

I looked at Ian. "He's turned."

I retrieved the crowbar from the floor. Ian picked up a chair. He nodded at me as I stood by the elevator call button. I nodded back and pressed it. Seconds later the doors slid open and an undead Barry lunged out into the lobby.

Ian swung first, bashing Barry on the side of the head with the chair. It was plastic so it didn't do much damage, but it did throw Barry off balance, giving me a chance to take good aim with my crowbar.

Thwack.

Once. Then again.

Barry's knees buckled and he stumbled to the floor.

I raised the crowbar over my head and brought it down one more time with skull-crushing force.

Barry fell face-forward to the ground, well and truly dead.

We dragged his corpse back into the elevator. I hit the down button and quickly stepped back into the fourth-floor lobby before the doors slid shut.

Ian put his arms around me. "You okay?"

"I think so." And I was, considering we were in the middle of a zombie apocalypse. I'd just had the best sex of my life and suspected I'd met someone who might actually qualify for a long-term relationship. Just goes to show online dating is nothing compared to real life experience when it comes to *really* testing compatibility.

LATER

Michael Marshall Smith

I remember standing in the bedroom before we went out, fiddling with my tie and fretting mildly about the time. As yet we had plenty, but that was nothing to be complacent about. The minutes had a way of disappearing when Rachel was getting ready, early starts culminating in a breathless search for a taxi. It was a party we were going to, so it didn't really matter what time we left, but I tend to be a little dull about time. I used to, anyway.

When I had the tie as close to a tidy knot as I was able, I turned away from the mirror and opened my mouth to call out to Rachel. But then I caught sight of what was on the bed, and closed it again. For a moment I just stood and looked, then walked over towards it.

It wasn't anything very spectacular, just a dress made of sheeny white material. A few years ago, when we started going out together, Rachel used to make a lot of her clothes. She didn't do it because she had to, but because she enjoyed it. She used to haul me endlessly round dressmaking shops, browsing patterns and asking my opinion on a million different fabrics, while I halfheartedly protested and moaned.

On impulse I leaned down and felt the material, and found I could remember touching it for the first time in the shop on Mill Road, could recall surfacing up through contented boredom to say yes, I liked this one. On that recommendation she'd bought it and made this dress, and as a reward for traipsing around after her she'd bought me dinner too. We were poorer then, so the meal was cheap, but there was lots and it was good.

The strange thing was, I didn't even really mind the dress shops. You know how sometimes, when you're just walking around, living your life, you'll see someone on the street and fall hopelessly in love with them? How something in the way they look, the way they are, makes you stop dead in your tracks and stare, and how for that instant you're convinced that if you could just meet them, you'd be able to love them forever? Wild schemes and unlikely chance meetings pass through your head, yet as they stand on the other side of the street or the room, talking to someone else, they haven't the faintest idea of what's going through your mind. Something has clicked, but only inside your head. You know you'll never speak to them, that they'll never know what you're feeling and that they'll never want to. But something about them forces you to keep looking, until you wish they'd leave so you could be free.

The first time I saw Rachel was like that, and now she was in my bath. I didn't call out to hurry her along. I decided it didn't really matter.

A few minutes later a protracted squawking noise announced the letting out of the bathwater, and Rachel wafted into the bedroom swaddled in thick towels and glowing high spirits. Suddenly I lost all interest in going to the party, punctually or otherwise. She marched up to me, set her head at a silly angle to kiss me on the lips and jerked my tie vigorously in about three different directions. When I looked in the mirror I saw that somehow, as always, she'd turned it into a perfect knot.

Half an hour later we left the flat, still in plenty of time. If anything, I'd held her up.

"Later," she'd said, smiling in the way that showed she meant it. "Later, and for a long time, my man."

I turned from locking the door to see her standing on the pavement outside the house, looking perfect in her white dress, looking happy. As I walked smiling down the steps towards her she skipped backwards into the road, laughing for no reason, laughing because she was with me.

"Come on," she said, holding out her hand like a dancer, and a yellow van came round the corner and smashed into her.

She spun backwards as if tugged on a rope, rebounded off a parked car, and toppled into the road. As I stood cold on the bottom step she half sat up and looked at me, an expression of wordless surprise on her face, and then she fell back again.

By the time I reached her, blood was already pulsing up into the white of her dress and welling out of her mouth. It ran out over her makeup and I saw she'd been right: she hadn't quite blended the colors above her eyes. I'd told her it didn't matter.

She tried to move her head again and there was a sticky sound as it almost left the tarmac and then slumped back. Her hair fell back from around her face, but not as it usually did. There was a faint flicker in her eyelids, and then she died.

I knelt there in the road beside her, holding her hand as the blood dried a little. I heard every word the small crowd said, but I don't know what they were muttering about. All I could think was that there wasn't going to be a later, not to kiss her some more, not for anything.

Later was gone.

When I got home from the hospital I phoned her mother. I did it as soon as I got back, though I didn't want to. I didn't want to tell anyone, didn't want to make it official. It was a bad phone call, very, very bad. Then I sat in the flat, looking at the drawers she'd left open, at the towels on the floor, at the party invitation on the dressing table, feeling my stomach crawl.

I was back at the flat, as if we'd come back home from the party. I should have been making coffee while Rachel had yet another bath, coffee we'd drink on the sofa in front of the fire. But the fire was off and the bath was empty. So what was I supposed to do?

I sat for an hour, feeling as if somehow I'd slipped too far forward in time and left Rachel behind, as if I could turn and see her desperately running to try to catch me up. When it felt as if my throat was going to burst, I called my parents and they came and took me home. My mother gently made me change my clothes, but she didn't wash them. Not until I was asleep, anyway. When I came down and saw them clean I hated her, but I knew she was right and the hate went away. There wouldn't have been much point in just keeping them in a drawer.

The funeral was short. I guess they all are, really, but there's no point in them being any longer. Nothing more would be said. I was a little better by then, and not crying so much, though I did before we went to the church because I couldn't get my tie to sit right.

Rachel was buried near her grandparents, which she would have liked. Her parents gave me her dress afterwards because I'd asked for it. It had been thoroughly cleaned and large patches had lost their sheen and died, looking as much unlike Rachel's dress as the cloth had on the roll in the shop where she'd bought it. I'd almost have preferred the bloodstains still to have been there; at least that way I could have believed the cloth still sparkled beneath them. But they were right in their way, as my mother was. Some people seem to have pragmatic, accepting souls, an ability with death.

I don't, I'm afraid. I don't understand it at all.

Afterwards I stood at the graveside for a while, but not for long because I knew my parents were waiting at the car. As I stood by the mound of earth that lay on top of her I tried to concentrate, to send some final thought to her, some final love, but the world kept pressing in on me through the sound of cars on the road and some bird that was cawing up in a tree. I couldn't shut it out. I couldn't believe I was noticing how cold it was; I couldn't believe that somewhere lives were being led and televisions being watched, that the inside of my parents' car would smell the same as it always had. I wanted to feel something, wanted to sense her presence, but I couldn't. All I could feel was the world round me, the same old world. But it wasn't a world that had been there a week ago, and I couldn't understand how it could look so much the same.

It was the same because nothing had changed, I supposed, and I turned and walked to the car.

The wake was worse than the funeral, much worse, and I stood with a tuna sandwich feeling something very cold building up inside. Rachel's oldest friend, Lisa, held court with her old school friends, swiftly running the range of emotions from stoic resilience to trembling incoherence.

"I've just realized," she sobbed to me, "Rachel's not going to be at my wedding."

"She's not going to be at mine either," I said numbly, and immediately hated myself for it.

I went and stood by the window, out of harm's way. I couldn't react properly. I knew why everyone was standing here, that in some ways it was like a wedding. Instead of gathering together to bear witness to a bond, they were here to prove she was dead. In the weeks to come they'd know they'd stood together in a room, and eaten crisps, and would be able to accept she was gone. I couldn't.

I said good-bye to Rachel's parents before I left. We looked at each other oddly, and shook hands, as if we were just strangers again. Then I went back to the flat and changed into some old clothes. My "Someday" clothes, Rachel used to call them, as in, "Someday you must throw those away." Then I made a cup of tea and stared out of the window for a while. I knew damn well what I was going to do, and it was a relief to give in to it.

That night I went back to the cemetery and I dug her up.

It was hard work, and it took a lot longer than I expected, but in another way it was surprisingly easy. I mean yes, it was creepy, and yes, I felt like a lunatic, but after the shovel had gone in once the second time seemed less strange. It was like waking up in the mornings after the accident. The first time I clutched at myself and couldn't understand, but after that I knew what to expect. There were no cracks of thunder, there was no web of lightning, and I actually felt very calm. There was just me and, beneath the earth, my friend. I simply wanted to find her.

When I did I laid her down by the side of the grave, then filled it back up again, being careful to make it look how it had. Then I carried her to the car in my arms and brought her home.

The flat seemed very quiet as I sat her on the sofa, and the cushion rustled and creaked as it took her weight again. When she was settled I knelt and looked up at her face. It looked much the same as it always had, though the color of the skin was different, didn't have the glow she always had. That's where life is, you know, not in the heart but in the little things, like the way hair falls around a face. Her nose looked the same and her forehead was smooth. It was the same face.

I knew the dress she was wearing was hiding a lot of things I would rather not see, but I took it off anyway. It was her going-away dress, bought by her family specially for the occasion, and it didn't mean anything to me or to her. I knew what the damage would be and what it meant. As it turned out the patchers and menders had done a good job, not glossing because it wouldn't be seen. It wasn't so bad.

When she was sitting up again in her white dress I walked over and turned the light down, and I cried a little then, because she looked so much the same. She could have fallen asleep, warmed by the fire and dozy with wine, as if we'd just come back from the party.

I went and had a bath then. We both used to when we came back in from an evening, to feel clean and fresh for when we slipped between the sheets. It wouldn't be like that this evening, of course, but I had dirt all over me, and I wanted to feel normal. For one night at least I just wanted things to be as they had.

I sat in the bath for a while, knowing she was in the living room, and slowly washed myself clean. I really wasn't thinking much. It felt nice to know I wouldn't be alone when I walked back in there. That was better than nothing, was part of what had made her alive. I dropped my Someday clothes in the bin and put on the ones from the evening of the accident. They didn't mean as much as her dress, but at least they were from before.

When I returned to the living room her head had lolled slightly, but it would have done if she'd been asleep. I made us both a cup of coffee. The only time she ever took sugar was in her last cup of the day, so I put one in.

Then I sat down next to her on the sofa and I was glad that the cushions had her dent in them, that as always they drew me slightly towards her, didn't leave me perched there by myself.

The first time I saw Rachel was at a party. I saw her across the room and simply stared at her, but we didn't speak. We didn't meet properly for a month or two, and first kissed a few weeks after that. As I sat there on the sofa next to her body I reached out tentatively and took her hand, as I had done on that first night. It was cooler than it should have been, but not too bad because of the fire, and I held it, feeling the lines on her palm, lines I knew better than my own.

I let myself feel calm and I held her hand in the half light, not looking at her, as also on that first night, when I'd been too happy to push my luck. *She's letting you hold her hand,* I'd thought, *don't expect to be able to look at her too. Holding her hand is more than enough. Don't look, you'll break the spell.*

My face creased then, not knowing whether to smile or cry, but it felt all right. It really did.

I sat there for a long time, watching the flames, still not thinking, just holding her hand and letting the minutes run. The longer I sat the more normal it felt, and finally I turned slowly to look at her. She looked tired and asleep, so deeply asleep, but still there with me and still mine.

When her eyelid first moved I thought it was a trick of the light, a flicker cast by the fire. But then it stirred again, and for the smallest of moments I thought I was going to die. The other eyelid moved and my fear just disappeared, and that made the difference, I think. She had a long way to come, and if I'd felt frightened, or rejected her, I think that would have finished it then. I didn't question it.

A few minutes later both her eyes were open, and it wasn't long before she was able to slowly turn her head.

I still go to work and put in the occasional appearance at social events, but my tie never looks quite as it did. She can't move her fingers precisely enough to help me with that anymore. She can't come with me, and nobody can come here, but that doesn't matter. We always spent a lot of time by ourselves. We wanted to.

I have to do a lot of things for her, but I can live with that. Lots of people have accidents, bad ones. If Rachel had survived she could have been disabled or brain-damaged, so that her movements were as they are now, so slow and clumsy. I wish she could talk, but there's no air in her lungs, so I'm learning to read her lips. Her mouth moves slowly, but I know she's trying to speak, and I want to hear what she's saying.

But she gets round the flat, and she holds my hand, and she smiles as best she can. If she'd just been injured I would have loved her still. It's not so very different.

ABOUT THE AUTHORS

FRANCESCA LIA BLOCK is the author of many acclaimed books, including *Dangerous Angels: The Weetzie Bat Books,* as well as the recent titles *Pretty Dead* and *Wood Nymph Seeks Centaur: A Mythological Dating Guide.* Visit her on the Web at francesca liablock.com.

STACY BROWN teaches writing at a major metropolitan university. She is the author of four nonfiction books. Her erotic romance short story is published in the *Merry SeXmas* Anthology, and *Electro Deluxe* is a stand-alone story at Ravenousromance.com.

ELIZABETH COLDWELL is the former editor of the UK edition of *Forum* magazine. Her stories have appeared in anthologies including *Best SM Erotica 1* and *2; Yes, Sir;* and *Naughty Spanking Stories 2.* She believes bad boys need to learn to play nice.

S. M. CROSS has been writing since the age of twelve, but Sue at last got down to the business of submitting her work somewhere in her forties. With short stories published in *Zahir,*

Peeks & Valleys, Entropy, Foliate Oaks, Sofa Ink, and the *2008 Contest Winner for Silent Voices, Volume IV,* she has decided the writing life is the only one worth living, although for practicality's sake she keeps her day job as a speech pathologist to pay the rent. And she loves zombies!

DANA FREDSTI is a San Francisco mystery writer and former B-movie actress who has lived many of the experiences she writes about in her sensuous fiction. She has traveled throughout Europe, and worked in the uncharted wilds of Hollywood as a screenwriter, a script doctor, an award-winning documentary producer, a stunt woman (her background is in theatrical sword-fighting), and actress in more than one cult classic. Along with her best friend, she created a mystery-oriented theatrical troupe in San Diego, which formed the basis for her Murder for Hire mysteries. She's written numerous published articles, essays and shorts, and is active in the Northern California chapter of Sisters in Crime. She has a deep passion for all things feline, and for many years has worked with her beloved tigers, leopards, jaguars, and other exotic cats at an exotic feline conservation center. Another love is the sea; she adores living by the beach, surfing, strolling the strand, and beachcombing. Her many friends know she can always be tempted by bad movies or good wine, preferably combined. When she is not hard at work writing or preparing for the coming zombie apocalypse, she can be found doting on her cats or swordfighting with her Irish lover.

STACEY GRAHAM is multitasking wife and mother of five daughters, and resides just outside of Washington, D.C. When not writing about her love life, she can be found sitting in attics conducting paranormal investigations and waiting for the other thing that goes bump in the night.

LOIS H. GRESH is the *New York Times* bestselling author of four novels and sixteen pop science/culture books from John Wiley & Sons, Random House, and St. Martin's Press. Her books have been translated into many languages and are in print worldwide: Italy, Japan, Spain, Russia, Germany, Portugal, France, Brazil, Thailand, Korea, China, Estonia, England, Canada/French, Finland, Poland, Czech, etc. In addition, they are often featured in *The New York Times Book Review, USA Today, Entertainment Weekly, Science News, National Geographic, Physics Today, New Scientist,* and *U.S. News and World Report,* as well as by National Public Radio, the BBC, Fox national news, The History Channel, and many other television and radio programs. Lois's teen novels have been endorsed by the American Library Association and the Voice of Youth Advocates. She's the author of dozens of published mystery/suspense, dark fantasy, and weird science fiction stories. She's been nominated six times for national fiction awards.

R. G. HART has published short fiction in several anthologies from Pocket Books. His latest sale is a paranormal romance novel to Sapphire Blue Publishing, writing as R. G. Hart, entitled

Bachelorette: Zombie Edition, due out later in 2009. Russ is a graduate of the Oregon Coast Professional Fiction Writers Master Class, and the Oregon Coast Short Story Workshop. His instructors have included Dean Wesley Smith, Kristine Katherine Rusch, Gardner Dozois, and Ginjer Buchanan. He is an accomplished public speaker, having achieved the Advanced Toastmaster Silver Award (ATM-S) in his Toastmaster International Club located in his hometown of Vancouver, British Columbia. Russ has been president of the Great Vancouver Chapter of RWA for the past two years and is committed to continuous learning and publishing as a career.

BRIAN KEENE is the author of more than twenty books, including *Darkness on the Edge of Town, Urban Gothic, Dark Hollow, Dead Sea*, and many more. He also writes comic books such as *The Last Zombie* and *Dead of Night: Devil Slayer*. His work has been translated into German, Spanish, Polish, French, and Taiwanese. Several of his novels and stories have been optioned for film, one of which, *The Ties That Bind*, premiered on DVD in 2009 as a critically acclaimed independent short. Keene's work has been praised in such diverse places as *The New York Times,* The History Channel, The Howard Stern Show, CNN.com, *Publishers Weekly, Fangoria Magazine*, and *Rue Morgue Magazine*. Keene lives in the backwoods of Central Pennsylvania with his wife, sons, dog, and cats. You can communicate with him on the Web at www.briankeene.com or on Twitter at twitter.com/BrianKeene.

KILT KILPATRICK is the pen name of an Irish author sometimes called "the Ferris Bueller of San Francisco." When he's not writing sexy stories for Ravenous, he is a nonfiction writer, public speaker, Bay Area event organizer, and, somewhat oxymoronically, a biblical historian and atheist activist. He is linguistically promiscuous; he is conversant in Irish Gaelic and bits and pieces of about two dozen other languages, including Welsh, Breton, Hungarian, Japanese, Arabic, American Sign Language, Cherokee, Klingon, and Elvish. He loves reading, movies, dancing, sex, and has been a saber fencer for more than twenty-five years. He lives in San Francisco with his steady girlfriend and number-one fencing partner, Dana, who is also a writer. And yes, he does wear kilts. If you know anybody like that, it's probably him.

JAN KOZLOWSKI fell in love with the horror genre in 1975 when the single drop of ruby blood on the engraved black cover of Stephen King's *Salem's Lot* transfixed her into purchasing it. She became obsessed with zombies the first time she saw Romero's masterpiece, *Night of the Living Dead,* in all its black-and-white majesty at the local drive-in. She began writing horror for her own amusement almost immediately, but didn't begin publishing until she sold her first story, *Psychological Bacchanal,* to the EWG E-zine in 1997. Her short story, "Parts Is Parts," won awards in both the International Writing Competition sponsored by DarkEcho's E-zine and Quoth the Raven's Bad Stephen King contest. Another short story, "Stuff It," was sold to an independent film producer and went into production as a movie short called *Sweet Goodbyes*. She has also sold fiction to Erotinomicon and Sage Vivant's CES.

MERCY LOOMIS graduated from college one class short of an accidental certificate in folklore. She has a bachelor's degree in psychology, but don't hold that against her. Her favorite pastimes include hobby gaming, road trips, and studying ancient history. See what she's up to and find links to her other work at mercyloomis.blogspot.com.

JEANINE MCADAM has published more than twenty-five short stories with the Dorchester Media "true confession" line of magazines during the past two years. Working as a reference librarian for seven years, Jeanine has helped patrons find great fiction. In her profession as a technology trainer, she wrote instructional materials and contributed to technology newsletters. When she began inserting romance, intrigue, and a touch of horror into the manuals, she knew it was time to start her career as a short story writer.

GINA MCQUEEN is the author of *Opposite Sex*, which she describes as "*Freaky Friday* with fucking." She is also rumored to be horror legend and literary zombie hero John Skipp in drag. Ya never know.

LORI PERKINS is the editorial director of Ravenous Romance and one of its founders. She has been a literary agent specializing in horror and erotica for two decades. She is the author of four nonfiction guidebooks and eight erotica anthologies. She just broke up with her zombie boyfriend.

REGINA RILEY writes everything from paranormal fables to steampunk chronicles. She prefers to pen complex plots, often with hilarious consequences. When not wasting time goofing around on the Internet, she writes from the heart about life, love, and the merriment of happiness. Her novels and novellas can be found online at Sugar and Spice Press, Phaze, and Lyrical Press. Aside from her wicked imagination, Regina believes her life is pretty pedestrian. She resides in North Carolina, although her roots spread a bit deeper thanks to a military upbringing. She is an identical twin, and has been happily married for thirteen years to a wonderful and giving husband. She also shares her home with a brood of moody cats. To learn more about Regina, visit her on the Web at www.thebackseatwriter.com, and feel free to e-mail her at regina@thebackseatwriter.com.

ISABEL ROMAN has been writing for four years and loves just about every second of it! Historical paranormals caught her eye (and ear) when she realized the vast conflicts inherent in historicals, and her deep and abiding love for all things paranormal. Nurturing a love of all time periods, she plans to explore as many as she can with as many couples as she can. Isabel is the author of Ravenous Romance's *The Dark Desires of the Druids* series, which features a Ravenous Rendezvous, *The Tryst*, as well as a full-length novel, *Murder & Magick*.

JAIME SAARE is a wife and the mother of four rambunctious children who turned to writing as a way to escape the fulfilling yet oftentimes overwhelming world around her. What began as a hobby became something more after her first story was completed. Currently she resides in the wonderful state of Alabama, where she was also born. When not kid wrangling, catering to the hubs, or writing something horrifying or erotic, she enjoys the simple things in life, including shooting a game of straight eight, listening to her favorite band (NIN), reading an excellent story, or partaking in a good (and she does mean *good*) horror movie.

STEVEN SAUS injects people with radioactivity at his day job, but only to serve the forces of good. His work has appeared in print at *Seed* magazine, *Andromeda Spaceways Inflight* magazine, and is due to appear in *On Spec* magazine. A story of his will also appear in the DAW anthology *Timeshares*. He also has several flash fiction works in the online magazines *365 Tomorrows, Everyday Weirdness,* and *Quantum Muse.* He blogs at http://ideatrash.net, and he can be found at www.steven saus.com.

MICHAEL MARSHALL SMITH is a novelist and screenwriter. Under this name he has published three novels—including *Only Forward* and *Spares*—and more than sixty short stories, winning the Philip K. Dick, International Horror Guild, August Derleth, and British Fantasy Awards. Under the name Michael Marshall he has also published five internationally bestselling thrillers, including *The Straw Men, The Intruders,* and, most recently, *Bad Things.* He lives in London with his wife, son, and two cats.

VANESSA VAUGHN has published erotic stories in numerous anthologies, including the award-winning *Best Women's Erotica* and *Best Lesbian Erotica* series from Cleis Press and the Ravenous Romance collections *Power Plays, Experimental,* and *Rekindled Fire.* Some of the many things that turn her on include zombies, mayhem, panic, and Stephen Colbert's brains! Turn-offs include sledgehammers, shotguns, and other weapons capable of decapitation.

JEREMY WAGNER has thousands of worldwide fans who worship his words. He has recorded six albums, two MTV videos, and has toured in sixteen countries with his bands, Broken Hope and Lupara. Wagner has written lyrics to more than seventy published songs, as well as dozens of short stories, four novels, and magazine features. Wagner's fiction has received praise from *New York Times* bestselling author Peter Blauner and *Rolling Stone* journalist Katherine Turman. Wagner now writes his own monthly column for the music webzine *Chronicles of Chaos*. His column, "Jeremy Wagner's Grotesque Blessings," is already a hit with music fans and writers alike. Wagner is currently finishing work on a zombie novella and revising a new novel.